Fata Morgana

Thomas J. Radford

Fata Morgana

Thomas J. Radford

TYCHE BOOKS LTD.

Published by Tyche Books Ltd.
Calgary, Alberta, Canada
www.TycheBooks.com

Cover Art by James F. Beveridge
Cover Layout by Indigo Chick Designs
Interior Layout by Ryah Deines
Editorial by M.L.D. Curelas

First Tyche Books Ltd Edition 2019
Print ISBN: 978-1-989407-01-1
Ebook ISBN: 978-1-989407-02-8

Author photograph: Devin Hart

This book was funded in part by a grant from the Alberta Media Fund.

This book was going to be dedicated to Nel & Violet, because this is their story. But they're both dead, so this one's all mine.

Unless . . .

Chapter 1

"Filthy starchies." The Kelpie on Nel's right turned her head and spat into the sawdust covering the floor. Spittle was flying fast and loose from the maw, drool hanging from the fleshless lips and dagger-teeth. A courtesy really.

Despite the show, her drinking companion hunched low over her vessel, head parallel to the table. This one had a stain of red on only one side of her face, mottled scales, whatever passed for birthmarks on Kelpies.

Mother must have spilled her wine on this one when she was a wee hatchling. Wrong colour though.

The cause for her not-quite-friends, her companions who didn't remind her of Loveland Quill at all, was the true-to-their-name, starch-pressed sailors marching into the drinking hole. It was long forgotten bells after sunset with only firelight and gas-flares to fight off the gloom. Plenty of patrons were deep in their cups and some already kissing the timbers.

Prime recruits.

"And how are we this evening, lads?" One of the recruiters sauntered over to their corner of the dank and gloom. The Kelpies both ignored him, the Troll just belched in his general direction. It might have been intentional. Might not.

"Cups are looking dry," the recruiter noted. The man had eyebrows, Nel found herself spotting. Hairy caterpillars, two of them, that appeared to move independently of one another in opposite see-sawing directions. Because of that she found herself meeting the recruiter's eyes.

Hells, call it what it is, the press-ganger's.

"And you, lass?" He held up a coin, tarnished and dull and already with several sets of bite marks. "You've the look and the mark of a sailor. Work's scarce, we all know it. The fleet is always on the watch for experienced hands. Might even be a rating in it for you if you were to volunteer."

Nel didn't look away, starting to push her tankard forward. The recruiter's grin widened as he dropped the coin into cup. It made a clang as it hit the bottom.

Empty after all.

"That's a quarter silver mark," Nel said, rolling the cup, making the coin swirl with the dregs.

"Man, or woman," the recruiter said, "could do a lot with a coin like that."

"Could do," Nel shrugged. "Could buy a horse or a cow, if they've a mind. Or book passage from here to the middle of the High."

"Figure it would buy you a room here for six weeks," one of her companions threw in.

"Be the longest I'd ever stayed in one place since I was a wee one," Nel rolled her eyes. She set the vessel and its coin down flat and began driving it with one finger. "Thing of it is, folk who take this coin don't get to spend it, now do they?"

The mug grated along the coarse wood of the table as she pushed it closer to the edge.

"Gotta pay your own way when you join up, lads and lasses," Nel addressed her drinking companions. "Can't sleep so a hammock's a must. Got to have a belaying pin. And the uniform, because we must be neat and trimmed and ever so pretty, mustn't we?"

Nel looked up, her chin low to the table, on eye level with the cups, meeting the recruiter's eyes. The lip of the cup with the coin teetered over the edge, tottering on a lean. Nel leaned back, folding her arms and nudging the table leg with her foot. It was enough; the press-ganger went to grab. A server got there first, plucking the falling vessel out the air before it could shatter on the ground. They swept past with a glare at Nel's group as they burst into raucous laughter.

"Best be chasing that one, limey," Nel chuckled. "Or they'll be taking that from *your* pay!"

"I like you, human." The wine-stained Kelpie slapped her on

the back.

"It wears off," Nel muttered, pushing herself to her feet. The room only swam slightly. *Good, might have a chance of making it back to my room without heaving in the bushes then. Assumes I can remember where is my room but life is an adventure, right?*

"I thought you cut from the same cloth as them," the Kelpie motioned towards the recruiters who were pressed three to the bar trying to retrieve the lost mark. The servers pled ignorance.

Might even be telling the truth there. Not my problem though.

"But you are welcome at this table any night," her new friend proclaimed.

"Beat you at cards," Nel reminded her. "Weren't such happy about that a few hands ago."

"A price I am happy to pay tonight," the Kelpie bared her teeth. "And it will not happen again."

Nel snorted. "Be seeing you soon then."

Making friends with Kelpies, she thought as she made her way into the crowd. The gloom wasn't too bad, smoky overhead and muddy timbers underfoot, but few gave her more than a glance and that suited her just fine. Her room was outside. A long walk. Too many people that way. Nel paused to lean on the bar. Just for a moment.

"Buy you a round?" This from a Korrigan seated just down from her. Their perch put them on eye level with Nel. Female and maybe half the age of Nel's former crewman Jack. She'd seen this one around before, played a few hands with her at the card table. Name escaped her right now. Had green hair though—was that an affectation or an affliction? Or was she just seeing things?

"Have I said no before?" Nel said.

"Never offered before. But a performance like that deserves a toast and you just lost your cup."

"A worthy sacrifice," Nel agreed. "One I'd happily make again."

"To worthy sacrifices and unworthy beer," the Korrigan lass toasted. She winked. "Can't stand the cheap stuff. Tastes like what you step in."

"To beer and song and oceans, then," Nel said, the first thing that came to mind, "so long as none of them are flat."

"That's a good one," her benefactor said. "I'll have to remember it."

"You're not a sailor then."

"Not even if you paid me."

"Avoid the streets after last call," Nel advised. "The walk home is the pressers' favoured hunting ground. Plenty a sailor was one who walked out happy and woke up at sea."

"One for the walk home then?"

"As long as there's coin to spend there is no walk home."

"Excellent, Barkeep, a round of the good stuff, top of the shelf there."

SHE WAS RIGHT. There was no walk home. The drinks and cards carried on through the night and into what passed for morning. The dark of the morning anyway. Her nameless Korrigan friend turned out to be a better card player than Nel was, bordering on a shark. Woman couldn't hold her liquor though, snoring loudly with her head thrown back, leaning against someone who had been a stranger only a bell ago. Nel was the only one awake when Loveland Quill arrived. She wished that weren't the case. She had no desire to speak with her former navigator and the look on his face made it clear he was equally disgusted by what he saw. But it wasn't the first time he'd visited the tavern. Far from it.

"What now?"

Nel didn't remove her boots from the only other stool, meaning there was nowhere for Quill to sit. He seemed to have no such inclination anyway, throwing down scrap paper onto the table beside her.

"Table's wet, Quill," she told him.

"Read quickly then," he suggested.

Nel sighed, flicking up the corner of one. The whole sheaf was fighting a losing battle not to roll up into a scroll. Only the lower half becoming sodden in spilled beer was preventing it.

"Running steel and coal to Scallop. Been there, place is a miserable coastal shipyard. Fishing and water tubs. Sometimes it rains so much you can grow fish in the tubs."

"The ship listed requires officers," Quill said.

"So?"

"You prefer the other?"

Nel read it, if only to appease the Kelpie. She snorted and

crumpled it in her fist. "Quill, this is to run tender on a barge storing dried manure in high transit. You want to stick your maw into a ship piled with dried dung bricks you be my guest."

She threw the note away. "Where do you find these?"

"The board on the town square. And the other by the merchant docks."

"Meant to leave them there for other folk to read."

"Few others can read. I intended for you to read them and I did not care to try and attempt to move you from your . . ."

"Yes?"

Quill shrugged.

"Well, read them and don't intend. We done?"

"Ships and sailors rot in port, Vaughn."

Nel squinted at him. "Since when do you care?"

"Since I began to lose respect for you."

"That hurts my feelings, Quill."

"I would see it stop."

"I would see more beer. Have a drink with me, Quill. Damned all else to do here." She waved to the bartender, fishing through her pockets.

"This is your plan?" Quill was incredulous. Nel ignored him, passing over what had to be the last coin either had to their name. The bartender gave her two foaming tankards, carried over in both meaty hands. They were huge, the largest the tavern sold and bigger than Nel's head, both of them.

"Ain't a plan, Quill." Nel stood, taking the vessels and holding one out. "Take your damned drink or I will."

Quill didn't, so Nel put it down on the table. But she didn't release her grip on it. She raised her own drink, coughing as she inhaled a swallow bigger than she should have, spilling beer down her front.

Waste of good beer.

"You think this will help?" Quill sounded angry. "This . . . this is the answer?"

"It's my answer, Quill. Don't have to be yours. Don't have to be a good one. Just gotta be."

Quill made no move to accept the offer.

"Take the damned thing, Quill, or I'll find someone who will." She gestured around her table. Her Korrigan card player was gone, Nel realised, probably slunk home to count her winnings.

There was a man she didn't recognise on the floor and someone she might have punched the night before next to them. None were capable of managing speech, let alone drink.

Quill stared daggers at her. He did reach for the tankard, and Nel released her grip. With deliberate precision he raised it in front of himself, then upturned the vessel and emptied the contents on the floor.

Nel stared blankly at the spreading puddle. "Well done, Quill. Really, well done."

Quill slammed the empty vessel down hard on the bar, making half the tavern turn to look. "You are a disgrace to your ship, Vaughn."

"Ain't got no ship, Loveland," Nel retorted, matching him name for name. "Or did I miss something? Seems I recall telling you to save her."

"I tried to save *her*!" Quill seethed. "*Her*! I made a promise. Or did you forget that too?"

"And how did that turn out?" Nel glared at him. "Who'd you save, Kelpie?"

Quill hit her. As hard as he could. Nel was sure her face was broken, the whole side of her face stung, and she could smell singed flesh. Hers. And she was lying on the floor. How did that happen?

She pushed herself back to her feet and turned to her former navigator. He was cradling his punching hand. From the way he was holding it he might well have broken *his* bones on her face.

Nel broke the oversized tankard on the top of Quill's scaly head. The pewter tankard crumpled and tore in her hand. Quill reeled but didn't go down like she had. The Kelpie could take a punch better. Maybe she was getting old.

They stared at each other in mutual loathing for a long minute. Quill turned and vanished into the crowd. Everyone stopped paying attention.

Nel took her broken vessel and shouldered a seat at a table. Her poor tankard was empty, a pathetic lining of foam was all that remained to her.

Waste of good beer.

The drink in Nel's hand had been sour and barely cold. Cheap and nasty. Everything that drink could do wrong. But it had been hers, and now it was gone. She nursed what was left, holding it protectively in the crook of her arm, hood pulled low over her face. People passed by her chosen corner but few gave a second look. She sat with legs pulled tight against her, arms wrapped around them. Safe and secure.

Nel didn't look up as a commotion stirred through the crowd, even as it drew closer. She didn't care. It didn't concern her. Then it did. People in her space. Too close. Too loud. Hit one with her drinking vessel and they stopped being loud.

The quiet was almost bearable.

Until that scaly hand reached out and plucked her from her safe and secure corner, dragging her to her feet. Her drink spilled from her hand, soaking into the rushes on the floor. She stared forlornly at the criminal waste, but not for long as she was pulled away from her corner. The room spun around her and she might have fallen if not for the hand pulling her relentlessly forwards, her feet staggering along under her. Cold air hit her face and she realised they were outside. Light stabbed at her eyes; street lamps. It was night time. How many nights had there been since they'd returned to port?

"Get off me, Kelpie," Nel swatted at the hand, dragging her heels into the dirt. Stumbled and fell, landing in the dirt and the mud and looking up at her former navigator. Only it wasn't Quill. Was the barman's goons, the hired muscle that rolled out the drunks in the morning. Backlit by the inside of the tavern and blocking the way inside.

"The hells is your problem?" she demanded of them. Sounded fine in her head. Didn't make much sense to her ears though. Just noise, mushy noise. The words were slurred and her tongue thick when she tried to form more. Drunk? One could hope. Then the drink wouldn't have died in vain.

"Take a walk," one of them told her.

"Got a room here." Nel made it to her feet. Somehow. More, the words sounded like words. The kind people used. "Paid up till week's end."

"Week ends tomorrow."

"Paid up till tomorrow then."

"Walk it off and come back," another told her. "Let you back in when you won't start a fight."

Nel made to throw her tankard at them. Her hand came up empty. She stared at it, confused.

"You take my drink?" she pointed at them.

"Walk it off," was all the reply she got. They turned away. Shut the door on her. No more light.

Nel sighed. Alone again. At least the ground was comfortable. The stars were bright tonight, she mused. Bright silvery pinpricks in a midnight canopy. Piper would have liked that. He would have liked it a lot. Stars so big and so bright you could almost touch them.

"Hells," she said. The stars were street lamps.

"Walk it off," she repeated. Seemed good advice, best to take it. Feet first, upright then one in front of the other. How hard could that be?

Boots clipped on the cobblestones. Sounded like horses' hooves. Reminded her of nails on deck. Deck always had scratches from them. Kelpie used to pace the length. Only there was no more deck to scratch. Maybe no more Kelpie to scratch them neither.

Where was she? Roads led to the town square. Quill had been trying to take her there for days. Maybe weeks. It was all one messy blur in her head. But that was fine. That was the plan. Not being able to tell. Not to think. Not to feel. There was a pounding in her head.

Hangover came early. Or not? Hells, an actual hammer. Who's working at this hour? A blacksmith? Don't see no forge. That the square?

The far side led to one of the municipal buildings. Whatever passed for government in Vice; legislation and clerical duties were not Nel's strong suit. Fancy ceremonial doors of self-grandiose importance right now struck her as nothing better than a convenient place to relieve herself. The thought made her grin, almost laugh. But her throat was dry and the chuckle died silently. The sound was coming from there as well. Nails on wood. Made sense.

Skipper.

The hells was that? Who's yelling? That big shadowy thing, what's that now?

Quill's notice board? Where he goes every day. Big wooden thing. Square. Solid. Bits of paper stuck to it. Fine, let's see what Quill wants to see. Read the pretty pictures and look at the squiggly lines. Someone was just here, where'd they go? Just me? Good, don't want no one watching for this.

There. Better. So much better. Where's the board now? Belongs to me now, I figure. Ah, there. Paper. That. Stay still, damn you. Like looking at the waves. Floating. Spinning. All in motion. Never did like water. Did I? Can't remember.

Skipper.

Shut up. Reading you, aren't I? Focus! Quill wanted to show you something, right? Jobs and such. Ships and runs and coin at the end. Need coin. Everyone needs coin. Coin pays for bits and pieces and makes all the hurt go away.

She pulled one off, tearing it in half. That was bad. Quill would be mad. That seemed important. Be all right though. Everything would be all right.

Just put it somewhere safe. Look at it later. Try again, not so fast this time. That one's pretty, got colours on it. Like ink-work almost.

It took her a moment to realise what she was seeing. Vice's authorities would post decrees and pronouncements. Sometimes jobs would be posted there, particularly urgent ones. Quill said that, Nel remembered knowing that. It was out of long habit that her eyes scanned the various parchments and banners nailed to the wood.

Another moment to comprehend it. And longer still to react. She took a hurried step, almost stumbling, and closed the distance to it. Hand on the wood, solid, comforting, taking her weight. Holding her up. Eyes pressed up against it. It was the only way she could make it out.

Words and phrases jumped out at her, twisting ad nauseum. She grabbed the top of the board with one hand, feeling splinters under her fingers and not caring.

All rights and responsibilities . . .

. . . of maritime purpose . . .

. . . beholden and bequeathed unto . . .

. . . referred to as the captain, one . . .

. . . henceforth to be known as the Tantamount . . .

The deed and title to the *Tantamount*. Nailed unceremoniously to the wooden framing. A deed written on the actual skin of the ship's Captain.

Her ship.

Her captain.

Chapter 2

THEY DID LET her back in, after her walk. Found herself a quiet spot at a dry table. The table was dry because she'd scrubbed it herself. Ripped the sleeve off her shirt and rubbed her knuckles half-bloody making sure what she had spread out would not get wet.

You went and died on me, Captain, was all Nel could think looking at the tattooed deed. *Don't need to pickle you as well, though I'm not sure you would have minded.*

Bottle me, Nel. If I should die adrift in the black or the lanes. Bottle me in brandy. Barrel me in rum and cask me in whiskey. And send me home to see my girls. And make sure the crew don't go tapping the keg. No tapping the captain on his own ship. It's a rule.

Had he actually said that or was her mind playing tricks? Sounded like something Horatio would have said so he might as well have.

"Then here's to you, Captain. My captain." Nel rolled the deed up, tucking it inside her shirt, as secure as it could be. She didn't think about what was touching her skin. Her mind was still far down in drink for it not to matter.

In the morning it would matter. The light would come back and burn her. There would be pain, pain in the head and the heart and wherever pain found a home for itself.

Someone sat down opposite her. She realised then the table was empty. People were giving her a wide berth. Couldn't fault that.

"Not tonight," she said, figuring it was one of her card playing companions. "Got no coin for games."

A cup was pushed towards her. More a goblet really. Filled with wine.

"That ain't my drink."

"Not such a waste if you knock this one over. Hurts less if you hit me with it too."

"Don't feel like wine, felt like beer," Nel grumbled, eyeing the dark red liquid.

"If you don't want it then—" the voice broke off as Nel downed the contents in a long swallow. She pushed the cup away.

"Saw your spat with the Kelpie. Making friends?"

Nel shrugged. Was too long ago to worry about that. Another cup appeared, or the same one refilled. Sneaky servers, this tavern. She took it but didn't drink so fast. Could already feel the first.

This first. There were other firsts. Earlier. First.

Nel finally looked up. Wasn't much to see, with eyes swelling shut from stray bar fights and rock-fisted Kelpies. Drink was taking care of the rest nicely, made everyone else look prettier. This one had long hair, bearded. Hood up to keep the rain off and the eyes out.

Don't know you, don't care to know you neither.

"Making friends," she said, hearing herself slur the words. "That's how I got here. Making friends . . ."

"Sounds like a tale."

"What's it to you?"

"I like tales."

Nel squinted at him. Now that she thought about it, he reminded her somewhat of Sharpe. Castor Sharpe. And meeting him had been the bane of her and the *Tantamount*. That was how the tale went. Her hand went to her chest, touching the rolled-up deed under her clothing. Didn't feel like much, had to reassure herself it was still there.

"Remind me of someone," she said, swirling her finger and taking a general stab at them.

At least two of them now, maybe more. Triples. Gotta be pointing at one of you.

"A good memory, I hope."

"Not even a bit," Nel leaned back, pulling one leg up so she had somewhere to rest her head. Made the room stop spinning, somewhat, resting her head on her knee. "But you're not him. He's dead."

"Ah, well, I'm not, so that's just as well."

"Who are you then?"

"Who do you want me to be?"

"Sound like him. He was an infuriating bastard too."

"Terribly misunderstood fellow, I'm sure."

Nel's only response was a snort of disdain. She twisted her head halfway to look at him side-on.

He could be Sharpe, she thought. *Lose the beard, clip the hair. Leave me out in the sun to dry out for a week.*

There was still wine in the cup. She took care of that.

Was that even my cup? Maybe two weeks.

The late-night movement was happening. She saw some of her regular drinking partners preparing to make the move to the next bar. Meaning this one was about to go dry. That wouldn't do. Nel got up to join the nightly procession. Safety in numbers, there was.

Nel swayed, putting hand to table. It was a straight line between her and the door. Her friends were leaving. A straight line.

Damnit.

"Hells, woman, how much *have* you drunk?"

"Don't you use that word!" She turned, too fast, too sharply, pointing at not-Sharpe, trying to stab him with her finger. She missed and had to steady herself before she met the floor.

"That's my word," she said to them. "Don't you be using my word."

She almost fell, from the pointing. The pointing and the yelling. Not-Sharpe grabbed her by the shoulders. Nel stared at them, all close and in her face.

"You really do look like him."

"Vaughn!"

That was a Kelpie voice. One of her drinking buddies. Red Scale, perhaps. Or Short Stuff.

No, Short Stuff is a Korrigan, not a Kelpie. Very bad to mix the two up. Very bad.

It wasn't either of them though. It was Quill. Pushing his way through the crowd of drunken patrons towards her. Not someone she wanted to see. Not now. Not ever.

"Hells."

"Nel," the man holding her said.

Nel pushed him away. It turned out he was the only thing holding her up. The floor leaned in to kiss her.

SHE WOKE UP in pain. Blinding, stabbing pain, going in through her eyeballs and trying to poke its way out through the back of her skull. Needle-shaped lightning carrying chisels and hammers. Cracking her skull from the inside out. Daylight. Nel rolled over, hand searching for the pillow to cover the pain. There was no pillow but her hand found something else. Blankets, twisted and knotted. Hair. Not hers. A shoulder. Definitely not her.

Hells. Not alone.

Nel groaned, fighting to open crusty eyes. The sun was invading the room through glassless windows. Nothing to keep it out. The noise of the street carried up. Wagons. Shouting. Noise. The only quiet thing was Quill.

She'd seen the pose before; legs folded back, hands clasped in front of him. His head was bowed, what passed for his chin resting almost on his chest. His eyes were closed.

He wasn't that quiet, either. His breath was raspy, in and out through his nostrils.

Nel sat up and the room spun. When she opened her eyes, she was staring up at the ceiling. Cobwebs. So many cobwebs.

"Slower," Quill's voice told her. "I suggest slower."

She took his advice, sitting up slowly. Inch by inch, keeping her head down, eyes focused on her knees.

"Quill," she said when she felt it safe to talk. "Where the hells are my boots?"

Her feet were bare. Cold, even.

"Under the bed."

"Get them for me."

"No."

She didn't reply. *So much for that plan. Under the bed? Stupid place for them. Have to stay there. Not going in after them.*

"Why am I in bed?"

"I put you there. Would you have preferred the floor?"

You always this mouthy, Quill? What else did I forget?

"What's he doing there?" she asked.

"Who?"

"Hells, Quill, there's only three of us here."

When she looked at Quill, he was grinning. Broadly.

"You don't smile, Quill. Looks wrong on you. Make it stop."

"I cannot."

"Plough you then."

The smile grew wider.

"Remind me what happened," Nel sighed.

"Ask your friend."

"Don't have any friends."

"You have at least one."

"You don't count. Never meant a single nice thing I said about you."

Even that couldn't knock the smile off Quill's face. "I was not referring to me."

A groan beside her. Her friend was stirring. Nel closed her eyes, leaning forward on her hands. She didn't care to look at whoever it was.

Her friend made a raucous go of getting up. There was a cough, mixed with a groan of pain.

"Lost a tooth," they said, voice thick and slurred. Then, "Half a tooth. Damn, woman."

She heard Quill laugh.

Nel steeled herself to look up. Mercifully, the room stayed level. She took in Quill's idiotic grin as she turned to confront her *friend.*

And forgot everything else for a moment.

Castor Sharpe stared back at her, pressing a cloth stained red against his mouth. His cheek and jaw were black and purple, mottled day-old bruises, visible even under the beard. The beard was new; she truly hadn't recognised him with it. Hair was longer too, and Nel didn't like it, looked like his face was hiding. In fact she felt a deep, simmering resentment just looking at him. Enough to forget about the hangover that was trying to force its way out from inside her skull.

Sharpe held up a broken fragment of white. Presumably the lost tooth.

"What happened?" Sharpe directed his query at Quill, his tone half accusing.

"She happened," Quill pointed.

"Yes, but—"

"She kicked you," Quill elaborated. He was still grinning. "In the face."

"My tooth."

"Presumably you will grow another."

"Don't work like that, Kelpie," Nel sighed, rubbing at her temple.

"Ah, truly? Unfortunate. Then you will be wanting this back?"

"Is it morning? Why is it morning?" Sharpe peered at the window.

"You fell asleep."

"She kicked me. In the face."

"Yes."

"Did she kick you?"

"I removed her boots. The kicks were less painful."

Quill clapped his hands together, rubbing them gleefully. "And now who would care for breakfast?" he asked. "Perhaps more drink? We must celebrate."

His smile only grew wider at their mutual groans.

QUILL BROUGHT THEM stew, a pot he carried and set upon wrapped cloth and served into wooden bowls. Maybe it was just hunger but the stew was good, thick and hearty with diced root vegetables and chunks of what might have been goat meat. If not Nel didn't feel inclined to ask what. The food settled her stomach but set the wheels in her mind turning.

"You don't eat much," she said to Sharpe.

He looked guilty, cradling his bowl between both hands, mostly picking at it with his spoon. "Don't feel so good," he said. "Smell's good, but making my head ache worse for it."

Sharpe had never been much of an eater, Nel recalled. *Always went through the motions, but . . .*

"Where'd you get the food, Quill?" She turned the bowl and scraped the dregs into her mouth.

"The kitchen."

"Thought you were out of coin."

"You were out of coin. I have been working."

"Where?"

"At the docks."

At the docks. Quill hates the docks. Lifting and pushing crates. Always said it were beneath him.

No wonder he kept bringing jobs. Should have just left without me.

Except Quill hadn't left.

Nel put her bowl aside. Her stomach rumbled in protest at the action. It had been a while since she'd eaten. Properly. She could make out bones in her arms, all knobby and angular. Not eating made the drinking easier, made the coins go further. Made the day after the night before harder.

"Thank you," she said.

Quill's eyes narrowed on her suspiciously.

Sharpe offered her his mostly untouched bowl. No more words were exchanged until she'd finished that as well.

"You ought to be dead." She handed the bowl back to Sharpe.

"Never was good at doing what I was meant to be," he said quietly.

"Tell her what you told me," Quill said.

Nel pulled her head back so she could stare at them both. "You been conspiring again."

"Quill found me," Sharpe said.

"I did not find you," Quill corrected him. "I was not looking for you."

"Found each other then."

"I'm so happy for you both," Nel said. "Now why ain't you dead, Castor?"

"First name," Sharpe nodded. "Means I'm in trouble."

"Such names should not be spoken," Quill agreed.

"Better left unsaid."

"Would you two . . . ," Nel sighed. "Ain't nobody in trouble, not yet. But don't make me put my boots back on. Where've you been, Sharpe, if not dead?"

Sharpe's fingers drummed on the bowl. Tap, tap, tap. A nervous habit he hadn't shown before. There was a pattern to it. And a distant look.

"Got picked up by the *Mangonel* after the battle. At Rim."

"Thought you were on the other ship. The one they dropped you on."

"Was. Didn't care for me much there. Not the best luck, me and ships." Sharpe's voice was light. Like always. The same mocking tone. But forced. "Wanted to string me up. Tried to . . ."

Sharpe reached up, rubbing at his neck. There was an abrasion there. Rope burn. *More than tried then.*

"Tried to hang you," Nel said, not unkindly.

"Yes," Sharpe said, eyes distant. Haunted. The ghosts of memories.

Hells, but I don't wanna know. Got enough shades of my own without . . .

"Nel . . . I saw," he turned to her. "I saw the *Tantamount* burning. The bodies. I saw . . . floating in the black . . . I . . ."

"You weren't there," Nel said. She found she had to look away. The memories were painful enough. She'd done all she could to drown them. But not just that. The naked emotion on Sharpe's face. It was painful to look at. And not something she'd expected to see.

Or him, for that matter. Ever again.

"They sent me to the *Mangonel.* Your friend, former captain. Heathen. Questioned me."

"How . . . no, what? What'd they ask?"

"All about you. Wanted to know what I knew, how to find you. Where you might go. Didn't care much about anyone else, your captain, she—"

Nel interrupted. "Not my captain."

"Yeah. Well, couldn't tell 'em what I didn't know. So after a while she started believing me. Guess it didn't make a difference though. Passed along to another ship. And they found you anyways. I don't know . . . I couldn't see . . . didn't know. But there was a battle. I got out. That's when I saw . . ."

Nel made the mistake of looking back at him.

"I saw you all die."

I didn't die.

I let everybody else die.

"She told me you were dead."

Sharpe's voice. What is that? Disbelief? Anger? Hysteria?

"It doesn't matter what she told you," Nel said, harsher than she'd intended. "None of it matters because it's all done. So Heathen and the rest of them can go—"

"It wasn't Heathen," Sharpe said. "It was Violet."

Chapter 3

Stars like tiny pinpricks in a black cloth. An endless ocean of black. Other meaningless clichés. Half-grappled thoughts that ran fleetingly through her head. Drifting. Ever drifting. All she knew was cold.

Light and mist surrounded her. Not the cold light of the stars, light reflected, light refracted, bouncing off the water that surrounded her.

Water? Mist? The water fell, off the edge of the world. Over her, but she remained. Drifting, twisting. Occasionally another world would pass across her horizon. Large, impossibly distant. Solid. Unreachable. Beautiful. Surrounded by a thousand tiny lights. Mere pinholes in a smothering canopy of black.

And eventually all those tiny pinpricks merged into one larger glob of light. Floating overhead. Blinding her.

"You're lucky to be alive."

The fall. Something . . . heavy. Being swept off the deck of the ship. Nel Vaughn's face, the deck of the Tantamount *shrouded in smoke.*

"All things considered."

A green-scaled hand, clawed . . . thaumatic energy crackling. The skipper . . .

Drifting.

Violet opened her eyes and sat up. She fell back down, a strangled cry erupting from her body. She hurt everywhere, from the tips of her fingers to the roots of her hair. She felt herself starting to curl up and forced herself to stop. Moving hurt. Not moving wasn't much better.

"Easy, easy," a voice told her. Young, male, somewhat familiar. She felt something soft and warm being applied to her brow. A towel maybe. Was it wet or was she sweating? She couldn't tell. "You were bitten by the cold before we found you. You made it through with all your extremities but only just. Lie still, your body needs a moment."

The same voice turned away from her. "Go tell the captain she's awake. Aristeia will want to know too."

The sound of a door opening and closing. Drawing deep, slow breaths, Violet opened her eyes again. She didn't remember shutting them but must have. Slowly, the world around her came into focus. A cabin, shipboard from the cramped confines and layout. A wooden cot below her, sweat-soaked, coarse woollen blankets. A man beside her, young, closer to her own age. Dark hair streaked with copper in the flickering lamplight. He wore a sailor's practical garb, but cut with a hint of severity and pressed free of wrinkles. His face was smooth, beardless. Soft hands, she realised. Not a proper sailor's.

You look familiar . . .

"Who . . . ," was all Violet could voice before her cracked throat failed her. She broke off into a fit of coughing.

"Niko, Miss," he told her, offering a wooden cup. She took it and drank greedily. "Niko Kaspar, ensign. On behalf of my Captain, welcome aboard the *Fata Morgana*."

Violet could only stare at him. It must have been enough to convey her confusion.

"You're aboard an Alliance ship, Miss." He took the cup from her and refilled it from a jug on the bedside table before offering it back. "We found you out there, drifting below Vice."

Violet drank again, desperate to ask about the *Tantamount*, the captain, Gabbi, the skipper . . . the last thing she remembered came back to her. The skipper turning away from her.

"I suggest you don't say anything." Kaspar squeezed her shoulder. "Strongly suggest. You're not well. Do you follow?"

Do I follow? The last thing I saw . . .

The door opened again. A new voice.

"Ah, Ensign, I see our patient is awake. Excellent. I've been looking forward to speaking with her."

"Yes, sir." Kaspar stood, moving aside to let the newcomer pass. "Brandon and I will be outside if you need us."

"I doubt I will, my boy, no need for the two of you to tarry."

"Aristeia insisted, sir," Kaspar told him, apologetically. "We'll be outside."

"Yes, yes, as you wish. Out with you then."

"Pleasure to meet you, Miss," Kaspar inclined his head to Violet. "Unfortunate though the circumstances of our first meeting may be."

He held her gaze for longer than seemed necessary, not blinking. Violet recognised him then, but found her voice was still too raw to voice her discovery. The voice in her head struggled to say it for her.

You . . .

The newcomer took Kaspar's recently vacated seat, folding his arms across his lap and leaning forward, smiling. "I'm so glad to see you awake and well, little one. We have so much to talk about. How are you feeling?"

"Elder," Violet managed to find her voice for the traditional word. The last thing she'd expected to find aboard an Alliance ship, aside from herself, was one of her own.

Especially one with seven tails.

"Raines, little one. Arlin Raines. Perhaps you . . . perhaps the name is familiar?"

Raines, the seven-tailed fox. The one who refused to return home.

Yes. Your name is familiar.

I know who you are.

She nodded. "I know who you are," she managed to say.

Raines smiled brightly. "Excellent. Most excellent. And you, little one, what shall we call you?"

Violet hesitated, using the moment to try and sit up in bed. The ensign, Kaspar, had been trying to tell her something. A warning. They'd met, back at Port Border. But why would anyone care about that? There was no sense in lying to an elder. "Violet. My name is Violet."

The bright gold eyes flickered at that. Just a flash. "Violet, you say? Not . . . no, Violet, of course. You are a long way from home, child."

Child. That's insulting. I am not a child.

"*You* are a long time from home, Elder." It was blunt; the words surprised Violet. Time was she never would have spoken to an elder that way. But he didn't seem to take offense.

"Indeed I am and better for it. Returning home would be so tiresome, such a waste of time, of experience. Tradition is such an archaic shackle, a tedious pantomime I have neither the time nor inclination to pander too. I see no reason for my odyssey to come to an end because some long-in-the-tooth ancient decrees it should."

So many words. Who does he think he's talking to?

He shrugged. "But I do go on, child. How are you feeling? You were not long for this world when we pulled you aboard. You had been adrift for some time—the majority of the battle, I should think."

Violet put a hand to her head. It was throbbing. "The battle . . ."

"Is over," Raines anticipated her question. "You would be wise to turn your attention to the present."

"Did any—"

"It would be best," Raines interrupted her, "if you were to recall that you first came aboard the *Tantamount* at Port Border. That prior to that you had never set foot upon that ill-fated ship. Do you understand what I am saying?"

Violet looked at him. This was the second time someone had tried to warn her. She made to pull back the blankets covering her and put her feet to the floor. The room shifted the moment she did so. Raines caught her by the shoulders, pushing her back towards the bed. Her whole body was shaking.

"We will speak again, little one. When you are . . . stronger. And I would be most interested in hearing your impressions of this vessel. I had a hand in its design. When you are stronger, of course. More yourself. Until then."

STRONGER TOOK ANOTHER day. Possibly two, she lost track. Violet slipped back into unconsciousness not long after Raines left her bedside. She dreamed of darkness. Of glittering eyes staring back at her from that featureless black. On occasion she woke, her throat dry and parched or when more basic needs refused to be ignored. Every time there was one of two young men by her bed. She might have been flattered if not for the Alliance colours they wore. But they tended to her without rancour, brought her water and gruel, all she could manage. Once there was another figure, not much more than a silhouette. She heard someone call them Captain. Or was it Skipper?

Not my Captain. Not my Skipper.

Not your ship.

After a handful of those waking moments she awoke properly. Clear-headed and in more or less control of her aching body. Her feet went where she asked them to and no one objected when that was outside her room.

"Captain said to show you the ship, I guess we show you the ship," Kaspar led the way through the narrow corridors of the *Fata Morgana*. She disliked the silver hue of everything, of glowstones. It seemed forever since she'd seen proper colour. It made her eyes itch and she rubbed at them constantly.

"The old fox just wants to show off his work to one of his own," Gravel, whose real name was Brandon, said from behind. Violet felt small sandwiched between the two young men. Gravel was junior in rank to Kaspar but the two bantered like friends rather than comrades, like Piper and the skipper had used to.

They did that before. On Port Border. Where you first met them.

"Watch your language, Brandon," Kaspar still admonished him. "Try and at least act as if you're proud to wear the uniform."

"Pay me to sail, not to act. And I don't think she's going to be offended by me referring to Raines as the old fox."

"She might be offended if you talk about her like she's not here," Violet muttered.

"Now that's an entirely different matter," Gravel chuckled. "Which way, Niko? Up or down?"

Kaspar looked up and down, ceiling to floor. "What do you think? Down to the pumps in engineering or across to the main deck?"

"Up and down are all relative. Up and down, left and right. Port or starboard?"

"What are you talking about?" Violet sighed.

Kaspar turned around to face her. "This isn't a normal ship, Miss. Not like any you'd have been on."

"I've been on a few," Violet told him. "Alliance ships aren't so different."

"This one is," Gravel said.

"He's right," Kaspar nodded. "And you can thank Raines for that."

"Old fox has some crazy ideas."

"Some brilliant ideas."

"Same difference."

"Anyway," Kaspar shook his head. "It's easiest if you think of the *Fata Morgana* as the halves of two separate ships, fixed together." He cupped his hands. "Sweep away the masts and join the two together like so."

"But that would never work," Violet frowned. "No masts means no sails. How would you push the ship anywhere? What would the navigator work with? And where would the ballast go?"

"Through that centre-line where the ships meet, with a thinner lining in the outside cladding." Kaspar led her forward to a hatch and the galvanised stairs leading down to it. "This part's a little tricky. It's easier if you just see for yourself."

He started climbing, unfastening the hatch and disappearing through it. Violet put a confused hand to the railing.

"Go on," Gravel encouraged her. "I'll be right behind to catch you if you fall."

"It's just stairs," Violet said. They'd been headed down, several decks, and unless the ship was bigger, far bigger, than she'd guessed, they should almost be down close to the keel and ether line.

The closer she got to the hatch, the heavier her body felt. At first she dismissed it as an effect of the effort on her weakened self, but then she recognised the familiar feeling of being too close to a ship's etheric ballast. And as she stepped down through the hatch the world flipped. She fell, or rose, she wasn't sure, and someone caught her. Kaspar's arms set her down gently on what should have been the ceiling, except she was standing on it. And when she looked down she saw Gravel, halfway through the hatch in that ceiling, which was the floor she should was standing on. Two different worlds of up and down collided, right through the middle of the ship. Her eyes wanted to roll back into her head, couldn't quite figure out where to look. She had to take a moment.

Lucky you're being held.

Gravel performed a half somersault, rolling out of the hatch and landing on his feet next to them. He stood up, not bothering to hide his smile. Violet resisted the urge to smack him.

"This way," Kaspar said. "Raines will be down in engineering. He'll want to see that you're up and about."

Down? We just—which way even is down?

They found the elder Kitsune amongst the pumps and pistons. One deck up from where up and down disagreed. A thin haze of smoke lingered in the belly of the *Fata Morgana* and the slick and stench of oil clung to everything. There were more moving parts than Violet could comprehend a ship needing. It was more like the inner workings of a clock tower than any ship Violet had ever been on.

"Child, little one, how are we today?" Raines exclaimed, taking her hands and peering closely into her eyes the moment they found him. He had a roll of parchment in one hand. "You are feeling stronger, yes? More like yourself, perhaps?"

"Yes," Violet said, feeling like it was the correct answer.

"Excellent, excellent. Tell me then, what do you think of my creation? This is mine, of course, all mine. Years in the making, the first of many, one would hope. A new generation of ships. New ships for . . . for new times. Exciting times are upon us, child, exciting times."

Raines paced as he talked, becoming more animated with his hand gestures.

"It's . . . different," Violet thought was a safe choice of words.

"Yes," Raines turned, holding up one finger. "Different. This is the key. Different is the deciding factor, one must never allow oneself to become trapped in the mire of traditional thinking, of the tried and conservative way of conduction. Different. Exactly. A different drive, a different skin, even the ballast for such a vessel as this must be different. So many opportunities to branch out and explore new possibilities."

"This here," Raines beat on the inside of the hull with his knuckles. His touch echoed, creating a knocking effect that lingered.

"Metal, you see? Have you ever see a ship made of metal? A heart of iron has this maiden, as tough as those who crew her. They sing songs you know, of wooden ships and iron men. A romantic wistfulness of an era that never really was. What will they say of this lady and those aboard? Songs yet to heard being composed as we speak. But this hull," Raines spun, his eyes bright and shining as his voice picked up pace, "lighter than anything ever before constructed. It has to be, you see. Lighter and yet durable, like the crew! Hammered into ship, moulded for a purpose. There is a progression, a small ship, a small iron ship, no, that would never work. No, no, no. But this, this expanse of air and space, this flies true."

Violet found herself nodding, while admitting to herself that she had little actual comprehension of what Raines was saying. Elder he might be but beyond that she couldn't say what if any wisdom he might possess. She thought he might go on forever but something distracted him.

A fine line between genius and madness.

"Something is bothering you?" Raines asked.

"No, no, sorry," Violet apologised, aware her attention had drifted.

"You've been rubbing at your eyes." Raines tilted her chin up with his finger. "A problem, yes? Perhaps since you woke up."

Violet nodded.

"Ah, forgive me, I had not thought," Raines sighed. "Had not considered it. Not surprising, though."

"We can take her to the surgeon," Kaspar offered. "Won't take long, hasn't been too busy of late."

"Nonsense," Raines waved his hand in dismissal. "A surgeon? A doctor, they call themselves? A simple cutter, more like. No, nothing the fellow could do. This is a simple case of exposure. Your eyes, yes, and other extremities. It is the blood flow, you see. Eyes are rather complex mechanisms. What you consider a pulpy orb is much more detailed, of lenses and foci, bits and pieces that perceive colour and shadow, all arranged just so. Your eyes were mostly likely damaged from spending so long in the cold black amongst the mist."

Violet reached for her face, clapping a hand over one eye in alarm. "Damaged? Like, permanently? Blind, eye patches, stumbling-around-in-the-dark damaged?"

Calm down, calm down. Breathe.

Raines frowned at her outburst. "You have been having trouble, yes? With your vision, perhaps your depth perception. A lack of colour, perchance?"

Violet nodded, still covering one eye. "Can't see colour. I

thought it was . . . the stones, normal. It's not?"

"An easy fix, you will be relieved to know. Your eyes should restore themselves, in time. A few days if you are lucky, more likely weeks but possibly months. However, I do possess the means to correct your vision in the present, a compensation. Not one I carry on my person, I should say, but you will no doubt visit my workshop soon enough. We can see to you there. Until then, I do believe the first officer is the one expecting you."

"I'm to bring her to Aristeia," Kaspar confirmed, touching Violet on the shoulder. "Those were her orders, once you were done speaking with her."

"Must run, must run," Raines said, as if to himself. He looked round at the trio. "Do you hear that hum? What is that? What have those meddlesome trolls done? Never feed the trolls, never ever ever. Kaspar, do show our young guest around the rest of the ship. We'll talk later, little one. I'm curious as to what you think, most curious."

Kaspar said something in response which Raines didn't seem to notice. He was already in motion, his lips moving and hands gesticulating, clearly thinking aloud. Kaspar shook his head, pulling Violet along by the sleeve of her shirt, though he allowed his arm to drop once she started walking in step.

"Crazy old fox," Gravel shook his head wryly.

"Is he crazy?" Violet asked. "Because to me he was making the sense that's not."

"He built the ship," Gravel said. "Dreamed her up and convinced workmen madder than he to build it just so. And it's fact she sails truer than anything either side of the Lanes but I'm not the one to ask how. I know to leave well enough alone."

Kaspar led them through the long and cramped corridors of the *Fata Morgana*. At Violet's best guess they were headed somewhere towards the centre of the ship. It struck her as an odd place to find an officer.

"Are we going to the bridge?" she asked.

"The bridge is a little different here," Kaspar explained, stopping to heave open a door. It swung open like the hatch of a bubble. The entirety of the ship seemed to be made of metal, causing sounds to bounce and echo loudly. They stepped through and Gravel secured the door behind them, swinging the wheel shut. *More and more like a bubble*, Violet thought.

"The whole ship is different," Violet said.

"Depends what you're used to," Kaspar shrugged. "If you grew up in a mine like Brandon did then . . ." Gravel made a face at him and Kaspar's words trailed off.

"Anyway," he said, "the bridge is this way."

The bridge was presumably the room at the end of their current corridor. Violet glimpsed it briefly when the door in front of them opened for someone to emerge from inside. A hive of activity, officious-looking, harried people in pressed uniforms.

Ahead of her she could see Kaspar visibly tense. His gait became stiffer, hands almost clenching into fists. She felt Gravel shuffle up beside her, almost protectively. He had the same look to him.

"Mors Coldstream," Gravel whispered to her under his breath. "Stone-cold killer, they say. Except they call him a duellist to his face. Mors works for the captain, but he's Aristeia Quinn's second."

"Keep quiet, both of you," Kaspar hissed. He raised his hand in a crisp salute as Mors approached. Gravel did the same.

"Someone doesn't know how to salute an officer," Mors Coldstream drawled, looking Violet up and down. The man was tall and whip-like thin, lank black hair framing a face tinged almost grey. His lips pulled back in a smile that was almost rictus, exposing sharp teeth. Too sharp, they looked to have been filed. On his cheeks were matching twin scars, almost perfectly in line with his mouth.

"This is the survivor we took aboard, sir," Kaspar said stiffly. "She's not enlisted."

"That's hardly an excuse," Mors said. Violet didn't look at him, her attention was focused on what Kaspar had just said.

Survivor.

Meaning the *Tantamount.*

You knew that.

You just didn't want to think that.

But it wasn't just that filling her belly with cold sinking dread. Mors Coldstream. She'd heard the name, though she couldn't recall where. The man was a duellist, a killer, as Gravel had said. Dozens of deaths from those duels, duels that only ever had one outcome. The scars on his face, the Luscan smile, were said to be self-inflicted. The only scars he had, despite his chosen profession. And more than that.

Violet knew who his Captain was. Raines, but Kaspar had mentioned someone else. Violet knew that name too.

"Are you listening to me, girl?" Mors said loudly. Very slowly, refusing to let her arm tremble as it so desperately wanted, Violet raised a hand to her brow.

The languid, icy look never left Mors' eyes. "Respect for the Guild carries only so far. See that you instruct her in proper etiquette aboard this ship, Ensign. The gunnery crews have already shown they need the practice."

Mors laughed at his own words, as he walked past them down the corridor. Gravel was the only one to watch him go.

"You need to tell the captain," he said angrily to Kaspar.

"Let it go," Kaspar told him.

"If you don't, then I will. You can't let him threaten you like that."

"I said let it go," Kaspar said wearily. "The captain knows . . . he knows enough. You know who they put in charge."

"Didn't have much choice in that matter," Gravel muttered.

"No, we don't," Kaspar said, veering off course. "Now let's go make ourselves known to the first officer, Miss Aristeia Quinn. And Miss Violet, be good if you do salute her this time."

"Do you call her Skipper?"

"What?" Kaspar looked at Violet in surprise.

"This woman," she said, "Aristeia. Do you ever call her Skipper?"

"No," Kaspar shook his head firmly. "Never."

They call her the Gunner's Daughter.

Do you remember why?

Chapter 4

THERE WAS MORE to Sharpe's story. Clearly. Nel could have imagined much of it, if she had the imagination left. His escape. Meeting Violet, where she was. How he'd found her. How he'd found his way back to Nel and Quill. So many questions.

The answers weren't going to be found at the bottom of her cup. Just as well. She didn't want to know them.

Sharpe was with her. Quill had disappeared. Some mouthful about errands to run. Perhaps his shift on the docks had come up. Nel felt his absence. There was nothing but the cup in her hand to distract from the looks Sharpe was giving her.

If she'd had a mirror she knew her face would look like Sharpe's. Looking at her like that. A look she wasn't ready to deal with yet. Distractions were few and far between. And Sharpe wasn't the only one watching her either.

Bouncers were keeping an eye on her. That was fine, they didn't look so big now that she was sober and she didn't feel like picking a fight with them no more. Korrigan lass from some night or the other was running another card game. Still had green hair so that hadn't been just the drink. Stumpy was all in for the game, the club-footed Troll's meagre pile of coins pushed into the centre. Korrigan lass waved to Nel, beckoning her over. She shook her head back, no time for games, nor the coin. She got a lewd wink in response, a knowing look at Sharpe. Nel winced. It was the kind of look Gabbi would have given her.

Gabbi. Captain. Violet. Sharpe.

Supposed to be dead, but you're not. Thought you were dead. Put you out of my mind. Accepted it. Moved on.

She grimaced at the drink in hand. *Ok, maybe not.*

You're alive. But everyone else ain't. Yet you say Violet's alive. Except we got no idea where in the hells damned black she is. So where does that leave us?

Staring at the bottom of our cups. That's where. Same as before but worse.

Her other hand drifted up, without thinking. Nel frowned. Something was missing. She patted down her shirt. Wasn't imagining it. The deed was gone. Searched the rest of her clothing, almost frantic now. Nothing. Finally in her boots, she found something, a rolled-up scroll, scrappy and torn, tucked into one of them. She hadn't even noticed when she pulled them on. But what she pulled out was not the deed. No. Not even close. One of the jobs Quill had brought her.

Staring.

I just imagine that? Some drunken fancy? Hells, was it a dream? Something meeting Sharpe triggered? I thought he came after . . . but . . . Hells.

I don't wanna think about it.

Captain left her to me though.

The Tantamount.

Violet . . .

"Why didn't you tell them?"

"Tell them what?" Sharpe asked her.

"You said you didn't know." Nel leaned over the table. "But you knew. Vice, Cauldron, maybe more. You knew where we'd been, where we were going, where we laid our cargo. You could have given them something. And I can see how hard they tried to get you to talk."

"This . . . fell on my face," Sharpe grimaced, pointing. "And got kicked in it. Didn't think of that other thing, honestly."

"Hells to that. You ain't stupid. That stupid. You held out. Why?"

"Am I that much of a mystery? I really gotta explain that to you?"

"I chose the ship," Nel said loudly.

Sharpe just stared at her.

"Chose the ship over her," Nel went on. She had to. "Made Quill choose too. Chose for him. Then we lost the ship anyway."

"That wasn't your fault," Sharpe said. He had to say that. It was what you said.

"The hells it wasn't. I made a choice."

"And if you had to choose again?"

Nel swore, throwing the half-full cup across the room. It shattered and stained the wall.

"You'd do the same again," Sharpe said.

"Yes." Nel looked down at her hands, clenching her fists until her nails dug in. Almost drawing blood. "Damnit, Sharpe, what the hells are you doing here?"

"I wasn't looking for you," Sharpe said.

"Then why did you come here?"

"I needed a point of reference." Sharpe managed a small smile. "They didn't let me have a window, and Vice was the only place I could say for sure the *Fata Morgana* had been. I was hoping to track where they went next."

"Track them?" Nel asked.

Sharpe nodded.

"Track the ship you were on," Nel repeated. "Escaped from. Yet you didn't catch where they were when you took your leave?"

"It didn't go well, my leaving," Sharpe looked down. "Not a chart plotter, Nel. Doubt I could have looked out at the stars and said where we were anyways."

"Where did you end up? After, I mean."

"Char. Coal mining strip of a town."

"Never heard of it."

"Neither had I. Didn't stay long."

"And now you're here," Nel said.

"Nel, I didn't come here alone . . ."

Quill chose that precise moment to make his return. He barged his way through the other patrons unapologetically, ignoring any complaints directed his way. He requisitioned a stool, sitting at the head of their table, declining to seat himself alongside either of them. He took in the mostly full pitcher and fresh spills suspiciously. Nel dared him to berate her again. He didn't.

"You have told her?" Quill said to Sharpe, except making it clear it was not a question.

Sharpe winced.

"You have not," Quill frowned.

"Told me what?" Nel asked.

"Was getting there. Important things first. Like the girl."

"Ah," Quill conceded, to Nel's surprise. "Yes. And now?"

"Yeah, now. Fact is," he turned to Nel, "they sent someone after me."

"Who sent who?" Nel said. *Said he wasn't alone, didn't he?* "Who is someone? Who's they? And what do you mean after?"

"That was a pitiful explanation," Quill growled.

Sharpe threw up his hands. "Spent the last months trying not to talk to anyone, Quill. Keeping shut is my new habit. You want to tell it? You tell it."

"I will. He is being hunted. An assassin or bounty hunter. It matters little, actually; they will be from the Guild. They will be capable. They will be coming for him." Quill slapped the table. "That is how you tell it."

"The Guild?" Nel repeated.

"Aye." Sharpe ran a hand through his hair, a new habit. Nervous one. Maybe the long hair was as foreign to him as it looked to Nel. It was at the awkward in-between length sailors despised. Too short to tie back easily but long enough to be a problem.

"And how do you rate a Guild agent, Sharpe?" she asked. "I didn't buy you being part of that the first time. Ain't buying it now."

"Not me, so much as who wants me."

"And who wants you? Heathen? Captain Raines? Anyone else even know you?"

"Aye, they do, I guess. That'd be bad enough, only it gets worse."

"Gods damnit, Sharpe," Nel growled in frustration.

Sharpe turned serious. "I know, I know. They picked up my crew almost as soon as we stepped onto the docks. I barely turned around before it happened."

"Your crew?" Nel stared. "Since when do *you* have crew?"

Quill made a sound of disgust. "Have you two truly discussed nothing while I have been gone?"

"And where the hells *have* you been, Quill?" Nel asked.

"Looking for his crew."

"What crew!"

"Powder," Sharpe said. All eyes turned to him. "Swayne. Boxing. Java. Yarn. Chit. Horse."

"Your crew," Nel said. She looked longingly across the room, to where the servers were sweeping up the shattered remnants of her last drinking vessel.

"Those are fleet names." *The kind you have to be given. Trade in your old life for a new name and turn your back to the world.*

"You forgot one," Quill said.

"Didn't forget, Quill," Sharpe said. "Just holding it back for last."

"What's the name, Sharpe?" Nel squinted at him.

"Stoker."

"Gods damn you, Sharpe, there anyone you don't plan on dragging back in?"

"I didn't have a whole lot of options," Sharpe told her, defensive but sticking to his guns. "Not a line of people waiting to help out. You were gone, both of you, all of you. So I thought. Else I would have come looking. I left Violet there. Wasn't supposed to happen like that. So I meant to go back, and not alone."

Nel shook her head. "You already said you don't know where she is. Hells, how'd you even know where to find them you're with now? *I* didn't know where Stoker took them, not even where to look."

Sharpe exchanged a guilty look with Quill. It was quick, furtive. Obvious.

"You two," Nel growled.

"We discussed some options," Quill told her unapologetically. "At Rim, after we played ferryman. Sharpe, Stoker, and myself. The captains of the other . . . *ships.*"

"Few of the folk from Rim, too," Sharpe added. "Those that were willing to leave."

"That include our captain?" Nel asked pointedly.

"It did," Quill told her.

"Don't remember being asked to attend," Nel said. "Or being told about it afterward."

"Captain Horatio could have forgotten," Sharpe said. It was a reasonable point.

"You were upset. Afterwards there was no point in informing

you," Quill said. "The fewer people who knew . . . the fewer people knew. And at the time you were . . . yelling."

"I remember the yelling," Sharpe mused. "Fondly, rather."

"The fondness fades," Quill told him.

"What happened to your crew, Sharpe?" Nel asked. "Seems we're struggling to stay on topic here. And what's this got to do with you being chased?"

"Thing about the crew," Sharpe started to say.

"They're all Draugr," Nel said.

"How did you—"

"Wasn't a big leap, Sharpe. Story. Out with it."

"That's the point, Nel," Sharpe said. "Draugr. Second I was off the ship it looks like they were pressed. No one to speak for them and if they tried to speak for themselves . . ." He shrugged.

Nel leaned back. *Damnit.*

"Don't think it was a coincidence either," Sharpe said. "A few hours later they came after me. Tried to jump me in an alley."

"Your ship is gone too," Quill added.

"What do you mean gone?" Sharpe frowned.

"According to the harbour clerk it departed several bells ago. It did not lodge a destination—few ships do in Vice. But it was under new command."

"You find out who?"

"I did not bother."

"It even your ship?" Nel asked. "No, don't bother, I don't care."

"Still a hard woman, Chanel," Sharpe told her quietly.

"Again with the not caring." Nel waved down a server, acquiring a new mug. It came with a warning from the establishment. Her last chance. Seemed about fair. She poured herself another drink.

Quill slapped his hand over her mug. "He is right," the Kelpie told her before she could do anything about it. "You were always hard. You have never before been callous."

"And?"

"And the girl is alive. Do you intend nothing?"

"No."

"No," Quill repeated. Eyes narrowing, breath hissing out. Clawed fingers tightened over the rim of her mug.

"Nothing to be done, Quill," Nel said. "Got no ship and no

crew. Crew's dead. Captain's dead. Got no idea where Violet is even if that weren't the case. So it's just us, the three of us. No plan, no options, no hope."

"That is not nothing."

"You're right," Nel agreed. "That's less than nothing. And good for as much."

The liquid under his hand started to bubble. Then steam. Then froth. It boiled over in a heady wash, geysering up between his fingers. Quill swept it off the table in a fit.

"Sharpe has a crew," he started to say.

"Sharpe had a crew," Nel said. "Locked up. Probably shipped to the far corners of the lanes by now. Sharpe had a ship. That's gone too. And still got no idea where Violet is. Can I make this any clearer for you? Want me to write it down for you? Draw you a pretty picture? Or you rather I just smack you upside your scaly head again?"

Quill leaned back, pulling away from her. "The captain would be disappointed in you."

"Well, he's dead so he don't get no say."

"I disagree."

Quill adjusted the strap of his satchel, the one thing he'd had with him when the *Tantamount* died. His maps, his charts, the only things he actually cared about. All inside. And one more thing.

He placed the deed to the *Tantamount* on the table, rolling it out flat. Carefully. Almost gentle.

"Where did you get that?" Nel heard the tremble in her voice. Could feel the same quaver in her words.

"From you," Quill said. "A better question might be, where did you get it?"

"Hells," Nel leaned back. *Not a dream then.*

"From me," Sharpe said. They both turned to him.

"I had that on me," he explained. "When I escaped. Only . . . I lost it. When things went wrong."

Quill frowned. "There are holes in this story. How did it come to be here then? You are sure you lost it?"

"Damned sure." Sharpe was staring at it with near the same fascination Nel had felt. "You don't forget something like *that*. Not when you know what it is."

"I found it pinned to a damned board," Nel growled. Eyes up, looking at Quill. "The same one you've been visiting."

"Perhaps someone intended you to see it," Quill suggested.

"Or you."

"Maybe neither of you," Sharpe said. "Last I saw that I was on the *Morgana*, still wearing prison shiny and squatting in a bucket."

"And you came by it how?" Quill asked.

"Courtesy of your former captain," Sharpe said to Nel. "There was . . . an accident aboard. Something went wrong. They had to call for help. She turned up. Gave me that. Gloated. Felt like gloating, real knife twist."

"That doesn't make any sense," Nel said. She reached out, touching the deed. The captain's own skin. Still sort of felt like him. Thin and leathery. All dried up but still tough. Upside down so the letters didn't read right but she knew what they said.

"It makes sense," Quill voiced his disdain. "A petty insult."

"Not so petty, Quill," Sharpe said quietly. "Nothing about it was petty or small-minded."

"Seems cruel," Nel said. "Don't remember her as ever being cruel."

"Our encounters with her would suggest otherwise," Quill disagreed.

"Always had her reasons why she did what she did," Nel shrugged. "Never did things just 'cause she could."

Quill and Sharpe kept talking but Nel drowned out their words. Just meaningless noise in the background of the crowded room. Her fingers traced the words on skin, the pretty pictures, the names.

Man couldn't sign his own back, she recalled with half a smile. *Had to get it stamped.*

Got fancier since then, he had it touched up. Wonder who he got to do that?

Captain had been particular about who he let see the deed. Unorthodox though it was. Still legal though. Secure even. But at some point Horatio's vanity or sense of grandiose had gotten to him.

Added a fancy border. Calligraphied some of the lettering. Even put in a crest at the bottom there. His own damned seal and coat. Hells, Captain, ever the flair . . .

But it wasn't just the deed to the ship. It was Horatio's will too.

He'd left it to her, of course. Everything. Even the crew, listed by name in some cases. It wasn't a gift. It was the responsibility. Or something near enough.

Doesn't mean nothing though. All gone now.

There was a message from the captain to her, hidden between the lines of legal script. If you knew how to look.

If you knew where to look, you could read too much into anything. Stars, flights of swallows, the cast of a throw of bones, or the remnants of tea leaves.

There was a message waiting for Nel, and for once it wasn't going to be found at the bottom of a mug or with her eyes to the sky. It was much plainer.

Captain of the Tantamount, she thought. *Never wanted that, begged him not to saddle me with it. Wouldn't matter a damn to him that there is no* Tantamount.

Didn't matter the first time either.

This ship is as good as any other, Nel. It's the crew that make her. Or near enough.

Near enough.

Hells, Captain.

The deed to the *Tantamount*. A ship that no longer existed, and flayed from the skin of a captain who no longer walked among the living. They must have pulled his body in and found the deed after the battle. Why though? Maybe Nel was wrong, maybe it was done just to be cruel. Was hard to fathom another reason. In some ways it was just a horrific reminder.

But then it was always meant to be, weren't it? Right down to the wording.

Her fingers drummed the table, close to but not touching the deed now. Nel's eyes tracked her restless fingers, quickly shifting out of focus, then falling on the deed itself. Following the lines of the illuminated borders. Costly work. Maybe the captain had won a big game prior to this. Or maybe it simply explained where all his share of coin had gone.

Sloppy work in that edge though, blobs of colour. Looks like someone spilled paint. Must have hurt like . . .

Nel frowned, leaning forward.

Staring.

"Sonofa—"

She stood upright, kicking the chair back.

The other two jumped up with her. Sharpe wide-eyed and rushed, Quill immediately suspicious and cautious.

"What?" the Kelpie demanded, casting about the room. "What is it? What happened?"

"Look," she pointed at the deed.

"At what?" Quill peered, then met her eyes. "I do not see?"

"Me neither," Sharpe said.

"It's right there," Nel pointed. Still the confused eyes.

"This could be much simpler," Quill grumbled. "You could, for example, simply tell us. I am not so familiar with this as you are. I do not see—"

"Oh, for the ever-loving . . ." Nel turned around a moment, putting her back to them while she gathered herself. She pointed again. "There. That's not meant to be there. That was never there."

Sharpe leaned over the table. He shook his head. "Just looks like scratch to me. Blobs of colour."

"Not blobs," Nel told him.

"No," Quill frowned. "Flashes. Such as . . ."

"Such as a ship might use," Nel finished.

"Trader code," Quill observed. "Not the Alliance colour wash. The captain? A final message?"

"Captain didn't have that put in there," Nel said. "Fact is, it looks . . ."

"Fresh," Quill finished for her. "The rest of the tattoo is faded."

Nel winced. "Aye."

"Someone added that?" Sharpe said. "You're saying. After . . ."

"After," Nel confirmed.

"Heathen gave that to me," Sharpe said. "She was very sure to give it to me. I thought it was her way of twisting the knife."

"It may still be," Quill muttered.

"Not now, Quill," Nel told him. For once the Kelpie held his tongue, though his face gave away what he was thinking.

"What does it say?" Sharpe asked. "Never had the time to learn trader code properly."

"Says it plain and simple," Nel said. "Three coloured dots, same as a signaller. Run through three of the borders, here and here, gives a location."

"And the fourth? I just see two dots. Blue and red. Didn't think traders use blue."

"They don't," Quill confirmed. His eyes narrowed.

"Alliance use it," Nel said. "Blue and red just means *boats return*. Could be nothing."

"Or not," Quill grumbled.

"Meaning what?" Nel asked him.

Quill ground his teeth, reluctant in coming forth. "The colours. Mixed together make . . ."

"Purple," Nel said.

"Or violet," Sharpe said. "Violet."

"Or . . . yes," Nel agreed. She met Quill's eyes. "It's a stretch. Thinking this came from Vi."

"It did not." Quill's look was fierce.

"I agree with Quill," Sharpe said quietly. "This came from Heathen, if anyone. The deed and the message both."

"This place," Quill traced the air above the other three borders with his finger, "I know it."

"Just like that?" Nel asked. "Don't have to look at none of your fancy star paintings?"

"It is a cold sun," Quill told her, without, for the first time Nel could recall, any malice in his voice. "It is well known. The sun is cold, the mist is thin. The people are lawless. Ships do not go there."

"Sounds like," Nel said, "at least one ship does go there."

There was silence around the table.

"What a pity," Quill said, staring at Nel, "that we do not ourselves have a ship."

"Worry about the ship later," Nel told him. "First we get a crew. Stoker and the others, that's what we focus on. Then we get a ship. Then we get Violet."

"We?" Quill asked. "There is a *we* in this now?"

"Shut it, Quill. You're already involving yourself so don't go trying to drag tail now."

Quill snapped his teeth at her. Probably Kelpie for something. Nel didn't pay it much mind.

"What are you saying, Nel?" Sharpe asked.

"The hells you think I'm saying, Sharpe? Said it yourself, Violet's alive. Don't care a damn about the rest, she's alive, and you can take me to her then we're getting her. Need a ship and a crew to do that. So let's get a crew." She scowled at the man. "And stop using my name. Making my damned hangover worse."

Quill chuckled at her rant. His hissing, rasping laugh.

"And you, Loveland," she pointed at her navigator. "Not. One. More. Word."

Quill chuckled. He did have one more word.

"Finally."

"This bit here," Sharpe tapped it with his finger, drawing glowers from both Nel and Quill. "That's a Guild symbol. But this next to it, don't know it. What's it mean?"

Nel told him.

"It's a shellback."

Chapter 5

"First Officer Aristeia Quinn," Kaspar announced, stepping to the side and clasping his hands behind his back. "Ma'am, this is the captain's associate."

Violet frowned at Kaspar's words. Associate, so that was the way it was. Why then the warning about her first meeting with Kaspar and Gravel. And what Raines had said about when she came aboard the *Tantamount*.

Not when you came aboard, when you were to say you came aboard.

The woman with her back to Violet must be the first officer. The skipper. Aristeia, a woman no taller than Violet with severe cheekbones and greying blonde hair. Her uniform was cut to be sleeveless, a variation Violet had noticed amongst the crew. Temperatures were high inside the metal vessel. Aristeia's showed off leanly muscled arms and red and raised tattoos.

Aristeia Quinn, she knew that name. Stories told in the skipper's voice were coming back to her: a hard woman, one who never questioned orders. One who never stopped to ask. In service to the same master and commander as Mors Coldstream, aboard this strange new ship.

Aristeia spared a glance for Violet and Kaspar but didn't otherwise turn from conferring with her officers on the bridge.

A bridge unlike any aboard any ship Violet had ever been on. Fully enclosed, yet more metal and glittering with reflected light.

Where her captain had kept his bridge manned by a bare handful there were a dozen uniformed sailors present. They occupied stations, work benches whose functions Violet could only guess at, arrays of levers and cranks, turn wheels and piping. Prisms covered numerous surfaces, not to provide illumination as she'd first thought, though they did that as well. But images danced over the highly polished surfaces, images that had to be coming from outside of the room.

The first officer finally faced her, grim and in a mood. The woman had scars, more than Violet had seen on any one person. They formed patterns, what Violet had mistaken for tattoos. They weren't the kind you got from being the normal rank and file.

The gunner's daughter.

Everyone in the High Lanes had heard of Aristeia Quinn, of the Alliance. Not everyone knew her name, but all knew her reputation.

The first to steer a ship through the Eye of the Needle, victor at the battle of Misty Bells and more. The woman was famous. And famously ruthless too. Sailed with a crew of hardened shellbacks, everyone handpicked. And everyone a killer.

This woman, Violet thought, *she would have scared the skipper herself.*

She did scare the skipper.

She felt her knees go out under her, collapsing in a boneless heap on the floor. A hand on her arm, Gravel, cursing softly, hauled her up.

"You've heard of me," Aristeia observed.

Struck dumb, Violet shook her head in an affirmative. She thought she might have collapsed again if not for the hands steadying her.

She felt the woman's eyes on her, threatening to break down whatever defences she might have left. She cleared her throat.

"Leave us."

The bridge crew paused only a second before departing.

"Ma'am?" Kaspar voiced an interrogative.

"You two as well, Ensign."

"Ma'am," Kaspar's response was as crisp as his salute. Gravel squeezed her arm once before following his friend out the room. Leaving Violet alone. With her.

"You are wondering," the first officer said when the sound of the door being sealed receded, "I can see that. Your time in the black was disorientating. That is not uncommon."

Still mute, Violet nodded. She drew a shuddering breath.

"Am I so terrifying to you, girl?"

Violet meant to respond, but her voice came out a squeak. And that made her angry.

"Good." The first mate turned away, taking slow paces, not at all concerned about putting her back to Violet. "I'm pleased even the Guild can show proper deference. Raines is not the best ambassador for your organisation, invaluable though he is. Raines was also the one who insisted you be brought aboard. I was surprised you survived at all. But it means something to the man, and his goodwill means something to my superiors. A small price to pay. As one of his own, Raines has vouched for you, for your continued good behaviour, your parole, if you like. You understand the concept of parole."

"Aye," Violet managed to say. "Aye, I do."

"Good," the first mate repeated. "The ship you were placed upon, that was destroyed while attempting to flee from Port Border, she sailed as the *Tantamount*. It was originally known by another name, a name still recorded in the Ledger of the Deep. Are you aware of this name, girl?"

"No," Violet said, without even thinking. "No, ma'am," she repeated, "I wasn't."

A different name?

Aristeia nodded. "There was no reason you should. Renaming a ship is not something to be done lightly. One cannot just blot out a name written in the Ledger. But Horatio Phelps did rename his ship, years ago. The *Tantamount*. Few ships know only one master like she did. What was your role aboard her?"

Violet flinched at the sudden question. *Ledger of the Deep? What the hells was that? Skipper never mentioned . . .*

"Cabin girl, ma'am."

"Why? For how long?"

Violet knew not to answer the first question. "Not long, came aboard at Border. Half the crew was new hands. Ma'am."

Aristeia turned away from her then, clasping her hands behind her back. The raised scars were highly visible. The left arm bore the stencil of a bird in flight, the right had three slashes like claw marks.

Violet looked away before she was caught staring.

"As Raines said; your assistance in the pursuit was invaluable. We'll speak more later, girl. Ensign!"

Violet flinched at the sudden bark of command. Behind her a door opened, Kaspar appearing crisp and smart.

"Ma'am?" he inquired with a salute.

"Take the girl back to her quarters. She's free to move around, provided she is accompanied at all times, with the usual restrictions. See to it."

"Aye, as you say."

Kaspar stepped up to her, steering her out of the bridge. The first mate faced away the whole time.

"Kaspar," Violet said when the door shut behind them.

"Yes?" the young man asked her.

"What happened . . . what happened to the *Tantamount?*"

"She went down. With all hands still aboard her."

STRANGE AS THE *Fata Morgana* was it still boasted a galley. Sailors had to eat and the ship still had those.

But on a ship without sails, are they still sailors then?

It was her first look at the crew as a more cohesive whole. Unlike every other ship Violet had known, there was a communal space set aside for meals. Where other crew would lounge around the open decks or huddle below carousing in hammocks and amongst cargo, these were jostled together, cheek and jowl, in tight-fitted tables and benches. The seating was bolted to the deck floors, narrow and utilitarian, the ceiling low, and the walls spaced just far enough to accommodate and still let people pass through the aisles. Even a low buzz of conversation filled the room, bouncing and echoing off the metal walls.

The cook gave her a wooden bowl, porridge and ship's biscuits. People stared at her as she passed with her meal, then turned back to their own conversations. A curiosity, but not much more.

Triple baked and twice that.

The crew was a mix, lots of humans and Kelpies. But also Korrigans and Trolls. Men and women, though she still couldn't tell with the Kelpies. A female Korrigan twisted to look at her, then whispered something to her neighbour. Laughter followed. Violet tried to ignore that but all she felt was small and alone.

There was even a pair of Dunnies, the only folk she saw smaller than her. Barely two feet high and brown furred. Long horsey faces too. Or maybe it was her imagination. When she sat down she couldn't find them again in the crowd. And apart from Kaspar and Gravel, everyone had significant years on her. Seasoned and grizzled and meaner for it.

"GOES IN YOUR mouth, Miss Violet," Gravel prompted her as she spent an age turning over one of the biscuits, staring at it listlessly. "Helps if you've got teeth but won't do your teeth no help, as it is."

"Had hands," Violet said.

"What?"

"Cook. Had hands, not hooks," she said.

"Why wouldn't he have hands?" Gravel asked, exchanging a look with Kaspar. "More so, why would he have hooks?"

"Alliance cooks have hooks for hands," she told him. "Everyone knows that."

Another look. "That a thing?" Gravel asked Kaspar. "We ship out with the wrong fellow?"

"Don't believe everything you hear," Kaspar said.

"Except now I can't help but think of some poor handless fellow wandering the docks looking for our ship."

Violet dunked a biscuit in the porridge. The gruel was thick, stood right up in the bowl. Biscuit stayed there.

"Not hungry?" Kaspar asked her.

Violet shook her head. She twisted around, looking at all the other diners. No one looked back at her, or if they did meet her eyes it was by accident and glowering followed.

"What do they all do?" she asked quietly. She rubbed the palm of her hand, tattooed and calloused. Still scarred from rope burn too. "No ropes. No lines or sails to tend. What do they all do?"

"Plenty," Gravel told her, crumbs falling from his mouth as he dug into his own meal. "Still got winches, more of them in fact. That's why you see so many knuckle draggers here. Why it takes so much to feed them too," he waved as a murderous glare was directed his way. "All about gas and pressure. Lots of levers and gears involved. Things that go clank until they don't."

"A lot of them are marines," Kaspar said.

Tell it to the marines.

"Soldiers," Violet nodded.

"More soldier than sailor," Kaspar agreed. "You look tired. I think we should take you back to your room."

Violet shrugged. It wasn't even her room. Not really. So it didn't matter.

"Brandon, bring her bowl." Kaspar rose to his feet, stepping out of the bench seating. "In case her appetite comes back. Don't *you* eat it though."

Gravel held up his hands in denial. "Never crossed my mind, sir. Not for a moment."

"I don't mind." Violet pushed her bowl towards him, biscuits stacked on top. "Not hungry."

"You need to eat," Kaspar told her. "Still healing."

She just shrugged.

"Here, Miss Violet," Gravel reached to help her up. "Let's get you—" He gave a yelp and snatched his hand back, shaking it frantically. Violet flinched away too, a sharp snap on her shoulder where he'd touched her. There was a round of snickering from the other crew.

"The hells?" Violet grabbed at her shoulder, glaring at an abashed Gravel.

"Static charge," Kaspar said quickly. "Builds up from all the dry air. Metal makes it snap like that."

"Aye, that," Gravel muttered, looking down at his front. He'd spilled the bowl. "Was my clean shirt too. Damnit."

"Wasn't that clean," Kaspar said. "Let's go."

They steered Violet out, out of the eating area and away from the *Fata Morgana's* crew. All of them just sat there, like it was nothing. Enjoying their meal. But they could though, they were still alive to do it.

The first mate's words started echoing, like the sound in that room. Noises, repeated, echoing, buzzing in her ears.

All hands aboard her.

No survivors.

The words kept running through her head. She saw the faces of the crew of the *Tantamount*. They passed in front of her, one by one, again and again. Smiling, laughing . . . crying . . . screaming. She could hear them screaming. That was all she could hear. It filled the ship, filled her head. She wanted to scream to drown the noise out.

Violet grabbed at her head, wrapping fingers through her hair until it hurt, but it didn't stop the noise. She stumbled and fell, colliding with the narrow corridor, except she wasn't the only one. Kaspar and Gravel were both thrown violently from their feet, the ship rolling onto its side and taking them all with it. Kaspar cried out but Gravel went strangely limp, curling up into a foetal position and clutching weakly at his head. Kaspar went to his friend's side as the ship righted itself. Watching them, Violet realised she could still hear the scream, a cry, and that she recognised it.

Different as the *Fata Morgana* was there was still a method to its mad layout. So while her escort was distracted, Violet ran. She ran down the corridor, expecting the shouting to begin and follow her any second now. But so far nothing. She ran to the end of the corridor. Then a staircase, spiral and headed upwards. Then so was she. A wheeled door like one would find on a bubble. She spun the wheel and pushed against the fitted door. It swung open reluctantly with a sucking sound. And beyond that lay a hatch, opening, as best she could tell, onto the outer deck. And what would the outer deck of this strange ship look like? She was about to find out.

Flat. Featureless.

The outer deck was a smooth and flattened plane, broken only by the harsh angle of what on another ship would have been the bridge or the wheel house. There were canopies of curved, hammered metal but for the most part there was nothing. Everywhere she turned, nothing. She stood alone on an empty metal plane against a starlit background.

Stars, she thought. *Which stars are they? Where are we? Where am I?*

She ran out onto the centre of the deck, looking up and around, turning all the while, trying to see anything familiar. The stars were bright, as bright as anything she could remember. And there was hardly any mist to obscure them. And the wailing cry she'd been hearing rocked the ship again.

Something white and massive filled her vision, looming up over the *Fata Morgana*. A ray, not a school like she'd seen before from the *Tantamount*, but a single, solitary ray. And it was well matched in size for the *Fata Morgana*. She couldn't tell how big the ship she had her feet planted on was but it felt bigger than the

Tantamount.

Than it was, girl. The Tantamount *is gone.*

The lone ray circled the ship, rolling and looping. Its cry, its song made the metal under her feet vibrate and rattle. So much so that she didn't hear Niko Kaspar behind her.

"You need to come back inside!" He grabbed her wrist and spun her around, pulling her eyes away from the spectacle.

Kaspar's eyes were wide. He was breathing like he'd run hard after her. Some distance behind him she saw Gravel, tottering on unsteady feet. The side of his head was lit by a trickle of blood, almost the only colour to be seen and vividly red for that. Everything else was shades of black and grey.

"Come inside," Kaspar pulled on her arm. "The captain doesn't need to know, not about this, but you need to come inside now!"

Violet planted her feet stubbornly. "The ray," she twisted and pointed with her free arm. "What's it doing?"

"We don't have time for—" The ship twisted under them again, and Violet would have fallen if Kaspar hadn't been holding her arm. Gravel did fall to the deck, cursing, but got back up again. The ray disappeared from sight but the song continued.

"If it doesn't stop they're going to open fire on it." Kaspar grabbed her around the shoulders and started moving her in the direction of the hatch. "You don't want to be out here, you don't want to see."

"Why?" Violet twisted and struggled but found herself held firm. She was still weak, she knew. "Why would they open fire on it? Why?" The last word was practically a scream. They passed Gravel, and he waved them on groggily, falling into step. He pulled the hatch shut and sealed it behind them.

"Why?" Violet shook her head, leaning back against the corridor wall. "Why?"

She wasn't even sure what she was asking. Kaspar held her by the shoulders. She heard gunfire, deep and throbbing. With each salvo she felt a hum and a vibration in the ship's bones. A tingling in her feet, distracting her from the ray's cry.

"Why?" she repeated, clutching at Kaspar's wrist.

"It keeps happening," he said. "Rays follow the ship. We try and avoid them but if they get too close, if they endanger the ship . . ." His words were punctuated by another salvo.

Violet looked away from him, and she felt herself sliding down the wall. Kaspar knelt with her.

"Please believe me," he told her, "when I tell you I am only trying to protect you. My orders are to protect you. You didn't need to see what's happening out there."

You? Protect me?

"Don't need you to protect me," Violet whispered. "Don't need anyone to."

"You've got someone all the same. Brandon, give me a hand here. We're taking her back to her room."

The cry had stopped. So had the guns of the *Fata Morgana*. There was only silence outside now.

CHAPTER 6

NEL REMEMBERED THE last time she'd been to the Draugr pens on Vice. Crowded and dirty, with customers and stock. The word sat uncomfortably with her. But it was hard to think of a better one; the rows of silent, listless Draugr seemed barely aware of their presence. But what if they were? Not something she wanted to think about.

It hadn't been an enjoyable experience last time. This time she'd come with a mind to buy, only the kind of buying that didn't pass with coin.

"All right, where are they at?" she asked.

"No idea," Sharpe said. "Quill?"

"They are with the new arrivals," Quill told them.

"Take us to them," Nel said.

Quill pulled his hood across his face, stepping through the mud that made up the paths between stalls and pens. In no way was he trying to conceal his identity, only to keep out the worst of the stench.

"Here," he said after minutes of trudging. It was a roped off section of the markets, Draugr of different shapes and sizes standing idle in rows, swaying and, in at least one case, sinking. Nel didn't recognise any of them immediately, certainly not Stoker, but they were dressed like sailors. At least two had tattoos she would have associated with that life. All of them looked rough, the falling-apart-might-have-been-dug-up kind of rough.

Greying skin that didn't move the way healthy flesh should, eyes liked smoked glass, clouded and unerring. And blackened extremities, the tips of his fingers and the point of his nose, the signs of congealed blood. They shouldn't be alive.

But then they hadn't been for a long time now.

"Help you folks?" the attendant asked them. A Vodyanoi, bringing a flicker of distaste to Nel that she tried to hide. Didn't have good experiences with their kind, nor was she in the charitable mood.

Especially seeing as I intend on robbing you blind.

"Looking for labour," Nel said. "Of the pretty kind. Heard ships in the High have been running with these for a while now."

"Aye," the attendant said. "Some do, merchantmen mostly, though the Fleet runs with them too. Hard to find what you're looking for out here though. Most of these are tagged to ship back into the High anyway. Big demand at auctions there."

"What about these?" Nel pointed. None of the Draugr had reacted to them yet, but she'd made Sharpe keep well back and behind her and Quill. No sense tipping their hand if they could avoid it.

"Ship out the day after tomorrow, headed for Castle. Big Fleet station out that way, plenty of trade lanes besides. Should fetch a premium."

"This one is prettier than the last one we looked at," Quill pointed to the closest Draugr. Nel had to concede that one had an impressive blonde beard, even braided down the middle.

"The facial markings," Quill went on, "they are your kind's mating plumage, yes?"

"I'll give you some mating plumage, Kelpie," Nel warned him. "The black and blue kind. Really attractive amongst *your* kind, ain't it?"

"I do not care for the other markings," Quill pronounced, ignoring her. "So drab. Boring. I am bored. Come, we should go."

With that the Kelpie turned on his taloned heels, stepping back through the muddy trail as delicately as he could, holding the hem of his cloak up. Sharpe did a take at Quill's disappearing act but followed him, leaving Nel and the attendant alone.

"Bloody factors," Nel said to him. "Always looking at the wrong parts of the deal."

The attendant nodded sympathetically.

Nel hefted a purse, weighted with coins, in one hand. It was almost all of Quill's dock wages. His ill-temperament was in no way acting. He did draw attention to himself on the way out, mostly the attendant's but some of the Draugr eyes too, eyes that weren't meant to be curious. One in particular stood out. Nel finally spotted Stoker at the back of the mob. That was all she needed. Almost.

"Do me a favour," she said as she bounced the bag. "Want to bring my captain through, see if there's merit in taking on some of this lot. Can you see it that these ones in particular don't get loaded until then? Not asking for special reserve or nothing, just a hold off on your duties."

"Seems acceptable," the attendant said, eyes moving up and down with the bag. "Can't make any promises on sale though. Have to make the purchase worth more than the run to Castle. But I can make sure they're loaded up last—maybe your captain can talk my factor's language. Best I can do."

"Captain's got deep pockets when he wants something," Nel assured him. "Likes to play the long game too. Just need a day or so to sort business and bring him around here."

"Think that can be arranged, then."

"Good man," Nel flicked the bag his way. "Watch for us tomorrow. Plan to be back."

"Aye, I'll do that. A pleasure, Miss."

Nel joined Quill and Sharpe outside. The Kelpie was still simmering.

"Whatever your plan I hope it does not involve coin," he said to her. "Because we have none. At all."

"Calm your scales, Quill," Nel said. "We got what we needed."

"That was them," Sharpe told her. "All of them. We're lucky."

"I know, saw Stoker. Was keeping to the back."

"Yarn was up front. The pretty one with the beard. That Quill liked."

Nel smirked. "Don't have long. So this is going to have to happen fast. Tonight even."

"You have a plan?"

"Enough of one. Going to need a few things though."

"Such as what?" Quill asked.

"A ship would be helpful. All well and good breaking a crew out of lockup, wouldn't be the first nor the last to do that. Don't do much good if when the chasing starts we have nowhere to run.

"So," she opened the floor to them, "who's got ideas on where we can liberate ourselves a ship?"

Not surprisingly, it was Quill who spoke up. "I may have something."

FLYING. NO, FALLING. Cold. So cold. She couldn't move. Trapped in ice, limbs frozen solid. And always falling; she never stopped. Frozen and falling, and she couldn't even scream.

Violet jerked upright, that scream choking her. She gasped, drawing deep and desperate mouthfuls of air. Her throat burned, the memory of ice so sharp and contrasting.

"Violet?"

The voice came from outside her door. She didn't have a door. There were no doors on the *Tantamount. Removed, the captain said. Years ago.*

Violet drew another breath, raising a hand to her chest. Heart hammering, hand shaking. She couldn't steady either one. That made her angry.

The door creaked open, dark hair, tied back. All slick and shiny with grease. *To keep it from getting caught in the machines,* a voice in her head told her.

She tried to place the face, the grey touching off an ugly thought, something she didn't want to think about. Her eyes were getting worse. The voice wasn't helping much with the face. She tried for the name.

Kaspar. Niko Kaspar.

"Bad dreams?"

She nodded mutely.

"May I?" He gestured to the edge of the bed. Violet nodded again, pulling up her knees and hugging them to her chest under the blanket. Kaspar took a seat by her feet, legs hanging off the bed.

"They call it the Falling. The Falling Sickness, Frozen Falls, Winter's Kiss, but usually just Falling. Lots of people get it, sailors often. The ones that fall overboard and live through it."

"I know what they call it, and I didn't fall overboard," Violet glared.

"No, you didn't," Kaspar's voice was calm.

Probably meant to be reassuring. Condescending prat.

"Sometimes it helps to talk," Kaspar suggested.

Violet hugged her legs closer, resting her chin on her knees.

"It happened to me," he said at length.

Violet turned her head to face more in his direction.

"I don't like talking about it either."

She snorted. "Prat."

"You can do better than that."

"Alliance monkey," she whispered, so softly he wouldn't hear. She heard though. Heard the words spoken in a dead Kelpie's voice.

"I remember reaching," Kaspar said, his eyes distant. "Trying to grab hold, hold fast. Anything. There wasn't anything. It's the first thing I do now. Hold onto something. Make myself open my eyes. See all the colours. See the things you don't see in the mist. I call them, name them, until I convince myself I'm not falling."

"Does that work?"

Kaspar shrugged. "If it doesn't I start screaming."

Violet laughed, weakly.

Kaspar studied her now. "The captain . . . Raines, vouched for you. More so, the first mate agreed to it. Why?"

"Don't know."

"Do you know him? He seems to know you. From back home, maybe?"

"Home isn't like that."

"What is it like?"

Violet studied the tops of her knees. "Where do I come from?" she said at length.

Kaspar frowned, his brow furrowing in confusion. "Shouldn't I be asking that?"

"Not me, stupid." She looked up at him. "Kitsune, where do we come from?"

More frowning. "Never thought about it. I just assumed . . ."

"We never tell," Violet told him. "Never."

"Never?" Kaspar smiled.

"Never," Violet said. "We're mysterious. All . . . mysterious-like."

Kaspar's eyes narrowed. "Are you baiting me, Kitsune girl?"

"Maybe. How many of us have you seen? Ever?"

"Not many," Kaspar admitted.

"How many?"

"A handful, a dozen, maybe less."

"We never grow old," Violet said. "Never get sick, neither. You ever see an old Kitsune, Kaspar? Ever?"

"Haven't seen enough to be sure. But none older than Raines, for certain."

Raines, Violet thought. *He ought not be here still. He's seven-tailed and too long from home. Powerful old. Powerful friend to have, if he was your friend.*

"You're teasing me, Kitsune girl," Kaspar smiled at her. "Don't think I don't see you doing it."

She shrugged shoulders still stiff from the cold. Or maybe just the memory.

"You're an easy to one to tease. All stiff and formal-like. All Alliance-like."

"That a bad thing?"

"Could be worse. Known some Alliance folk."

"Good folk?"

"Might have been. All dead now."

Kaspar appeared taken aback for a moment but it didn't take him long to regain his composure. He took another moment to look around the room.

Yes, we're alone. Door's shut even.

"You remember how we meet, Kitsune girl? Back on Border, during the riots."

Oh, I remember you.

Violet nodded.

"That doesn't seem strange to you, us meeting back there and then you ending up here, after being pulled out of the black?"

"Except we didn't meet," Violet said, smiling at the immediate frown that marred the ensign's brow. "Gravel and I were doing the meeting. You were doing the interrupting."

Kaspar laughed. "I'm so sorry. But I remember your Kelpie friend doing the interrupting. Now he was a mean-looking sailor."

"Quill," Violet said. She felt her lip quiver. "He's dead now. Like all of them."

Kaspar sighed, running both hands through his hair, pushing it back in a nervous habit. "Aw, hells, I'm sorry, Violet. Didn't mean to bring up bad memories."

"It's all right," she said. "It's all bad memories. Not your fault."

"It does get better," Kaspar said.

"Yeah?" Violet said. "When does the falling stop?"

"When someone catches you."

Violet made a face at him. "Sick of being rescued. Don't wanna be the one being rescued no more."

"Sounds like a good start," he assured her.

"Happened to you, right?"

"Getting rescued?"

"No, falling into the black."

Kaspar nodded, not saying anything.

"Tell me."

"And in return you'll tell me all your secrets, Kitsune girl?"

"No."

"That hardly seems fair."

"Life isn't," she told him. "Not on the High or in the Free."

"Fair call," Kaspar nodded. "All right, there was a ship. I fell off it. Crew barely got it turned around before I froze to death out there."

"You lose anything?" Violet asked him. "To the cold, I mean. Extremities or . . ."

Kaspar met her gaze without flinching. "Nothing important."

The contest held for a moment, then Violet's resolve broke. So did her face and she started laughing. Kaspar smiled ruefully, maybe the closest he got to laughing.

He's the serious type, this one. Surprised he even knows how.

"I'll get us some cards," Kaspar said, wiping at his eyes. There were tears. "Good way to pass the time. Can already tell you've the face for it."

CHAPTER 7

"THAT IS THE one." Quill pointed.

"Why that one?" Nel asked, tugging her hood lower on her face.

"Because we have a chance of stealing it," Quill said. "And with so few of you to act as crew, we require a ship of modest size."

The ship Quill had chosen was a sloop. Almost more brig-like though, with two masts rigged for squares and headsails. Small enough to be manageable but she'd be fast. Looked to be a shallow draught too. Wouldn't be much stow for provisions or cargo. Nel would never have looked at this kind of ship with her former life in mind. But that was just that, a lifetime ago.

"We managed the *Tantamount* with less," she said.

Quill shrugged. "We were not attempting to chase down an Alliance warship at the time."

"Ten gunner," Sharpe commented from behind folded arms. "Not much to be going after the *Morgana* with. Even worse if we have to worry about big blighty."

Nel winced. "Could we not refer to the dreadnought as *big blighty?*"

"Why not?"

"Disrespectful."

"One assumes we will not be trying to outshoot your former prison ship," Quill interrupted, to Nel's relief. "Though it would not be the first time we attempted such lunacy."

"Second thoughts, Quill?" Nel asked. *Second thoughts—given how quickly you took us here makes me wonder if you haven't been eyeing her up already. New career for you, Loveland Quill, pirate. Liberator of unsuspecting ships. Bane of trader captains across the Free Lanes.*

That was uncharitable, she chided herself. Quill had been working the docks. Would have seen all the ships coming and going.

Seen them and wanted one for himself.

Quill declined to reply, changing the subject again. "Even for a ship that size, the two of you will not be enough. Not for a voyage of any length, not should we require any sort of manoeuvring to finally be rid of this place. We will need more hands."

"Gonna be getting more hands," Nel said. "Get hands, get ship, leave port. In that order."

Quill shrugged, unwilling to argue the point.

"Nothing to say?"

"Much, but I will wait until after we leave. I assume we plan never to return here, Vaughn. Vice is lax with its laws but I do not believe we will be welcome if word of this gets around."

"Only in trouble if we get caught, Quill."

"There a plan for staying out of all this trouble?" Sharpe asked. "Other than dreams and fancy?"

"There's a plan," Nel said. "Comes with some risks."

"Risks for who?"

"Wouldn't risk anyone I liked, Sharpe."

Quill laughed.

"That's . . . not very comforting," Sharpe told her.

"Funny you should think that."

"So who does it involve?"

"Draugr," Nel told him.

"You mean Stoker and the rest," Sharpe said.

"Aye, former Alliance midshipman Stoker. That's who I meant."

"I don't follow."

"But Draugr do."

"Is this supposed to be making any sense to me?"

"Could do, if I explained it some more."

"Ah," Sharpe nodded. Waited. Expectantly.

Nel let him. "Not so much fun to be on the other side, is it?"

Sharpe grimaced. "Fair play, Chanel."

Nel growled at him.

"Skipper," he corrected himself. "Soon as we get you a ship."

"Tell it to the marines," she grinned.

Sharpe stared at her hard. Nel took immense satisfaction in that.

"Marines take orders even better than Draugr," she said. "Sailors take a bit more yelling but they'll move with the mob. Simple creatures, really. Gonna make that work for us."

"Tell it to the marines," Sharpe repeated.

"Exactly. Ship we're chasing is full of marines, shellbacks at that. Need to start thinking that way."

"Something else we might tell the marines," Quill ventured. There was reluctance in his voice.

"Got a story for us?" Nel asked. She hugged her arms to herself. Because it was cold. Not because they were shaking. Drying out . . .

"We do yet possess one . . ." Quill considered, "*friend* on this world."

"Friend of ours or a friend of yours?" Sharpe asked pointedly. "Wouldn't be more drinking buddies now would they?"

"They would not. Nor would they consider you a friend. And given our endeavour . . ."

"Speak your mind, Quill," Nel sighed.

"Jack," Quill said shortly.

"Hells."

Korrigan Jack.

The Kelpie was right. She hadn't considered Jack. Nor had she caught sight of her former crewman since they'd made landfall in a cracked bubble.

"You been keeping tabs on him, Quill?" she asked.

Of course he has, wouldn't have suggested it otherwise.

"I believe I can find him, yes."

"Do that," Nel said.

"Jack's still around?" Sharpe asked, annoyed. *Really doesn't like not being the one in the know.*

"For now," Quill said vaguely.

"Something you ain't saying," Nel said. "Out with it."

"Jack is a somewhat blunt instrument," Quill told her. "Who

nonetheless has his uses. When properly applied."

Generous of you, Loveland. Times must be even more desperate than I thought for you to be keeping Jack in mind. Didn't think you ever forgave him for the rats.

"And you can get him to sign on? Don't need to ask him?" Sharpe said.

"He's crew, so yeah, Sharpe, I trust him. More than I trusted you."

"And what you just said? About not wanting to risk anyone?"

"Anyone I like," Nel shrugged, which earned her a sibilant laugh from Quill. Might even have been approving. "So Jack comes along. Wouldn't feel right otherwise."

Besides, what might the lad get up to if we did leave him here?

"Looks like these fellows made port recently." Nel inclined her head at the ship they'd settled on. "Good for us in that the crew probably scattered to every grimy drinking hole on the cheap side of Vice."

"You know them all then?" Quill asked.

"Stow it, Loveland. Won't be setting sail without us, is what I mean. Bad part is they might be low on provisions."

"We'll manage," Sharpe said. "Just the three mouths to feed."

"Four," Quill corrected him.

"Four, right."

"It's going to be tight," Nel said. "That trade ship moves for Castle tomorrow morn. Means we have to go in tonight and take *this* ship straight after. Else things get messy. Lots of attention messy. We don't want that, especially not in Vice."

"Indeed not," Quill agreed.

"This plan of yours," Sharpe said. "Planning on sharing it yet?"

"With you? Not even a little. Quill, think you can track down Jack by tonight?"

"Track down? Yes, I know where he can be found."

"Good. Grab him last though, don't want him knifing no one when we go back into the stalls. That would be bad."

"That . . . would be best," Quill said.

"Best laid plans," Sharpe muttered.

"Exactly," Nel said. "This is our last night on Vice. Don't nobody get themselves knifed. That's not part of the plan."

"Wʜᴀᴛ ʏᴏᴜ ᴅᴏɪɴɢ?"

Kaspar ignored her, her and the card game he had been neglecting to join. His attention was focused on the papers he held. Half a dozen loose leaves that had been bound in twine.

"Best be leaving him to it, Miss Violet," Gravel advised her. "Ensign don't like to be disturbed when he's reading his love notes. At full attention he is."

At this Kaspar did look up, his face descending into its habitual scowl lines. "Shut up."

"Changed much have they, sir? Those squiggly lines there, since you read them the other day? And the day before that and the week before—"

"Fine," Kaspar rewrapped his letters and pulled his chair over to join them. "What are we playing?"

Gravel smiled and dealt him in.

"Who are they from?" Violet asked. "These love letters?"

"They're not—" Kaspar caught himself. "They're about things back home. Folks and events. Only one to gets new out here."

"Ain't news when you've read them so much you've rubbed the ink off," Gravel said. "And how is our Mikel? Still stationed out at Saddle?"

"Who's Mikel?" Violet asked.

"That would be Mikel, Miss Violet," Gravel told her, pointing at the letters. "Marine lad, stationed back in the High. Writes to me and Kaspar. To Kaspar anyways, but sometimes the ensign will read to me. And beautiful letters he writes too, our Mikel. Like flowers they are, at least they look as much to me. Don't make any other kind of sense."

"Who's Mikel?" Violet asked again. She gave Kaspar a look. He was still ignoring her.

"Manliest of men, Miss Violet. A marine he is, as I said, with the muscles and the marching. And also the letters and—"

"Brandon," Kaspar slapped his letters down. "Are we playing or not?"

"*We* are." Violet played a high card, beaming. "If you can beat that."

Kaspar did. Unnecessarily, in Violet's mind. Turned out he had cards to spare as he won the next two hands as well.

She hated losing. Hated. So she changed tactics. "So what's in the letters?"

Kaspar flushed. "Nothing."

"That's a lot of time you spent reading nothing."

"It's hard. For me."

Gravel laughed.

"It's not funny, Brandon," Kaspar glared.

"Certainly is, sir. Least you can read, however it might make you feel."

"You know what I mean."

"I don't know what you mean," Violet pushed him on the shoulder. "Stop talking circles. Tell me about Mikel."

"Why?"

"Because I asked, that's why. You rather I asked Gravel? Gravel, what does—"

"I don't . . . read well," Kaspar gestured, waving his hand in front of his face.

"Read better than me, sir," Gravel studied the cards. He carefully played his next.

"Letters don't stay still for me when I read," Kaspar said, his skin flushed. "They move, like the ship. Worse when the ship moves too. It takes me longer than it should to make sense of words. Even when I've read them and know what they say."

"That why you read them again and again?" Violet asked.

Kaspar shrugged. "I work at it. Sometimes it's easier."

Gravel grinned at him. "I think you just like to—"

"I saw you play that double card there, Landsman," Kaspar interrupted. "Think you should be taking that turn and skipping a round."

Violet laughed, nudging Gravel. "And you thought he weren't paying attention."

Gravel's discomfort was covered by the ringing of a bell. Three tolls, the change of a watch. Kaspar gathered up the cards, looking up and waiting until Gravel returned all the cards he'd been holding. Kaspar stowed the cards and his letters in a satchel, making sure it was secure before hanging it from one of the hooks in Violet's cabin.

"No more games," he said. "We actually have work to do. And that includes you, Miss Violet."

"It does?"

"Assuming you know how to walk the black?"

Violet gave him a long, slow grin.

THE *FATA MORGANA* was unlike any ship Violet had ever been on. In all honesty that hadn't been many, and only the *Tantamount* had she spent any considerable time under sail. The *Morgana* didn't have sails, nor even timbers, for the most part.

Being different came with its own set of problems, something Violet could relate to. A rueful thought. The *Morgana* was a misfit, one of a kind, but the kind that was celebrated as a step forward.

Not an outsider reviled. Progress. Celebrated and admired for being different.

The skin of the ship was metal, both copper and iron. Metal sheets warped and wrapped around cold hammered ribs. And it was filthy.

Gravel was across from her, feet planted to the outside of the deck, gripping his safety rope with both hands. There were two more sailors further down from him, more focused on their jobs, that of scraping the corrosion from the outer hull.

Violet was looking up. Or maybe it was down, the difference still confused her. Above was the stars, calling to her, pulling at her senses. The stars held all her attention. Out here it was quiet, the noise that filled the insides of the ship was muffled, out here she could breathe.

Violet leaned back, tilting her head until all she saw was black and mist and stars. The rope was rough and tangible between her hands, the coarse fibres rubbing against the scars on her hand. Literally her anchor.

Violet sighed, breathing in cold air. Tightened her grip on the rope. Still there. And she had a job to do.

At her feet was the gritty black rust that plagued the ship and needed to be scraped off.

"I thought it was supposed to be red," she called out to Gravel.

"What?" Gravel answered, confused.

"The rust." She rolled her head over to him, meeting nervous eyes. He clearly didn't like being out here, despite the rope.

Silly boy, the ether's holding his feet to the deck, to the hull, one plane, two, a dozen, he's not going anywhere. The rope isn't even necessary.

She checked. The rope was still there. However unnecessary.

"The rust, the corrosion," she said. "Isn't it red? Or green sometimes. This is just black."

Gravel made a face at her, smushing his features up. "It is, it's just the light you're standing in. It looks red from here and the sooner it's gone the sooner I won't have to stand here."

Violet looked down. The rust was definitely black, black and gritty against a grey hull. Everything was shades of grey and silver.

It was like being below deck, in the Lanes, rooms lit by glowstones only. The notion brought to mind dreams, things half-remembered and hazy, absent colour and sound. Violet thought of the last time she'd void walked, trying to patch the hull of another ship, before a rush of water almost swept her away.

Violet leaned back, arching her back and neck until all she could see was black and mist, the shroud pierced by tiny pinpricks of starlight. She felt the memory of cold on her arms, enough to make the hair bristle, but it was only a phantom feeling. She really didn't feel the cold anymore. But being outside again, looking up at the black, that felt right to her.

As long as your feet stay planted to the ship.

Sound carried out here, no bustle of the interior to muffle it and no noise from outside the envelope to muddy the background. She could feel vibrations through the hull though, a constant buzz from the workings of the ship. And something else. A pattern, almost.

Shrill whistling interrupted her thoughts, bosun's whistling, the piping short and sharp.

"Change of plans." Gravel grabbed for her hand, pulling her along. He held onto his rope, stepping vertically as they were reeled in.

"What? Let go, I can do it myself." Violet tried to pull away. Gravel held on, probably for the best as letting go would have thrown her back.

"Ray sighting," Gravel told her, looking over his shoulder. "Means back inside. If we change course now we might avoid them but we don't want to be out there when the ship turns. Planes get all messy and these ropes are long enough to float you outside the short spaces of the envelope."

Not again, not again.

Violet shook her head, pushing down on the idea of the black.

Of falling. Her moment of tranquillity was gone, the only sound and pattern she could make out now was booted feet running along the metal skin.

The ray's song grew louder. It had to be a big one. Not from the rising sound but from the shadow that passed over the ship, something big enough to put itself between the ship and the nearest star. Light arced out in response, the ship's weapons firing on the ray. But they couldn't have much of an angle on the creature unless . . .

The ship tilted right under her feet. Violet stumbled, fell, and then the ship wasn't there anymore. She grabbed frantically at her tether rope, her mind spiralling as she felt herself start to drift.

No, no, no, no!

Something inside her head was screaming, she felt the cold lapping at her heels. Could she be that close to the edge of the envelope already?

A jolt went through her whole body, arm almost pulled out of her shoulder, numb skin, then solid ground under her feet again. Fingers entwined in hers.

"Come on, Miss Violet," Gravel told her, holding her hand tight. "Don't be doing that now. Inside we go."

CHAPTER 8

"WHAT'S HE DOING?"

Nel turned her head to follow the sound of Jack's voice. The Korrigan and the Kelpie. And her.

Jack, soot stained and blistered, reeking of burnt hair and leathers. Quill, back against the void, clawed hands clasped in front of him, just staring. How many times had she seen him like that? Praying, meditating, ignoring the rest of the world. How long since he'd even moved?

"Crying."

"Kelpies don't cry. Can't." Jack stated it as he would have normally done. But there was nothing in the words.

Kelpies cannot shed tears, so you will be crying on the inside.

Damnit, Piper, get out of my head.

For the hundredth time Nel ran her gaze and the tips of her fingers against the broken spider web of cracks on the bubble's curving wall. As yet she couldn't feel any abrasions inside, but if she could they'd likely be dead. Just three more frozen bodies drifting away.

The bubble was broken, almost a third of it riven with fractures. Gods only knew what was keeping it intact.

Gods only . . .

Nel ran her hand across the densest cluster of cracks again, pushing hard. They didn't shift, not even a flake moved at her touch. But her fingers tingled, numbness, just at the tips.

How is he doing that? This ball should have cracked hours ago.

And it was more than that, she realised. They were drifting ever closer to Vice, another hour maybe and they'd be back on solid ground.

And, best case scenario, they'd be stranded there.

The alternative meant shipping out in the brig of an Alliance ship.

If Nel turned her head, faced away from the docks, she would still see the smouldering remains of the Tantamount. *Burning up whatever remained of the air in its envelope. For all intents and purposes it was gone, gone with all hands going down with it.*

Nel kept her gaze fixed firmly ahead, watching Vice grow larger until the bubble dropped, none too gently, onto the rim of the flat world.

Glass flew in all directions, flung away from the three of them. A last gesture from Quill or the result of him releasing whatever cantrip had been holding the thing together. The glistening fragments rained down around them, settling in a ring, tiny prisms that caught the light just so. Nel dropped to her knees amongst them, drawing a gasping breath of air.

Air that had been running out, growing thick and heavy inside the bubble. That was all it was, she told herself, as she drew breath after shuddering breath, just the air. Just breathing. Nothing else.

She fell, landing on her side, clutching her stomach. She didn't remember being hit, being injured, but she must have been. So much pain there.

Shadows fell across her face. Jack looking down at her.

"Where are you going, Jack?" She heard Quill's voice when the shadow moved away.

"Leaving."

"But where?"

"Somewhere."

Silence.

"You coming, Kelpie?"

More silence. A long, sibilant, indrawn breath.

"No."

Heavy footfalls. Fading quickly.

On the edge of her eyeline, Quill settled in a crouch, hands clasped in front of himself again. He stared resolutely at those hands, hands that trembled and shook so firmly did he grip them against themselves.

Nel drew another shuddering breath and fought not to curl up into a little ball.

"EXPLAIN TO ME again, how this will work," Quill muttered from behind her. That was Quill, never happy unless he was complaining. Didn't help that he made some valid points when he did.

More valid than usual this time.

"Alliance ships run with Draugr," Nel said. "Can't run the complicated jobs but you find them a repetitive enough job, they can manage well enough. Frees up your deckhands for all else. Less crew per ship, means more ships, been pushing that way for years. Just takes some trial and training to find those jobs what Draugr can do."

"How does one train a Draugr?" Quill asked.

"With candy," Sharpe told him. "Sour lemon rocks, the kind you suck on till your face puckers up 'cause they'll crack your jaw if you bite down on them. That's why the poor beasties look the way they do. Lemon candy."

Quill glared at him.

Sharpe grinned. His humour had been coming back. The tide was out on whether that was a good thing. "Tell me I'm wrong," he said.

"I cannot. But that does not mean I believe you."

"Stranger things are true, Mister Quill, stranger things."

They'd parked themselves on a small rise, where cobblestones gave way to muddy and over-trodden trails. It was an ugly spot where dead-end streets ended in drunken, tottering buildings but it had the ideal vantage over the Draugr pens and the roads leading down to the harbour.

"This is taking too long," Quill muttered.

"Takes as long as it takes, Loveland," Nel told him.

"Kind of agree with Quill," Sharpe admitted. "Sitting still, waiting, makes me nervous."

"We haven't done anything yet," Nel scowled. "Nothing to be nervous about."

"You haven't. I'm on the run. Wanted man. Being hunted."

"By who?" Nel snorted.

"The Guild," Quill told her reproachfully. "Or have you forgotten already?"

Nel winced. Truth was, she had.

"And we're sure about that?"

"*I'm* sure," Sharpe said. "There were a few . . . incidents, along the way. Things that happened, happened wrong."

"You didn't mention this."

Scowling. "A lot's happened, Nel."

Nel bit her tongue. Seemed the wisest response.

"More than likely this hunter was responsible for what happened to your crew," Quill said.

"That," Sharpe nodded, "and more."

Yeah, makes sense, don't it. And I just happened to find my old captain's deed nailed to a board here. Convenient. Except I probably wasn't who was supposed to find it.

"They're coming," Sharpe whispered, unnecessarily hoarsely.

And as of now the Draugr were beginning to file out of the compound. Neat orderly lines if not marching in step. There a dozen or so minders with them. *Pipers*, Nel thought with a grimace. The creatures responded to the notes en masse. It was an efficient system.

"I still do not see why we waited until they began loading," Quill turned to her.

"Not loading, Quill," Nel watched the procession. "Just wanted them out of the buildings. Didn't want to go in after them."

"That would have seemed simpler. Stoker and the others could simply have walked out with us once we found them."

"Would have been seen. Paid the man off for a reason, mean to get my return. They'll be the last ones out, on account of them hoping some rich dandy captain is going to swoop in and buy them. So we know where to look. And grabbing them from the tail is a sight more easy than hunting down the whole line."

"Clever," Sharpe said.

"Until we are seen anyway," Quill pointed out. "Or do you intend to dispose of the guards? This is not your first rescue attempt, either of you. Correct?"

"You steal ships, we rescues princesses," Sharpe told him.

"That's how the world works."

Nel kept counting off Draugr as they marched. She was over a hundred now. "Speaking of princesses," she said. "Plan doesn't require you being here, Quill. Fact is you'd be more useful tracking down Jack."

"I know where he is," Quill assured them.

"And where's that?" Sharpe asked.

"The town square."

"You sure? Won't have moved on?"

"I am sure."

Nel frowned. *Town square? Worry about that later, Jack is Quill's problem. Focus on yours.*

"We need to get the whistles," Nel reminded them, singling out the pipers.

"Not all the whistles," Sharpe pointed out. "Just enough for a dozen or so likely lads. If we take them all we'll be leading a procession back to the docks. Be a grand sight but won't help us with your plan."

"Good distraction though," Nel said. "Hopefully it won't come to that."

"And the rest of your plan?" Quill asked. "Where do you plan to obtain the uniforms?"

"Don't need the uniforms, Quill," Nel said. "Just raincapes and colours. There's a store not a few blocks away, can get what we need there. This isn't a daylight job so that will get us by."

Quill looked sceptical. "Perhaps."

"Meet us between here and the docks," she told him. "I'll have a pretty blue dress just for yourself by then."

"With a bonnet and bow," Sharpe added. "And you'll look prettier than a songbird in spring."

"If this works . . ." Quill sighed, a rather tepid response Nel thought. "Never mind. Very well, I will see you both later. Until then."

The Kelpie slipped away, leaving Nel and Sharpe alone.

"That was unexpected," Sharpe said. "Is he getting more agreeable in his old age?"

"No," Nel told him. "Ain't that."

"What then?"

"Violet," she said simply. "He'd never say it but he wouldn't deny it either. He's dark . . . over what happened to her. Learning she's still out there, that we . . . left her out there, it won't sit right with him until he puts it right."

Easier for him. He has a chance to make it right. Not sure I ever can.

The pens looked to be mostly empty now. Time to make their move. She motioned to Sharpe.

Sharpe nodded. "Always liked that about Quill," he said as they started down the hill. "Never knew where you stood with him but he did have his own code. Respect that in a fellow."

"Don't think any of us really understood Quill's code," Nel frowned. "Except maybe the captain. Maybe Piper too, come to think of it. Both always knew which way Quill would jump before I did. Hells, maybe it was just me."

"It wasn't just you," Sharpe's voice was dropping as they drew closer. Little more than a whisper.

"He blames me, Quill does. For what happened to Violet."

"Was it your fault?"

"It was my choice."

"Those aren't the same thing."

"Same result."

"Hard to argue that. So let's steal some bodies, hey? And then we can move on with getting our girl back."

Sharpe pulled his hood up and together they slipped quietly towards the back of the Draugr procession.

"STILL HAVING BAD dreams, my furry little wench? The nightmare kind, not the wanton kind." Gravel played a card on top of hers, scoring the round. Violet made a rude sound and played another card without paying much attention. Gravel was a snarky little street urchin. She liked that. Made him easier to talk to. Easier than the stiffer and more formal Niko Kaspar.

"Ain't yours, snipe, and at least one of us can grow hair."

Gravel laughed good-naturedly and cleared the cards. It was his turn to shuffle.

"Remind me to kick your boy in the shins about running his mouth too," Violet said.

Gravel missed a deal, sending a card off the table. He swore and bent to retrieve it. "The game is euchre, little fox, we're both going alone. And Kas ain't my boy."

"Spoilt for choice there, but he still runs his mouth."

Gravel shrugged. "He can keep it shut, more than you think anyway."

Violet didn't answer.

"Don't be all mad he told me about your night terrors. He used to have them himself not so long ago."

Violet looked up from her cards. They were bad anyways. "He said he went over the side once."

"Didn't say much else, right?"

"No. Yes. Some."

"Sounds like our Niko."

"So what happened? How did it happen?"

Gravel shrugged.

"Oh come on," Violet said. "You know, I can tell."

"Never was good at saying no to a pretty lady." Her playing partner placed his cards face down on the table, leaning back and folding his arms.

"It was two years ago," Gravel mused, his eyes becoming distant as he brought back old memories. "Kaspar was fresh out of officer school, and I still had the tar of the docks on me. As far as the brass and braids were concerned, we were expendable. That old fox Raines, he'd come up with a new idea. Something brilliant, they all said, a way to sail a ship without sails. A ship that could sail from the Edge to the Morgana. Barmy, I thought. Absolute madness. But the brass and braids went for it and built the damned thing. Then they just needed some idiot to shake it down. And that," he picked his cards up again, "is where our dashing young Niko and I came in."

"How?" Violet asked. "This ship . . . it's like nothing I've ever seen. Even heard of. How did you—"

"How did a bilge rat like me and a bright shiny pup like Kaspar end up stealing her maidenhead?" He grinned at her.

"Don't be an ass."

"They needed volunteers. The original was nothing like this. It was an open-decked sloop with Raine's contraption bolted to it. Proof of concept they called it. And that concept didn't need much in the way of crew once you took out the rigging. Just a couple of people nobody would miss much. Kaspar volunteered. I didn't get so much say."

Violet nodded. "So your trip went wrong?"

"Aye," Gravel shook his head. "Aye, you could say it went

wrong. We didn't know it at the time but we weren't the first ones to test this . . . concept. First boat they sent out never came back. Second one exploded, somewhere out near the belts. Exploded, lass, less than a week into their shakedown."

"How long did it take you?"

"Your faith in me is touching, lass," Gravel reproached her.

"Can't build the drama when I can see you survived," she told him. "And it had to work at some point 'cause we're sitting in the middle of it playing cards to talk about it."

"Aye, spoils the ending, don't it. Trip was meant to last two weeks in that bucket of tin and gears. Had enough supplies for three, broke it in one, and didn't make it back for a month, maybe longer. Got hard to tell near the end there."

"So?" Violet demanded impatiently. "What happened?"

"Broke the old fox's damned engine, didn't we? Well . . . I broke it," he grimaced. "Kaspar didn't make a big deal about that in the final report but that's what happened. Broke the engine and we drifted off course. We managed to pull together a sail and catch a solar back home eventually. Luck of the black, really, weren't nothing astounding on our part."

Violet shook her head. "You're the worst storyteller ever to climb a ship's rigging. How in the hells did Kaspar go over the side?"

"Trying to fix the engine I busted. Like I said, they bolted the piece of scrap to the hull, had to dangle him over the edge to try and fix it. Not that we could. Line got snagged and he had to cut himself free, wasn't enough pull from the ether to hold him in so he fell right through the envelope."

Gravel shuddered. "Damned scary," he admitted quietly. "Seeing him drift off like that. We had no steering at that point, wasn't a chance in all the Lanes I could have gone after him. He managed to grab the end of the line and pull himself in, but it was a damned close thing. Seemed fine at the time. Wasn't till after a day or so that he felt the falling. Hard lad, I guess, when he needs to be."

"How long?" Violet asked. "How long did he have the night terrors for?"

"Too long," Gravel said uncomfortably. "Whose deal is it?"

"Yours," Violet said, watching him carefully. She suspected Gravel was cheating—he always dealt her too many black cards.

That and there was another deck mixed in. She had pairs of the same card several times. Violet rubbed at her eyes. Her eyes ached and her hands trembled. Then Violet cursed as she realised she'd missed Gravel dealing. She took up her cards.

Blacks again, damnit.

"Happened to me once," she said as they played their hands. "Fell through the envelope, ended up at the end of my rope."

"Good story?" Gravel asked politely.

"Running an ice cargo. Started melting and we sprung a leak. Leak burst when I was fixing it."

"Wet fur," Gravel nodded. "Must be heavy, nor your best look."

Violet glared at him and slapped a card down.

"You've the worst luck, Miss Violet," Gravel said, shaking his head at her latest play. "Or would you like me to go over the rules again?"

"Blame the dealer," Violet said, waving her cards at him.

"So how many times you fall off the ship, lass?" Gravel sighed when he saw her hand. "Just the two times? With the ice slip and what when we found you all frozen and stiff in the black? Weren't the same, surely."

"Weren't the same," Violet snapped.

"Heard stories about Free Lanes crews."

"Yeah?"

"Aye, meant to be devious and unscrupulous-like. Running all sorts of ill-gotten and underhanded goods. And meant to be good at what they do. Never thought they'd be shipping frozen water and falling sodden over the side."

Violet threw her cards at him.

"Played a lot of cards with the ensign," Gravel said, picking up what she'd thrown. "Wouldn't believe it but the lad's got a temper on him too. Gets frustrated just like everyone else."

"Why wouldn't I believe that?"

"'Cause of how he carries himself aboard here, all prim and proper. Yes sir, no ma'am. Aye Captain. Saluting just so and always neatly pressed. A proper officer and a gentleman."

"All an act then?"

"Not an act," Gravel frowned. "More a side of the lad."

"Seen the other side have you?"

"Talk a lot with a fellow when you're marooned aboard a

broken ship."

"That's not what marooning is. You're thinking of adrift," Violet pointed out.

"Aye, thanking you kindly, lass. I surely was. Adrift and desperate for distraction. Man might confess all his secrets, if he has any to tell, that is."

"Who confessed? You or the prim and proper gentleman?"

"Not much to tell about myself, truth. Grew up in a mine and got named after what we pulled out of it."

"And the ensign?"

"Started talking in his sleep. Right embarrassing really, moaning his dockside sweetheart's name and then waking up and realising he was stuck on a boat with me. Been having nightmares ever since."

Violet bit back a laugh. Gravel grinned at her as he deftly played out the next hand.

"Don't try too hard to hold back, lass, your face might crack."

"*Your* face might crack."

"Cracked long ago, I'm afraid. Think that's why ma gave me up so young."

CHAPTER 9

THE REARMOST MINDER never saw Sharpe. Never even heard him coming. By the time he was grabbed and with an arm wrapped around his windpipe it was too late to make noise. He did struggle, kicking the cobblestones, but no one came to help. Nel crept up on the second, taking him down just as quietly. The third one had a torch. They made sure to wait before trying for that one. A sudden change in the light could alert the whole group. Not what they wanted at all. Nel went through the pockets of her mark. Nothing useful, nothing like what she was looking for.

"Nel." Sharpe's voice, distinctive in the night. Hopefully only to her.

"Find something?"

"Pretty little bird caller." Sharpe dropped in beside her, held up a collection of clay whistles strung together on a leather cord.

"You're sure?"

"Aye, I'm sure, colour coded, these ones go for this up ahead there. They're the ones we want."

"Which one tells them to fall in and follow the piper?"

"This one, but breaks down to groups."

"And you're sure?"

"Want me to sound them out?"

"Hold the thought, Castor."

A ghost of a smile on his face in the dark. Nel shook her head ruefully. That was the easy part done.

"You realise we don't need the whistles to make these particular Draugr dance," Sharpe said as they crept forward. "Not sure dancing is in their repertoire, but asking nicely might work better."

"Whistles aren't for them," Nel said. "Whistles are for when it all goes wrong and we need a distraction."

"Think that's likely?"

"More than likely. Counting on it."

"This plan of yours . . ." Sharpe mused. "Anyways, what comes next?"

"Fellow with the torch," Nel pointed. "One of us grabs him, other grabs the torch. No shadow puppets. Not part of the plan."

"I hear you. Prefer the torch or the man himself?"

"Been eyeing up the torch."

"Colour me surprised. Fine, let's make this quiet."

"Quiet but not the forever kind of quiet," Nel said, hand on his arm.

"Don't like killing, Nel," Sharpe grimaced. "Maybe you hadn't noticed."

Nel shrugged. Truth was, she hadn't thought about it, at least as far as Sharpe was concerned.

Sharpe jumped the guard. He threw up his hands, letting the torch go. Nel grabbed it before it dropped too far, then turned to put a knee into the man's side. He went down just like the other two; with muffled choking sounds. Sharpe dragged the body to the side of the street, propping them up against some steps. Nel kept pace with the Draugr procession, keeping the torch thrust in front of her. Anyone looking back should be blinded by the light, at least enough not to be able to identify her.

They were coming up behind Stoker's group now. Last in line, just like Nel had been promised. That was gratifying. One of them turned around, one with enough facial muscles left in working order to look surprised. She heard Sharpe jogging up beside her, finger pressed to his lips. Their spotter turned back, kept marching. Didn't so much as nudge his fellows.

Good man, don't need no jabbering Draugr sailors ruining our surprise. Going to be tricky enough to slip away as it is.

"Pass me a whistle," she told Sharpe.

"You want the two-note call," he told her. "Fingers over the first and third hole, then just the second. Two pipes. Tells them to head home, should do an about-face when they hear it. Yours is the group up the front, if I'm reading the colours right. Tell my group to march double time, them at back ahead of us. Should be enough of a muddle."

"They teach you those tunes growing up?" Nel asked. Her words caused Sharpe to pause for an oddly thoughtful gaze at the whistles he held.

"Suppose you could say that."

"Useful skill."

"Not hard to learn. Could teach you if you want."

"Show me this is gonna work and we'll get to that."

"You can read notes?"

"I can read," Nel scowled.

"I meant music."

"Ah, then no. Learnt the bosun calls, though."

"About the same," Sharpe conceded. "But you have to learn it the hard way, no writing it down."

You think I got time to look at papers on the deck? Nel bit back saying as much. Sharpe still made her wonder. The man was a collection of skills and bits and pieces of knowledge but there was some glaring gaps when you started looking at the whole. *I'd wonder more except I know there ain't no answers there.*

"Going up front," she told him. "You let Stoker know the plan and be ready to run. I blow then you blow, got it?"

"Aye, aye, Skipper," he winked at her.

Nel shook her head, wondering if she'd missed something. She hurried her pace, passing the Draugr. Clapped Stoker on the arm as she passed. He made eyes at her but didn't so much as open his mouth.

Good man, Stoker, always did like him.

And that was it, she thought. She could see the Draugr ahead of her, groups of about twenty in each, squad-like. Another dozen guards or minders or handlers, however you thought of them. They must have been slowing because she caught the odd disgruntled look back their way. Pushed their luck as much as they dared. She set whistle to her lips and blew, just like Sharpe had said to.

She heard him do the same behind her, then the Draugr immediately in front of her broke into a brisk trot. Not quite a run but more than their minders were expecting. She heard shouts of alarms, throwing her own voice into the mix to add to the confusion. There was mayhem when she saw more bodies coming her way, the lead group sauntering back the way they'd come and no one seemed prepared to get out of the way. Nel dropped her torch and belted back down the cobblestones to Sharpe and Stoker.

"Aye, all right lads and ladies, follow the piper, this way, this way, mind your heads," Sharpe called out, quiet but loud enough for Nel to hear. Her eyes were still half-blind from the torchlight but she found them, tucked into a side alley. Sharpe kept them moving. They'd targeted a dry goods and sundry store three streets over. There were no words exchanged until they'd put distance between them.

"Skipper," Stoker said with what might have been a grin. There were teeth showing and lips pulled back. "Sight for sore eyes, you are."

"What about me?" Sharpe asked.

"You're a sight," someone else said. Half the Draugr were speaking over one another.

"To make eyes sore."

"Your eyes are sore?"

"Only when I check to see if thems still there."

"What took you so long, Sharpe? We was waiting."

"Didn't expect to see you again," Stoker said to Nel. "Heard the worst. Was sorry to hear it."

"Not the worst," Nel told him. "Just not much better. Keep moving, got to get you all dressed then find ourselves a ship."

"What's wrong with what we're wearing?" someone asked. *Hells, have to find out names soon as we get a chance.*

"What's wrong or what's left?"

"She say find a ship? Sharpe, you lose the ship as well as lose us?"

Sharpe winced. Even in the dark Nel didn't miss it.

"Don't worry," she told Stoker. "Got a new one all picked out for us."

"You coming with?" he asked her.

"Planned to. That all right with you?"

"Pulled my frozen body out of the black, Skipper. Happy to have us both on the same ship any day."

"She thought you were me," Sharpe told the Draugr

midshipman.

"Did ya?" Stoker asked.

"Thought no such thing," Nel said. "Where'd you even hear that?"

"Careful, Sharpe, gonna get yourself locked up again," the jeering came.

"Locked up." Nel slowed to a stop. "Aw, hells!"

"What?" Sharpe stopped with her, looking around anxiously.

"Jack," she said grimly. "Just figured it out."

Figured out why Quill was so sure where he was and wasn't going nowhere. Damnit.

Sharpe's face was vacant for a moment, then caught up to her. "Go find them," he said. "We'll manage. Meet you at the docks."

"You sure?"

"Yes. Go get your crew."

Nel looked over at the rest of them. All staring at her. Her new crew, she realised. "Won't be long," she told them. "Don't cause any trouble while I'm gone."

Sharpe cocked his head to the side. There was still yelling to be heard a few streets over. "Wouldn't think of it."

"YOU DID NOT waste much time. Finally you find quarters suitable to yourself."

Korrigan Jack stirred from his cot, blinking up at the shadow-covered grate. His cell was below street level, that one grate letting him look out onto the foot traffic. Not that there was much at night. Refuse piled up against the back of the gaol, runoff trickled or gushed into the cell depending on the weather. He could make out the silhouette of a hunched figure against the night sky. Tapered head, legs that bent the wrong way, lashing tail. There was a clink when they moved, a sound familiar to Jack, that made the scars on his wrists ache. Chain. Coils of it looped over the shoulder.

"Kelpie."

They both waited but neither seemed inclined to say anything further. Finally Jack relented.

"What'd you want?"

Quill peered down at him. "How did you manage to acquire accommodations such as these, Jack? One must almost admire your efficiency in the matter."

"Stabbed someone. They screamed a lot. Ended up here."

"This screamer, they offended you in some way?" Quill asked.

"No. Never met them before."

"No? I assume they died then."

"Probably did. Wouldn't be such a fuss if they didn't."

Quill considered this, nodding thoughtfully. "Vaughn has found us a new job. We are going after the ones who attacked us. Shall I extract you from your predicament?"

"No."

"No?" Quill echoed his surprise. "You wish to remain? Here?"

"Room's fine. Got some rats under the bed. You should stop by again. For dinner."

Quill scowled. "Perhaps you did not understand. We are going after the one who killed the cook. I thought that would be of interest to you."

"Why?"

"Revenge."

"Won't bring Gabbi back," Jack said. "No point."

"You will remain here then? You will be sent to a prison, Jack. Perhaps a mining camp."

"That's the idea, Kelpie."

"You wanted this?"

"I understand this," Jack shrugged.

"I do not understand you, Jack."

"Never liked you neither, Quill."

"That is not what I meant."

"Still don't like you."

"We intend to steal a ship. It will require crew. Vaughn is greatly opposed to involving others. This is one of the few things I would consider you useful for."

"You stole ships before, Kelpie."

"A criminal exaggeration. It was but one time."

Jack shrugged, going back to lay down on his cot. The bed creaked under his weight.

"I truly do not understand you, Jack."

"You're ugly."

"What?"

"You're ugly, Kelpie. That's why I don't like you none."

There was a scraping sound from the street above. Quill stepped into sight again, dragging a barrel of fish. From the smell they were none too fresh. The Kelpie pushed the barrel in front of the cell grate.

"Goodbye, Jack. I will look you up after we are done. I look forward to it."

"Oi, Kelpie!" Jack called out.

"What?" Quill's voice carried back, full of suspicion.

"You're still ugly. Just 'cause I can't see you don't change that."

There was silence from outside. Then the sound of another barrel being dragged across the street.

Jack chuckled.

"THAT," VIOLET PEERED down the length of the deck, "is a lot of big guns."

Another day, another tour. Always there was a new part of the ship to see. Today it was Kaspar guiding her. She'd asked to see the gun deck. On a trader ship it would be the secondary cargo hold and also where most of the crew hung their hammocks. In fact there would be almost no guns to speak of, guns being less valuable than cargo in the trader scheme of things.

On the *Fata Morgana* it was a different story.

"Actually, for a ship this size, we're considered under-gunned," Kaspar told her, leaning his shoulder against a post running from floor to ceiling. "We should have two to three times as many cannon, but all the ship mounts is thaumatics."

"How many are there?" Violet asked. These were the same guns they'd been killing rays with. Raines said it was due to the fluids in the ship's pipes. The fluids that were actually gases, mist. The way they moved, the *dynamics* he said, of what happened inside the pipes was similar to the mating call the rays put out. Not something audible to her ears but the rays could hear it from leagues around. And it was getting them killed.

And not just rays.

"Twenty a broadside," Kaspar said. "A few mounted in the stern and a half-dozen large calibre lances in the forward battery."

"Why no cannon?"

"Weight," a sharp voice interrupted them. The pair of them jumped when Mors Coldstream emerged out of the shadows behind them. "Cannon weigh twice what their counterparts do and require shot and ammunition. This is a much more elegant solution."

The half-breed looked them both over, fixing his eyes on Kaspar, who stood rigidly at attention.

"I don't believe the girl should be here."

"Apologies, sir," Kaspar said stiffly, "but she has the captain's permission to move around the ship while under escort."

"And that freedom extends to the gun deck? Curious. Regardless, this deck is under my control and I don't want her on it. Are we clear?"

"Yes, sir. We'll be going then."

"A moment." Mors' hand flicked out and grabbed Kaspar by the shoulder. He drew one of his duelling wands with the other.

"You have some problem with thaumatic weaponry, Ensign?"

"No, sir." Kaspar looked straight ahead.

"No?" Mors chuckled. "Come now, be honest with me, Ensign. What are the tactical advantages of cannon over a lance?"

"Range, power," Kaspar answered quickly, then winced.

"True." Mors took a step to the side, tracing a pattern in the air with his wand. "A traditional cannon has a superior range and possesses more raw power than a lance. But what you fail to consider is the trade-off. A lance requires a single gunner, a cannon needs a small crew. A cannon requires reloading after each shot, a lance does not. A lance is a far more accurate, indeed, more elegant weapon."

"The accuracy and efficiency of a weapon relies largely upon the skill of its user, sir," Kaspar replied.

"Yes," Mors grinned. "Oh yes, it does. I couldn't agree more, Ensign. But we seem to be at something of an impasse, you and I. How shall we settle this?"

The duellist made another small circle with his wand, sharpened teeth bared eagerly. "There was an attempt, many years ago, before wands and thaumatic diversions became common, to develop hand cannons for soldiers. Single-shot, and then little more than a club. You can see why a thaumatic approach was more favourable. A core premise of this ship is the minimal effect a broadside of cannon would have on it. I look forward to the day when we test the theory."

"I have every confidence in the ship and its crew, sir," Kaspar told him.

"Unfortunately, the feeling is not mutual. You are aboard this ship because of the role you played in her development. I have yet to see evidence you deserve that placement. I wish you to prove me wrong."

Mors held up his wand, the weapon spinning lazily between his long fingers.

"Kaspar, let's go," Violet tugged on his arm.

Kaspar took a deep breath, standing his ground. "With respect, sir, the captain has banned duelling aboard the ship."

"Not on my deck, Ensign. Not here. And as you can see, the captain is not *here*."

The muscles in Kaspar's jaw bunched. "Sir . . ."

"Let me make it clearer for you, Ensign." Mors strode to a small metallic locker mounted near the door. He unlocked it with a set of keys from inside his jerkin. He retrieved a wand and threw it in Kaspar's direction. Kaspar caught it one-handed.

"You are not leaving until we settle our disagreement. Are you refusing an order from a superior officer to do so?" Mors struck a pose, wand levelled at the ensign.

Kaspar stared at the weapon in his hand. Violet glared and stepped in front of him. The Luscan blinked his black and white eyes at her in lazy bemusement.

This is his deck, his guns. Which means he shot down the Tantamount.

"Get your pointy flash stick out of my face or I'll find somewhere to stick it."

"Violet!" Kaspar tried to push her out of the way. She set her feet and shouldered him back.

Mors' head pulled back in surprise, but the smile didn't take long to reappear. "My now, this is becoming interesting."

He reached behind him and retrieved a second wand, dropping it at Violet's feet.

"Pick it up, little girl," he told her. "Let's see if you can back up your mouth now." He grinned at Kaspar. "Don't worry, Ensign. You're free to help your little friend. You're going to need each other."

Mors drew his second wand and held them crossed in front of himself as Violet snatched up the one he'd thrown.

"This is a bad idea," Kaspar told her, holding his weapon low.

"Lots of bad ideas on this ship," Violet found herself saying, "this one's just a little less bad."

Mors made the first move, flicking his wands out in either direction. Violet ducked and heard Kaspar grunt in pain. He hadn't moved fast enough but she saw him rolling for cover. *Tougher than he looks, then.* Violet put her back against a post, listening.

Mors was quiet but she caught the scuff of his boot against the deck. She edged around the post, sending off a badly aimed shot in his direction. Mors leaned aside easily.

Not going to be that easy.

A bang, a knock on wood sounded to her right. Kaspar caught her eye, pressed out of sight against a post of his own, and motioned down the deck. There was more cover that way. She moved when he did, keeping her head low and eyes fixed on her destination. Wand fire ricocheted near her feet to the accompaniment of Mors' laughter. Violet tripped, tucking her shoulder into a roll and scrambled behind one of the lances. Breathing hard now. She looked for Kaspar. There across the deck.

He made a complicated series of gestures with one hand. More pointing. A circling. Then pointed down.

Violet shook her head. Kaspar repeated the hand signs.

"I don't know what you mean!" she mouthed, over-emphasising the words. Kaspar scowled back at her. He stood up and swept his weapon across his cover before ducking back down hurriedly.

"I expected better of you, Ensign!" Mors called out, his voice echoing down the gundeck. "Your father was an excellent duellist, so they say. How did all of that talent fail to make its way down to you?"

Kaspar's face was mottled, red and purple. Violet could see him grinding his teeth together, knuckles tightening around the borrowed weapon.

He's clearly baiting you, are you going to be stupid enough to fall for it?

Kaspar stood up, his pride stung by whatever barbs Mors had flung his way. Violet didn't doubt the Luscan had known exactly what to say. She looked away but couldn't close her ears to the cry of pain that came all too soon. Hook, bait, and trap. Which meant Mors would be coming for her now.

Just you. All alone. No one to save you.

"Hells," Violet muttered, staring at her own wand. She didn't even know how to properly use the damned thing. Hadn't understood what Kaspar had tried to signal to her before. Only left one option really.

"I give up!" she called out.

There was a silence.

"You . . . give up?"

Mors' reply sounded incredulous. She could only imagine his face. Violet rolled the wand out onto the deck where it could be seen by all.

"You can't give up!"

"I forfeit," Violet repeated her claim, rising up, holding her hands where they could be seen. She could see Mors now, he was only a few feet away. Kaspar too, half bent over, ashen faced and down on one knee. It was a hard choice as to which of the two of them was more confused.

"That would be the end of it, Coldstream."

Behind Mors stood Aristeia Quinn, the first mate. Violet hadn't heard the woman arrive, nor could she guess how long she'd been present. The woman had hard eyes though, hard eyes that were hard to read.

"Unacceptable," Mors flashed his teeth.

"I suggest you accept it, my friend," Aristeia told him. "A forfeit would be a legitimate outcome to an actual duel. Which of course this is not." She looked meaningfully at Kaspar.

"Of course not, sir." Kaspar raised a trembling hand in salute. "Nothing of the like."

"Nothing of the like," Violet copied his gesture and words.

"*Captain* wants a word, Mors," Aristeia told the other. Mors seemed of a mind to ignore her as he stormed up the deck, snatching up the loaned wands from the floor. "Until later," Violet heard him say to Kaspar as the boy climbed to his feet. Violet moved to help him while the two officers left abruptly. He waved her off.

"Never saw the forfeit coming, Kitsune girl," he eyed her. "Didn't think that was in your nature."

"Mors didn't neither. Gonna irk him more than anything else would."

"Almost didn't work," Kaspar said. "If Aristeia hadn't have reined him in like that—"

"You damned fool," Violet told him, brushing at his clothes. "He got you all fired up and wide-eyed stupid, and you let him."

"Aye," Kaspar winced, "aye, he did. And I did."

"Why did the mate pull him up like? Didn't think she cared for neither of us?"

"Aristeia follows orders, lass. Raines wants you looked after. Captain says to look after you, first mate looks after you. Simple as that."

"Then we should tell the captain what happened."

"No," Kaspar shook his head, grabbing her shoulder. "No, we should not do that."

"And why not?"

"Duelling is banned aboard the ship. Aboard all ships. Worth your life and career in the service to be admitting to it."

"Mors didn't give you no choice!" Violet protested.

"Aye, and he knows I can't tell the captain either. I said it was banned, didn't say it don't happen. Just doesn't get talked about."

"He trapped you. All officer-like. You can't duel and you can't not duel."

"Aye, that's how it is, lass."

"Stop calling me lass," Violet pushed him.

"I should start calling you furry wench like Brandon does?"

"Don't do that neither. What was that about your father?"

"Nothing." Now it was Kaspar's turn to look away.

"He some kind of famous?"

"No."

"What was he then?"

"He was my father."

"That's not an answer."

"And he's not a duellist."

Chapter 10

Quill was halfway to the docks when Nel encountered him. He was alone, a fact that didn't sit right with her.

"What happened?" Nel asked him without preamble.

"Nothing happened," Quill shrugged, adjusting the wrap that covered his shoulders and head. "Where is Sharpe? Have you misplaced him already? Did your rescue attempt not go as planned?"

"Went fine and Sharpe's fine. Waiting. Where's Jack?"

"Locked up."

"I know he's locked up, Quill, figured out that was what you were hedging about. It's Jack. Shouldn't have expected nothing else. You were supposed to do something about that. So tell me now why you didn't and why Jack ain't here."

"No."

"No?" Nel repeated, drawing out the word. "Loveland, we ain't got time for you to get belligerent on me and—"

"That is what Jack said, Vaughn," Quill interrupted her. "I told him what we intend, he wanted no part of it. He said no."

Nel stared at him. "No ain't good enough, Quill."

"This is Jack we are talking about. When does *good enough* become a concern?"

"Hells damnit, Quill, this was your idea. Never mind, I'll see to Jack." She pushed past Quill, back the way he'd come.

"And what am I to do?" he called after her.

"Follow me, you miserable snakeskin. What else did you think?"

She didn't look back to see if he was. Didn't look at anything till she got to the square. Market vendors, carts, barrels, and stalls, all gone for the night. Nothing but the rotting produce that couldn't be sold. To be expected for that time of night. Looked different sober.

"Jack?" she called out, probably too softly. "Where you at?"

She heard the clack of clawed feet on cobblestones. Quill had decided to follow her after all.

"Where's he got to, Quill? You sure you didn't break him out."

"Quite sure."

"Then where?"

Quill pointed. To a barrel of overturned fish.

"You're joking with me," Nel glared at him.

Quill shook his head, once to each side.

"Of all the—" She bit off the rest of what she might say and began kicking at the loose fish with her boot. The smell made her gag.

Week old fish, oh the stench of it. Don't even care for fish.

"Jack?" she called out, as the tops of the bars to his cell appeared. "You in there?"

There was no answer.

"If this ain't Jack," she warned Quill. "Then I've a mind to take them anyways. And they'll be bunking with you, Kelpie."

"Your threats are unnecessary," Quill told her huffily. "The cell belongs to the Korrigan. The fish are a recent addition, but I consider it will be an improvement."

Nel looked down through the bars, saw Jack looking up at her. He had a half-eaten fish in one hand. The other half was being ground up in his mouth.

"The hells are you doing, Jack?"

"Helping," he told her, not bothering to swallow before speaking. The sight only made Nel want to gag more.

"That's disgusting," she said.

"So is the food here. Except for the rats. Rats are ok. Better than fish. Don't like fish."

"Then stop eating it."

"I'm hungry."

"Jack, you're coming with me. Cook'll make you a proper

meal. Soon as we got ourselves a ship."

"Who's the cook?"

"Don't know yet. Haven't picked one."

"Think I'll stay here then. With the rats."

"Don't think, Jack. Ain't never been your thing."

"Don't wanna go," Jack said stubbornly.

"Don't care what you want, Jack. I say you're going so you go. And I say the Kelpie is gonna make that happen." She waved at Quill. It was time to do the thing. And the sooner they got away from the fish the better.

"Stand away from the window, Jack," she warned him. For a blessing the Korrigan did as she bid and backed up into his cell. Quill stooped down, wrapping a length of chain around the bars. He eyed Jack cautiously as the prisoner munched on his fish. He stepped back, holding the length of chain. About a dozen feet of it.

"Where'd you even get the chains?"

Quill shrugged.

"Fine. Tie it off," she said.

Quill surveyed the market.

"Our options appear to be limited."

"Find something," Nel told him.

"I will attempt to make do then." Quill took a step away, the chain still dangling from his fist. He seized on a nearby tarp-covered wagon, stooping down to wrap the chain around the axle several times. Nel was impressed. The Kelpie didn't have to crawl under, what with the way his chicken legs folded back. Just crouch and bend at the hips.

"This will do nicely." Quill straightened, raising one hand. Blue sparks, he was all set to perform. The wagon lifted off the ground, several inches at first, then a foot, tilting uncertainly.

"Having trouble there?" Nel asked.

"It is an awkward shape," Quill admitted, his voice rasping through clenched teeth. "A moment."

He lifted his other hand, in an invisible balancing act. Not for the first time Nel was reminded of the oddities of thaumatic scaling. The stronger the practitioner the more they struggled with small objects and fine control. Quill was more used to billowing canvas than pushing a cart.

"Do you need to lift it?" she asked aloud. "It has wheels,

couldn't you just push it?"

"No!" Quill snapped, his shoulders stiffening and his stance widening. "I could not!"

Meaning you didn't think of that until I said it, more like. Fine, Quill, just break the boy outta the jail so we can be gone.

Quill sweated, floating the cart until the chain went taut. Having found the limit he brought it back, then sent it flying across the market square in one savage push.

The action tore the axle free; the axle and half the wagon floor, scattering its contents over the square. Nel had to cover her mouth with the crook of her arm. Fish. The wagon had been filled with fish every bit as rancid as those blocking Jack's cell.

"Damnit, Quill!"

The Kelpie navigator turned and glared at Jack's cell. Or perhaps it was just Jack he was directing his animosity at. The Korrigan stared back, chewing his fish. The bars were still in place, though one had been bent out of shape. There was no way Jack was fitting through.

"No one appears to have noticed," Quill observed.

"No one has noticed," Nel repeated incredulously. "No one noticed the bloody cart of rotting fish being thrown across the square?"

"It's late," Jack offered. "Folk are sleeping."

As if solely to prove them both wrong, Nel heard the sound of raised voices. Yelling.

"Or not," she growled. She reached for her wand, aiming for the mortar around the bars. Jack flinched, retreating into the darkness of his cell.

"Godsdamnit," she muttered, knowing the charge in her weapon wasn't near strong enough to damage the bars. She clenched her fingers around the hilt in frustration. But it did give her an idea.

"I'll be staying here then," Jack surmised, still keeping a cautious distance from the window. Even with bars missing it was going to be a tight squeeze to get him out.

"The hells you are, Jack," Nel told him. She wrestled with the hilt of her weapon, unscrewing the pommel. The charged crystals inside slid out into the palm of her hand, tingling with pins and needles where they met bare skin. Two of them. Might be enough.

Might.

"Stay back," she pointed at Jack, wedging the hardened ammunition in the base of two of the bars. There was enough chipping and pitting around the set to get them in there. Marks where prisoners over the years had forlornly scraped at the bars. Hopefully done their bit to weaken them.

Just enough for this to work. Be up the river if we don't.

"What are you doing?" Quill sounded alarmed, watching Nel pummel at the bars and her makeshift charges with her fist.

"Improvising," she said, backing up. She could hear the commotion getting closer. The ruckus they were about to cause wouldn't make them hard to find. "The crystals, blow 'em."

Quill stared at her. "This is—"

"Just do it, Kelpie!"

". . . not going to work," he finished stubbornly. "They require heat to do what you intend. How am I to create heat?"

"Just . . ." Nel raised one hand, wriggling her fingers. Quill narrowed his eyes back at her.

"Damnit." *So much for the brilliant idea. Had a damned torch too, left it with Sharpe.*

"The lamps," Jack said.

"What?" Quill snapped at him.

"Gas lamps," Jack pointed, as best he could. Then made a face. He appeared annoyed at himself. A moment of self-recrimination.

"Quill," Nel ordered. "Get the lamp."

Quill got the lamp. He did so by extending one hand towards the nearest lamppost and ripping it thaumatically from the ground. The Kelpie had lost his patience but also his control. He and Nel both jumped aside as the gas-filled fixture shot towards them. It crashed into the wall of the gaol. Whether by accident or design the gas erupted in flame, engulfing the bars and the crystals Nel had mined there. From inside there was a bellow from Jack. If he hadn't already regretted his words he did now.

Nel covered her head with both arms, shielding her face and curling her knees up. There was a flush of heat from the gas fire, not bad but noticeable. Hopefully enough to . . .

The booms went off, one after another. Boom and crack. Loud and echoing off the brick and mortar of nearby buildings, bouncing off the cobblestones, clear as a ringing bell.

Quill was coughing. Nel's ears were ringing, and she spat out a mouthful of grit and dust, waving her hand to clear the air in front of her face. But the crystals had done their work: the bricks and mortar around the bars were cracked and gone. Scattered fragments lay all around. The bars were still in place but a few solid kicks finally dislodged them.

"Up and out, sailor," Nel ordered Jack. The gap was bigger now, big enough for him to make his escape. If they were quick.

Jack was slow, far too slow for her liking. He came to the window, now a hole in the wall, placed his hands out onto the street level. He looked up at Nel, his greasy and grey-streaked braids hanging over his face.

"Why?"

"I need you, Jack," she said.

"Don't nobody need me," he shook his head.

"Gabbi did," she told him. "She needed you then. Like I need you now."

"You ain't Gabbi."

"No. I ain't. Ain't nobody here Gabbi, but I'm still your damned skipper and you're my damned crew. And I need my crew, sailor."

Jack made a sound. A small one. The kind a child might make when finding a missing piece of a puzzle. He started to climb out.

"Give me that," Nel caught his scrabbling hand as it clawed in the dirt, seeking a purchase. "Quill, come help us."

Quill helped and together they pulled Korrigan Jack free from the prison. The three of them stood a moment, breathing hard lungfuls of smoky air.

"And now we run, boys," Nel told them. "We've a ship to catch."

THE SERVANTS, OR maybe assistants was a better word, that occupied Raines' lab were called Mandragora. Twisted little creatures. Not twisted as in they were cruel or malicious, but twisted in that they resembled the twisted lattice-work of vines and roots. They were all brown, from dark and dun-coloured to tan to the hue of sand grains. And tiny, none more than two feet in height and some were half that, smaller even than the Dunnies she'd seen in the galley. Their eyes were huge in proportion to the rest of their face, like water droplets dabbed on their faces as an afterthought. Somehow both deep and liquid, perhaps to make up for an almost non-existent nose and the tiny mouth. And their hands; the fingers were like extensions of their twisted root-tuber arms. Hairy tendrils that refused to confirm to any set design.

They were, Violet thought, intensely interesting.

The same could not be said about her. They universally ignored her, scurrying around the lab on whatever business or errands consumed their attention.

"The new glasses are satisfactory?" Raines asked her.

"What?" Violet jumped. She touched her face self-consciously. Raines had provided a pair of eye-glasses. His own design, naturally. The lenses were tinted to compensate for her not being able to see colour. It turned out, as Raines had explained it, all colour was in fact hues of other colours. The part of her eye that saw red had been damaged. The glasses compensated.

"Oh, yes. Thank you. I can see colours again. Not walking into doorways no more."

"Anymore," Raines correct her.

"Never seen them anywhere else," she said, ignoring the lesson, watching one carry a beaker of frothing liquid from one apparatus to another. A beaker half the size of itself—though if the task was strenuous the Mandragora didn't show it. But what did show was the colour, a welcome change. Being able to see colour again made Violet feel . . . whole. Like something had clicked into place. Made her pace as well. The workshop was filled with things to look at.

"The Mandragora are native to the Fata Morgana. Not the ship, rather the Fata itself, a small moon precisely," Raines told her, then considered his own words. "Perhaps not native, rather, originated from."

"I meant on this ship," Violet clarified, examining a spinning top. Like a child's toy, only with arms, metal rods with weights attached. It bobbed and dipped with the flow of the ship, never losing its balance on a single point. *Inside the Fata. The other Fata, Morgana to the Fata.* "Only inside this room."

"They do leave on occasion," Raines assured her. "When there is cause. They are simply more comfortable here, kept occupied. Also, the ship is technically a vessel of the Alliance Fleet. As such Aristeia Quinn wishes to maintain her own brand of discipline aboard. Myself and the Mandragora do not fall under that blanket. Stop!"

Violet froze, fingers against a glass canister. It was filled with mist, but of a colour she'd never seen before. Active and coiling, looking for an escape. And it had followed her finger as she traced it up and down the outside. The canister rocked at her sudden touch, flinching like she had.

Raines stilled and righted the object, holding it steady for long moments before he released it. "Curiosity is a desirable trait," he told her. "But some things do not reward the curious. Mist from the Fata, for example. The same mist inside the mechanisms of this ship. Very dangerous, but very useful. Under the right circumstances and discipline. Would that *this* substance was so malleable. And speaking of discipline, I have heard about an incident between you and the master-at-arms, Mister Coldstream."

"Weren't no incident," Violet said quickly, turning away from him.

"No?" Raines' voice followed her. "Mors Coldstream has a formidable reputation, like many aboard this ship. I for one would not want to find myself facing off against him on a duelling field. If I were to stoop to duelling, that is."

"Duelling ain't allowed on your ship."

"Nor is it advisable, unless one were, shall we say, rather proficient at it."

"Man wouldn't be so fancy up close." Violet remembered something, a battle fought aboard the deck of a ship. Not a duel with proscribed rules and practices. "Hard to hit someone with a wand when they're up in your face."

"Indeed. An unconventional approach can overcome many obstacles. It does not pay to overlook the little things, or the little ones." Raines regarded the short-statured creatures fondly, emphasising his point. "This ship was first conceived within the Fata. It seems appropriate we should carry a piece of that realm aboard, to accompany the name."

"What do you mean by realm?" Violet asked, still watching the minions go about their tasks. For that was what they were, she realised; Raines' own private entourage. No wonder the skipper . . . Aristeia, didn't like for them to roam. "How is the Fata a realm? Isn't it just . . . distant?"

If you consider a year's voyage each way distant, it may as well be a realm unto itself.

"A distant centre, very much so," Raines agreed. "Realm is a way to say . . . define . . . an area of which conditions, rules, the environment . . . is not what we consider normal. The Lanes operate under one set of conditions, a calm summer's night. The Fata is a winter storm. A maelstrom, child, of activity. Of energy."

Raines held his hands together, making a cupping motion. "All of it contained within a very small area, relatively speaking."

"And how does one go from such a maelstrom to such a ship?" Violet heard herself asking.

"A pertinent question," Raines said. "One observes a process, one attempts to replicate it."

"And was one successful?"

"Success is but a succession of failures," Raines shrugged. "The latter but a progression of that prior. And success often comes in places unlooked for, or in fact disguised as something other than what we expect."

"I don't understand," Violet admitted.

"The key is not to be afraid of failure," Raines told her. "Failure is always an option. It is something that can only occur when one makes an attempts. Thus, it follows that failure is vastly preferable to not making any attempt at all."

"Your first attempt was a failure, and the next ones after that."

"Yes?" Raines peered at her intently. "And which attempts would these be?"

"Your test craft," Violet said, hoping it wasn't meant to be a secret. She wondered if Gravel's lips were as loose as Kaspar's. "One . . . exploded. One lost. The other just broke."

"Ah, yes," Raines' voice carried his disappointment. "That. But no matter. Worthy attempts, all of them. The next attempt was the proof of concept. As it turned out the maelstrom was best observed from . . . outside. And here we are now."

"People died," Violet reminded him.

"People die all the time. Consider fire, a primitive tool, but an essential one. How many conflagrations and singed fingers were suffered before it was mastered and brought under control? Lessons to be learned there, child. Imagine the alternative," Raines began to pace. "Stagnation, forever frozen in the troughs of progress. That is what our people have come to. Yours. Ours."

"Our people?"

Raines nodded, his tails fanning out behind him as he walked.

He stopped, turning abruptly on his heels, pointing at her.

"Two tails," he said. "One more and you'd be expected to return home. Wasteful."

"How is it a waste?"

"Ships and sailors rot in port," Raines said mockingly. "An apt saying. One would not think to look for wisdom amongst common sailors but neither should one overlook it. Discoveries made by failure, by accident, perhaps even overheard. Apt. The purpose of a ship is to sail. It has no business lying dormant, restrained by ropes and papers, by nonsensical traditions. How are we any different?"

Violet's eyes fell on Raines' tails. Seven. Seven tails. She'd never seen the like, not outside of home. Raines had said so himself, he was long past the point of return.

"Knowledge," Raines said. "Discovery, opportunity, potential. All of it wasted by a feeble tradition. Why? Why return home?"

"To share," Violet said. "Or . . . it's all lost. Everything you are . . ."

Lost.

"Ah, but there is the crux," Raines said, his eyes bright, animated. Almost fevered. "All that we are. I could be . . . *so* much more. I am so much more than those who walk the familiar paths. Look where we are. They call this the *Free Lanes*. Still uncharted, undiscovered. Still waiting to be found. Potential. I have seen that potential, crossed it, from the Fata Morgana to the Edge, the very *Edge*. This is where I choose to stay. This is where I choose to be."

Violet shifted uncomfortably.

Raines asked her, "Is the Alliance a bad thing, in your opinion?"

"Seems like."

"And by contrast the so-called Free Lanes would be better."

"Free, ain't they?"

"Hardly," Raines told her.

Violet looked at him, perplexed.

"You, you have spent most of your time travelling these free worlds. Tell me, what are some you have visited?"

"Vice," Violet responded immediately. "The flat world. Border, Crossed. Spent a week at White Cast and then ended up at Cauldron."

She frowned. That was wrong. White Cast was in the High

Lanes, named for the traders' beacon ships used to navigate there. She'd never been. Who'd put the idea of it into her head?

"The worlds you speak of are not for the faint-hearted. Vice is free, as you say, the freedom of anarchy and lawlessness. Now Cauldron, not too dissimilar from many places in the High Lanes, if on a much larger scale. Both run by autocrats who use intimidation to control their holdings."

"I don't . . . know anything about that."

"Ah, well, let me enlighten you then. You see, Cauldron sits along a moderate-sized shipping lane. Nothing unusual there, it makes no sense to establish a community in the outskirts of nowhere. But shipping attracts raiders, smugglers, deviants of many kinds. Eventually one rises to the top of the pile and asserts themselves. What was this one called?"

"At Cauldron? I . . . don't know."

"Ah, curious, mysterious even. But there will be someone. Perhaps several someones but power will always be concentrated in the smallest available number. It is the way of things. The way of progress. And potential."

"Maybe." Violet threw herself back in the chair. This wasn't a conversation, or an argument. It was a lecture. A point of view being imposed.

Pay attention.

Her head hurt. Violet pulled off the glasses, dropping them in her lap and rubbing at her eyes. A black and white world.

"Do you understand why I led the crew to believe you were my associate? Part of the Guild?" Raines asked her.

Violet shook her head. Staring at the glasses. Already dirty and smudged, she noticed.

"To keep you safe," Raines said. "The aura of the Guild carries a certain protection, which I have extended to you. It will keep Aristeia and her ilk from looking too closely into your past. This much I can do for . . . one of my own."

One of my own.

"As an associate of the Guild you are safe, you have a future. As the long-serving cabin girl of a forgotten ship, you do not."

"But I am that girl," Violet looked up. "I was, I mean. Not some Guild . . . anything."

"You cling to your past," Raines told her, relentlessly. "Who you were. Preconceptions. Ignoring potential. Your own potential."

Violet snorted. "What potential?"

Raines turned and beckoned to one of the Mandragora. The creature brought something over, wrapped in sail cloth. It was oddly out of place for the elder Kitsune's workshop. So mundane and commonplace.

"I see great potential in you, little one. I see the person you could be, a person I very much look forward to meeting in the future."

Violet sat up, not looking at Raines. There was no potential, no future. There was nothing ahead of her.

"A memento from your past," Raines held out the offering. "But perhaps it can help guide you towards your future. I would have discarded such a bauble, this repository of a bygone era, but it has a unique property I believe could bring out what I see in you."

He let the covering fall. It was Horatio's sphere, the one the captain had given to her back on the *Tantamount*. It was cracked, the mist inside dull and wispy. The ship listed to one side, adrift.

Violet reached out to take it, her fingers brushing the polished curve of the surface. It was warm. Raines covered her hand with his, pressing her fingers down around the sphere, squeezing them with his. She felt her hand start to grow warm. And glow, pale, almost blue. Sparks.

"So much potential," Raines told her. "Just waiting, inside of you." He held up his other hand. It was wreathed in sparks, jagged bolts that orbited his fingers. "Just waiting for you to accept it. To be who I see you as."

Raines let go of her, and the thaumatic effect vanished. No glow, no sparks. But the cracks in the sphere were gone.

"You may keep the bauble," Raines told her. "I believe we are done for today."

Chapter 11

"Ain't never seen one of them before."

"Pretty."

"Was talking about the glass ball, Niko."

Kaspar gave Gravel his long-suffering look. Violet was coming to know it well.

"But the lass is easy on the eye too, sir, whatever you meant."

"You're doing it again." Violet put the globe away, tucked inside a pocket. Her fingers still buzzed whenever she touched the glass, and she could feel it, a solid weight against her skin. The glasses were likewise tucked away. Much as she welcomed being able to see colour again, Violet found they strained her eyes. She needed to take breaks. "Talking about me like I can't hear what you're saying."

"Aye, and when we say it so well it's no wonder you hear. But we've a present for you, little Miss, and we'd be crushed if you didn't hear so from ourselves."

"Brandon has a present for you," Kaspar corrected.

"So *you* don't have a present for me?" Violet pouted in Kaspar's direction. "Now I am crushed."

"I says it's from both of us," Gravel shrugged, "and the lass heard that so that's how it is."

"What is it?" Violet stopped her teasing of the young ensign, who already looked grimmer than a Lane storm. "Can I see?"

"Aye, it's a sight, to be certain," Gravel said. "Much like

yourself, and yourself is where it belongs, given—"

"It's a pearl earring," Kaspar interrupted. "Tradition, for those who survive a shipwreck. Stupid custom."

Gravel sighed, his moment spoiled. "Aye, as he said. Could have let me finish saying such but apparently he's not of a mind." He held out a scrap of cloth, canvas, likely once part of a sail. Violet took it and unwrapped several layers in her hands. As Kaspar had said, a pearl earring, ghostly pale and translucent and hung from a brass hook.

Violet reached up, tugging at her earlobe between finger and thumb. There was a problem, something missing.

"I don't got nowhere to put it," she said.

"Rare girl," Kaspar mused, "all that sailing and ink on your skin. But not ring nor a hoop to show for it."

"Always seemed odd," Violet admitted. "Poking holes in yourself to hang shiny things from."

"Says the girl with painted skin?"

"Got just the few. And they're pretty."

"Ever so pretty, Miss," Gravel agreed. "But I've thought on that, came prepared even."

He held out his hand, palm out, revealing a needle and a candle.

"You want to stick holes in my ears," Violet said, staring at the implement.

"Just the one," Gravel said. "Wouldn't make no sense to do both, not with just the one earring."

"Which ear?"

"Figure you might want to pick that yourself. Don't have to be an ear, neither."

"It doesn't?"

"Could be the nose," Gravel tapped hers. "Lip too, maybe tongue, might make eating hard though. Don't recommend anywhere else. Might catch on your clothing."

"Where else would you—" Violet stared. Then recalled an image of a shirtless Piper. The man had had numerous piercings, not just confined to his face. And he had worn a pearl earring too, though of a different colour.

The idea didn't seem so unappealing when she recalled that. Just like Piper's.

Her gaze fell on the needle. Less appealing, but still more so than a few moments ago.

"How's this work?" she asked.

"Heat the needle, pop the ear, and thread the pearl," Gravel shrugged. "Easy as pie."

"You ever make pie?" Violet asked him.

"Seen it made plenty of times," Gravel assured her. "Seen this done too."

"You do your own?" Violet pointed to the three small silver hoops in Gravel's left ear.

"I did them," Kaspar folded his arms. "That's why they're all in the same ear."

"Don't follow," Violet said.

"Brandon did the ones in the right himself. Made a mess of it. Bled for a whole day because he used a needle too big for the job."

"Didn't look so big," Gravel said. "Didn't hurt none either. Just never knew there was so much blood in a man's ears."

"You do it," Violet pushed the needle towards Kaspar. "Don't want blood on my clothes."

"It washes," Gravel said.

"You doing the washing? You any good at washing blood off? You know how many times I've had to wash blood out of my—"

Gravel held up his hands, sighing. "As you wish, little Miss."

Kaspar lit the candle, then pulled a cork-stopped flask from somewhere on his person.

"What's that?" Violet asked.

"Rum," Kaspar said. "Strong stuff, too." He pulled the cork and dropped the needle into the vial, shaking it around before fishing it back out. He then began heating it over the small candle flame.

"Fancy a swallow?" Gravel offered her the flask as soon as Kaspar had put it down. Violet took one sniff and her eyes began to water. Strong. She pushed it away, to the lad's amusement.

"Dab some on your ear," Kaspar told her, holding the now red-hot needle through half the sail cloth wrapping and holding out what was left to her. "The rum should burn off any nasty so you don't take sick."

"And the needle does the rest?" Violet did as she was told, still eyeing the red-hot metal sliver cautiously. She wanted to back out but a voice in her head wouldn't let her.

"You don't want your ears to take sick," Gravel assured her.

"Look right silly without your ears, you would, and then nothing to tuck your hair behind."

"Stop scaring her," Kaspar said, shuffling over. He held up the cork. "I'm going to put this behind your ear so I don't stab your neck when the needle goes through. Ok?"

Violet nodded, not at all comfortable. She took a deep breath and held it as the cork was pressed against the back of her earlobe, held tight by Kaspar's hand.

"One . . . two . . ."

He never counted three.

"Sonofa—" Violet jerked away from Kaspar, clutching her ear. The ear he'd just stabbed with white-hot lightning doused in vinegar. Alcohol her bright, fluffy tail!

"Hells!" Violet swore, feeling something damp on her fingers. She looked at them and saw red. "Bloody hells!"

She glared at Kaspar, went off on another blue tangent for a full minute. "There's a hole in my ear, damnit!"

Kaspar stared at her, his eyes wide like dinner plates. "That was . . . the idea."

"That hurt," Violet cried. "That really, ploughing really hurt!"

"I'm . . . sorry?" Kaspar faltered. He shoved Gravel next to him. "And what are you laughing at?"

Gravel clutched at his stomach, gasping. "Can't breathe," he wheezed out. "Can't . . . gods, but that's the funniest thing I ever saw. And look . . . the needle's still in you. In your ear. It's stuck in the cork!"

Gravel howled with laughter, rolling around on his perch hysterically. Violet aimed a savage kick at him while trying to dislodge the cork from herself. Gravel didn't notice and she was no more successful with the needle and cork.

"Here," Kaspar reached for her, making Violet recoil.

"Don't you touch me!" She raised her foot to kick him if he tried, hopping away from him as best she could.

"Think you've done enough, sir," Gravel gasped, wiping tears from his eyes. "Gods, lass, did you cry this much when you got your ink done?"

"Shut your face," Violet told him. Her fingers wouldn't grip the needle, too slippery with blood. Was it meant to be bleeding that much? Surely that was too much blood. Surely.

"I'll go," Kaspar held up his hands wearily. "I think we've done enough here. Brandon, we have the watch."

"You have the watch, sir," Gravel corrected him. "I'm with this shrieking siren, at least until the next bell turns."

"Right," Kaspar frowned. "I'd forgotten. Well . . . carry on."

"Aye, sir, carrying on," Gravel saluted him. "Enjoy your watch."

"Want me to help with that?" Gravel asked when Kaspar was gone, pointing to her face. "You were a mite harsh on the ensign, but he must have hit some sore spot for you to be carrying on so."

"Fine," Violet said, tensing as he took hold of the cork behind her ear. His hands felt hot against her skin. She expected more pain but there was none yet.

"Hurry up," she told him impatiently.

"Easy, lass, got to get the earring through first. Otherwise this was all a waste and would be a shame to waste a scream like yours. Language too, never heard the words come from such a pretty face. I know hussies and harlots you could turn red. Where'd you ever learn such colour?"

"Is there much blood?" Violet wanted to know.

"A drop, that's all." Gravel stepped back from her, holding up the piercing instrument. "All done now, lass. And the pearl is pretty, if I do say so myself."

"Hells," Violet shuddered, resisting the urge to reach up and feel for herself. She didn't want to see any more blood. She could feel the earring though, an odd weight, just on the one side of her face. Felt like she was listing to one side, which was silly. Barely weighed a thing. Just felt heavy. Unfamiliar.

"Looks odd," Gravel told her, echoing her thoughts. "Drags your ear down. Should even it up, pop the other one too."

"No," Violet shook her head. The movement sent her new earring shaking, knocking against her skin. It was going to take some getting used to.

"Hells," she said, holding it still with two fingers. She spied the vial of rum next to her, still corked. Lucky she'd remembered to do that; she had a use for it now.

"That's truly not for drinking," Gravel warned her as she raised it up. Violet ignored him and swallowed half the contents. It burned hot and fiery down her throat, bringing a flush to her face. And another laugh from Gravel so she downed the rest of the rum. It was smoother the second time.

"Works for drinking just fine," Violet told him. She considered the empty vial, then shrugged and replaced the cork, tucking it inside her shirt.

Give it back to Kaspar later.

"I worry for my ears now that you've taken to liquor," Gravel said. "Be stripping the rust right off the hull with just your tongue come our next walk. Where'd you learn to cuss like that anyhow?"

"Before," Violet said. She frowned. Hadn't been thinking about the skipper too much of late. But there she was, all bright and vivid in her mind. Redheaded and stern disapproval on her face. Reaching for her that last time . . .

Red, like the blood on my hand ought to be.

Violet rubbed her fingertips together till the blood dried and crumbled off.

Except the skipper didn't reach. She let me go. I saw. I remember.

"Don't wanna talk about it," Violet said.

"Aye, as you like," Gravel shrugged. "There's a look on your face, though."

"What look?" Violet glared.

"Lonely," Gravel said. "You look like I felt, way back when. When I first came up from the mines, didn't know nobody. Not a friend nor family to my name."

"Don't need a friend," Violet said.

"Aye, that's what all folks without friends say. Everybody needs friends. Even Mors and Aristeia got each other. And I've got Kaspar, bless his heart. For all his faults as an officer, he's a good lad. Had my back since those first days so I try to do right by him."

"You are friends," Violet said. "That's . . . odd. That is odd. For an officer and a sailor to be friends like you two."

"Why's that?"

Violet looked Gravel up and down. There was a rush in her head, the spirits going straight to it. "Because he's better than you."

Gravel shrugged, the words missing their mark. "Aye, so I've heard. Fact is I didn't know squat about being a bluejack, couldn't read colours or tie my own shoes with nought but a nest knot. Niko taught me all that. Took me under his wing."

"Charitable of him," Violet said. "Won't have done his career any good though."

Gravel shrugged. "Didn't quite fit in amongst the officers, even before we joined this lot. Wasn't mean enough. Didn't like giving orders much. Kept to himself where he could."

"What's his secret?" Violet asked.

"Secret? What secret?" Gravel said. Too quickly.

"Everyone's got them. A secret."

"Secret of Niko Kaspar is he ain't his own man," Gravel said. "Got pushed into the fleet life and never got a say about it. Been lonely ever since."

"Got you, hasn't he?"

"Aye," Gravel said slowly. "But . . . well, sometimes it ain't enough, you know? Like it could all be taken away from you. Just like that. Lost to the black."

Changed my mind, bluejack. Don't like your words. You can go back to shutting your face. Don't need a friend.

"You look lonesome, lass," Gravel said quietly.

"Shut your face," she told him out loud.

"You're a mean drunk," he replied. "Won't be offering you any more bottles."

"Fine."

"Come on," he stood up and held out his hand. "Got something to show you."

Violet looked at him, all suspicious.

"What?"

"Come on," he repeated. "Been wanting to show you for a long time. Now is good, assuming you're done bleeding on the deck."

He pulled Violet to her feet before she could even touch her ear.

"ARE WE MEANT to be back here?"

"No," Gravel looked back at her with glittering eyes. "No, we are not."

Back here was the cargo deck of the *Fata Morgana*. It was far smaller than the *Tantamount's*, which had in fact covered an entire deck and often spilled over from that. Gravel had led her deep into the bowels of the metal ship, towards the stern if Violet had managed to keep her bearings, which wasn't easy since they'd crossed over the plane twice. A roundabout way to get to something Violet suspected was strictly off limits to her.

And not just to stowaway little girls. Dockside mining orphans aren't high on the chain. Whatever it is, he's not meant to be here either.

Violet grimaced, shutting down the thoughts. She had to hold onto the wall to keep from falling over. The change in direction and the after effects of the drink. Any more and she'd struggle to lie on the floor without holding on. Whatever it was had best be worth it.

They stopped in front of a bulkhead door. The *Fata Morgana* was extremely compartmentalised, making the most use of the multiple plane layout and enclosed interior. Gravel spun the wheel, the door opened outwards.

"Ladies first," he gestured.

"Ain't no lady," Violet muttered as she stepped past him. Gravel just grinned at her. She held one hand on the doorjamb, taking a moment. The ship was swaying. Or maybe the drink, and the dark wasn't helping.

"What are we looking—" Violet bit off the last word in a strangled squawk as something dive-bombed her. She dropped to the deck, grabbing for whatever was suddenly caught up in her hair. Hot breath and sharp claws scrabbled at her face as she tried to fight it off or get away.

She became aware of deep, uncontrolled laughter. Her assailant vanished at the sound, leaving Violet gasping on the floor. Violet reached up to touch her face, expecting it to be bloody and ruined. Instead she found it more or least unmarred.

"You scared him."

"Scared him?" Violet cried. "The hells was that?"

Gravel stood in the doorway, backlit by glowstones in grey and silver. His silhouette was hunchbacked, one shoulder grossly malformed and moving all its own. Violet stared.

That's . . .

"Bandit?"

An uncertain chitter greeted her inquiry.

"Bandit, get over here, you mangy rodent!"

The loompa dropped to the deck and closed the distance in a single bound, wrapping trembling, wiry limbs and tail around her. The impact rocked Violet onto her back and she crushed Bandit to her chest, an embrace that must have squeezed the air from his small lungs from the wheeze he gave off.

Violet didn't care. She hadn't thought about Bandit since coming aboard, a guilt that made her cradle him all the tighter.

For a moment, just for a moment, it was all right. She was back in the hold of the *Tantamount*. She could smell Gabbi's cooking mixed in with the acrid smell of loompa fur. She could hear Quill and the skipper bellowing at each other across the deck, almost drowned out by a shanty Piper and the captain had sparked up.

In a moment those all faded away, into dust, into the black. Gone.

They're all gone.

Except for the smell and feel of Bandit's fur against her face.

When Violet felt she could let go, that the only other member of her old crew wouldn't vanish like so much dust in the air, she realised there were tears streaming down her face. She hoped Gravel couldn't see them.

"Thank you," she whispered.

Gravel shrugged uncomfortably, but still smiling. "Came in with you, poor thing that he is. More than half frozen to death and scrawnier than me when I first signed up. Didn't think he had much of a chance but he's a tough little furball."

"Who else knows he's down here?"

"Just the right honourable Niko Kaspar. Didn't approve, of course. He never does."

"Thank you, Gravel, thank you both."

"Well, don't thank me too much, little lady. Our friend has to stay down here. Half the crew would spit him just for the practice and that's not even including Coldstream and Quinn."

"This is a wonderful surprise," Violet stood up. Bandit perched on her shoulder, a familiar weight she hadn't known was missing.

Gravel chuckled. "Worth it for the look on your face. Before and now. You're a sight prettier when you smile. Less so when you're spiteful."

Violet flushed, remembering her words not so long ago. Could blame the drink but it was more than that. "I'm sorry," she said.

"Makes all the difference, lass. Fact is you can't hurt my feelings much but prefer if you didn't try so hard at it."

Violet hung her head. *Hells, what did get into me?*

"Enough of that. That's only half the surprise you've seen." Gravel rubbed his hands together conspiratorially. "We have to go right to the end here."

Gravel led the way with Violet and Bandit in tow, the loompa riding her shoulder, the opposite one to her new jewellery. It felt right somehow, balancing her out.

"Is that—" Violet stopped, squinting in the dark. They'd come to a mostly empty area of the hold, which was sectioned off into compartments. There was a ship inside, a small tender, tarped over.

"Aye, the *Fata Morgana's* grand-daddy, wrinkled wee thing it is."

It was small, Violet thought. Very small, for two people to spend a month on. The mast had been lowered to make it easier to store but she could make out that the tarp covering it had once been the makeshift sail. Under that she glimpsed a bulkier, less elegant design of the pipes and coils that festooned much of the *Morgana.*

"Would it still sail?" she asked.

"Probably," Gravel said. "Wouldn't want to have to test it again though, once was enough."

"Kaspar fell off that."

"Aye, he did."

Violet frowned at it. How had it gotten in here? It was too big to be lowered in from the deck above. The deck above was enclosed, anyhow. Part of the hold must open up to the black, for loading and unloading purposes. Strange design.

"Come on, that's not what I was looking to show you."

Gravel led her further in, to an out-of-the-way corner of the hold. Whatever stores were kept here were bulky and little used. A layer of dust covered everything, sending Bandit into a fit of sneezing. Her guide stopped her in front of one of the darker shadows. Something bigger than both of them.

Violet let her eyes travel from the feet, almost round and featureless, up to the more sculptured torso, where she could make out individual muscles, almost lifelike in their detail. Finally the face, almost a blank slate again, but for the two deep-set eyes. There was no trace of colour now but Violet had seen them lit from inside. Blood and red in colour. She never thought to see them again.

"Where did this come from?" she asked. She rolled her shoulder, realising Bandit had vanished from his perch.

"Can't tell you that one," Gravel admitted. "Truth is, he's a scary fellow to be staring down inside or outside of a ship. Had the pleasure once before, during those riots on Border. Didn't realise the fellow was a paying customer until I stumbled across it looking for a place to rest my head one day. It's something though, ain't it."

"It's . . . something." Violet reached out, the tips of her fingers brushing the obsidian golem's carved chest.

Onyx's hand closed around her wrist. Just like that. Violet tried to pull away, but she was held fast, the grip solid, if not crushing. She glared furiously at the construct. It had moved just the once, seemingly lifeless again. But it wasn't letting go.

"What happened?" Gravel rushed up, staring at the black polished hand.

"Grabbed me," Violet scowled, tugging harder with her free hand.

"*How* did it grab you? It's never moved for me, I would have sworn it didn't move. What did you do?"

"Maybe it just remembers me," Violet gritted her teeth. She braced her feet and tried to push the arm up instead. It wouldn't move, as solid as the statue it pretended to be.

"Remembers you?"

Violet ignored that. "Find me a hammer, a tool, something." She jerked her head. "Bandit, smash, go fetch."

Bandit was gone off into the darkness. Gravel cast about, looking perplexed.

"I don't understand," he said.

"Don't need to understand, just need to break the dumb rock." There was a cry from the darkness. "Go see what he found. Go!"

Gravel jumped at the barked order, leaving Violet alone with the golem. She stared up at the face.

He could crush you just by flexing his wrist.

"All right, you big, dumb rock," she leaned in as close as she could, "do you remember me? I'm the one who dropped you off the *Tantamount*. I watched you float off into the mist, and if you don't let me go by the time my friends get back with the biggest hells damned hammer you've ever seen, I'm going to watch them smash you into pebbles. You hearing me, you dumb slab of granite?"

The head shifted, she would have sworn to it. Twisting just a bit to look down at her. Condescending. Mocking. Daring.

"Fine," Violet swallowed, hearing Gravel coming back. "What'd you find?" she called out impatiently.

"This," he held out a satchel.

Violet scowled. "I asked you to find a hammer, not a lady's purse."

"Easy, lass," Gravel made a pained face. "It's a caulker's kit, got hammers."

"Little ones?"

"Metal ones. But more importantly," he dug around inside, "chisels."

"Ha!" Violet exclaimed. She turned a gleeful expression on the golem. "Hear that, crag face? Chisels. Now let go right now and maybe I won't carve my sign in your backside."

Gravel winced. "Violet, maybe don't be jibing the golem. Not when it's holding you like that. What if it . . . squeezed?"

What if?

"It won't," Violet kept glaring at Onyx. It didn't squeeze. Nor did it let her go. "Fine. Gravel, start chiselling."

Gravel stepped up, hammer and chisel held in either hand. "I think the old fox wanted this thing. For all I know he might have made it. Maybe we shouldn't . . ."

"Give me the hammer then," Violet held out her free hand. "I ain't staying like this and I ain't being found stuck to this walking landslide neither."

"Fine, I'm chiselling," Gravel muttered. He set the point of the chisel at the joint of one of the fingers and started tapping away.

Gravel. Little rock. Think you can take down Onyx?

Bandit climbed atop Onyx, dragging a second hammer, making his way to the smooth head. Violet grinned when the loompa started making ungainly swings at Onyx's face with a hammer half his own size. She focused on that.

Not doing so much but I warned ya, crag face. Don't says I didn't.

"This isn't working," Gravel said. "I'm not even scratching it."

"Hammer harder," Violet suggested pointedly.

"I'm hammering plenty hard."

"Then get a bigger hammer."

"Why? So as I can smash your hand too? This isn't going to work."

Violet growled, shaking her head.

Shouldn't have . . . shouldn't have drunk. Can't think . . .

He's right. You saw Piper and Jack pound on this thing with all they got. It didn't bother it none at the time.

"So what? I just stay like this?" She wiggled her fingers.

Gravel grasped her arm under the golem's fingers and pulled, hard. Violet yelped, smacking at him with her free hand. Bandit screeched from his high perch, brandishing his weapon on protest.

"Oi, stop that! I tried, it don't work."

"Damnit," Gravel muttered, leaning one hand on Onyx's. He reached up to brush hair damp with sweat out of his eyes. "Violet, I'm going to get you out, ok."

"Yeah, how?"

"Could you . . . maybe turn yourself around?"

She stared incredulously. "See this here? This here whole kind of the problem? I can't turn nowhere!"

"Maybe just shut your eyes then," he suggested.

"No! What are you thinking on trying? Whatever it is, I ain't taking my eyes off you."

Gravel muttered something under his breath. "Fine," he ground out. "Just don't be saying nothing about it."

He raised one hand, his face descending into intense lines of concentration.

"That your thinking face?" Violet said.

"Shut up," Gravel told her. "This ain't easy."

Violet held her tongue. Then she felt it. Hair standing on end, an extremely unpleasant feeling when one had more hair than should be standing. And saw it, a pale blue light against the white, starting to emanate from Gravel. Filling the air with that crackling sound she'd always associated with Loveland Quill. With . . . thaumatics.

Gravel reached out, hands held close together, fingers almost clawed in tension. He held them as if they were an oversized extension of Onyx's already prodigious fingers, and started to pry them open. The golem creaked and groaned in protest but one by one Gravel dragged each finger free. Violet snatched her hand free and stepped away, staring wide-eyed. The glow dropped. She expected Onyx's hand to snap shut again but it remained open, frozen and splayed.

"Are you . . . meant to be able to do that?" Violet asked,

rubbing her hand. "You didn't want me to see . . ."

Gravel shrugged, backing away from the golem. Bandit gave a squawk when he realised he'd been abandoned and jumped to rejoin them. "Don't nobody know I can. Except you and Kaspar."

"You two," Violet shook her head, "you real tight with your secrets, aye."

"Aye," Gravel admitted. "Let's go, afore we get ourselves in more trouble."

"Think anyone'll notice himself posing like that?" Violet indicated the grasping golem.

Gravel winced. "Aye, except I don't wanna think about it."

Chapter 12

"THE HELLS DID you do?" The first words out of Sharpe's mouth when they arrived just shy of the docks, breathing hard. "Half the city is woke up."

Nel scowled at him. Didn't care for the tone, nor for the words Sharpe was using—sounded too much like something she'd have said.

"Blame Jack," she said. "Got himself locked up. Again."

"Jack," Sharpe stared past her, squinting in the flickering torchlight. "Good to see you again."

"Huh," was all of Jack's response. He eyed up the half-dozen Draugr contingent behind Sharpe. Didn't seem impressed.

"Anyone here not gotten themselves locked up recent?" Stoker asked, stepping forward. He had a loosely-tied bundle of clothes thrown over his shoulder, a pick and mix affair.

"You get everything?" Nel asked.

Stoker looked to Sharpe. "Did we? Seems we've acquired a few costumes here. Still not sure what the run is here? You planning on anymore breakouts tonight?"

"Just the one," Nel told him. "Got a pretty lady I'd like you all to meet and you have to dress the part to make introductions." She knelt down and started investigating what they'd brought.

"Should be enough," Sharpe told her. "Grabbed what looked promising and hustled. Didn't feel like a good idea to get caught with our breeches down given all the yelling."

"Breeches stay up," Nel told him firmly. "Dress quick, all of you. Seems like we woke the neighbours."

"This," was Quill's considered opinion, after they finished

dressing, "looks ridiculous."

The Kelpie wore his hooded cloak with a roughly modified vest in Alliance blue and white glimpsed beneath. It was the closest they'd been able to find for Quill's frame. By contrast, Jack, Sharpe, and their Draugr contingent appeared the more genuine. All wore hooded rain capes draped around their shoulders and pulled low, covering more ill-fitting and makeshift uniforms, though this time in the dark green and black of Alliance marines. Nel wore the same colours as them but hers would pass closer inspection. There just hadn't been anything suitable for the Kelpie's lean and angular body in the slop boxes they'd raided, and he'd never pass for anything other than a deckhand or officer.

Quill is right, Nel thought. In the harsh torchlight, their party looked ridiculous and had little chance of passing inspection. But there would be much less light down by the ships and with any luck it wouldn't come to that.

"How do I look?" Sharpe asked, puffing out his chest. His sense of humour was coming back, she noted. Truth was he had the build to pull off this role.

"Just play your part," Nel told him. "A marine Captain. You should be able to manage that."

"Just another face for you to wear, lad," Stoker told him.

"Put my face on same as all of you," Sharpe replied. "One saggy cheek at a time."

"Could use some help putting mine on," said another of the crew. *Java,* Nel thought. "Things aren't where I remember them being. Not just the face neither."

Gallows humour.

"Quiet in the ranks," Sharpe told them. "Remember, you're in the army now. Less talking, more marching."

"Marines are still fleet," someone corrected him. "We don't march in the fleet. We sing."

"Sing it loud," another added.

"For the blind!"

"And louder for the deaf."

"And loudest for all the ones we left behind," Stoker finished.

"Not the best start to your career," Nel told a frowning Sharpe. "Maybe we promoted you too far? Might have to bust you back to sergeant."

"Sergeant Sharpe," Stoker grinned. "Got a favourable ring to it."

"Captain no more," the one with the beard said. *Yarn, that one I know.*

"You wanna be captain, Nel?" Sharpe asked her.

"No."

"Then keep on saluting me, lass. Call it lieutenant and meet you halfway. Now, if you'll excuse me, got some yelling to do. Hells, this better go better than the last time."

"Just get a move on, Castor."

Sharpe had the grace not to answer her jibes, striding up to the boarding ramp of their chosen ship. *Dancers Poignard.* The name made Nel sigh. Well down the ladder as far as ships of the line went. Whoever had named her had barely deigned to adhere to the Alliance convention.

The Poignard Dances would have been closer. Hells, sounds just as trite. Maybe we can rename the damned thing, almost worth the hassle. Wonder if Quill would go for it again?

"All hands!" Sharpe bellowed, aiming his voice up at the decks. "I want to see your pasty tar-speckled faces lining the docks before I finish counting. And I don't count so high since Three Peaks."

A small wiry figure holding a lantern bobbed above the railing. "And who in the Seven Hells are you, greenjack? What do you want?"

The other members of this bell's watch were gathering now. Nel counted three. If they were extraordinarily lucky that could be the sum total of crew left on the ship. The rest might be dispersed and carousing in town.

"It's almost the dead man's watch, laddy," the man called out again. "Ain't you got some buttons and brass needs polishing?"

"Lieutenant Castor Sharpe, third squadron, marines." Nel's teeth caught as Sharpe identified himself. Using his real name probably wouldn't ring any bells with this crew but it seemed a daft risk to take, defeated the whole point in using disguises in the first place. "I'm here to secure this vessel before our passenger arrives."

"Passenger? What passenger?" the watchman objected. "It's the middle of the bloody night! Skipper ain't said nothing about—"

"Then I suggest," Sharpe stepped up the gangway, closing in

on the trio of noticeably smaller sailors, "you go wake him up!"

The sailors were momentarily cowed, shrinking back from the much bigger marine officer. The lead watchmen made a hurried sign to one of the others, who scurried off towards the stern of the ship. That was where the captain would be. So there was at least one senior officer still aboard.

"How many of your crew have returned?" Sharpe forged ahead.

"Returned? They meant to be returned?" the watchman stumbled.

Sharpe rounded angrily, or a good convincing of it. "Half my men are out rounding up your useless crew, sailor. What drunken rat holes have they crawled into that they haven't made it back to your ship yet?"

"On whose orders are they returning?" the captain's shrill voice echoed over the deck. "What are you doing on my ship, Lieutenant?"

Sharpe turned his head to acknowledge the dark-haired woman, even if she hadn't bothered to don more than a nightshirt before storming out onto the deck.

"Commander," he saluted her. A calculated insult. A ship this size was too small to be commanded by an actual ranked Captain, even if they were generally referred to as such by all aboard. It had been Nel's idea but she wanted to strike Quill for it when she heard him chuckling softly beside her.

The woman scowled at Sharpe furiously, managing a respectable affronted dignity while the wind whipped her shirt around.

"Sergeant," Sharpe bellowed. Nel grimaced but marched briskly up the gangway, coming to stand beside her *lieutenant*.

"Orders," Sharpe held out his hand and Nel placed the pilfered papers in it.

"From above," Sharpe said, offering the rolled parchment to the commander. The woman took it, looking up from under what Nel could see was grey-streaked hair. She didn't look for long. *Good, papers aren't much better than the rest of us.*

"Who's this passenger?"

"Need to know, Commander," Sharpe said, his tone implying the obvious.

"If they're on my ship then I need to know,"

the *Dancers Poignard* commander growled at him.

"Then you can ask them yourself," Sharpe shrugged, smiling evilly. "They'll be here within the next bell, along with the rest of my men and whatever sorry remnants of your crew they've managed to sober up."

The commander glared. "Best be watching your mouth, greenjack," she said, dropping the sailor slang for marine. "I don't care who your damned cargo is, on my ship you show me my due or I'll have your back flogged till you run crimson."

Sharpe continued to ignore her. "I count seven of your crew present, Commander. Is that all of them currently aboard?"

"Aye," she said warily. "Why?"

"My men and I have to secure the ship before our guest arrives. You'll all wait on the docks whilst we make our inspection."

The woman cursed. Nel took a moment to admire her extensive vocabulary. It took another exchange and more cursing before the commander led her increasingly surly crew down to the docks. Nel and Sharpe stood in front of them, doing their best to block their view of Quill and the Draugr as the Kelpie led the makeshift marines up the ramp.

"Your marines' footwork needs work," the commander said bitterly. Nel held her breath, waiting for some exultant shout of discovery but it seemed just the woman getting her sour kicks in.

Quill appeared at the top of the gangway. The plan called for them to board the ship and somehow keep the crew stranded on the dock. Yet Quill looked genuinely agitated. Jack was next to him, looking mean and ugly by contrast. Perfect marine, though it most likely wasn't all acting.

"We have a problem," Quill called, louder than was needed. Sharpe exchanged a concerned look with Nel, before regaining his composure.

"Anything you'd like to tell me, Commander?" he put an edge in his voice.

The woman eyed him coldly. "Got one in the hold."

"One of your crew?"

The commander didn't answer.

"And you didn't think to—" Sharpe bit off his words in disgust. "You stay here! Sergeant, come with me," he bellowed.

"You found someone?" Nel whispered hoarsely to Quill as they drew closer.

"They have a man secured below deck," Quill said.

"How secure?"

"Secure."

"This is a problem." Sharpe glanced back at the milling sailors on the dock.

"No, this is good," Nel shook her head. "Gives us an excuse, gives us time."

"You want to cast off?" Sharpe said. "What about this prisoner?"

"That's going to be their problem, but later."

"We could retrieve them and—" Quill started.

Nel interrupted. "No, take too long and we don't know why they're locked away in the first. We need to go fast, or this crew might start thinking. Worse, woman might read those papers. Give the signal."

"How much sail do you need?" Sharpe asked Quill.

"The main will take too long. The headsail will suffice. Just tend to the ropes and keep them off."

"Right. Which one is the headsail?"

"I'll take care of it," Stoker rescued him before Quill's reaction took voice. "Horse, with me."

Horse, Nel filed the woman as she and Stoker moved towards the bowsprit. *Easy to see why.*

"I'll get the ropes," Nel told Sharpe. "You be useful and hold the ramp."

Sharpe took his post, placing himself large and directly across the gangway, looking down at the Alliance crew and out into the docks. Nel kept to the centre of the ship, staying in the shadows of the rigging though it was doubtful she was visible to anyone below. She took her knife and went to work on the lines holding the ship to the dock. She got them all but for the barest threads. None of the about-to-be-former crew could see but the lines would fail the moment Quill launched the ship.

She held her breath, waiting for the shouting to begin when the Draugr unfurled.

The sail dropped open. The murmuring of complaints echoing from the docks rose, reaching a much higher pitch. Voices were raised, there were shouts, then the distinctive clap of sheets filling with thaumatically conjured wind. There was Quill, arms raised on the bridge, casting the faintest halo of blue and white light. The ship lurched under Nel's feet, rocking her as Quill applied pressure, forcing the sloop to strain against the lines. They began snapping in audible twangs, one after the other, leaving curled and frayed ends dangling into the water. The sailors ashore stared as their ship sailed away from them.

One, quicker of mind than his fellows, made a sprint up the gangway. Sharpe raised his arm to strike, bare-knuckled, other hand clutching his wand's hilt, but Quill's next surge drew the ship away from the dock, sending the gangway tumbling into the waters between. The sailor fell with a despairing shriek, arms flailing and clutching at air until he hit water.

The commander was yelling orders, the crew a disorganised mob but keeping pace along the wooden platform. There wasn't much running room but until they were clear there was still the threat of being boarded. Someone pitched a makeshift missile in Quill's direction. It fell short but worried Nel nonetheless. She joined Sharpe, wand drawn, waiting to repel boarders.

The acting marine lieutenant was firing shots at the pier, aiming low and for the feet, seeking to trip up the sailors. Nel joined in, targeting those who were closest first. The ship picked up speed, clearing the docks, leaving its former crew stranded at the end of the pier, staring after them forlornly. The commander stood at the very edge, just far enough away to make her expression indiscernible but Nel didn't have to imagine very hard. She'd been the one on that pier before. Same damned Kelpie stealing the ship too.

Sharpe put his wand away, one hand on the railing.

"That," he spoke slowly, "went better than I expected."

Nel nodded her head. "I expected something to go wrong. Right at the last minute."

"So did I."

They felt the ship start to shake under their feet. The Draugr had dropped the mainsail. A momentary vibration rattled the ship as Quill wrested the ship free of the water's surface tension, sending them skyward.

"Industrious bodies, are they not," Quill grimaced from the bridge. "You were right."

"Hoped as much," Nel said.

"You were not sure?"

"Was pretty sure."

They all reached for handholds as the *Poignard* angled sharply upwards, its etheric plane not yet able to overcome the much more powerful pull of Vice. Nel watched the Draugr carefully but after a moment the creatures all froze in place, immobile and secure, waiting for the ship to level off.

The ship climbed higher and higher. Glancing back, Nel could still see the landscape at an unnatural angle to themselves and yet her sense of normal up and down began to reassert itself. A few minutes after, and the world appeared level, the Draugr took up their duties. It was eerie, watching them move, slowly and somewhat stiffly, but they did echo the real flesh and breathing sailors they were acting in place of.

Sharpe gazed at Nel sidelong. "It worry you?"

"What?"

"Look at them. Not doing a half bad job. Wouldn't take a lot for them to replace an actual crew. Maybe all over."

"Draugr ain't never gonna replace good sailors, Sharpe. Even this lot. And they're special. But we run into real trouble and we'll all wish we had a few more warm bodies."

"You didn't want more."

"Still don't."

"Put some weapons in their hands, wonder what sort of soldiers they'd make," Sharpe mused.

Nel frowned. As far as she knew the concept had never been tried.

Far as I know though? If Sharpe here just thought of it then somebody else must have.

"Thought you were against Draugr."

"Against . . . what happened out there. Not against what these are, how they can be used. There's a difference."

"Ever think that sorta thinking is how out there happened?"

Sharpe frowned, oddly contemplative. His repose was broken by a banging from belowdecks. Nel and Sharpe turned to each other. Atop the bridge, Quill's posture straightened alarmingly. The ship dipped for a moment before he regained his poise.

"Vaughn!" the Kelpie yelled down at her.

"Aw, hells," Nel ran a hand through her hair in frustration. "We forgot about the damned prisoner!"

Chapter 13

"ARE YOU STUPID?" The flat of Kaspar's hand slammed into the wall, right next to her head. Violet turned her head from the close-up of that white-knuckled appendage to the face of its owner. *Angry suited Kaspar,* she thought. His face was all mottled with indignant rage, nearly a match to his copper-toned locks, maybe redder than usual through her glasses. *It was like when Mors Coldstream had him all fired up*, she thought. Only different. A different kind of angry.

"Are you?" he repeated. "Are you that hells damned stupid or do you just enjoy tempting fate? I've known guppies with more sense than you!"

"I don't see what you're so upset about," Violet said. She made to walk away; Kaspar's other arm blocked her. She was caught between the two of them.

"You were in the hold, you and Brandon."

"He tell you that?"

"It doesn't matter."

"Exactly, it doesn't. So why are you so worked up?"

"I can't protect you," Kaspar spoke quietly, his voice still tightly controlled, "can't protect either of you. Not if you carry on like this."

"Nobody saw us," Violet said. "Nobody has to find out. Nobody will find out. And besides . . . I don't need you . . . to protect me."

She smiled as she said the last part, reaching up to touch his cheek.

Kaspar glared at her, dropped his head closer. "Do you know who it was that found you out there? Me. I was the one who sighted you, floating out there, half frozen to death. I know what that feels like, remember? I know just how close you came to dying."

"My hero," Violet turned her head, grimacing. "Do you know why I was out there, Niko? Because I trusted someone to look out for me. To protect me. Ain't gonna do that again. You don't need to worry about protecting me because you can't protect me. No one can."

She put her hand to his chest and pushed him away. He caught her hand, not about to let it go either.

"And what about Brandon?" he demanded. "You happy to drag him down with you? If he'd been caught in the hold with you—"

"With your secret golem cargo?" Violet cut him off. "Is that what you're worried about? I know what that thing is, Niko. Seen it before."

"You should stay away from it. You both should."

"You don't think your thaumatic friend can take care of himself?"

Kaspar flinched, releasing her hand and taking half a step back.

"Yeah," Violet stepped up to him. "I know, he showed me. Down in the hold."

"He shouldn't have."

"Yeah? Why not?"

"Because he's not registered," Kaspar whispered harshly. "Nobody else knows about it, Violet! If they did . . ."

"They'd take him away," Violet nodded. "Take him away to some training camp, turn him into a navigator or something."

"You don't get a choice, not if you have talent. Not in the Alliance, in the High Lanes. They need people like that. So much they take that choice away from you."

"Yeah, they do. And that's your big, bad secret, isn't it, Niko? That's what you're keeping from the captain."

"Violet," Kaspar whispered, his voice low so it wouldn't carry. "The captain can't find out. Not Raines, nor Aristeia. No matter what else, they can't know Brandon is thaumatic, do you understand?"

Violet frowned. "It's a secret, I get it. You can trust me to keep it."

What's twisting his britches about it so much?

Thaumatics are everywhere, all types. Meant to be registered, sure, but not the end of all high water if you're not.

So, why?

"And what about you, cabin girl," Kaspar said then. "You think I don't know your secret?"

"Mine?" Violet asked. "What the hells do you think you know about me?"

"You didn't join the *Tantamount* at Port Border," Kaspar told her. "And you're no Guildsman. How many Kitsune cabin girls are there? You were with *her* from the start."

"From the . . . no, how . . ." Violet put a hand up in protest. "Where did you hear that?"

Kaspar shook his head. "It doesn't matter, Violet. If people found out, if Aristeia or Mors even suspected . . . if any of them guessed any of this . . ."

You sound like Raines. Isn't that interesting?

"Why are you protecting me?"

Kaspar stared at her, eyes bright, wide, still worked up. He didn't answer.

She changed the angle of the question. "Why is Raines protecting me?"

He leaned in, lowering his voice. "I don't know. But they can't find out, none of it. They can't know."

They, they, they. Who are they?

Violet tilted her head to look Kaspar right in the eye. "So you keep my secrets and I'll keep yours. Sounds fair."

"You," Kaspar whispered, "are going to get us all killed."

"Don't you trust me?" Violet asked.

Don't you trust me?

"No."

"And why is that?"

"You're inconsistent," Kaspar said. "You're hot then you're cold. Yes then a no. Sometimes I want to know you. Other times I don't think you give a damn about anyone, even yourself. So I don't trust you."

"Am I that hard to figure out?"

Kaspar didn't answer. He did lower one arm, offering her a way out.

Violet took the opportunity. She leaned forward on her toes and planted her lips on his. Kaspar's eyes widened, surprised, too much to respond in any way until after she pulled back.

One way to keep him quiet.

"Figure that out," she told him.

TAP, TAP, TAP.

The tapping echoed through the ship. Violet couldn't get it out of her head.

Tap, tap, tap.

She woke up to it, went to sleep to the sound of it. She dreamed it. It was driving her out of her mind.

Three bells into the twilight bell, the dog's watch, or whatever it was called on the *Morgana*. She'd given up on lying there, asleep but not dreaming, awake but unaware. Swinging her legs over the side onto the cold metal floor. The cold had started to bother her of late, whenever she felt herself drift off into a place that wasn't quite here, where she wasn't herself. Right now the sting of cold metal made her flinch but cleared her head. It was dark, silver lit, but the world had that little flush of colour, tinges of red and orange that had been missing.

There is no colour though, not really. Only the black.

Her minders still slept, Gravel on his back on the floor, one arm thrown up over his head, breathing through his nose and snoring because of it. He hadn't shaved in several days, the scraggly whiskers on his face almost endearing.

Kaspar always slept on his side, Violet had noticed. It was how he went to sleep and how he stayed until he woke. He'd fallen asleep during more than one late night card game, rolled onto one side or the other in the cocoon of his hammock or chair. Or tonight, in the corner of the too small cabin. His face was rarely restful, more fitful, like he was snatching at sleep itself. His arms wrapped around himself, hugging his shoulders and his legs pulled up towards his chest. Not quite curled up into a ball but he wasn't far from it.

Ever defensive and protective, that one.

Neither of them stirred when she moved, despite Kaspar's

insisting that they all stay. He'd been cold and chilly to both of them until sleep had taken him. Avoided looking at her. But if either were awake they were watching through half-shut eyes and keeping quiet about it.

No one moved to stop Violet as she padded down the halls of the ship. Sometimes they would, barring access to parts of the ship or preventing her from going a certain way. Other times they let her do what she wanted. If there was a pattern to the way the crew handled her, she couldn't make sense of it, other than Aristeia and Mors, who both resented her. Quinn and Coldstream. The first mate's name reminded her uncomfortably of the former Kelpie navigator, too familiar, too close for comfort. She preferred the first mate's given name and thankfully so did most of the crew. It was an otherwise ugly reminder of two people she preferred not to think about, a time she increasingly chose not to dwell on. Although the outright maliciousness of their hostility to her was new. So much more direct than what had previously been a mostly verbal conflict.

The tapping had taken her down a corridor, one on the underside of the bi-planar axis of the ship. It was hard to pinpoint the source, other than sometimes it was higher or lower.

Could the gravity plane be affecting the sound? Does gravity affect sound? If up and down are both the same thing, does the sound bounce when it crosses over?

As if on cue the world tilted with her next step. Colour gone, everything upside down. And she was falling again. She bit her fist to keep from crying out, focusing on the pain, grabbing for the wall with her other hand. Stumbling, trying to find her balance until everything made sense again, came right-side up. And then she was . . .

It was Raines' workshop, but different. Things had been moved. Instead of a Draugr on the table it was one of the Mandragora. A small and shrivelled thing, cut open and splayed out. Violet covered her mouth with one hand, feeling her gorge rise, an unhappily forgotten meal of biscuits and broth trying to make itself known. She must have forgotten her glasses again because everything was grey, silver, out of focus. Could have sworn they were on her face. Raines was talking, pacing around the table. Not to her. His words were muffled, like that time Jack had ducked her in the water barrel and she couldn't hear right after. He wasn't even talking to her.

"Who knows? How could we know? Maybe we did know. Unlike these, these . . ."

"What have you named them?"

"Goras. Dolls, much like. Mandragora, these natives. So mindless yet still they persist. Simple instinct. I wonder what would happen to them outside of their environment. Or if their environment . . . no, that would be . . . no."

Nothing made sense.

"These were taken from near your homeworld?"

"These? No, elsewhere. Far away. The centre. Yet not so different. We were wrong to think the Morgana was unique. There are . . . pockets. Eddies."

There were more jars. Canisters filled with the coiling not-mist. Barrel sized but made of glass. Violet ran her hand along the surface, watching the strangely foreign miasma bunch and follow after her fingertips.

"It's drawn to thaumatics. Ships can't go there. Not as they are now."

"And that's a problem?"

"An obstacle. To be overcome."

Violet turned away from the voices. She couldn't place the other speaker. Sounded familiar, but wrong. She couldn't explain why.

On the wall was a chart of stellar markings. Constellations and nebula. Oort clouds and rogue planets. And there . . .

"This is home," Violet froze, her fingers touching the spot. It wasn't on any charts, but she knew the way. They all knew the way.

"No," she heard Raines, sharp, decisive. "Not anymore. No longer. No . . . there's no point. The projections all say so. It travels along the cold lanes, finding its way. It will find its way there . . . home. And then there will be no home. Not even a memory."

Raines laughed. "At least now we know why. Simple. So close, so far. Never knowing. The irony."

"Where do your projections show? What will the next world be?"

"Not yours, you will be pleased to learn. Nor mine, not yet. Soon though. Or later, perhaps later, yes, but one day soon. But for now . . .”

Raines brushed past her. Violet started, not moving in time, but she barely felt his passing. Like he wasn't . . .

“There.”

“And where is that?”

“They call it Vintage. So quaint. The fleet must be told. Steps taken.”

“Will they listen?”

“They will listen. They will scream, they will protest, but they will listen. And then they will move. And do what needs to be done.”

“Will you tell them this is your fault?”

“It is not.”

“In a way.”

“Obstacles are to be overcome.”

Violet turned, trying to identify the other speaker. There was no one there. Nor could she see Raines. He'd gone, vanished. She spun again, trying to find him. So fast she made herself dizzy and stumbled. Her stomach lurched, dropping out like she'd left the envelope. Falling. The black. Again.

No!

Violet grabbed for something, anything. Her hands found a surface that was solid, flat, but she couldn't get a purchase. She lashed out at it, striking with her fists. Something jumped into her hand, solid, metal, cold. She felt the pain, squeezing her fingers around it. Something to focus on.

She opened her eyes. She was in Raines' lab. How she didn't know, last thing she remembered was being in her cabin. Asleep. Every intention of sleeping.

Raines wasn't there. Three Mandragora were, staring at her. Until they grew bored and returned to their duties, whatever they were. She was forgotten.

She sucked in a breath, staring at the object that had brought her back. Raines' canister. Metal and glass, brass chasing. Shiny.

Her face was reflected in the brass. Blurred, distorted. Almost unrecognisable.

Violet put the canister back.

How the hells do I get back without having to explain this?

Violet shrugged, both in her head and with her shoulders, moving for the door. Her footfalls sounded very loud to her. But there was no one else around.

And yet it wasn't just her footfalls either, there was a second set, lighter and more furtive, keeping pace with her but staying further back and . . . high? For how long now?

Violet turned on her heel, her bare feet barely making a sound on the ridged floor, glaring up at the network of pipes and tubing that infested the upper corners of all the *Morgana's* corridors.

"Get down here now," she said impatiently.

Luminescent eyes stared back at her from the darkness, bobbing and weaving as they stalked closer. Gradually more of the furry body emerged from the shadows, hunkered low and on all fours in the cramped crawlspace. The loompa, her fellow survivor and refugee, stared back at her cautiously.

"It's me, Bandit," she reassured him. "Just me. You can come down now."

He did come down, settling by her feet, staying low, rather than perching on her shoulder as she had come to expect. Had hoped for, if she was being honest.

Violet knelt down, holding out one hand, to which Bandit sniffed and batted at, again with the caution. Life aboard the metal ship was giving him a nervous disposition. Violet didn't care much for it.

"Was that you?" she asked, her voice low so that a whisper wouldn't carry. She was out of bed for that reason, the vagaries of how sound travelled. "Did you wake me up?"

Apparently not. Convinced it was her and her alone, the loompa took off, stopping at every turn and ladder to wait for her to catch up. The sound she'd been following had stopped, not enough to convince her it wasn't Bandit making it all along but she had no other leads to follow.

He led her into a different part of the ship, one she hadn't explored before. One, if she was being honest, she was not sure she could find again. Bandit took her through twists and hatches and two more crawlspaces. Either the loompa had no destination in mind and was lost or there was a reason for this circumspect route.

Could be both, could be just after his next meal. Might have been chasing a rat this whole time.

And then he stopped. At a door. Just stopped, stood up on two feet, waiting for her reaction. Nose twitching, whiskers quivering.

All expectant-like.

Violet stared. There was nothing remarkable about the corridor. It was featureless apart from the wheel-turn doors, three of them and nothing to set them apart. They could be anywhere in the ship—could be the brig or the galley or the head on the other side of those doors.

There was no explanation from Bandit, no hints or anything. He just sat there, waiting.

His part is done. Now it's on you. If you can figure out what that is.

She tried the door. Nothing. It creaked in protest, locked or stiff or maybe even seized. The sound of metal on protesting metal echoed down the corridor and she jumped away from it, smacking her back against the opposite wall and making even more noise.

"Who's there?" a voice from beyond the metal demanded. "Can't a fellow get some sleep without you lot marching to the beat for one damned bell?"

Violet clapped her hands to her mouth, frozen. Her heart was beating, its own wild march, and she was shocked the owner of the voice couldn't hear it echoing off the metal walls. She held still, immobile, waiting to see what would happen. Any moment now she expected the door to open and to be discovered. She started to move, slowly, quietly.

That was her plan. Bandit, unfortunately, wasn't in on the plan. Without so much as a permissive look to Violet, the loompa vaulted up onto the wheel, clinging awkwardly onto it, screeching and banging with one paw on the outside. Demanding to be let in or just making conversation, Violet couldn't tell. She could only listen and stare in horror.

She lurched forward, wrapping her arms around Bandit and trying to pull him free. He clung on, fierce, bit down on her hand when she tried to cover his mouth, shrieking the whole time. Muffled shrieks with his fangs in her skin but shrieking to the best of his ability.

"Hey, Bandit? That you?" the voice on the other side called out, shocking Violet. Bandit cried out in response, a triumphant trill.

"What's going on out there?" the voice demanded. "Who's there? What are you doing to my little friend? You better not touch him! Got the mange he does, plague, fleas, all sorts! One bite and your nethers will drop off, so you leave him be if you know what's good for you!"

The plague-ridden loompa wriggled free from Violet's grasp, resuming his banging and tugging on the locked door. She knew that voice. She knew it!

"Who are you?" she called out, shaking her head. She had to know now. Because it couldn't be true. Couldn't be.

"Who am I? Who're you? You're the one banging on my door, harassing my friends. Well, friend, just the one, which makes him all the more precious. And you—"

"Sharpe," Violet exclaimed. "Castor Sharpe!"

There was a pause. "Now . . . one of us is mightily confused."

Violet pushed up against the door, shoving Bandit aside. She tried the wheel again and it wouldn't budge, so she set her ear against the door itself. Bandit finally quietened down.

"It is you," she said. "But you're dead."

"I got better," came the reply, "but who're you? You're with Bandit, that's clear enough. But you don't sound big enough to be Piper nor wheezy enough to be the old man. Fact is you sound like a lass, only I've known many a lass in my day, that is to say more than one and—"

"Damnit, Sharpe!" Violet slapped the door. "How do I get this open?"

"You can't," Sharpe said, after a hesitation. "Violet. That's you, right?"

"Yes," Violet whispered, cheek to the door. "It's me."

"Damn, lass, but it's good to hear your voice. You don't know how much I mean that."

"You too." There was a catch in her voice. Made her not want to say anymore.

"Are you alone?"

"It's just us. Me and Bandit."

"But the others, your crew. How are you even here? Is anyone else with you, I mean. Is Nel . . . ?"

"They're dead," Violet said. "They're all dead. It's just me." She looked down at Bandit, the loompa's wizened little face, the black eyes. "It's just us."

She heard a sigh. "Lass . . . I am so sorry."

Bandit scratched at the door, claws on metal. It was a half-hearted gesture, simple noise making. He cried, a soft, mewling sound. Squeaks. Violet gathered him up in one arm, held him close with her back against the wall.

"Lass," Sharpe told her from the other side. "You can't stay. Can't let them catch you here."

Violet shook her head. Everyone was always telling her to leave, not to go. Be careful. Don't get caught. Bandit squawked at her, reminding her that Sharpe couldn't see her. "Not leaving," she said stubbornly. "Hells not. Not."

"You're going to get us both in trouble," Sharpe reproached her.

Violet laughed. "How much more trouble could we be in?"

"One of us is still wandering around freely so she could be in much more trouble yet. And don't let them see Bandit. He brings me snacks. I like my snacks."

"How did you get here?" Violet asked, laying her head back. She heard shuffling on the other side, imagined Sharpe mirroring her position. Backs against the wall. Just the two of them.

"I'm a prisoner. This is a cell. So they put me here."

"No guards."

"Can't have guards. Might talk to them."

"Talking is bad?"

"Very bad."

"What happened? How are you here?"

Silence.

"Picked me up, didn't they? Just like you. Found me on what was left of that ship out at Rim. Last one left. Didn't take too kindly to that."

"You took them all out? By yourself?"

"No," he said. "*I* was the last one left. They didn't know about you—the other ships got away. So it was just me. They made it count. Made it . . . made it hurt."

There was a tremble in his voice.

"I'm sorry," Violet said. She hugged Bandit, and he crooned to her. It wasn't the same.

"It's fine, lass. Knew what I was getting in for. Ended up here. And here's where you are. Not as nice as the last time you found me, felt like a warmer welcome."

"You were covered in ice."

"What?"

"When I met you. Covered in ice. Frost. You must have been freezing."

"Ah. True. Maybe it wasn't warmer."

"The skipper saved you. She jumped."

"I recall that."

"She jumped twice. After the battle. Turned out to be Stoker. But she thought it was you."

"Stoker made it? Good to hear. Liked him. Good man. Strange sense of humour."

"She didn't jump for me."

The bitterness in her own voice surprised her.

"What do you mean?" Sharpe asked.

"We were attacked. The ship. Under . . . there was a waterfall . . . they shot at us. The mast. I was in the mast and it fell. I fell."

Violet pulled her knees up close, resting her chin on them.

"She let me go. Let me fall."

"Violet, I—" Sharpe started to say.

"It doesn't matter." She got to her feet quickly. "It's done. It's over. She's dead, I'm not."

"You—"

"I'll be back." She put her hand on the door. "I'm not leaving you."

"Violet," Sharpe called back to her.

"I'm not leaving you."

Without you. I'm not leaving without you. Because she's dead. You're not.

Because now there was a plan. Not much, but the beginnings of one.

CHAPTER 14

QUILL FACED NEL and Sharpe. His arms were folded and his tail lashing. He stood between them and the prisoner.

"I am not happy."

That, Nel thought, *is about the funniest damned thing in the whole damned universe.*

"That!" Quill turned and pointed furiously. "What is that doing aboard our ship?"

Been aboard less than a bell and he's already calling it our ship. At least he ain't calling it his ship. Yet.

"Comes with the ship, Quill. You knew there was a prisoner aboard when we stole her. Too late to do nothing about it now."

"It is not too late. We are not yet over the falls."

"You want to throw them overboard?" Nel shook her head in disgust. Even for Quill that was detestable.

"They appear fat, fat like the cook. The fat ones float."

Nel glared at her navigator. Hard. "Don't be mentioning Gabbi, Quill. Not like that."

Quill matched her glare for glare. "I will speak of her as I have always spoken of her. The cook was fat and fat is how I will remember her. We do not need another fat one. We do not need another one of . . . of them."

"Of them, Kelpie?" Nel folded her arms. "You beating that dead horse again?"

"We have only just expunged the last of these from our ship.

139

Must we infest this one with more of your stray mongrels?"

"You'll hurt her feelings, Quill."

Quill flicked a suspicious glance at the female Korrigan who remained silent in her irons. "Her? It is female?"

"Yes, Quill."

"I am not happy about this."

"I couldn't care less, Quill. Get topside and make your unhappy self useful. Leave me to fix things down here."

Quill brushed past her, making dark mutterings.

"What was that about?" Sharpe asked. "Remember it being Quill's idea to fetch Jack. What's got him so antsy?"

"Doesn't like the strays. Never has. Natural order of the universe reasserting itself," Nel shrugged, waiting until Quill's stomping footsteps had faded out of hearing, taking a seat opposite their newly acquired prisoner.

"Give us a moment," she told Sharpe. He left her alone with the other woman.

"So," the prisoner said, "how're you looking to fix me, then?"

Nel did look the woman over before replying. Darker skinned than Jack, almost a walnut coloured tan, ears that were longer but narrower, and tightly braided black hair streaked with green. Some sort of affectation, most like, as colour like that couldn't be natural. Like Quill had been crude enough to point out, she could have been on the large side but then most Korrigan measured the same in all directions. She was dressed like a sailor which suggested she was part of the ship's crew, which raised the question, what had she done to get locked up?

"What's your name, lass?" Nel asked.

"Lock," the woman shrugged, with no appreciation for the irony. "What's yours?"

"Skipper."

"Ah," Lock chuckled. "That."

"Should I let you go, Lock?"

"Thought you were looking to throw me over. Prefer if you didn't."

"Kelpie was. I ain't him."

"You in charge then, I'm hoping?"

Nel kicked idly at a water cask with her booted foot. There were several of them stacked around a beam, held in place by loops of wire. One of them bulged out, the wire seeming barely long enough to secure itself where it was twisted into a crude knot.

She asked, "What'd you do, Lock?"

"Got caught."

Nel laughed, in spite of herself. "You realise my friends and I just stole this ship out from under your Captain."

"Figured that. Don't change my situation any. Still tied up down here. Couldn't go nowhere even if you did let me out."

"Guess not. How'd you get caught?"

The woman hesitated, then shrugged. "Got greedy, I guess. One too many things from the captain's cabin. Woman didn't appreciate that."

"I wouldn't neither." Nel headed towards the stairs. "Meet me on deck. We'll talk this out some more."

Lock held up her manacled wrists quizzically.

"Five minutes," Nel told her.

She made her way to the bridge. It jarred her how quick the journey was compared to her old ship. While the *Poignard* was not significantly shorter than the *Tantamount* that extra length resulted in a much wider and taller vessel. And in mirror fashion her crew was reduced to just a bare handful, a motley dozen.

Maybe two handfuls then.

She'd yet to ascertain if Sharpe would be of any practical use when it came to the ship itself. He hadn't been last time.

He juggled.

The Draugr also tugged at her memories, recalling setting out for Rim with a hold full of the creatures.

Hells, it was these same folk. If I don't remember them from above deck they must have been below. Got to stop calling them creatures too. If they can talk they ain't that. Real folk, they are.

Real people, Nel caught herself thinking. *But they had been real people. So where was the line between Stoker and other Draugr?*

Not my problem. This about Violet, getting her back and making things right, don't need to think about anything else.

"Shall I prepare a plank?" Quill interrupted her musings. "Or shall we dispense with such ceremony?"

"Don't test me, Quill."

"What did she do?" Sharpe asked. The man leaned against the railing, watching Stoker and the others work. They'd dropped the last of the sails and were making good headway if the rushing scenery was any guide.

Lad really is useless aboard.

"Theft and desertion, looks like," Nel said. "Attempted desertion anyway. Was dumb enough to get caught."

Sharpe nodded. "What's your thoughts?"

"I think we're stuck with her. Unless you want to side with Quill here."

Quill turned expectantly. Sharpe bobbed his head in consideration, fingers beating a tuneless pattern against the railing. "Not for those charges. Bad precedent."

Quill made a sound of disgust. "I believed we were done with this collecting of riffraff. Had I known otherwise I would have left Jack where I found him. Fine. Fine! Collect your strays, Vaughn. I no longer care."

"Good, because as soon as she works those shackles Lock is gonna be joining us up here."

"You expect her to affect her own release?" Quill did not bother hiding his scepticism.

"Woman palmed some wire off one of the barrels," Nel told him smugly. "If we hadn't stolen the ship with her on it she would have taken her leave already."

"A pity we did not wait just a bit longer then."

"You can wait now, Kelpie. Just you wait."

Enjoyable as making Quill wait was she had rounds to make. Starting with Stoker. She found him near the bow, checking lines on the headsail.

"Said it before, Skipper, but you're truly a sight for sore eyes," Stoker greeted her with what might have been a smile. "If my eyes could get sore no more, that is. Still, good to see you, lass."

"Stoker," Nel said gravely, as she took her first proper look at him. "You look terrible."

He did. The Draugr sailor's skin was drooping on one side of his face, the skin hanging loose and in folds. What little colour had been left to him was gone. The eyes were yellowed and shrunken, like sun-dried grapes. His clothing hadn't fared much better: pressed against his own decayed skin, the cotton and leather was falling apart. Could have been rot from the Draugr pens or just general neglect. He'd discarded the rain cape and coloured tunic already, neither suitable for ship duties.

"Haven't looked in a mirror for a while," Stoker confided, noting her study. "All a bit of a blur to me anyway."

"Your eyesight's going?" Nel winced.

"What? Naw, eyes are same as they always were. Eyes of a hawk, lass, world only makes sense from a distance. Was never a problem aboard."

"You're far-sighted."

"That's the fancy words for it. Always preferred the hawk part myself."

"You're falling apart, lad," Nel told him. "Does it . . . ?"

"Hurt? No, not in the sense that you're thinking. Feels slow, like when you wake in the morning after a hard night. Stiff and not sure how you got that way. Except you never loosen up. You stay that way, never getting no better. Forget things too. Maybe that's just me age catching up with me though."

"Never seen a Draugr age like you, Stoker."

"Ain't none like me, Skipper."

"No? I count seven others," Nel pointed down the deck.

"Ah, well, counting, lass. Too fancy for the likes of me. Leave that to yourself and those who've a head for numbers."

Nel chuckled. For all that he wasn't much to look at, she liked Stoker. Nothing so plain-spoken as a common sailor.

"Tell me about them," she said, leaning back on the brightwork and looking down the ship. "Your people. You sail with them all before?"

"Naw, just the two. Powder and Swayne there. Powder used to be a cannon monkey. Lad's a bit hard of hearing even before, stand to his left if you wanna make yourself heard. Swayne was a bosun. Keep her away from the cat and she's not so bad."

"And the rest?"

"Town folk, those who'd done some sailing or trading. Had names but we didn't care for them much so we gave 'em new ones. Lad with the crooked nose is Boxing."

"Good man for a tavern brawl?"

"Not sure. Shipping crate fell off and hit him in the face. That was the first round, could be he made a comeback but my coin is on the crate. Java, the short one there."

"The Troll?"

"Prefers Java, couldn't pronounce her last name. Too many what-you-call-thems."

"Syllables? Consonants?"

"Letters, I'm thinking. Being fancy again there, Skipper."

"My apologies," Nel grinned.

"See, you could have just said you were sorry," Stoker ribbed her. "Anyway, Java's not one to drink, not grog anyway, but I hear she used to be a right horror without her coffee. The black kind."

"Put her with Jack in the galley," Nel told him.

"As you like. After that we've got Yarn, man with the beard. Likes to talk, too, introduce you later but have your excuses ready. Chit is the reedy fellow and a soft touch for a loan. Horse is—"

"The one with the face?"

"Wouldn't be asking about that one, Skipper, not if you're squeamish at all."

"The face?"

"The name."

Nel raised an eyebrow. "Won't be asking then. Ignorance as they say."

"A warm feeling in cold waters," Stoker nodded.

Nel laughed. "Ain't no one like you, Stoker. Wasn't looking for crew but glad to have you here."

"Aye, seems you went from drinking alone to a merry band in short order. Could show the pressers a thing or two, I'd wager. As for me, well, maybe that's it. Not enough of me to be me, all being used up. Showing me age. Think I even saw a grey hair the other day. Hard to tell though, without the mirrors."

"And people call me hard," Nel said.

"And well they should, Skipper. Don't worry about me; I don't. Don't feel a whole lot of anything, truth be told. Should be a bother but it ain't."

Oh lad. Stoker . . .

"I'm sorry," Nel whispered.

Stoker shrugged. "It bother you, lass?"

Nel shook her head. "No, but . . . I know you. Most folk don't. How do people look at you? I mean . . . do they realise? How do you live?"

Stoker reached up, scratching at the top of his head. "Feel like you've asked me some of this before. Fact is, don't feel the need to talk to most folks, except for ones I know, like yourself. No reason to. Don't need nothing from them. Don't feel the cold, don't get hungry. Don't feel much of anything, really, like I said."

"That sounds . . . horrible. Like not living, at all."

"Aye, suppose it does. Except it doesn't. Or isn't. Just is. Might be a what-you-call-it, side effect, of not being alive. Talked about it with the lads and lasses. Talk to each other we do, great philosophical discussions. Last for days. Don't need to sleep, either. Not a great deal of sense of self-preservation left to us, we feel. Which is nice."

Sharpe came up to meet them. Stoker greeted him, clasping him by the arm and clapping him on the back. Sharpe did the same in return, his expression openly warm.

"Never thought I'd see you again, lad," Stoker said. "Said that now more times than I can count. Figured you for the black or the inside of a brig for the rest of your days. And that were the happy endings."

"Both, as it happened," Sharpe told him. "You're looking well. New shoes?"

"Aye, except I call 'em feet."

"Suits you."

"More than the foppish rags you had me wearing."

"All the Skipper's idea, Stoker."

Nel raised an eyebrow at them both. "You two didn't have time to bask in each other's company before now? Is this for my benefit?"

"Had a job to do," Sharpe said. "And I just do as I'm told. Speaking of which, still waiting on your friend, Nel."

Nel scowled. "Maybe if you found something useful to do you'd have less waiting."

"You're not wrong. Quill wanted me to ask after the children, Stoker. Ask you himself but he's too busy inventing new curse words."

Nel felt a flush of guilt, remembering the children of Grange, the ones who hadn't been affected like Stoker and most of the adults had. Made her look at Sharpe. Seemed it was one of those days where he was the better person. She didn't buy the part about Quill wanting to know.

"Well, last I heard," Stoker told them, "sent the ones we could off to what families they had, where they had. Apprenticed a few of the older ones."

"But not all, I'd imagine."

"No, not all."

"What happened?" Nel asked.

"To the winds, mostly," Stoker told her. "Off in small groups. Safer that way."

"How do you mean, safer?" Nel asked quickly.

"Learnt that one quickly," Stoker nodded. "Ain't quite Draugr, us lot, but most folk can't tell the difference. Safer to pretend to be but too many of us all together, well, draws the wrong kind of eye. Like what happened in Vice."

"Alliance?" Nel asked.

"Sort of. Pressers more, scavenger types. Still a demand for Draugr labour back in the High. Worth an enterprising man's time to round up any strays and ship them in."

"Folk are struggling and starving," Nel said. "Common folk, can't get a job for love or money and they're pulling in Draugr as a workforce."

"Because they can do three times the work for none of the pay," Sharpe reminded her. "Not a hard thought for anyone of means. Rich get richer and the poor get poorer."

"Hells," Nel sighed. *Hells, but . . . not my problem. Not why we're here.*

"Truth is, there's not much purpose left to us," Stoker waved towards where his fellow Draugr were tending lines. "Told ourselves it was all for the children but once we saw to them there wasn't much of a connection left. No reason."

"There were more than just you," Nel said. "You on this ship, I mean."

"Connections," Stoker said. "Those that had them, well, they had them. We didn't. More than a few of us. When Sharpe rolled through, desperate and begging for help—"

"I wouldn't have said desperate," Sharpe objected. "Nor begging."

"Hush you," Nel told him.

"He helped us, more than less," Stoker continued. "Remember your girl. Sounded like a good thing, a rescue. Seemed a fitting end to it all."

"An end?" Nel repeated, sombre. "Is that how you see this going?"

"Alliance ambushes waiting?" Sharpe pointed out. "Struggling Grange families and starving children? Perhaps another jail break? Another ballad of daring escapes, liberating grey-skinned sailors from the Draugr pens? All so we can be off to rescue our fair princess?"

Nel scowled at him.

"Spent a long time drinking in those tavern dives, didn't you, Vaughn?" Sharpe grinned. "Heard so many fireside drinking stories you started to think this was one."

Nel scowled harder. "Tell me how this story ends, Sharpe. When we sail into the mist of a cold sun with our crew of undying sailors to rescue a lost shipmate."

Not a damned princess. Hells.

"Badly, I'm expecting," Stoker suggested. "But I'd have no regrets. Makes for a better tale that way."

Sharpe winked. "With a heroic rescue, to be retold by firelight. Joyful reunions and a passionate kiss for our hero."

Nel snorted. "A kiss?"

"Aye, for Quill. But don't tell him, I want it to be a surprise."

At that, she laughed.

CHAPTER 15

IT WASN'T OFTEN now that Violet found herself escorted by both Kaspar and Gravel. Such days had mostly been confined to when she'd first come aboard and had needed help moving around. But it had been happening more and more now.

The order of the day was polishing. Her special status aboard the ship still didn't exclude her from mundane duties. Everybody worked. But that was fine, polishing and greasing the *Fata Morgana's* battery of wands was a familiar task, and preferable to polishing the outside of the ship. The mundane task let her mind drift off into other places.

Are they watching you or is Ensign Niko Kaspar watching you both? Hard to say. But how ever are you going to get back to Sharpe with pretty eyes like that on you?

Pretty eyes. Pretty lips too.

As it turned out, that place had no filters between her mind and her mouth.

"I'm sorry we kissed, Niko," she said. Both boys dropped their tools, Kaspar a belaying pin and Gravel a bag full of lard. Jaws fell too. Gravel spoke first.

"I hear that right?" he said. "There was kissing going on?"

"No," Kaspar replied quickly.

"Oh, right now, because kissing is something normal folk do."

"What's that mean?" Kaspar turned his glare on his friend.

"That you ain't normal, Kas," Gravel told him. "Look at you, been at this for an hour and not a sweat stain or a wrinkle on your pretty face. Tell me that ain't unnatural."

"That wasn't what you meant," Kaspar retorted.

"Aye, no? What'd I mean then, sir?"

"I didn't kiss her," Kaspar said sullenly. "She kissed me."

"You let her kiss you then?" Gravel exclaimed. "Why'd you go and do that?"

"I didn't *let* her do anything!"

Gravel retrieved his lard, shaking the mess in Kaspar's direction. "You shoulda told her. Sir." There was reprobation in his voice.

"Told me what?" Violet asked quickly. "What's to tell?"

"You gonna tell her, sir?" Gravel asked pointedly.

"Seems like there's a lot we could all be telling each other," Kaspar said. "Anything *you* want to volunteer?"

"Yeah, aye, that there are days when I wonder why I went back for you," Gravel told him. "Could have left you out there, make a fine frozen statue you would have. Except I didn't because when you're not wedging yourself proper on that stick up your wheelhouse you're a decent sort and officers like that shouldn't be left all alone in the black. And you," he turned to Violet, causing her to take half a step back as he levelled a finger. "There are days when I don't half like you either, Miss Violet. Not that you aren't a fine figure of a woman, lass, won't deny I've had thoughts about how our babies might look, adorable furry illegitimate mongrels they would be, no doubt. But sometimes you've a mean streak that feels like it ought to belong to someone else and when you're like that, like now, with what you said right there just to try and be hurtful, I don't much like you, not like you deserve.

"And that's all I have to say about that," Gravel told them both with a shrug.

"Furry babies?" Kaspar repeated.

"Wheelhouse?" Violet added.

"Aye, to both," Gravel folded his arms. "And is there anything either of you would have to say for yourselves?"

Violet and Kaspar exchanged a look. "I didn't say it to be hurtful," she said.

"No?" Gravel said. "Then why'd you say it at all? Been drinking again? You're mean when you drink."

"What? No! Because . . ." Violet struggled. Why had she said it? Seemed she couldn't even recall her own reasoning now.

"Maybe Gravel's right, do have a mean streak. Not sure I like that," she admitted.

"Besides, not like a kiss from Mister Wheelhouse himself means all that much. He's kissed me the once too, so don't feel so special."

"Oh for . . ." Kaspar buried his face in one hand. "That again?"

Violet pointed at Gravel, feeling her eyes about to pop. "*Him?*"

"It was stupid," Kaspar muttered. "There was grog. Lots of grog."

"Aye," Gravel grinned wickedly. "Though not much grog left after."

"Must you?" Kaspar sighed.

"Aye, I think so, sir. Apologies on account of my poor recounting, unless you'd prefer to take over the telling of it?"

Kaspar slumped down against the bracket he'd been polishing, waving a hand for Gravel to go ahead. For the first time Violet saw grease smear the whites of his uniform.

Gravel took to his telling with gusto. "Was after I pulled himself in after his trip into the black. Figured we'd earned ourselves a ration of rum, helps warm the blood too. Medicinal. Poor Niko, though, was all shook and trembling from his ordeal. Drank the rum straight without mixing it with the water first. Went straight to his head."

"You gave it to me," Kaspar complained.

"Aye, and I've never again made such a mistake, now have I? A bell later the young ensign was pouring it out, his heart and his eyes and every breath in his lungs. Learnt all about his family and how hard it was growing up him. About his pretty sweetheart . . ."

"Pretty?" Violet repeated.

"I never said pretty," Kaspar interrupted, making a face.

"Can't call them ugly now though, can we, sir?" Gravel put his hand to his chest in mock horror. "Wouldn't be right without them having a chance to defend themselves. As I was saying, Miss Violet, our friend here is distraught we'll never make it back, he'll never tell them how he feels and declare his true and undying love. Next thing is he's bawling his eyes out. Probably crying tears of purest rum, if I'm any judge. Try to console the lad and next thing I know he's making a sodden mess of my shirt and planted a fierce one on me. I tell you," he said to Violet, "fellow could get drunk just off the fumes of the ensign's breath this day."

Kaspar just glared at him. "You done now?"

"Aye, sir, done as done. And ain't I been a good friend to you since? Got us back in that creaking tub—"

"I got us back," Kaspar said.

"Pointed the way," Gravel said, with a sidelong glance at Violet. "Not a secret we had to resort to more traditional methods of navigation to make our return voyage. Must have figured that out. But I ain't said a word about it since, now have I?"

"Until . . . you just . . ."

"Aye, but Miss Violet here deserved to know. Didn't tell your pretty sweetheart now though, did I?" He gave Violet a meaningful look. "Met the fellow when we made it back. Wasn't lying before, for a man, all bearded and manly, very pretty fellow."

Kaspar sighed.

"I didn't know," Violet said, sinking down onto the deck on folded legs.

"Know what?" Kaspar said wearily. He eyed her expectantly.

"All . . . ," Violet waved a hand, searching for the right word. "Manly. That who wrote you all those letters?"

There was a snicker. Kaspar threw a balled-up grease rag in Gravel's direction. "Oh, shut up."

"Shutting up, sir."

RAINES PUSHED THE tea aside, a wisp of steam still rising from the drinking vessel. Wooden, durable, sturdy. There were leaves in the bottom of Violet's mug, shrivelled and liquid. The dregs, she supposed. Some people made a living divining tea leaves. Violet couldn't think how—to her it was just a damp mess.

Not that she was having any more success divining what it was Raines wanted with her. He sat across from her in his private cabin. A cabin that unlike most aboard the *Tantamount* was in fact private, due in no small fact to still having a door that both closed and locked.

Raines had sought out her company, or more accurately, summoned her. Kaspar had escorted her to his quarters and now stood watch outside the door.

As always, her eyes were drawn to the fan of tails spread out like plumage behind the elder. One couldn't tell from his appearance, Raines persisted in a somewhat indeterminate age, but his bearing was slow and measured. Very different to the manic eccentricity he had displayed before. She didn't know what to make of it entirely. All the elders at home were just that, elder. Venerable and considered. There was something about Raines that refused to be placed into that aged category.

Seven tails though. She hadn't seen the like since she left home.

Home. Where a seven-tailed fox should have long since returned.

"Tell me again of your time aboard the *Tantamount*, child."

"I didn't spend as much time aboard her as you seem to think."

"Did you not?" Raines brought his drinking vessel up, face momentarily hidden by the steam. He smiled as he set it down. "Perhaps you are forgetting who it was that suggested you spin such a tale."

"No."

"Do you believe that the first mate believes such tales?"

"I believe the first mate is not entirely forthcoming with what she believes," Violet said carefully.

"A sensible attitude. Belief is a precious and powerful thing. Wars have been fought over it. Wars have been fought over much less. Lives lost . . . worlds, well . . ."

"Are we at war, elder?"

"Perhaps."

Perhaps.

"I would like to speak of Draugr and golems, child."

There was a Draugr on the work bench next to them. The body was cold, stiff, like all Draugr. But this one didn't move. Dead and discarded, if it were ever truly alive.

Laid out in neat little rows. Bodies wrapped in sailcloth. Waiting to drift into the black.

Except him there is all kinds of naked. Right down to his bones.

The Draugr had been cut open. Examined. Maybe experimented on. By Raines. Violet had watched him do it.

The strangest part was . . . it hadn't affected her any. No blood, no pain, no squeamish rising of her belly. It wasn't so different to helping . . . Jack . . . aboard the *Tantamount.*

Violet winced, holding a hand to her temple. Her migraine was back. A side effect, Raines had said about her constant headaches. Stemming from her time in the cold black. Surely they should be getting better though? If anything it was worse.

"This ship has many unique qualities," Raines said. "But also its own challenges. I believe you took part in, what do they call it? Void walking."

"Treading the black," Violet nodded.

"Ah, curious. The black. Anyway, maintaining the condition of the exterior of this ship has become more of an arduous task than either the first mate or I am content with. Skilled crew members, such as we have aboard, should not be wasting their time on such mundane tasks. Unfortunately, they are essential. But also detrimental. Ships such as this would not be practical under widespread use unless we can address such issues."

"Is that what you're doing?" Violet asked.

Raines nodded at the Draugr. "This ship itself is an experiment. The labour shortage is nothing new. We have tried to address it several times. Golems, Draugr. The Mandragora," he pointed to the creatures who were bundling the eviscerated Draugr away, "were like this ship. First. A proof of concept. But not very practical.

"We have a golem aboard," Raines commented. "Have you seen it? A remarkable specimen, very unique. Carved from a shell of obsidian. A special commission, for a friend. You know the one I'm talking of?"

Violet felt her mouth go dry. She didn't answer.

You know the one.

"I will show you later. Golems are very useful, very useful indeed. Powerful, adaptable, but they require careful deployment and close supervision to be at their most efficient. Draugr were an attempt to alleviate that, a wider solution to a growing problem. A fraction of the cost compared to their golem cousins but able to manage so much more unattended."

Cousins? Violet wondered.

"However," Raines mused, "demand far exceeded our expectations. A victim of success. Over the last few decades Draugr have been pressed into many, many positions and roles within the High Lanes industries. So many that the Free Lanes have been stripped of what dregs did filter out to them and the shortcomings of the creatures themselves have become more apparent."

"A Draugr can't sail," Violet said. "They can't pull lines or trim sails. Can barely manage rigging. They can manage simple tasks but not complex requirements. A Draugr might build a wall, brick by brick, but not a water wheel or windmill. They could dig a hole but not measure so that it wouldn't collapse onto itself."

"Yes," Raines leaned forward, eyes bright. "This. So much of this. You do understand. There are indeed many tasks a Draugr cannot perform. But where do these words come from, little one? These aren't the words or thoughts of a girl with the veil of indoctrinated lessons still covering her eyes. Nor a cabin girl who might have travelled but never really seen. Which brings us to the question of whose words are you repeating?"

Violet frowned.

Just words, aren't they? You heard the skipper talk like that. The captain. All the big people. The big people with big ideas. Piper, Gabbi, Sharpe, and that Kelpie navigator. Scarlett . . .

Raines leaned back, stroking his chin. He continued to muse. "Like everything ever created, one must consider the inevitable applications. Everything in time comes to feed the war machine, whether directly or indirectly. Draugr, golems, these are no different."

He gestured around them. "This ship, how long do you imagine it took to construct? Ignore the theory and experimentation, the trials to reach such a design. How long to build such a thing?"

"A year," Violet guessed.

"Somewhat more, but in the near region. And time is . . . limited, once gone it cannot be made up. Now consider the crew aboard, how long?"

Violet frowned. "I don't understand."

"To make a sailor, perhaps fifteen years, from the moment they are conceived to when they begin to learn their trade. Perhaps another five before they are considered competent. Ten before they have the makings of an officer? Or twenty, perhaps, to determine a captain. A ship may require dozens or even hundreds of such souls. So a ship, in its entirety, is the product of hundreds of years of labour, carried out concurrently, but an immense investment of time. Not everyone is so patient."

"You want to replace that with your own creations?" Violet said.

"Me, I want no such thing," Raines denied. "But the question has been asked. For me, the challenge of the question itself holds the interest. I believe such a thing is possible. My Mandragora, golems, the Draugr, all are iterations of an attempted solution. All of which have fallen short," he smirked at the diminutive Mandragora bustling around the lab, "if you will permit such a poor joke."

"What are Draugr?" Violet asked, looking towards the door the Draugr had been taken through. "What were you hoping to learn from . . . that?"

"We are all the sum of our parts. Some have more, some function perfectly adequately without what others possess. Some parts are incompatible. It pays to refresh one's knowledge of the intricacies."

"But what *are* they?" Violet asked again.

"An evolution," Raines said. "A progression of an idea, the same way a cart follows a horse and so becomes a boat and then a ship. Golems to Mandragora to Draugr and more. I had designs on another iteration, a perfect medium and balance between all of them."

"What happened?" Violet asked.

"Distractions," Raines said. "Experiments sometimes possess . . . an internal compass all their own. They go in unexpected directions you had never anticipated. Sometimes these directions yield results of their own, sometimes not. Such is the wayward path of progress."

"Did you have a name for this experiment?"

"Perhaps," Raines said. "Sometimes you do not know what to call it until after the experiment has run its course."

Violet frowned. "Distractions," she said, parroting his own words. "But what are Draugr? Are they people?"

"Certainly not. They lack the essential defining qualities. Speech, fears, drives, free will, as an annoying concept as it can be."

"Then can people be Draugr?"

"Ah, the scientific approach," Raines' eyes sparkled, his voice quickening. "The other side of the equation. So . . . perhaps. Perhaps some people are Draugr but no Draugr are people. And if they become one then they cannot be the other any longer. Such is the crux. You follow?"

Violet frowned. "No."

"Ah," Raines tilted his head to the side, frowning. "I hear—best you hold on to something, child."

One of the Mandragora stumbled as the ship tilted. Violet heard the sound of the guns firing, the song of the rays in the black. It all happened at once but in slow motion. The Mandragora tumbled into the canister, the one Raines had said specifically not to touch. It fell, teetering off the workbench and then tumbling end over end. It didn't shatter, as she half expected it to, but the lid detached, spilling the contents.

It was full of air, the kind you could see. Like the mist outside but different, wrong and off. Tinged with green and yellow where there should have been no colour. Without thinking, Violet snatched the top, slamming it back on before more could escape. It latched on easily enough and she breathed a sigh of relief.

That was her mistake. The not-quite-mist seeped into her nose and mouth. Violet waved a hand frantically in front of her face, realising her error and trying not to breathe in more. Too late though. She grabbed onto the floor, unable to stand suddenly. Dizzy, aimless. Everything blurry.

What happened?

Where am I?

Who . . .

She felt herself slipping, falling through the floor. It was dark, cold, alone. She didn't like it. Falling. Falling. She reached out, trying to grab onto something, anything. Her hands felt huge, feet like tree stumps, giant footsteps and so much sound. But it was dark, she couldn't see, could barely feel. She wanted to scream in frustration but she had no breath, no voice, no mouth at all.

No, no, no. Not again. Not again!

She lashed out. In anger. In pain? Pain would have been welcome, it would have been a feeling. She sensed metal tearing, wood splintering. But still felt nothing. It was all so wrong.

Someone was shaking her, calling her name. Violet tried opening her eyes but everything was still dark. There were voices, talking over each other.

"What happened down here?"

"Did that thing do that? Gods . . ."

"Is she all right? What happened?"

". . . don't breathe it in . . ."

"I think she hit her head."

"Find some chains . . . make sure it's . . ."

"Sir, did you see . . ."

"Curious, very curious."

"This is bad. We need to make port. There isn't time. I don't think . . ."

"I am not a child!"

She grabbed onto those words. That voice. It sounded like her. Hers. Grabbing. Holding on. Kaspar. What had he said? Find something to hold onto. Something real. She reached out. Fingers searching. Grasping. Floor. Solid. Cold. There, carpet. Rough, bristles. Wooden leg, a table. Warm. Flesh. Fingers. A hand. Who?

Pain.

Black.

She sat up, gasping, clutching at her chest. The falling feeling, she'd hit the bottom now. A jolt to her chest, heart racing. She couldn't see, just darkness. Voices all around her.

Glasses, where were they? She needed to them, to see the colours. Without them the world was just black and white. Black and . . .

She clawed at her face, found hands there. Warm touch, something she could feel, cradling her. She covered them with hers, held tight. So tight she drew blood, hot and wet under her nails.

"Violet," someone was saying. "Violet, you're ok. Violet."

No. That's not . . . right.

When she opened her eyes, he was there. Holding her. The world was grey, but real. She could see him. He pulled back, sliding her glasses on and there was colour again. Blues and greens. And red.

"Your . . . hands," she whispered.

Kaspar looked at the backs of them ruefully, gouged and running red. "Might ask you to trim your nails, Miss Violet," he said. "Can you stand? Slowly now."

"I think so."

With help she made it to her feet, leaning heavily on the

ensign.

"That was . . . unexpected," Raines commented, holding the canister the Mandragora had knocked over in one hand. He eyed the creature with annoyance but considered what he held. There was a look on his face.

Contemplation. Or realisation.

Big words.

"Kas! You in here?"

Gravel burst through the open doorway, skidding to a stop, out of breath. He caught sight of Raines whose attention had snapped to him, angrily.

"Sorry, sir!" Gravel snapped to attention, chest still heaving. "First mate sent me, to check on you all."

"Yes, yes, well, we are fine, sailor . . . sailor . . . whatever your name is," Raines dismissed him, then thought better of it. "What happened? What is going on?"

"Was a ray, sir, a big 'un," Gravel said. "Gunners winged him and he had a right go at us. Did some damage to the underside, got breaches and worse."

"Worse?" Kaspar repeated. Violet's arm was around his shoulders. He tried to disengage himself from her and set her down in one of the chairs. She resisted, holding on tighter until he gave up.

"Yes, how do you mean *worse*?" Raines followed up.

"Breach in the pipes, sir," Gravel told them. "They're burst, venting gas into the hold, going to need some patches. Trying to shut the valves off further up ship."

"It's not gas, it's . . . never mind. Venting? I need to see." Raines tossed the canister he was still holding aside, indifferent to it now. It fell to one of the stuffed chairs, a soft landing but one Violet's eyes followed. Raines stopped at the doorway next to Gravel.

"The hold, you said. And a ray . . . never mind," he turned, as if remembering Violet. His eyes met hers, searching, but flicked away with a grimace. "Take her back to her room. Watch her, advise me if there appear to be any . . . symptoms."

"Aye, sir, be doing just that," Gravel told him. "Here, Ensign, give you a hand, she looks heavy."

Kaspar winced. Violet was still groggy, but she settled for leaning as hard as she could on Gravel as getting her own back.

She needn't have bothered, he was built more solid than the lightly muscled ensign. Even saying that it was only the narrow corridors that prevented him from carrying her like a maiden back to her room.

"Mate didn't send you," Kaspar whispered fiercely to Gravel as they lay Violet down on her bed. "The hells were you doing in the hold?"

"Haven't heard you swear like that in an age, sir," Gravel replied. "Was all true, things are bad down below. Gonna be limping in to port if they can't plug the holes there."

"All true?" Kaspar repeated sceptically.

"Aye, except for Aristeia, that part I made up."

"Obviously. You're off watch, should be in your hammock."

"Was worried, sir, obviously."

"About me?"

"Aye."

"You're an awful liar."

"Better than you, Niko."

"Can still hear you both," Violet complained, laying an arm over her eyes. She found she was still wearing her glasses. Made for uncomfortable resting. Why was she so tired? Shutting her eyes helped, could think clearer.

"Sorry, Miss Violet," Gravel apologised. "Relieved you're all right, is all. Both of you."

Violet smiled, still covering her face. "Bandit ok?"

"Aye, he is. Probably found some new hidey holes even, Miss."

"What happened, Brandon?" Kaspar asked.

There was a long pause before he answered, enough so that Violet lifted her arms to see Gravel's face when he answered. "The golem, one in the hold. Went berserk. Or maybe not, went for a walk maybe. Tore a path through things that mattered. Things are a mess down there. Ray showed up not long before we started making smoke signals. All a bit of a mess."

"That's impossible," Kaspar said firmly.

"Aye? Which part? 'Cause it all happened. Familiar territory, Niko. Unless they fix what got broke, we're adrift again."

CHAPTER 16

RUMOURS RAN THICK and fast on a ship—sailors liked to talk, loose lips and sinking ships aside—and the retellings of what happened grew wilder with each day. Something about marines, Violet suspected. Gravel loved to talk too, fed it all back to her, much to Kaspar's annoyance. She was tempted to try and send a tidbit or two back but a little voice in her head told her not to be so mad.

"Like the last tavern after the shortest shore leave," Gravel said. "Knee deep in water and tar and air not fit to suck on."

He was talking about the hold, around where the ray had hit the ship. Wounded and in pain, its death throes had seen it fly headfirst into the hull.

"What's wrong with the air?" Violet asked.

"Stuff in the pipes," Gravel shrugged. "What makes the ship go round and round."

"Ship's going round and round but not round the right way," Violet said, eliciting a grin from Gravel. It was true—the ship hadn't settled right and couldn't hold a straight course, worse than a drunken sailor on his way home.

"Aye, air's not too healthy here aboard. How's your head, Miss Violet?" Gravel asked her. "Not making you dizzy and sickly with all this motion?"

"No," Violet insisted. "Was that stuff from Raines' office what made me all . . ."

"Flopsy?" Gravel suggested.

Violet scowled at him. "Terrible word."

"Don't know any fancy words, Miss Violet, perhaps the good ensign could share a few, hey, sir?"

Kaspar ignored them both.

"Rather he shared what's in the pipes," Violet said. "Bet he knows."

"Mist," Kaspar said shortly. "And it's not a secret."

"Mist ain't dangerous to breathe," Violet objected.

"Can be. There's mist and then mist."

Violet considered this. "Like what Raines had in his workshop, all bottled up?"

"That wasn't mist," Kaspar told her.

"Fancy words," Gravel nodded. "Always figured mist was just mist, myself."

"It can be miasma," Violet grinned, getting into the banter.

"Never could tell the difference."

"One you find in the black, the other you find near worlds and such where it mixes with the clouds and all."

"Ah, clever. Which is which though?"

Violet touched the side of her nose, conspiratorially. Gravel mimicked her in response.

Kaspar sighed again. The long despairing sigh of the long suffering. "That's not even remotely accurate."

"Leave us simple souls our folklore, good sir," Gravel told him. "Don't have time for all that fancy book learning you of the leisure time do."

"Are we going to make port?" Violet asked, changing the subject. Tease him too much and Kaspar would sulk and swear off on the two of them, citing official duties or some such rot. Better to keep him around as their window into the officers' camp. "Ship's as banged up as you say then we must need to set down."

"We do," Kaspar said. "Problem isn't the repairs though, we can fix what's broke easy enough. The problem is putting back what was lost, refilling the pipes that make the ship go . . . round." He made a face, realising he'd fallen into their wordplay.

Violet and Gravel exchanged wicked grins at his dilemma. "So fill them. Just mist, ain't it?" she said. "Plenty of that outside."

"Not the right kind."

"Should have brought more of the right kind then," Violet told him.

"We did," Kaspar said. "Barrels of it, sealed tight in metal drums and all the gaps coated in tar. Whole stock room of it."

"All of which, most of which at least, got smashed up at the same time the pipes burst," Gravel said.

"By the ray?" Violet asked.

"That's the official words we've been told to sing along to, aye."

Violet looked down at her hands. *So . . . not just my imagining things. Big rock really did get loose. Smashed things up good. Not good for much else, are you?*

Are you?

"What now then?" she asked. "Captain must have a plan?"

"Called for help, flares and signals and that," Kaspar said. "Seems to think someone's around."

"And if not?" Violet asked sceptically. Privately it seemed ridiculous that the captain or first mate would even consider asking, let alone *calling* for help. Seemed too . . . proud, if nothing else.

"There's a place we can go," Kaspar said. "Out of the way, fix the pipes and fill the tanks. Only it's not safe."

"What's that mean?"

"Means it's not part of the Alliance," Gravel said. "Right, Niko?"

"That's part of it." Kaspar nodded.

"All dark and lawless and uncivilised is the Free Lanes," Gravel made a face.

"Be there soon," Kaspar said. "And then . . . we'll see."

"Enjoying the view?"

Violet traced the incoming horizon, the dock-world of a backwater planet whose name had already slipped her mind. It grew steadily larger, the mist chased away by the *Fata Morgana's* encroach.

"It doesn't feel right," she told Kaspar.

"What do you mean?"

"This," she waved her hand in front of the polished crystal, the planetary landscape reflected in it. "The perspective is wrong. The way the ship moves, I feel it, and then I see this, and this is wrong. It's wrong."

"You're not the only one to say that." Kaspar stood at ease, rocking back and forth on his heels with the pitch of the ship, hands clasped behind his back. "Not enough that we're listing. Maybe something else is lost, with all this metal and glass between us."

"It is."

"It's an odd thing for you to say that."

"Why?"

"Because we pulled you from outside, Violet. Frozen and cold. I would have thought if anyone would have wanted something between them and the mist, it would be you."

Cold. Falling . . .

"So you thought wrong," Violet said. "Can't be the first time."

"I see the ice still has some melting to go."

You don't know cold. You don't know it at all.

Violet grabbed at her head, knuckles massaging her temples. The motion knocked her glasses askew, the fragile wire frames almost bending from her reflexive actions. The glasses made everything worse, staring out at the world through scratched and tinted filters. Worse but better, because without them there was no colour. They made her nose hurt, leaving painful indentations on the bridge. She probably looked ridiculous too. The pain made her short-tempered and snappy. She knew it made her that but it didn't stop her snapping at people. At Kaspar and Gravel.

"And how are you today, little one?"

Violet turned, leaning against the hull of the ship. Raines stood a few feet away, hands clasped behind his back, studying her intently. She disliked it when he looked at her like that.

Like some peculiar specimen in some jar, some pretty butterfly pinned to a board.

"Better," she said.

"You do indeed look more sure of foot, more flush with colour. You are recovered from your latest incident? The glasses are helping your vision still? Well, one could presume so. However, the proof is in the undertaking, so they say."

"Sir?" Kaspar inquired.

"I would like you to accompany the shore party, little one," Raines explained, addressing Violet. "The first officer is leading a search of the more lurid elements of this port. A distasteful task, some would say, myself among them, but I believe it would be beneficial for you to accompany them."

Violet stared. "Why?"

"You will of course accompany our young friend, Ensign," Raines continued as if she hadn't spoken. "You and your companion sailor friend. I believe he is attending to preparations towards such manners now."

"As you say, sir." Kaspar nodded respectfully.

Prat, Violet thought, folding her arms. She couldn't imagine a reason why Raines wanted her to go ashore. He might be one of her own kind but the way he treated her made her skin crawl sometimes. Like one of his experiments.

Still . . . if she was allowed ashore there would be opportunities.

Opportunities for what?

Her hopes took a beating when she was confronted with the sight of Aristeia Quinn. Her encounters with the woman hadn't been pleasant so far, but they had been minimal. Now they'd be making landfall together.

Leanly muscled, covered in scars. Deliberate scars, something Aristeia and Mors had in common. They were like tattoos, only carved into her flesh. Pale skinned like a lot of humans who spent time in the mist, dark hair just touched with grey.

Wooden ships and iron men. Iron women, more like.

They never call her skipper.

Skipper or no, when Aristeia gave orders the marines moved. Like freshly greased clockwork. And it was marines, not sailors, that made up their party.

Marines were like soldiers who sailed, rather than sailors who could fight.

Someone had once told her that. The *Fata Morgana* seemed to have a few of them, these marines. All tough and big and mean-looking. A mix of all distaff sorts. And armed, all for the shore party.

"Am I to understand that the girl is coming ashore?"

Aristeia had noticed her.

I got a name, lady, Violet thought, but held her tongue.

"That is the way of it, Mistress Quinn," Raines said. "I would be most appreciative if you would include young Violet and her companions in your expedition today."

"*Her* companions?" Aristeia repeated. "Last I heard both Brandon and Kaspar sailed under our colours, on this crew."

"Yes, indeed. Perhaps we can discuss this later, but suffice to say they have been . . . delegated the chore of looking after my young friend for such time as she is with us."

"Have they now."

"Yes, now perhaps a word in private, first officer?"

Aristeia allowed herself to be drawn aside by Raines, some distance from Kaspar, Violet, and the marines. The woman gave Violet several long, cold looks as Raines spoke at length, occasionally nodding. Whatever he relayed, the woman showed little reaction. It was a welcome relief when Gravel appeared, a distraction if nothing else.

"Where have you been?" Kaspar asked him.

"From one end of the ship to the other," Gravel squinted at them. Violet guessed he'd been down in the hold or some other dimly lit part of the ship and his eyes were still adjusting. She hadn't been able to make time to see Bandit herself, let alone Sharpe. Gravel always seemed to make time for the loompa. "What's this fuss about? Are we going ashore?"

"We are," Kaspar nodded. "All of us."

"All?" Gravel stared. "Us? Her? *Her*?" He cast a meaningful look at the first mate. The woman didn't miss the reaction and Gravel flinched at her frown in his direction.

"Hells," he cursed under his breath.

"Damnit, Brandon, be more careful," Kaspar winced. "Stand to."

Gravel fell in alongside his friend, overly stiff and attentive as the first officer strode up to them, booted feet loud in the metal corridor.

"Keep a watch on her," was all she said, but both boys snapped off parade-worthy salutes. The woman's eyes lingered over Violet but she made no further comment.

They took a tender to the surface of the planet. A reassuring wooden vessel, oak and pine, timbers and pitch with rope and sailcloth. Violet crouched down in a nook, her fingers stroking the grain of the planks. So reassuring and familiar. The sail flapped until someone adjusted the boom, cold-faced marines sat silently, leathers creaking and the occasional restless foot.

"The mist is thin here," Aristeia could be heard saying to the navigator. "Don't let us slip off the pathway."

The mist is thin.

It was a blue sun, the planet orbited. Dangerous to look at directly while still in the black but Violet risked a glimpse. The surface of the star, massive even in the distance, roiled like an ocean of white caps. Blue and white. Somehow colder than the black.

Violet thought about asking why it wasn't the *Fata Morgana* herself making port. But the answer seemed obvious. They didn't want anyone to know they were there.

That explained the silence. The anxious look on Gravel's face and the tightly controlled grimace on Kaspar's. Aristeia wasn't going ashore to visit or secure supplies. There was no trading intended. She had a mission, one that required both secrecy and a significant armed presence.

Yet somehow it was still permitted for her to tag along.

Curious and curious still.

Aristeia's raptor stare fell upon them again. Wordlessly, she passed two utilitarian wands to Violet's minders. Gravel accepted his clumsily, Kaspar tucked his through his belt without comment. The first mate leaned close to him, passing on something Violet couldn't make out. Kaspar just nodded, his face still pale and taut.

"Nothing for me?" Violet said. Aristeia ignored her.

"You ever even used a wand, Miss Violet?" Gravel asked her.

She looked pointedly at the weapon in his shaking hands. "You ever even?"

"Shot the head off a wooden man once," Gravel said. "Took it clean off."

"A wooden man?" Violet repeated.

"It was a bucket," Kaspar said. "Shiny."

"A shiny bucket?"

"Very shiny," Gravel agreed. "Weren't even aiming for it."

Violet looked over the side of the gunwales. Below she could start to make out details of the dockside town. The town was still shadowed, not much more than silhouetted buildings, but on the horizon, sunrise was beginning. A razor's line of the most brilliant blue and white against the black, punctuated by a starburst of brightest yellow fire.

Colours. Missed you all.

She jostled the glasses on her face. Still didn't feel right, how they sat, how she saw through them. Like the ship, only more personal. But the colours, those were worth the niggling inconvenience. Just needed the headaches to stop.

Too much in your head. That's the problem.

"Are we still in the Free Lanes?" Violet asked.

"This is Port Autarch," Gravel told her. "Name of the town. Maps call it the Cold Night, 'cause it is. So yes, it is."

"Should I know that?"

"No reason you should. No reason anyone should have to. People avoid the place, and the place would be a whole lot better if someone were to nudge a comet around about the town square."

"I've seen that happen," Violet told him. "It's not pretty. Not a solution either."

Gravel shrugged. "Town square is where they hang people."

"Criminals?"

"No. Examples. Don't have to be criminals to be one. Don't take them down, neither. Just leave them there until there's nothing to take down."

"You sound familiar with it," Violet said.

"We've been here before," Kaspar told her, his voice solemn and quiet. "Not just us, the *Morgana*. It was our last job. We didn't get to finish before we were called away."

"Called away to do what?"

Kaspar shrugged. "Raines."

"When was this?"

"A few months ago."

"And now you're back. Why?"

"If we're lucky, I know why," Gravel said.

He might have said more but like everyone aboard he had to grab for a hold. The tender shuddered, tipping to one side. Something had hit them.

"Brace!" Aristeia called out. "All hands down!"

The vessel tipped the other way, deliberately, Violet thought, as the world turned downside and they were looking up at the ground. At township and harbour and unforgiving rock. They shuddered again. An impact, Violet realised, something had hit them. A hole caved in one side of the boat, and a marine grabbed at his thigh as splinters gouged into it. Another gave a strangled shriek, cut off mid-cry as he was thrown clear off his seat and the thin envelope. He tumbled for a bit, cartwheeling, before the pull of the planet caught him and he disappeared to earth.

Someone's shooting at us.

Hells.

"Take us down! Now!"

Violet grabbed on, she wasn't sure as to what. The wood under her feet didn't feel so reliable now. It was breaking, coming apart at the seams. And going down.

The envelope was starting to fray. She saw broken timbers and ropes, anything not tied down, fly from the boat and vanish. Debris that would drift or fall, depending on which side it had exited. There was no up or down anymore. They were spinning.

"You alive there?"

Violet opened her eyes, not realising they'd been closed to begin with. She was lying on the ground, grass under her hands and feet, staring up at the sky. Grey sky.

The colours were all gone.

Violet raised a hand to her face, found everything where it was supposed to be. Nose, chin, lips, but no glasses. No colours.

No headache either, but everything else hurt.

"I'm alive." She sat up. Kaspar was kneeling in front of her, Gravel peering over his shoulder in concern. The marines were scattered around them, in various stages of getting to their feet. The remains of the tender were nearby, the bow crumpled and so many splinters.

"More than can be said for our stalwart boat there," Gravel said what she was thinking. "Be needing another ride back to the ship."

"Can't they come get us?" Violet asked. She pinched the pearl still hanging from her ear between thumb and forefinger. *Broke the big boat and now the little one too. How many more boats we got left? Getting to be a habit.*

"They might have to," Kaspar grimaced, looking up into the sky. "But let's hope it doesn't come to that."

"What happened?" Violet said, letting Kaspar help her up. "Something hit us?"

"The locals," Kaspar said. "Don't care much for the Alliance."

"And we made such a song and dance for them too," Gravel said. "Coming in flying our colours and such."

Kaspar shrugged. "Navigator softened the landing. Took a shaft through the chest for their troubles and bled out soon after.

Couldn't leave even if the boat had stayed in one piece. We'd be dead if not for them though, all of us."

"Can the ship . . . would they shoot at her too?"

"The *Morgana*?" Gravel chuckled. "Big steely-skinned monster *pretending* she's a ship. Like to see them try. She'd shoot back, more than like. Be messy."

"You want that?"

"Not with myself in between I don't," Gravel said.

Makes sense. Explains why they sent us in like that too. One more reason anyway. Still doesn't explain what we're doing here though.

Aristeia was calling her marines to order. She marched over to the three of them.

"You all survived," she said, stating the obvious.

"Thanks to your navigator," Violet said. "I'm sorry."

"Don't be. Man was dead before we hit the ground. If he'd done his job right that never would have happened, so save your concern."

"But I thought—" Kaspar started to say.

"You thought wrong, Ensign." She glanced over her shoulder at her marines, stark uniforms that stood out even to Violet's colour-blind eyes. "We need information, this lot would attract too much attention. You three head into town ahead, sound out the locals. Report back here within four bells."

"Aye, sir." The boys both saluted and responded in unison. Aristeia's attention lingered on Violet again, but she didn't give the woman a response.

Until Aristeia's back was turned.

"And where are you gonna be, lady?"

The first mate's back stiffened into a rigid line. Violet wouldn't have been able to resist turning around to respond in her situation; Aristeia did.

"Nearby."

The woman walked back through her marines, one and all they fell into step behind her, carrying the already stripped contents of their craft. All but two managed it on their own, those that could not hobbling along with support. One remained. The navigator who had died before impact.

"Best be going then, right, sir?" Gravel rolled his shoulders. "Got a town to inspect and locals to incite."

"As you say," Kaspar nodded.

Violet took one last look at the wreckage. The sun had risen, she could feel what should have been heat on her back right now. Except it was cold, like a winter day. The chill before the frost. She'd always loved dawns, where the night gave way to blue and purple shades before dissolving into the warmer colours of day. But now she only saw grey. Shades upon shades of it.

Stupid colour.

Chapter 17

Nel had promised an appearance from their reluctant stowaway crew member. That appearance had never arrived.

"Damnit, woman, are you trying to make me look stupid?" Nel growled at Lock. The Korrigan ignored her, head and hands intent on the hopelessly bent length of wire she was still probing her restraints with.

"Give me that," Nel said in disgust, snatching the makeshift lockpick away. She knelt down and set to work. "I thought you knew what you were doing."

"Never said I knew nothing about this."

"Your damned name is Lock!"

"Best I could come up with on the spot, Skipper!"

"Hells damnit, woman." Nel glared at the chains. She was having no more luck. Bad enough she had to leave Quill and Sharpe back on deck to come see what was taking so long.

Shouldn't have acted so damned smug about it. Thought I was being clever. Too damned clever. That'll teach me.

She could feel the tumblers through the length of the wire, the tip catching but not releasing them the way it should. Nel bit down on her lip, refusing to acknowledge the fact that she had little idea what she was doing.

She heard footsteps behind her.

"Go away, Quill," she said without turning around.

Something clattered down beside her, something metallic.

"From the captain's cabin," Quill said. She heard his footsteps track back above deck.

Nel ground out some of the previous captain's colourful language before snatching up the key. Not surprisingly, it was a perfect fit.

"You and me," Nel pointed at the woman. "On deck and now."

"So long as there's grog I'll follow you."

Nel stopped, one foot on the stairs, twisting back to her. "Hells, I know you, don't I?"

Lock shrugged. "Had drinks a few times."

"More than a few—you fleeced me at cards," Nel scowled. "You took me for so much I almost sobered up."

Lock winced. "Sorry?"

"Don't be. Had it coming. Could have saved me the mother of all dryings if you'd taken the rest of it the same night. Come on, up top, may as well introduce you to folk. But no more gambling," Nel pointed, "got enough headaches without my crew indebting themselves."

They emerged into the bright sunlight, dawn breaking and the sky burning all kinds of red gold. It had been too long since Nel had seen a sunrise. She couldn't recall the last time she'd been on water to catch the light reflecting on one. And that was a shame.

Piper would have loved this one.

She saw Quill at the bridge, doing his best to ignore them. Jack and Sharpe waited for them.

"Who's this?" Jack asked bluntly.

"Who're you, old man?" Lock asked right back.

"I'm Sharpe," Sharpe introduced himself before Jack could reply, extending his hand. "Castor Sharpe, former marine in the service of the Alliance."

"And now?" Lock seemed reluctant in taking his hand.

"Now?"

"Yeah, now. What do you do now?"

"Ah. Well . . . ," Sharpe looked at Nel. "Good question. What am I now, Skipper?"

"Cabin boy," she deadpanned.

"Cabin boy?"

"Can you sail?"

"Not in the slightest."

"You want to be Jack's assistant?"

"Castor Sharpe, cabin boy," Sharpe announced.

"Then who's my assistant?" Jack asked. "Her?"

"No," Lock said flatly.

"You smell funny," Jack told her.

"That would be soap, Jack," Nel told him.

"Soap," Jack repeated. "Be in the galley. Tell my assistant."

"You get used to him," Sharpe said once Jack's back was turned.

"Why would I want to?" Lock asked.

"Because I still haven't decided what to do with you," Nel said. "Unless you've a request?"

"Turning around and dropping me back at the docks not being one of them?"

"Wouldn't be healthy or helpful for any of us. Unfortunately for you there's not much but a few archipelagos between us and the edge. Which means you're coming along for the trip."

"Trip to where?"

"About to discuss that with Mister Quill," Nel said. "Sharpe, take a tour around. Our new friend can go with you."

Sharpe raised his brows at her. "Might be she knows her way around the ship better than any of us."

"Good point, she ought to take you. What'd you do here, Lock? Don't have the hands for a sailor."

"What?" Lock looked down at her hands.

"No tattoos," Nel said. "Not nearly enough callus and no scars that I can see."

"Cargo," the woman said. "I was a clerk. Am a clerk."

"Ah, the rebellious life of a scribe," Sharpe nodded. "I hear that will get you locked up."

Lock gave him a quizzical look, perhaps trying to decide if he was being serious.

"Take a walk," Nel said.

"Aye, Skipper, walking as ordered," Sharpe said, steering Lock away.

"Your tendency towards homing strays is frustrating," Quill told her when she joined him on the bridge. Stoker was with him, giving her a questioning look. "I always thought it was the captain's peculiar madness."

"Keep yourselves quiet," Nel told him. "Quill's opinion notwithstanding, we might end up offloading her at the first opportunity. No reason to send her off with tales of overly eloquent Draugr."

"No danger of that, Skipper," Stoker grinned. "No danger at all. I'll pass the word. Quiet-like."

"If that is your intention then why release her at all?" Quill demanded.

"Haven't said what my intention is. And I let her out because it means less chance of her bearing ill will our way, that's why."

"You do not even know why she was locked up," Quill said.

"I asked. Nothing that worries me."

"And you believed her, of course."

"Records will be in the log books, Quill. I'll check if it worries you so much. And no matter what it is, I can't see her causing trouble on a ship full of strangers in the middle of a crossing. Woman doesn't strike me as stupid."

"She is an unknown factor," Quill said. "I suggest you get rid of her at the earliest opportunity."

"Get rid of, Quill?"

"Put her ashore. Nothing more."

"That's always your argument. It change your mind if I let slip that Jack agrees with you?"

"What?"

"Doesn't like her either. Says she smells funny."

"Jack . . . she . . . smells?" the Kelpie's eyes bulged.

"Soap, Quill."

Quill frowned at her. "I have a course to plot," he told her abruptly. "And I will require a summary of the ship's provisions. I must know if we will require any stopovers to sustain our journey and its return."

"Return trip," Stoker winked. "Sounds hopeful."

"That's what I keep him for, Stoker," Nel said. "Beacon of hope, our Quill. Got Jack and Sharpe looking the ship over. Let you know what they find."

"Good," Quill said. "For now we can maintain our heading to the horizon. At the very least, this time we are not being shot at."

"See?" Nel said. "Beacon."

THE FIRST GLANCES they received were wary. Then furtive, then fearful. People drew away from them in whispering huddles. It was not the sort of attention Violet was used to receiving. In fact it made her realise how little attention she normally received when she went anywhere.

Children should be seen, not heard. But some children are not even seen.

Not a child, Violet thought angrily. *Just me alone now, can't afford to be no child. Just me.*

Don't be you.

"Been here before?" she asked to break the silence.

"Aye, didn't get so many looks last time though," Gravel said. "Get to ourselves more."

"What were you doing here?"

"Investigating."

"Why? What for?"

"Rumours," Kaspar said. "Stories that come out of this port are dark. Brutal."

"They don't like Alliance," Gravel muttered. "And here we are, all dressed up to say hello."

"Kaspar," Violet stopped in the middle of the street, turning in a half circle, her head on a swivel.

"I see it," he replied, only confirming her suspicions. His hand was rigid at his side, kept far enough away from his weapon to be obvious.

"See what?" Gravel eyed them both. "I don't see nothing."

"That's it," Violet said. "Everyone's gone, gone inside. We're alone."

Gravel looked around, voicing choice dockside words. Kaspar grabbed his friend's hand when it reached for his belt.

"I wouldn't do that," Kaspar told him.

Their isolation was already over, but then they'd never been alone to start with. The townsfolk had just realised it before the three of them had and made themselves scarce. They were surrounded now, figures stepping out of alleyways and around corners. Maybe a dozen, too many folk and too few options to think about causing trouble.

"Now what do we have here?" one called out. Violet couldn't identify them at first glance, somewhere halfway between Korrigan and Troll.

Could be a half-breed, could just be ugly. Smells ugly, even from here.

"Alliance pretty boys," they said. "And so far from home. This one's pretty enough to be a girl. Does your papa know you're all out wandering in the dark like this?"

"Not looking for trouble, sir," Kaspar told him, taking half a step forward, clearly intending to do the talking.

"Sir?" The lead henchman looked around at his fellows. Violet had mentally named him Trog, unable to make up her mind about his background. Names didn't seem forthcoming and names were important. Trog's sub-henchmen were as much a mixed bag as he himself—Violet didn't count more than three the same.

"You hear that, lads, boy called me sir. You all remembering that for later now, yeah?"

Violet very deliberately stepped onto Gravel's foot, stopping him from taking the half step forward to stand next to Kaspar. The sailor half staggered, but not noticeably, glaring down at her. She shook her head in warning.

"See, not looking for trouble, and going around dressed like that," Trog pointed at Kaspar's crisp white uniform, "is asking for trouble. We don't care for lime and starch round here, pretty boy. So what did you think were gonna happen, dressed up so?"

"Kaspar," Violet stepped forward now.

"It's all right," he said.

"No," she shook her head. "It's not. And I ain't gonna get took again."

"Don't see many of your sort around, little lady," Trog inclined his head to her. "Didn't think there were many of yours with the Alliance at all."

"Not too many to start," someone else called out.

"Aye, that's true," Trog agreed. "Shame that. Tell you what, Miss. Seeing as how you're not dressed like your friends here, I'll make the assumption that you're not with them. Fallen in with bad company, as it were. So let's say you just . . . step aside. And we and the boys conclude our business here, never minding you. How do you say?"

For a moment, Violet considered the offer. Actually considered it. After all, what loyalty did she owe anyone else right now? Where had it gotten her in the past? Anyone she might have actually cared for or felt a bond to was gone. The problem was though . . .

You can't count on anyone but yourself.

She snatched the wand from Kaspar's belt, swinging it in a wide cast. The bolt hit Trog right in the forehead, knocking his head back. He hit the dirt of the street, kicking up a cloud, and didn't move. Neither did anyone else.

Violet whipped Kaspar's wand back the other way, striking a second henchman in the shoulder. Not such a good strike, but at least it was his weapon arm.

Shouts all around them now, a yell she recognised as Gravel's, and more brightly coloured lights flashed through the air. She started to pull Kaspar towards a side street. There was an opening there a moment ago but she saw more people rushing towards them now. Reinforcements, things going from bad to worse. Kaspar's uniform rumpled in her hand, coming loose, and she lost her footing then found herself flat on the street, being pressed down.

No, she thought, *not again, not again.*

She fought to free herself, seeing only white, and realised it was Kaspar atop her. He let her up, offering his hand. The sound of the chaos was over, Violet realised, except the moans of the injured.

"Unorthodox," Aristeia appeared behind Kaspar. The first mate had a staff slung over her shoulder, shod with copper ferrules at both ends, one of which drifted smoke. "But effective."

Violet batted away Kaspar's outstretched hand and pushed herself to her feet. "What just happened?" she demanded.

"Marines happened," Gravel told her. He was clutching at his thigh, limping slightly. "Surrounded the folk who surrounded us. One of them got me good, too."

"They weren't aiming for you, Brandon," Kaspar told him. "You just didn't duck in time."

"Aye, sir, huge comfort to my leg, that is. Perhaps next time if you could let us know to be getting down that might save the other one? I have some words you could use. Might shout them, even."

"You knew?" Violet turned an accusing stare on Kaspar. She closed in when he didn't respond immediately. "This was planned, wasn't it? What she, what Quinn said to you on the way over. You knew!"

"Easy, Miss Violet," Gravel tried to pull her back, calm the situation.

"No," she shook off his arm. "I want an answer. Were we bait? Was I?"

"Not bait, little girl," Aristeia told her. "A distraction, if it happened."

"What did you expect to happen?" she demanded.

Kaspar looked away. "Aristeia to do her job. Like she always does."

Unable to help herself, Violet's eyes found the woman. Scarred. Smirking. Surrounded by her marines. They were trussing up the ones who'd attempted to waylay them. Captives bound.

"Now what?"

"Now, I'd wager," Gravel told her, "we go after the big fish."

"And who's that?"

"Few of these bully boys on this world," Gravel pointed to the prisoners. "Smugglers and no good traders. Pirates. But there's always a big one at the top looking down on everyone. In this port he calls himself the Night Cricket."

"As in the bug?" Violet asked, to be sure.

"Not the most traditional of names," Kaspar said.

"You be quiet, still mad at you," Violet told him. "Why? What's it mean? There a story? Must be a story, what is it?"

"Probably is," Gravel agreed. "Not sure as I know it though, or could do it justice. Who knows how these things get started?"

"Stupid name," Violet said.

"Aye, well, you tell them that. If you can find them."

"Ever tried hunting crickets, Violet?" Kaspar asked her. "Not that easy."

"Remember telling you to shut up," Violet told him.

"Kill if you have to," Kaspar said.

"What?"

"That's what she said," Kaspar said. "Aristeia. Kill if we have to. To protect you."

He pushed past her, without explaining any further. Violet turned to Gravel for that.

"What they both said, Miss Violet," Gravel elaborated. "They want you kept well, the captain and Mistress Quinn there. Which means . . . no holding back from us."

Yet they're not worried about putting me and us in harm's way, are they?

She said as much, trying to gleam something from Gravel's reaction. But like always he was much as he appeared. "Might have been the plan, might not. Might just have been Aristeia and the lads making the most of what they saw. The first mate is a cold hard one, Miss Violet. Just stay this side of her, less shade here."

"You're saying this is her good side?" Violet was sceptical.

"Saying she's got much worse than what she's shown."

CHAPTER 18

THE TOWN HALL, or whatever the tall building that dominated one face of the square was, appeared to double as the town prison. Metal bars were set on all of the ground floor windows and shutters covered the top. An iron-banded double door of dark hardwood covered the entrance. It looked designed as a makeshift fortress, something to exert authority on the township around it.

Aristeia's marines were drawn up in front of it, as if they intended to lay siege. A languid, unhurried siege. The marines stood in doorways and peered around corners, with a few flanking Aristeia in the empty street, uncovered and open in front of the building. They appeared to be waiting.

"Now what?" Violet asked. "Do they knock? Wait for the Cricket to come out? Or shall we just make camp and sing songs?"

"Impatient lass, aren't you?" Gravel said.

"Kaspar," Violet addressed the ensign. "What do you know?"

The boy shrugged. "Aristeia doesn't tell me her plans. But she will have one."

"Guess you two have that in common."

"Should have brought Mors along," Gravel suggested quickly. "Could challenge them all to a duel, honourable-like."

"Don't think they're the honourable types," Violet said, not bothering to be specific about who.

"It's all relative," Kaspar said.

183

"Meaning what?"

"Nothing, stop talking. Pay attention."

"To what?"

"Don't know, but you'll miss it, I'll miss it. You're distracting." There was a touch of irritation to his voice that Violet found she enjoyed. Another crack in the ensign's shiny facade.

"Something's happening," Gravel pointed.

Shouts and shots fired from inside the town hall. Aristeia and her towering bodyguards stirred. The woman went so far as to remove the staff from her shoulder and plant the butt in the ground.

"Sounds like a mutiny," Violet suggested. She moved to get closer for a better look but Kaspar held her back. When she turned to berate him she missed what happened next. A brief cheer went up from the marines, cut short at a gesture from Aristeia. Violet heard the crash that preceded it and the groans that followed. By the time she looked back it was over.

The front door to the town hall was open, both halves swinging out wide. Between them stood Mors Coldstream, wands in both hands as he walked out onto the street.

"When did he get here?" Violet demanded.

"There's always a plan," Kaspar told her quietly. "Guess we weren't the only distraction."

Mors' target was obvious: the prostate and crawling figure in the middle of the street. Looking up, Violet could see the blown open shutters from the second floor. They'd been thrown out of the building. Probably by wand-fire.

"Is that the Night Cricket then?" Violet asked. Mors had reached them, kicked them over onto their back and had one booted foot planted on their throats. Aristeia and the marines were moving to join him. A half-dozen, a squad, rushed past them into the town hall.

"Wouldn't be betting against it, Miss Violet," Gravel said. "You know what this means though."

"No," Violet said grumpily, watching as the figure, a woman, middle-aged and weathered, was hauled up by two marines. "What does it mean? What happens now?"

"Watch," Kaspar told her.

Violet resisted the urge to kick him. He was lucky he'd taken his wand back. Aristeia and Mors were talking. Mors looked past the woman, over her head, directly at Violet. His eyes narrowed and her skin crawled because of it.

"There," Kaspar pointed.

Atop the building the squad of marines had reappeared. They'd reached the flag pole and had struck the colours of the Night Cricket, red on a black field. They were raising the Alliance's own now.

"And there," Gravel pointed. "Been watching us."

Violet squinted, knowing what to look for. It would have been hard to make out without knowing. The streaked grey of the hull blended in with the mist above to her eyes. Even with her eyesight as it was it was the first proper look she'd had at the *Fata Morgana* from outside. It was hard to focus on, wispy and transparent.

"Not there," Kaspar put his hand on her shoulder and adjusted her sight. "There."

He was right. The ship she'd been looking at wasn't the real *Morgana*, it was a mirage, somehow cast from the ship itself onto the mist. The real ship was directly below the imposter, inverted and buried deeper in the banks of mist. The twin hulls and double prows were just starting to break through.

"What are they doing?" Violet asked, watching the marines escort the Night Cricket and a handful of others towards the bodies. The bodies hanging from trees. The examples.

"Making a point," Gravel told her. "We don't need to watch this."

"Yes," Kaspar said. "We do."

Aristeia's eyes were on them. Watching. Judging. The first rope was placed around the first neck. The Night Cricket. No waiting around and no build-up. The woman's face was set, resigned. But showed no fear.

The intent was clear. Port Autarch was now part of the Alliance.

An example had to be made.

THERE WAS A handful of bottles in the captain's chest, underneath the bed. The chest had been locked but that wasn't hard to deal to. More logbooks. A hat, like Horatio had used to wear. Silk underclothes. Nel ignored everything else inside but for the hard liquor, one of rum and two of brandy. She sat them on the chart table, staring at them. All three were dusty, probably well aged. Unlikely to have gone foul—that was a criminal waste on a ship where favours were traded in sips and rations. None had been opened, the rum was still corked and the brandy was wax-sealed with the maker's mark. Not only pristine but of high quality.

No sense over-thinking it.

She tucked a bottle under one arm and held the other two by the neck. It was a short walk to Jack's new galley. He looked up at her. The room was still neat and tidy, not much sign he had taken to rearranging his new domain yet. Most of the cupboard doors and drawers were in some state of open, so he'd at least taken stock.

"Not right."

"What's not right, Jack?" Nel asked. The galley was smaller than she was used to. Smaller than the *Tantamount* which was in itself smaller than most of the fleet ships she'd served on. And galleys were small to begin with.

Going backwards in my career. Probably finish up stuck in a rowboat with just myself and Jack again by the end of it.

Not a pleasant thought.

"This ship. Ain't right. Not enough crew."

"Sailed with less before, Jack."

"Was different. Just had to keep going till we got back to the crew. Came back to them with a whole mess more than we left."

Nel shrugged. *Can't argue with the man when he's right.*

"Missing some crew," Jack went on. "Important ones. Ship needs them."

"I know, Jack. Don't need to remind me. But they're gone. I can't change that. I can't—"

"Don't mean that," Jack interrupted her gruffly. Quickly.

Almost too quickly.

Almost. Ain't no almost about it.

"Don't got a cook," Jack said, looking around himself. "Ship . . . needs a cook."

"Fine. You're the cook. You was the assistant cook, I just promoted you to cook. Java's your assistant, when she's not busy with other stuff. You get to tell her."

Jack scowled. "No doctor."

"Still you, Jack. But you're still an assistant. No promotion."

"Need a captain."

Those words stumped her. She turned away, looking out through the open doorway at the waves and foam over the gunwales. A little longer to the falls yet. They could take flight if they needed but Quill preferred the less taxing route. And he still needed some time to finish plotting their course.

"We don't need a captain."

"Ships need a captain."

"Well, we ain't got one."

"So who's in charge?"

"Me."

"So you're the captain, Skipper?"

"No. Don't call me that."

"Skipper?"

"Captain."

"Ain't calling you Captain. You don't listen when I calls you anyway."

"Good. What?"

Jack stared at her. "Night in the square. Called to you."

"When?"

"Few nights ago."

"When we found you?"

"Before."

Nel struggled with it. *The square? Hells, I barely remember the night before last. Too drunk to . . . aww . . .*

"You called."

"Yeah."

"I was . . . Jack, I'm sorry."

Jack blinked. "Yeah, well, you did."

"And I'm sorry."

"Fine," Jack grunted. "Just . . . yeah. That."

"Jack," Nel asked. "That why you didn't want to come? You thought we forgot about you? I forgot?"

"No."

"Part of my crew, Jack," Nel told him. "Don't want to explain to the captain where my crew went."

"What captain?"

"Figure that out later, Jack."

"Just don't go letting the Kelpie think it's him," Jack told her. *Captain Loveland.* Nel snorted at the idea. *That'll be the day.*

"Here," she handed over the liquor, remembering why she'd

come in the first place.

"What's this?" Jack asked.

"Rum and brandy for your stocks, Cook."

"Where from?"

"Captain's chest. Private reserve."

"Ah, emergency supplies then. This all of it?"

"All I've found so far. If there's more I'll bring it around when it shows itself."

Jack unceremoniously pulled the cork from the rum bottle. He took a sniff, his expression turning into one of appreciation.

"Good stuff," he said. "Strong. Put hairs on your chest."

Nel snorted.

"Not keeping none for yourself, Skipper?"

"No. Make me some coffee though when you find the stocks, black as you can."

"Haven't found none yet so it'll be black, for sure," Jack shrugged. "Keep the brandy for the patients. This can go in the grog cage. When I find it." He set the rum aside and replaced the cork. The smell of it wafted over, pungent and strong. The sort of wet that would still burn.

"At this point, I'd settle for some of your special blend even," Nel sighed.

Jack grinned at her, showing off an impressive collection of discoloured ivory. Impressive that someone who ate like he did still had teeth to show for it.

"You got a real thing for punishing yourself, Skipper," he told her.

"Still hauling your sorry hide from brig to port, aren't I?" Nel told him right back. "Gods, Jack, do us both a favour, I'm telling you this, as your skipper and your friend, eat a damned vegetable. Something green, leafy. Don't even wash it, just put it in your mouth and chew. As a friend, Jack."

"You don't make friends with salad," Jack said stubbornly. "Now get out, got coffee to find."

THEY'D KILLED ANOTHER ray this morning. Two watches ago—night and day had no real meaning aboard the ship, only the turning of the glass and the tolling of the bells. But it had been a while ago now. Days since they'd set up shop in this strange place. Taken over the whole world. Just like that. As easy as that. All because there was something here they wanted.

Something Raines wants.

But what do the rays want with us?

A lone male, if Violet remembered the markings correctly. A third to a half the size of the *Fata Morgana*. It was hard to judge size in the black when the horizon was so much mist and more black. Mors had shot it at the outer edge of the gunnery range, at the first opportunity. It had become standard practice to eliminate anything of a large enough size to physically threaten the ship but rays specifically seemed drawn to her. Her unique design; perhaps from a distance it looked like a ray, as well as sounding like one.

It was the third time it had happened. The third time since the first time, when she'd run out onto the hull. She felt numb to it now. Feeling numb was worse than feeling nothing, because Violet knew she should feel *something.*

"Is that how you started out?" Violet asked, looking up at the golem, standing still as the statue it resembled. "You start out with blood and fleshy, all feelings and tears? Then you turned to stone, bit by bit, piece by piece? That what's happening to me, crag face?"

Onyx didn't answer her. It never did.

Violet shifted, finding her whole body had stiffened and locked. She sat on the floor, knees pulled up and arms wrapped around. Maybe she would turn to stone herself staying here. She went to say to Bandit, "I wonder what turns first," and found he was gone.

Violet listened and heard the faint scrabblings and scratchings; Bandit was chasing prey. Even aboard this ship there were rats, perhaps even more than on others with the pipes and recessed places for them to sneak aboard and hide in. It amazed her that no one else ever heard Bandit, he was too big and too loud to be mistaken for a rat.

But then I didn't hear him till I knew to listen. There's that.

Mors would kill him if he heard him. Aristeia too. The captain . . . Raines would cut him open. See what makes him work.

Rats. Rats make him work.

Violet laughed, surprising herself. The sound echoing off the walls made her do it again.

What would I find in you? she wondered, eyeballing her rocky foe. There was no eyes where there should be eyes. Just blank holes. She'd even tried sticking her fingers in there once. Nothing. She remembered them being red. Red eyes. Now nothing.

What makes you work? What is inside of you?

The golem hadn't moved, not since that one time. Except it had. Its hand was no longer raised, finger wrenched open. It was back hanging down by its side.

But why did you move that one time? Because of me, but why?

Do you remember me?

Do you know who I am?

A chirp beside her. The loompa, standing up on back legs. Freshly caught rat hanging from his mouth. Two more black eyes watching her.

"Come on," she said to Bandit. "Visiting hours are almost over."

"You ever write poetry?"

"Not that I recall."

Violet turned over the paper in her hand. Not paper though, sail cloth. Cotton or linen, she couldn't say, but marked with what looked like charcoal. Big letters, all curvy and linked up. She had no idea if the words were any good but it looked pretty.

"Could start, pass the time."

"Be asking for a quill and parchment next visit then."

Violet chuckled. *Quill. Ha.*

That thought was pushed aside quickly.

"Don't need parchment, got walls."

There was a grunt in response to that idea.

"You need to get away."

Violet made a face. "I said no."

"You're allowed to say no. That's fine. Voice your opinion and that. Just do what you're told. And get."

Violet frowned, turning around to show her displeasure. The steel-lined and riveted door she had her back to didn't care. Cold and unyielding as before. Sharpe's voice carried through just fine but nothing else got through.

"I said I'm not going and I meant it," Violet said. "Not until I can get you out. We'll go together. You, me, Bandit."

She still had no idea how to go about that. There was no way into Sharpe's cell, not that she'd found. No key she could steal. And no way off the ship after that. She'd looked while they'd been on Autarch but hadn't found anything promising. Certainly no ship the two of them were capable of managing by themselves.

"Sounds nice, lass. But you should still go, while you can."

Don't talk to me like I'm a child.

"Where would I go?" Violet leaned her head back. She folded the love letter up, tucking it inside her shirt. Fingers brushed the other thing in there, the captain's sphere. It felt sharp today, a brief shock, a tingling. She wrapped her fingers around it and the feeling faded. Like everything faded. "I didn't have anywhere to be before the *Tantamount*. Was just me on my own. Drifting."

"Kind of the point of you, isn't it?" Sharpe said through the door. "Go out on your own till you're all growed up. Then head home and start pretending you know how the worlds work and what your place in them is."

"What do you know about it?"

"Raines," Sharpe said. "He talked about it a lot. Still does. Hated the whole system. Limiting, restrictive, archaic. A template for oppression designed to snuff out new thinking and reinforce the status quo."

"He said this to you?" Violet asked.

"Around me. In front of me. He never really talked to me. Never even used my name."

Violet shifted around. It was cold in this part of the ship. Her limbs would stiffen up if she didn't move around some. Felt like the cold was colder than it had been in the past. Maybe from being in the black so long? "How do you mean? He the one integrating you?"

"Interrogating?"

"Yeah, that."

"No."

"What then? Sounds like he did."

"Violet," the sound of his voice shifted. He was facing the door now. "He made me."

Violet swallowed a lump in her throat. Which was hard, her throat had gone dry. "Made you how?"

"I don't know how, Violet, but like you would a Draugr or a golem. Like that. Not like a real person."

Raines told you.

"Shut up," Violet twisted, facing the door, hand on the cold metal. "You are real. Real to me. You were real to the captain and the skipper and . . . you are real, hells damnit!"

She smacked the door with the flat of her hand. Made a noise, reverberating in the air. Covered up the sound of what she didn't want him to hear.

"You miss 'em, don't you?"

"No."

They're all dead.

And they left you to die.

Both of you.

"Doesn't matter." She put her back to the door again.

"Violet," Sharpe's voice sounded right in her ear. Must have been pressed right up against the door, talking into the cracks. "When you met me, when you found me . . ."

"In the black," Violet heard herself say.

"I was running. I ran as far and as fast as I could. To get away from him. From Raines. I ended up on Marching, caught up in all that happened there. And I couldn't . . . I couldn't not . . ."

Violet heard him slump down on the floor. "I couldn't leave. Like you were saying. But I think maybe I should I have. I think I made things worse by not leaving. And I don't want that for you."

"Why were you running?" she asked him.

"For the same reasons I want you to. And don't be stupid like I was. Don't get caught up in nothing. Or they'll find you and drag you back, just another thing in Raines' lab to prod and poke at."

Sharpe chuckled, bitterly, Violet thought.

Experiments. What experiments? What's he even want with me?

What would anyone want with you?

She studied her hand, clasped around Horatio's sphere. The ship inside moved about, occasional flickers of lightning flashing out, striking where her fingertips grazed. She'd tried, numerous times, to do what she'd seen Gabbi and Quill and others do without effort. But she couldn't move so much as a feather. Not without something else. Someone else. Now that she'd thought about it, every time she'd convinced herself she was getting powers, wizard powers like Piper had been wont to say, it had turned out to be someone else. Must have been the same that time in Raines' workshop. Him, not her.

If you're an experiment then you're a failed one.

She could hear Sharpe moving on the other side. "Does he talk about . . ."

"Who?"

Me?

"Scarlett."

"No," Violet said. "Why would he?"

"They knew each other," Sharpe said. "She used to visit his lab. When I saw her on Cauldron I thought for sure she'd recognise me. But she didn't. Didn't know me at all. But she knows who I am now."

"No," Violet shook her head. "She's dead."

"She's not."

"I saw her," Violet whispered harshly. "I saw her out there, in the black. She was dead."

Cold. Frozen. Falling.

Just like you.

"Raines told me she's looking forward to seeing me again," Sharpe said. "That she's coming here. To the *Morgana*."

"He's lying," Violet insisted. "She's dead."

Because you saw her die?

Like you did?

"He's not," Sharpe replied. "That's why you need to leave. And soon."

"And go where?" Violet asked, hearing the bitterness in her own voice.

"The Free Lanes."

The Free Lanes. A few hours ago this was the Free Lanes. You just helped bring the Alliance into a small corner of what used to be pirate sovereignty. Now you want to run there?

"Ain't gonna be no Free," Violet muttered. "Just the High. Eventually."

"Maybe. But not now. Not yet."

"You know what they did, below, on this planet we're circling?" Violet asked him. "They marched in and took it. The whole planet. Because there was something there they wanted. Not because of what was going on or how folk were being treated. The High Lanes, it's not a place. It's a thing, a thing what's coming for all of us. People are running below already. Only there's not gonna be anywhere left to run from it."

"The High isn't what's coming, Vi. It's just one more reason to go while there still is somewhere to go."

"Not without you," Violet told him. "Don't wanna hear any more about it."

"This is as close as you'll get to me," Sharpe told her. "And . . . hells. Violet, someone's coming."

Violet scrambled up, on her feet, heart pounding. "I don't hear anything."

"In the floor, the vibrations, never mind. Just hide."

But there was nowhere to hide. Sharpe's cell by its nature was in a dead-end cul-de-sac of internal corridors. Only one way in and . . .

Two glowing eyes in the dark, looking down at her. Bandit, squeezed into the pipes running through the top third of the wall. There was space up there. Not much but maybe enough. Violet could hear the footsteps now, grabbing hold of the pipes and hauling herself up as quiet as she could. The pipes felt strange under her touch. She could feel movement, wondered for a moment if they might burst or rupture. But they held solid and she squeezed herself into the crawlspace, slowing her breaths. Bandit's face was pressed right up against her, eyes huge in the dark. She gently, very carefully, brushed her fingers down his face. The eyes closed at her touch.

It was the captain. Not alone, two marines accompanied him, but the sight of the man himself was what made Violet's heartbeat faster. There would be no explaining herself if he saw her, even worse if she was caught trying to hide. Raines stopped in front of Sharpe's cell.

"Step away," he ordered. He didn't wait for confirmation, setting one hand to the wheel and turning. The door creaked open and Raines stepped inside, the door swinging close but not shut behind him. His guards followed him inside.

Was this it? Her chance? Raines wasn't alone, but the cell was unlocked. Overpower the captain and his guards, escape with Sharpe. There were other ships now, a whole town full of them. That should be enough.

Not much of a plan.

So what? Figure it out. Skipper always did.

You're not her. And she didn't. She left you. Was that her plan?

Fine. Not yet. But soon.

Violet rolled out of the pipes, slowly, setting bare feet to the floor. Quiet. She nudged Bandit, his eyes flashing open again. He jumped down too, darting out the open corridor. Violet cast one longing look at Sharpe's cell. She was tempted to listen but there was still nowhere to hide. She had to go now.

She got caught a hundred feet away. Almost screamed the ship down when he grabbed her by the arm. There was no hiding the alarm on her face.

"Been looking for you," Kaspar said, releasing her.

"Me? Why? What happened?"

"You're not supposed to wander alone," he reminded her. "What are you even doing down here?"

"Exploring," she said quickly. "Been here weeks and there's still places I don't know."

"This area is off limits."

"So?"

"So you don't come here, alone especially."

"Not alone." Violet pointed up. Bandit in the pipes again, above the ensign's head. Kaspar's face tightened at the sight, some barely restrained comment.

"Come on," he said. "We've got company. Need to make sure you aren't found *exploring* on your own when they step aboard."

Violet's heart lurched again. "Company? What company? Who? How'd they find us?"

Kaspar shook his head. "You'll see."

She's dead. You saw her die.

You saw her.

Didn't you?

Chapter 19

The chair creaked under her, legs even bowing a bit. Nel listened carefully for the sounds of splintering wood as she leaned it back just a little, placing her booted feet on the corner of the table. She didn't hear anything, so dismissed it as shoddy, inferior timbers used in the construction. Or maybe worn down in old age and hard use, like most things aboard a decent ship.

Not me, that's for sure. Been puking up every other meal on my liquid diet. And now I've got to eat Jack's cooking to put my weight back on. Gods below, done it to myself this time.

She looked at the cup of black sludge in her hand. It looked thick, soupy enough to rest a quarter mark on.

Taverns that see too much of the pressing gangs ought to hire Jack to pour their drinks. Won't nobody miss a shiny silver floating on top of their drink instead of sinking to the bottom.

Ah well. Here's to me then. To the first drink of whatever comes next.

Nel swallowed hard as she raised the coffee to her lips, closing her eyes and swallowing fast. She started coughing. Her guest had the good graces not to laugh.

"That as nasty as it looks?"

"Not so bad as I feared," Nel rasped, clutching at her throat. "Tastes all right. Just too damned hot."

"That'll get you burnt then," Lock said cheerfully, tugging on one of her green braids. She looked around, constantly, rather like a rodent. Her nose almost twitched too.

"What am I going to do with you?" Nel asked, setting the mug down to cool some more. Her tongue was scalded, almost numb. She could practically feel the skin blistering off already. The worst part was it was making her think of chilled beer or wine to soothe it.

Can't be having that, though.

"You should redecorate," Lock said. "Captain Flint didn't have much sense for fashion. You could do a lot with this room, this whole ship, really, if you put some time into it."

"If her taste was so poor what were you stealing from her?"

"Oh that? Boredom mostly. And silver. She had a nice set of goblets. And knives. Just the one spoon. No forks. Wonder what happened to them."

Nel recalled her own encounter with a drawer full of forks once, what seemed so long ago. She shook her head to clear away the fog of memory.

"What'd you want silver for?"

"To sell, mostly," Lock said. "I suppose you could melt it down and stamp coins out of it. Or even into bars and ingots if you had enough. Like if there had been forks. But selling seemed easiest. Least effort for most reward."

"To what end?" Nel frowned.

"Oh, to desert, why else? Seemed silly to go without taking it, so I did."

Nel stared. "That's not the sort of thing I'm used to hearing so . . . honestly."

"Why not? You found me trussed up in the hold, not much sense being dishonest about why I was there. Where are we going?"

"Off world," Nel said. "Then on to Haven." Haven was the world Sharpe had met up with Stoker. It was along their back trail and made a convenient heading, according to Quill. It was as plausible as anything to tell Lock until Nel figured her out.

Woman was locked up. Probably lying about why. Locked . . . hells, she got the imagination to lie about it?

"Haven? Been there, don't really care for it. Going anywhere else? Why are you making that face? If you're not careful it will freeze like that, that's what my ma used to say. Then she fell in a river, middle of winter. Really did freeze. Took a week before she could make another one. Face, that is."

"No," Nel said. "We're not . . . going anywhere else."

Lock sighed, tilting her head up to the ceiling. "Well, maybe someone will be. At least it's not an Alliance planet. Had enough of that lot. Can't talk to them. I mean, do I look like a sailor to you? Who in their right mind thought that was a good place for me?"

"You were pressed, weren't you?" Nel said.

"Yeah, stayed one hand too many at a card game and got knocked on the head on the walk home. You were right."

"I was?"

"About . . . you know, so long as there's drinks there is no walk home. Remember?"

"Right."

Lock shrugged. "Got a head for numbers and letters, not for whatever a ship runs on. But seems like they'll take anyone these days. Anyone they can get. Work is scarce but once you're in the High Lanes there's not so many options."

"So I hear."

"Wonder what they need them all for. The High Lanes."

"Sailing. Takes a lot of bodies to make a ship move."

"Never seen sailors like yours," Lock said.

"But then you don't sail, like you said."

"Not the sailing, but the coming and going at the ports, seen a lot of that. Draugr normally do the dock work, not the sailing."

Nel shrugged. "No one else wants to be a sailor, I guess. They don't complain much."

"Guess that's true."

"We can drop you at Haven," Nel said. "Think you'll manage fine there."

"I'm grateful. Maybe I can return the favour."

"Two favours," Nel said, eyeing the woman. "If you'd listened to my advice it would be three. Or maybe none."

Lock smiled. "Fair point. Looks like our time's up though, cabin boy wants a word."

It was Sharpe standing in the doorway. Man was still wearing his marine colours. Stepped aside to let Lock past him, watching her until she was out of earshot. He shut the door behind him.

"This a private conversation, Sharpe?" Nel asked him. She reached for coffee and found it had gone cold, congealed into a gelatinous form. Looked like black pudding. And about as appealing.

"A few words, now that we have the time." Sharpe took the seat Lock had recently vacated.

"By all means," Nel waved. "Make yourself at home."

Sharpe hesitated, frozen mid squat, then continued to plant his behind on the chair. It creaked, just like Nel's did, which gave her some amusement.

"Sorry, Captain," he apologised. Almost seemed sincere. Hard to tell behind the beard.

"Not the captain," Nel corrected him. "That hasn't been decided."

"Would you prefer Commander?" he asked with a grin.

"Not after the way you used it at the dock."

"I was technically correct," he reminded her.

"The best kind of correct," Nel agreed. "In the fleet."

"This is you reminding me we are no longer in either the fleet or Alliance Lanes?"

"Shouldn't have to. You look plenty smart."

"You're sweet. Think that's the nicest thing you ever said to me. Then why the obstinacy over being our captain then?"

"Haven't had the best captains myself. No hurry to be like most of them."

"Really," Sharpe didn't blink as he looked at her. "Captain Phelps was a good man."

"Aye, a good man. Doesn't make a good captain. Horatio was the kind of man who did the right thing for the right reasons and still got it wrong," Nel sighed.

"We'd be lucky to be remembered that way ourselves."

"Not if the Alliance writes our epitaphs. Be lucky if anyone remembers our names and don't spit on them."

"Most of your bad captains were Alliance fleet, weren't they?" Nel shrugged.

"That message from Heathen," Sharpe said. "I never would have found it."

"Probably not. What's your point?"

"Feels like she meant it more for you."

"Far as she knew I was dead."

"You sure about that?"

"Does it matter?"

"Taking a lot on a little faith here, Nel."

"Who else do you think she meant it for?" Nel asked him. "Violet?"

Sharpe blinked. "That's . . . not the worst idea."

"Now that doesn't make much sense either. Message there was meant for someone to follow it. You and Violet were already there, so it had to be for someone who wasn't. Heathen gave it to you, makes you the messenger. Except for the part where you lost it."

Sharpe rubbed at his face with his knuckles. "Are all you Alliance types so tricky and shifty?"

"Former Alliance," Nel reminded him, staring at the mug of coffee. Sharpe *had* lost the deed.

"You and your former captain both."

"The Alliance is rotten," Nel told him. "The kind of rot that spreads. Things I saw . . ."

"Made you leave it," Sharpe nodded. "A career officer, no less. If they'd have you, would you go back? Join the fleet?"

"No."

"Maybe you could fix it. Has to be easier from the inside than out."

Nel shook her head. "Da was a career sailor. Never amounted to much himself. Was proud of me, when I made third mate. Then second, then first. But the more I saw of those above me, less I wanted to be them."

"Never heard you talk about your father, or any family."

"Was a quartermaster," Nel told him, remembering. "Except not really. Other hands just called him that 'cause he did all the steward's work while the man was sleeping it off. Ran a card game on the side, most ships. Pocketed about the same coin as he would have that way."

I remember Da's games. Always rigged, said he was trying to teach us a lesson.

"Man never made officer," Nel said. "Was always bitter about that. Felt he was doing the work without the brass to show for it."

"What's he doing now?"

Nel shrugged. "Old bones, bad back. Took a dockside job. Customs. Tariffs. All the same as being a quartermaster, less thieving crew members trying to tap the barrels. Keeps the same card game going, I think. Keeps a rod under his desk for when bad players take exception.”

She made a face. “Took me for two months’ pay last time I saw him. No exceptions for family. Probably why Ma left him.”

“You see them much? Your family?”

“Not for the last five years,” Nel said.

“That’s sad,” Sharpe said.

“Made my choice,” Nel shrugged. “Found a new family. Trying to save what’s left of it.”

“That’s what the Free Lanes is all about, isn’t it?” Sharpe said. “Being able to make your own choices but having to live with them too.”

“Making it sound trite there, Sharpe.”

He grinned. “Prefer the Free to the High and I’ll say that to anyone who asks.”

“That’s your problem though, never wait to be asked.”

“Never was very good at waiting.”

“Found you doing nothing but waiting,” she reminded him.

“And for that I’ll be forever grateful. All right, I take your point. I’ll go be a pest in someone else’s ears.”

“Wait,” Nel said.

“Yes?” Sharpe paused, halfway out of his chair.

Nel held out her cup. “Tell Jack to send more of this.”

Sharpe took the cup. “I ever tell you how much I admire your bravery, Chanel?”

Nel scowled at him. “Get out.”

THE *MANGONEL FALLING* remained the biggest ship Violet could ever recall seeing. It was three times the size of the *Fata Morgana* and with its sails unfurled it masked out the stars in the black.

“Monstrosity,” someone said. “Stupidly big. Oversized tug. Couldn’t wallow its way out of a nebula.”

The last time she’d seen the ship it had been chasing her. Vice. The mountainous underworld. Before that it had carried the golem now sitting in the *Fata Morgana’s* hold. Was it so far-fetched that the Guildswoman Scarlett might be aboard? Plucked from the black the same way she herself had been? And coming to retrieve Onyx?

Someone else had been aboard the *Mangonel* too. Heathen, the skipper’s own former captain. Would the Kelpie recognise her? They’d never spoken but she might. And then what?

"You all right there, Miss Violet?" Gravel nudged her in the ribs. Violet winced, clutching her side. She almost fell but felt a hand on her shoulder steady her.

"Fine," she said. "Was just . . . somewhere else."

"You do that," Gravel told her. "Go someplace else in that head of yours. Getting all little-girl-lost on your face."

"Leave her alone, Brandon," Kaspar told him.

Gravel shrugged. "Was just saying. Gots to have imagination to do that, what she does. Always wondered what that would be like."

"All I'm imagining right now is that beastly thing ripping our panels off if it strays too close," Kaspar scowled, pointing at the faint shimmer around the *Mangonel.*

"Stupid big," Violet agreed with him. "Wouldn't worry though. They'll send over a tender rather than get any closer."

Kaspar nodded. "They'd better, wait, look, they're signalling."

Flashes of coloured light, a three-point signal repeated twice. Presumably there was an answer from their own ship because the next message was a standard one-two flash, acknowledgement and end of conversation.

"I was right," Violet said. "Officers away and en route."

Kaspar gave her an odd look. "You read Alliance signals?"

"They supposed to be secret?"

"That one wasn't but most trader folk don't learn them."

Violet shrugged, ignoring the obvious question.

Ain't that different to what we sent. Feels familiar almost, just like a foreign accent. Same rules, right?

Bigger it might be, particularly when right up alongside them, but the dry and creaking timbers of the dreadnought made it appear tired next to the sleek outline of the steel-clad *Morgana.* Their ship was clearly the faster, but the *Mangonel* wasn't meant for speed. It was meant to annihilate its target.

"Just like its captain."

"What about them?" Kaspar said.

"There," Violet pointed to the just launched tender. It was one of the assault types she'd seen at Rim. Like a stripped-down sloop, shallow and flat bottomed with an iron prow covering. Single mast with its own thaumatic driver. There were a half-dozen passengers, all Kelpies.

No Scarlett. She is dead. Has to be.

"Intimidating bunch of swamp turkeys aren't they," Gravel said.

"Please don't call them that," Kaspar winced. "If anyone heard . . ."

"Aye, there'd be squawking."

"Those are her old crew," Violet said. "From her old ship. Must be all that's left of them."

"Left of who?" Gravel asked.

"Captain Heathen. She's the tall one at the back," Kaspar told him.

"Ah, herself. Still wondering how a privateer ended up in charge of an Alliance ship. And such a big one, at that."

"She's a friend of the captain, I think," Kaspar told him. "Used to be in the fleet too. Before."

"Captain has friends now?"

"Are you trying to run your mouth into the brig?" Kaspar turned on him. "Or worse? You let Quinn or Mors hear you talking like that . . ."

"They served together," Violet said. "On the front. During the silk lane march. Back when they were trying to secure a trade route out to the Far Lanes. Trying to plot the end of the mist."

"How do you know that?" Gravel asked, a look passing between him and Kaspar.

"Met her before," Violet shrugged. "I think."

You know you didn't.

"She's been here before," Kaspar said.

"Had a big meet with the captain and officers," Gravel said. "Real hush-hush. Not long before we met you that first time, Miss Violet, back in—"

"Shut up!" Kaspar snapped at him. "Gods, you two, both of you." He was genuinely incensed. "Did it ever occur to either of you that if you want to keep a secret you don't go around running your mouth and letting everyone know you have a secret?"

Kaspar scowled at them both, hard enough that Violet and Gravel both hung their heads in admonishment.

"No secrets here, sir," Gravel saluted him, which only made Kaspar's face darker. "Just some idle chat from a couple of lowly deckhands."

Kaspar shook his head again, not even bothering to contradict his friend. He tugged at his uniform, pristine as always, but still brushing at imaginary dust and grime.

"I need to go to the deck and join the welcome party. Like Brandon said," another annoyed look, "all the officers will be there. Can I trust you, both of you, to keep quiet and out of sight and not be in trouble when I come back?"

"Aye, sir, quiet as a two mouses we'll be," Gravel said.

"Mice," Violet corrected. "Making the ensign's face purple there, use your words right."

"Aye, Miss Violet, quiet as two mices we'll be."

Violet laughed. Kaspar didn't. She thought she could hear his teeth grinding as he marched away. All parade stiff.

"Sad fact is most mice ain't too quiet," Gravel winked at her. "Your furry friend, I should say furrier friend, been eating like a king these past weeks."

"Haven't seen Bandit much," Violet realised, feeling a pang of guilt.

Haven't thought about him so much either. That's odd . . .

"Aye, not gone unnoticed. Little lad's been asking after you."

Violet gave him a wry look.

"I speak loompa," Gravel shrugged. "Useful and very much sought-after skill, it is. And he's not the only one."

"What do you mean?" Violet asked cautiously.

"Miss Violet," Gravel said reproachfully, "hard as it seems for you to believe, I am on your side. I'm the one who brings Mister Sharpe his food. And sometimes your furry friend comes by and says hello when I'm doing that. We're none of us stupid so it's not hard to figure you've been visiting."

"Sharpe," Violet said.

Not as clever as you think, are you?

"Aye, as I said, it's a useful skill. Not many folks around here can . . . talk loompa too, as it is. Fellow's been asking about you."

"I haven't been able to go see him," Violet said.

That was a lie.

"Got the feeling he was all right with that part. Was more concerned you might be thinking of doing something stupid. Like trying to see him. Things the good ensign might disapprove of rather strongly."

"What's she doing here?" Violet said aloud, looking out at the *Mangonel* again. Neither *Mangonel* nor *Morgana* struck her as a proper ship. One had too much of something and the other not enough.

"Captain called for help," Gravel shrugged. "Guess help has arrived."

"Thought that was what taking over that town was about?" Violet said. "How'd the captain even know she was out there, Captain Heathen I mean? Seems awful convenient she was just nearby like that, like she were just waiting for the call."

"Maybe. Our captain don't rightly confide in me, Miss Violet, can't tell you what you're asking."

Violet leaned back against the wall, the metal cool at her back. She found her fingers tapping a rhythm all of their own. The sound echoed and carried. Sound always carried far when the corridors were empty like this.

"You mean what you said? Just now?" Violet asked.

"What'd I say? Remind me, gentle-like."

"That you were on my side."

Gravel nodded. Didn't say nothing. Just nodded. Without hesitating.

"Gonna be quiet, ain't it?" she said. "For a little while. While officers and such do their talking."

"Aye." Gravel eyed her suspiciously, not missing her deliberate phrasing.

"Be good if we could go somewhere," Violet said. "Talk. Some place quiet."

"Talk," Gravel repeated.

"Aye," Violet grinned. "Come back to my cabin. We'll talk."

Gravel sighed, pushing a hand through his hair. "Far be it from me to turn down such an inviting invitation, except when you say talk I figure you don't mean talk."

"Oh, we'll talk," Violet assured him. "Gonna talk lots. Lots to talk about."

"Quiet-like?"

"Quiet as mice, Gravel."

Chapter 20

"WHAT'S THIS?" Nel stared suspiciously at the mug in her hand.

"Coffee."

Nel took another sip. "What did you put in here? Why does it taste good?"

"Salt," Java said. The Trollish-Draugr shrugged, a roll of over-developed shoulders. "And butter. Makes it smoother."

"This is *really* good."

Java beamed, giving Stoker a meaningful look.

"Done it now, Skipper," he said. "Lass will be making all sorts of concoctions in that galley now."

"Appreciate a woman with taste, is all," Java said.

"Oh, this woman appreciates," Nel assured her.

"Shame we don't run cold," Java told her. "Can't do better than a black watch cold press."

"What's that?" Nel asked. "Is that good? Last ship ran cold, what've I been missing out on?"

"Away with you, lass," Stoker told her. "Bother the woman in charge some other time. She's got things to do, skipper-type things. That need doing."

Java shrugged and left, taking the steps down with a swaying, bobbing motion. Half of it was her shorter than vertical stature, the rest was the to-and-fro of the ship on the waves. They'd yet to take to the air, still bound for the edge of Vice. Nel's orders, they still needed to take stock of the ship proper. And figure some notions out. Difficult notions.

"I'm keeping her, Midshipman," Nel warned Stoker. "The rest of you, don't know what your plans are but that one's mine."

"Stealing me crew, Skipper? Thought we was friends."

"We are. Trade you. You can take Sharpe."

"Beggin' your pardon, but I believe he came with me as well. That's two of mine you've gone pressed now."

"Fair point, you want Jack then?"

"On account of you wanting to put the wee Trollish lass in charge of the galley now?"

Nel made a face at Stoker. He wasn't wrong.

"Permit me a view to that show and the lass is yours."

Nel snorted. And took another sip. "This is *really* good, Stoker," she sighed happily. "If the rest of yours have half the happy surprise to offer I'll keep the lot of you."

"Might generous of you there, Skipper. Truth is I've been wondering what Yarn might be hiding in that there bird-nest but I'm not the one brave enough to take a comb to it."

"Him up in the stays, right?"

"Aye, face for the crow's nest. So the rumours say."

Nel counted four of the new Draugr crew up in the rigging. Yarn and Chit. The other two, she couldn't remember their names. Had some learning to do. Stoker made with the signalling and the sailors dropped the main; it billowed briefly before filling out and the ship rushed forward at a new clip. Nel found herself matching grins with Stoker. She had missed this, the rise and fall of a ship on the waves. And no one shooting at them.

"Decided what you want to be doing about your sober companion, Skipper?" Stoker asked.

And the grinning was gone.

The woman was down by the steps to the hold. Sharpe was down there with Boxing and Swain doing stock. Woman looked green, swaying but not with the motion of the boats. Like she'd forgotten how to stand. Nel waved to her, motioning for her to come up to the bridge.

Lock waved back. Stoker chuckled.

"Shush you, not meant to laugh."

"Truly she's not a sailor, that one, Skipper. Doesn't even know the signals."

"That was hardly a signal."

"Perhaps you should try the one to go away?"

"I'm about to make it to you, Midshipman."

"Be about my duties, Skipper. Best of luck with your decision making."

Nel sighed. Gesturing again at Lock. The woman got it this time, scurrying across to her, holding on for purchase wherever she could on the way.

"Your hair," Nel asked her. "Why's it green? No, never mind. Don't care. Don't sail well at all, do you?"

Lock shook her head.

"Keep your eyes on the distance," Nel told her. "Keep busy. Talking helps. Distractions."

"Not many to talk with here, Vaughn. Do I call you Vaughn still? Big Jack and the pretty boy call you Skipper, should I be calling you that?"

"Vaughn is fine. Big Jack?"

Lock shrugged. "Doesn't like me much. Nor his Kelpie friend."

Nel smirked. *Friend. Ha.* "They don't like much anyone, either of them."

"Seems to be the pattern here," Lock nodded. "Who's Gabbi then?"

Nel looked at her sharply. "Why you asking? Where'd you hear that?"

"From you. Couple of times, actually, when you were deep in your cups. And from Big Jack, when he was tossing around in the kitchen. Gabbi would and Gabbi wouldn't."

"Used to be the cook. Our cook. From . . . before. Jack liked her."

"Same way that marine fellow likes you?" Lock asked.

Nel didn't rise to that. "Gabbi was a friend," she said quietly. She looked out over the horizon. Nothing but blue sea now.

"Ah, sorry. Doesn't sound . . . didn't mean to pry there."

"It's fine," Nel told her.

"Won't help myself by saying this but I don't fancy you have a lot of friends, Vaughn."

Nel turned to the woman. "You trying to get on my bad side?"

"No, the other side. Figure I'm here, don't see a lot of other options."

"You trying to be my friend, lass?"

Lock shook her head. "No, don't think you have friends,

Vaughn. Just trying . . . not to be the other thing."

Nel snorted. *Now why does that sound familiar? Hells, last thing I need now is any more friends. The ones I got are all on this ship.*

"Come on," she clapped the woman on the shoulder. "Have a drink with me. The kind that doesn't put you to bed. I'll have Jack make you some of his special blend."

See if you still wanna be anyone's friend after that.

"WHY THE NAMES?" Sharpe asked. The two Draugr paused, frozen in mid-motion, the crate between them. They set it down before one of them answered.

"Got to have names." That was Boxing.

"But why those? Not regular names, are they? Your mother didn't name you like that."

"No." That was Swain.

"Who then?"

"Folk."

"Ship folk," Boxing added.

"Crew," Swain said for good measure.

"But why?" Sharpe asked. "Regular names not good enough?"

"You choose your name, Mister Sharpe?" Swain asked.

"Of course, figured nobody else would."

"Ah. Well, ours did."

"Get chosen," Boxing said.

"We like it that way."

Sharpe sighed. Inventory. They were meant to be taking inventory. Inventory was boring. And his workmates weren't much better. At least they were doing the lifting. The floor with his back to a post was much more Sharpe's preference.

"Skipper's got a real name. Jack. Quill. Castor."

Sharpe turned to the new voice. It was Lock, their Korrigan passenger. How long had she been there?

"Lock ain't a real name though," he said. "Seen any biscuits? Jack says there ought to be some."

"Real as yours," Lock winked. "And no, no biscuits."

"Sharpe ain't real," Swain said. "Not a proper name. Not in the fleet."

"Like Swain? Is Swain a real name?"

"Means bosun," Boxing said. "Like Skipper, only not."

"Right," Sharpe nodded. "What's a bosun thing?"

"That's a bosun," Lock pointed.

Sharpe sighed but the Draugr chuckled.

"Lass gets it," Swain said.

"Be careful with that barrel," Lock winced as the two Draugr made to heave it out of the way. "Filched some wire from it, might burst."

Boxing leaned down, running grey fingers over the staves. "Right again," he said. "Feels heavy, overfull."

"Rum barrel?" Swain suggested.

"Or brandy. Could be brandy."

"Never so lucky. Won't be brandy."

"Be a crime to spill though. And a mess to clean up. Best leave it for Stoker, officers know best."

"Which is senior?" Sharpe asked. "Bosun or midshipman?"

"Yes," Boxing and Swain nodded.

Sharpe sighed. He appealed to Lock but the woman was gone. Couldn't blame her. He heard footsteps heading topside and was tempted to follow.

"Real name?" Boxing asked.

"Not a fleet name."

"Could be a purser. Would suit a purser."

"Or a gaoler. Good name for a gaoler."

Sharpe sighed. The world made no sense. What was a poor cabin boy to do?

GRAVEL WAS VERY quiet after she'd said her piece. Elbows planted on knees, head in his hands. Not despairing, thinking. Brows creased in deep contemplation.

Violet waited, knowing she couldn't push him. More than that, if this went the wrong way, she didn't have a plan to fix it. It was up to him to say something, if not to her then to the captain and first mate. Or to Kaspar. Any one of them could put a stop to it, to what she intended. It was his duty, his responsibility to do just that.

But Violet didn't think he would. Or she wouldn't have told him she intended to break Sharpe out of the brig.

She'd told him everything else too. Everything since she'd first met the man. Sharpe, not Gravel. Everything that happened in between meeting the two of them and up until now. Why she couldn't stay. Why she couldn't leave Sharpe behind.

"You're mad, Miss Violet," Gravel said finally. "Touched in the head."

"Maybe," she said. Felt awkward, sitting across from him on the bed, legs pulled up under her. Like a little kid.

Don't wanna be a kid no more. Can't be. No room in this world to be.

"Say it works," Gravel said. "You and him make it off the ship. What then?"

"Head back to that town," Violet said. "Find a ship, make for the Free Lanes."

"You need a ship just to make it below," he pointed out.

"No, just a tender. It's not far."

"Two ships firing on you? No navigator. How far you think you'd get, Miss Violet?"

Violet took a deep breath. There was one thing she hadn't told him still.

How to tell him though?

Looking around, there was nothing obvious. She thought of all the things she'd seen people with the talent do. Forks and potatoes, tables, chairs, and boats. Blocks of ice, whole ships. Golems, even. Her room was sparse, the bed, the solitary chair that Gravel was sitting in, the deck of cards still splayed out from their last game.

Perfect.

She pointed at the cards, one arm, palm open. Gravel looked, half rose out of his chair to fetch them until she shook her head for him to stop.

I can do this, she thought. *Just a pack of stupid cards. Don't weigh nothing. So move, damn you!*

Nothing happened. Violet exhaled in frustration, slapping her hand down on the bed. It jumped half a foot off the floor, three legs at least. Practically rolled her off when it dropped back, leaving her facedown in the blankets.

She looked sheepishly at Gravel, found wide eyes staring back at her. "Still figuring that out."

"Black lanes, Miss Violet." Gravel shook his head. "I mean . . . for a wonder . . . when? How?"

"Don't know," Violet admitted, picking herself up. "Started to wonder, a while back. Friend told me, said I wasn't. But I guess I am. Like I said, still figuring things out. Don't work all the time. But enough. Maybe."

"The crash," Gravel blurted out, eyes popping wider still, "when we crashed on Cold Night. Should have done for us all."

"Kaspar said it was the navigator," Violet said. "I thought he was covering, for you."

"Aye, he was, except it wasn't. I mean, I didn't do nothing. Not then. Too busy holding on and trying not to soil myself. But you . . ."

"I don't remember," Violet said. "I don't . . . no."

"That happen to you much, lass? The not remembering?"

More and more. And maybe more than you know.

"Not the point," Violet steered them back. "I told you, Brandon, I'm getting Sharpe. Getting Bandit too. And getting off this metal tub. So the ways I see it you've got choices. Say that to the captain, say nothing, or say you'll help me."

"Why me?" Gravel asked her. "Why you asking me and not Kas?"

"Because I ain't got this thing figured out yet," Violet said. "And you do. More than me. So maybe between you and me we can figure it out. Enough to get us away."

"That ain't what you asked though. Still think you can do this all by yourself. So why me and not him?"

"Because I'm asking you."

"Not an answer, lass."

"Because he does his thinking behind his salute," Violet said hotly. "He's part of the fleet and I don't see him choosing me over that."

"Still sore over the kiss, aren't you?"

"I am not!" Violet snapped. "Ain't got nothing to do with—right, changed my mind. Don't want your help."

"Good, 'cause your plan is right stupid, Miss Violet," he told her matter-of-factly. "Not a matter of wanting so much as needing. Which is what you're saying anyways, that need is more important than want, aye?"

Violet squinted at him. "Shut up."

"I'll help you," Gravel said. "On two conditions."

Violet beamed at him. Felt like a huge weight had been lifted off her chest. Breathing and all that was easier sudden. "What?" she asked, trying to sound cautious. "What conditions?"

"Forget about heading back to that township. Both of us be better if we never step foot near there again. Got a ship we can take in mind. Much closer. Less holes in the plan that way."

"Ship? What ship? That ship? Your ship? That'll work?" The words tumbled out.

The ship in the hold. Down where Bandit lived. The one he and Kaspar tested.

Then lied about.

"Aye, it'll work. Most likely. More than likely. I think."

"And the other condition? What's that?"

"I go with you."

Gravel said it quickly, braced himself. Held his breath even while he waited for her answer.

Her answer came with a squeal, launching herself across the space between them, almost on to his lap. Violet wrapped her arms around him and squeezed. Squeezed the breath he'd been holding right out of him.

"You mean it?" She thumped him on the chest repeatedly. "You'll come with?"

"Aye, I mean, yeah, didn't seem so dangerous a moment ago." He stared up at her.

He has nice eyes . . .

"Didn't think you'd leave," Violet said. "Leave him, I mean."

"Aye," Gravel winced. "Kas, he's a good lad. But . . . you're right. Couldn't ask him this. Wouldn't be fair."

"You know what he'd say."

"Aye, I do. Be better off, I think, without us, without me. No more lies, no more having to protect someone. If I stay, there'll be questions, after you're gone. If I'm gone with you, they'll know who to blame and it won't be Kaspar."

"They won't blame him?" Violet hesitated.

"No, not when they've got the common deckhand to point fingers at. Lad's an officer. Not good to go around making examples of officers. Families get all funny about it."

They both ran out of words then. Violet was still on top of Gravel, almost straddling him. She grinned, right down into his face, grabbing him by the shirtfronts.

"Come on," she said. "Before you wise up and change your mind."

SHE'D WANTED TO be alone. It was more dignified that way. Small ship but small crew, all of them busy. Should have been easy. Hidden down in the hold. Lock found her anyway. It only took her an hour.

"Told you that stuff looked nasty."

Nel grimaced, wiping at her mouth with the sleeve of her borrowed uniform. She'd been planning on tossing the garment anyways.

Not the coffee. Everything but. And not eating since . . . hells, when did I? Been busy. At least it's still dark.

What little had been left in the cold pit of her stomach made the jump to the floor. The end of her dignity along with it. Nel grabbed for something to pull herself up, coughing and retching. She could feel sweat breaking out on her arms and face.

"Never again," she groaned, back against the packed cargo. "Never."

"Heard that from many a person," Lock mused. "Believed it at the time, same as the person who said it. Never known it to be true though."

Nel grimaced. Woman was right, most likely.

"You want something? Or just enjoying me making a mess of myself?"

"Came to get away," Lock shrugged. "Told you, no sailor. Water makes me queasy. Figured it might be better down here."

"It's not," Nel told her. "Air's bad. More sway. It's worse."

Lock sighed. "I'm stuck on this ship, aren't I?"

"Yeah. Afraid so."

The woman sank down, back against and legs out. "Your crew ain't right," she said.

"Never met a crew that are," Nel muttered.

"Yeah, but most crew . . . they're people. Folk. Yours aren't."

"It's all going that way," Nel shrugged.

"It is in the High," Lock said. "Everything's being sucked in and put to work there. This is the Free."

Nel frowned. Gave the woman a look. "What do you know about it?"

"Don't have to know anything, Vaughn. Can't ignore it unless you try."

"I've been trying."

"And what else are you trying?"

"How do you mean?" Nel sank down to the hold floor herself.

"You stole this ship, right?"

"Yeah."

"What for?"

"Needed a ship."

"Why?"

"Why do you care?"

"Because I'm on it!" Lock snapped.

Nel stared at her, not answering.

"I'm going with you, aren't I?" Lock said. "Whether either of us like it or not. So I have a right to know."

"Maybe you do," Nel said. "But that don't mean you get to know. And right now, this ain't the time to be having a go at me."

Her newest crew member stared at her. Nel wondered if she was going to have to get up for this, maybe knock some sense into the lass. But Lock backed down.

"All right. I get it. You don't know me. I understand that, but I don't know you either. Not yet."

Nel nodded. "That's fair."

"So tell me one thing, Vaughn," Lock said to her.

"And what's that?"

Lock broke out into a grin as wide as her face. "You and the marine, the one with the tall and shoulders. There's some boot knocking going on there."

Hells, why does everyone keep . . .

"Kicked him in the face once. With my boot. Knocked his tooth out. That count?"

Lock laughed. Loudly. "I'm starting to like you, Vaughn."

Nel shook her head. *You're right, don't know you at all. Need to look into that. Soon as my stomach settles. Hells, I miss Gabbi, gonna have to stare down Jack's cooking now.*

STARE DOWN SHE did.

"Did you cook that?" she asked Jack, raising her eyes from the slab of salted meat up to her new cook. "At all?"

"Don't need cooking. Been salted. Salt cooks it."

"That's not . . ."

"Salt burns. Same as cooking."

Nel frowned. It was hard to argue when Jack wasn't wrong.

Doesn't make him right though.

"Thanks, Jack," she told him. The plate shifted an inch or two as they struck another wave. Still with the waves. "Go tell Quill to get us in the air. Time we made some time."

Jack grunted, walking back out the way he'd come into the captain's cabin. Leaving her alone with her plateful of salted pork.

Nel hoped it was pork.

She decided she'd rather focus on the previous captain's logbooks for now. They were many and voluminous. Maybe the salt would finish cooking her dinner by the time she was done.

"Morning, Skipper," Stoker called as he shambled through the doorway.

"It's morning?" Nel looked around. Yes, there was sunlight. So, not dinner then.

"Aye, happens after night, mostly. Just have to hold on a bit longer sometimes."

Nel leaned forward over the desk, looking closer at Stoker. "Stoker, are you bleeding?"

"Don't believe so."

"Your feet are bloody." She half rose out of her chair in concern.

"What?" Stoker looked. There was a half-formed trail of red footprints following him in. He lifted one foot, studying it intently.

"Been down in the hold, Skipper," he apologised. "Believe it's wine. Must have stepped in some, feels like it's gone to vinegar though, to save us the tragedy."

Nel sat down, making a face at him. "You gonna clean my floor?"

"Believe that's a job most suited for a cabin boy, Skipper. Be sending him right along, I will."

Nel tried to hold face. She failed. Found herself laughing along to Stoker's silent smirk.

"What can I do for you, Midshipman? Have a seat."

Stoker tested the seat, rocking it gently. "Believe I'll stand, thank ye all the same. Got a wee problem that might concern you."

"Why not?" Nel sighed. "Everything was going so well." She reached for the book again, opening it up to a random page. A crew manifest. Former crew. She found herself smirking again.

Hells, hope the captain never wrote anything like this about us. About me.

"Been inspecting the guns and the armoury with young Powder, Skipper. On the one, we've enough small arms to repel, if not quite the arms to do the repelling with."

"And the other?"

"Been tryin' to find some shot for the big guns, lass. Skipper, I mean."

"There is none?"

"Not as we can find it?"

"Check the log books," Nel said. "Should be a manifest here somewhere. Got everything else so far."

"Would that be the one you're holding?" Stoker asked.

"No," Nel tossed it aside carelessly, reaching for another.

Stoker eyed the not insignificant collection of journals. "A mighty task you've set yourself there, Skipper."

"Feel free to help," she told him.

"Ah, would but me eyes, you see. Don't agree with the words and the squiggly bits. Too close to my face, you see."

Nel snorted. "Of course. Ah, this one's about crew discipline."

"Be needing that one, I imagine."

Nel frowned. "Never did. Brought it up once, captain shot it down. Didn't care for the cat, or the like."

"And you?"

"What do you think, Stoker?" Nel sighed, turning the page.

"Would never presume to think, Skipper. That's when all the bad things happen. Thoughts and the like. Bad ones."

"You think I'm a bad person."

"No, lass. Nothing of the sort."

"Hard though. Everyone says."

"Best officers make the worst choices, they say. Only they mean hard."

Nel eyed him over the pages. "Careful, Midshipman, feel a promotion in your future."

Stoker coughed. "Best be going then, got rounds to make. Unobtrusive-like."

"Yes, you do that," Nel waved to him. She'd come to empty pages; the logbook must be current.

Wonder if Lock's in here. Ah, here's the last one. Ten lashes. Tapping the . . .

Nel frowned.

"Ah, Skipper . . . ?"

Nel looked up, seeing Stoker standing in the doorway. The morning light was shining on him. Fellow was staring at his feet.

"Believe I was wrong," he said quietly. "Don't think it's wine after all."

"QUILL!" NEL CALLED towards the bridge. "Level her off!"

Stoker gave a wave to Jack. For appearances, he had the whistle. Ropes were pulled and their speed slowed. A glance over the side told her their altitude was about right, flying parallel to the water, a mast's height below them. They were still a few hours from the edge but Quill had already launched the ship. The breakers were getting too big for a ship meant for the black. Quill had chosen the expedience of using a rising crest as a ramp instead.

And Nel had just called him on it.

"This is not as simple as it might look," Quill told her and Stoker, descending from the bridge. He eyed the sails critically. "Make up your mind, either let us ride the waves or rise above them. Holding the ship here is tiring."

"Suck it up, Loveland," Nel told him. "I'm about to grant your dearest wish."

"We are throwing the Korrigan overboard?" Quill asked with false optimism in his voice. "I regret bringing him aboard already. You were right, the other one does indeed smell much better. I had in fact forgotten how fragrant his kind are."

His gaze moved to Lock, herself lounging against the brightwork and watching the Draugr work.

"That, my friend, is exactly what we are doing," Nel said. She rested a hand on her new wand. Charged and heavy, courtesy of Stoker and his armoury manifest. Small arms indeed.

"Exactly what?" Quill said. "I do not understand."

"Watch closely then," Nel told him. She gave Stoker a nod and he likewise made a few signals to his fellow Draugr.

She started her march towards the woman. Lock spotted her from a distance but didn't react until Nel drew close.

Studying Stoker and the others. Been more than a bit curious about them.

Now she knew why.

"Never seen Draugr used like this, ma'am," Lock said. "You could be on to a gold mine here. Except for them being pricier than water during a drought back in the High."

"Look over the side, Lock," Nel told her. "See that island over there? The small pretty one with the grass and the trees and the white sand?"

Lock frowned, leaning over the side and squinting at what Nel pointed at. She pulled back from the edge. "Aye, what about it?"

"Need you to swim for it. Assuming you can swim, that is."

Lock turned a faint shade of green. "Truth is I never learnt."

Nel inclined her head. "Well, that will make this the more challenging for it. That and the big waves. Jack!"

"Aye, Skipper?"

"Go check out the hold. Find me an empty barrel or crate. Something that will float. Mind where you step too."

Jack shrugged but didn't question, heading belowdecks to search.

"The water's salt," Nel said to Lock. "Saltier than most. Should help you float. Once you hit the water head straight for the island. Don't know what else might be in the water but I'd lay odds it swims better than you will."

"What's on the island?" Lock demanded. "Why the swimming? Why me?"

"Don't want to put the ship down there," Nel said. "And you because I say so."

"Why not one of the small boats then? Or the glass things?"

"Tenders," Nel said dryly. "We call them tenders, whether they're made from glass or wood or whatnot."

"Fine, why not one of those?" Lock scowled. "What's this all for?"

"Really haven't spent much time aboard ships, have you, Miss Lock?" Nel said. "At all. Jack, where's my barrel?"

"They're all full," Jack said.

"Full of what?"

"Useful stuff. Water, beer. Biscuits. Dung bricks."

"Very useful indeed, Mister Jack," Nel agreed. "What did you find, what's that you've brought up?"

"Pig pen," Jack held out the wooden framing. It was thin and lightweight, about two feet by three and just over a foot high. "Or maybe it was chicken. Smells like pig though."

"Very good, Mister Jack. Hand it over to our friend Lock here."

Jack shrugged and passed the cage over. Lock held it by the bars easily in one hand. "What in the hells is this for?" she said.

"For you, Lock, or whatever your name is," Nel told her. "You're in luck, actually. We both are. Jack's right, barrels are useful and so is what's in them. Cages are good, float even better. Many a pig or rooster lived when sailors didn't because they had them. Now," she turned and pointed to the side. "Get the hells off my ship."

"I don't understand." Lock took a step back, away from Nel. Away from the edge of the ship. The woman's eyes were wide.

"Been reading the captain's journal," Nel said. "And I ain't asking again. But I got one more thing I'll say. Swimming. Learn it fast. That water goes all the way to the edge of the world. It won't stop just for you."

Nel drew her wand, slapping it hard against her thigh. She raised her voice. "If she doesn't jump in the next breath any one of you is free to throw her off."

Lock's eyes darted between them, from Nel to Jack and then further afield. Stoker and his lot. Quill and Sharpe most probably. There was nowhere for her to go and she had no friends aboard. Lock held the wooden cage up in front of her, protectively. Nel raised her wand. And Lock jumped.

"Take us up," Nel called out, turning to face Quill. He was right where she expected him to be. Sharpe was next to him, shocked, where Quill was merely puzzled. She gave Stoker another nod, and he headed for the hold with Boxing and Swain.

"That was unexpected," the navigator said.

"*What* was that?" Sharpe shook his head.

"Do you have a problem with this?" Quill said to Jack.

"Why would I?" Jack frowned. "I didn't know her."

"Nor did any of us," Quill nodded.

"Smelt funny."

"We have discussed this. It was soap."

"Funny."

"Very well. I am taking us up. And away from here."

"You didn't even look," Sharpe said, grabbing Nel by the arm as the ship rose. "To see what happened when she hit the water. Let alone whether she made it to the island."

"Let go of me," Nel told him, not looking at him or the hand on her arm, "or you can jump too."

Sharpe held on, meeting her eyes, making his point. Then he let go.

"Since I first came aboard," he told her, "your crew have been telling me the same thing. Skipper's a hard woman. I believed it, but I never thought you were cruel."

"Since you first came aboard," Nel said, "there's a lot less of my crew than there ought to be. You came with trouble and it ain't left since."

She saw the fight play out on Sharpe's face. He seemed to have trouble keeping his emotions from showing these days. Before he'd been harder to read. That was the crux of it, what Nel had just said. She wasn't wrong.

"Why'd you do it, Nel?" he asked.

"Won't make the same mistake again, Castor, that's why."

She turned her back on him, making for the captain's cabin. Didn't feel right to call it anything but, certainly wasn't hers yet. Have to throw a lot more than one former prisoner over the side before she could start feeling anything about it. Did have a door though, she'd missed that, make a change not sleeping in a ready cabin where any folk could barge in. Less chance of being attacked by cutlery too.

It took less than a hundred heartbeats to dispel some of those illusions. She heard the door open and shut behind her, softly but deliberately, the latch clicked, loud in the empty ship.

"What?" Nel demanded, not looking to see who it was.

"I would talk," Quill answered her.

"Who's flying the ship?" she replied.

"I left Jack in charge. For all his faults he is a capable sailor. I believe he can handle a crew with no minds towards drink and debauchery or maudlin songs."

"Won't the ship drop out of the air?"

"Eventually."

"How long is eventually?"

"I believe we have a few minutes."

"As long as that?"

"I suggest we talk quickly."

"What do you want, Loveland?"

"This is a new side of you, this throwing of excess crew over the side. I am not sure I disapprove but I would know the thinking behind it."

Nel grabbed the captain's logbook off the table, holding it out to her navigator. He took it, turning it over.

"I was not jesting about what little time we have," he told her pointedly. "There is something relevant in here?"

"Captain was officious," Nel said. "Kept good records. Better than we ever did. Every hand aboard, every bale and sack of flour. Every punishment doled out and every half-measured bottle in the spirit cage."

Quill hefted the book. "All this in here?"

"Naw," Nel pointed, to the chest and the books now strewn about it. "Whole chest full of them. Like I said, officious."

"And the relevance?"

"No mention of our friend Lock. Not a one."

"You went through all of them? In the hours since we took possession? I trust you also considered that not being her actual name," Quill said.

"Aye, I did. Fact is, seen her around before. Shadowing me, buying me drinks even."

"I dislike her already, yet you still were unaware of her name?"

"Never asked. Never cared to. Seems obvious now though, don't it?"

Quill narrowed his eyes, the same eyes flicked around the room.

Aye, not so indifferent to abandoning your post after all, are you, Kelpie?

"Wasn't looking for me, not to be my friend or drinking buddy. Was waiting. For Sharpe."

"Ah." The long exhalation between clenched teeth told her Quill had caught up to her. "There *is* a prisoner though," he dropped the book down on the table. "The commander thought as much. What happened to them?"

"Stoker found blood. Chances are he either finds the rest of them dead to the world in a box or they've already gone over the side. A bold move, standing in for them, have to give our friend Lock that much credit."

"You are certain of this."

"Threw her over the side, didn't I?"

"I have been suggesting that for years, yet this is the first time."

Nel pointed to the deed, still unrolled on the table. "Guild symbol," she said of the more recent additions.

"What of it?"

"Wasn't there before. Part of the message. Guild's involved."

"Sharpe mentioned as much. The connection is what?"

"How'd the deed get to Vice. Quill? Sharpe didn't bring it. Heathen sent it. With who?"

Quill frowned.

"That was bait," Nel thumped the table. "Bait for me. For us. And we were meant to draw Sharpe out."

"That is . . . the most tenuous of threads, Vaughn. And you believe her, Lock, to be a Guildswoman, the Guildswoman sent after Sharpe?"

"I figured as much. You were the one who said it was probably Guild-folk who were after him. Figured Heathen sent Lock, and gave her that deed."

"That makes little sense."

"Plans inside plans. Everyone has their own game here, Quill. And we're all being played."

"And if you're wrong?"

"If I'm wrong . . . well, still won't say I'm sorry over it."

"No. You gave her a barrel."

"Chicken coop."

"Jack said it was a pig pen."

"Does it make a difference? I did it. It's done."

"I see. One last question then. What made you act? The log book? Her fraudulent name?"

"Never saw Lock go for rum. Always had the coin for the quality. Not used to slumming it with the likes of us."

"The likes of you," Quill corrected her. "What of it?"

"Aye, whatever, Quill. Point is, it stood out. Bit of a lightweight teetotaller if I'm being honest.

"Last entry here, fellow in lockup was there for tapping one of the rum barrels. Got lashes for it. Didn't see no lashes on Lock, and I know what to look for. And book says fellow, mind, not lass. So now that lass . . . she's swimming in the biggest drink of all. That's irony for you."

"Perhaps." Quill remained unconvinced.

Nel pointed at the still visible bloody trail Stoker had left. "See them footprints, Kelpie? There's your clue."

Quill studied the evidence. Tail flicked. He was annoyed. "And you do not begin by mentioning that?"

The ship gave a slight shudder. Nel saw the pitch of the cabin start to angle down.

"It appears that is all we have time for. Until later, Skipper," Quill inclined his head to her.

"Stop!"

The muscles in Violet's arms and legs almost cramped as she threw herself back, an inch, maybe two, before catching herself. Movement. Freezing. Whispering and shouting at Gravel all at the same time. All that tension in her body and it had nowhere to go. It yelled at her in protest.

Violet spun around, grabbing Gravel by the arms and pulling him into the crook of the bulkhead door. She resisted putting her back against it, feeling her tail brush up against the wall. Gently easing both their weights back, slowly so as not to make a sound. She clapped a hand over Gravel's mouth to quiet him. Violet shook her head at him, right in his face. His breath on her hand as he tried to suck air in, too loud, too noisy. Made her clamp his mouth harder. She tried to talk with her eyes, towards the open doorway. The glow. Voices. There were people that way, right where they wanted to go. Right outside Sharpe's cell.

It was Aristeia and she was not alone. The one doing all of the talking was the Kelpie captain, Heathen. Violet had only heard her talk that one time aboard the *Tantamount* but the sight was instantly familiar to her.

The words were muffled, Violet couldn't make any of them out, but she knew the tone. It wasn't a conversation, more that of someone speaking at a captive audience. Gloating. Every now and then there would be a word, little more, from Aristeia. Violet felt Gravel's arm spasm under her touch at the first, a flinching reaction. They were less than a dozen feet away. If the two women hadn't been so engrossed in their conversation they would have heard them coming down the corridor.

A conversation that seemed to be coming to a close. There was lull in the voices, then the ring of footsteps tracking towards them. They had nowhere to go and only shadows to hide in. Violet wrapped her arms around Gravel, pulling him onto her, so close she could feel his heartbeat and the damp sweat on clammy skin.

Whose it was, that she couldn't tell. Pulled them down together, in their little intertwined ball, small as could be. Gravel's arms were around her too, a precarious balance they both held, shallow breathing on her neck. Her chin resting on his shoulder, refusing to shut her eyes and look away though only one eye was able to see around his sailor's ponytail.

They're on board a friendly ship, not even on watch. A secure area of a ship, the brig. They won't be looking for trespassers. Carrying a glowstone, means bad night vision, only looking to put one foot in front of the other and not trip over themselves. Kelpie's have front-facing eyes, they look ahead, more so in a corridor like this. Won't be looking to the side. If Heathen comes through the door on the side closest to us then less chance of being seen. If it's Aristeia there's more.

Thoughts she barely recognised flashed through Violet's mind with every footfall. She felt calm though. There was nothing else to do other than let this scene play out. Not so for Gravel, she realised. He was holding his breath, waiting for it to be over. Waiting to be caught. Completely still.

That was bad, she thought. *Breathe. Now, before you have to. Breathing is loud, they could hear you.*

She hugged him closer, squeezing his chest, heard the slight exhale as the air left his body in surprise, the even quieter inhale right by her ear as normal breathing resumed. On the next breath Heathen and Aristeia stepped through the doorway, Heathen on the side closest to Violet and Gravel, as she'd hoped. The two weren't talking to each other, a silence Violet wished they had filled, but both stepped with the quick-footed marching of people who had places to be.

They despise each other.

The moment of passing was long and drawn out, broken only by the slamming jolt of the door shutting behind them. Aristeia didn't even turn to inspect it after the turn-wheel left her hand. The two disappeared around the corner of the corridor, the muted silver glow of their light soon following. After what she deemed long enough Violet tapped Gravel on the back and they shambled awkwardly to their feet, Gravel sucking in noisy breaths. He hadn't been breathing proper after all.

"They're gone," Violet told him. "You can let go of me now."

"Funny," Gravel said. "Seeing as it was you grabbing me

there."

Violet slapped him on the arm. "Weren't no grabbing, Brandon."

"As you say, Miss Violet."

"You ever going to drop the Miss Violet?"

"No, Miss," he said with a straight face. "Not likely I will."

"Get the door," Violet made a face at him.

"Aye, Miss Violet, getting the door."

She felt better with a closed door behind them, one less obstacle. That still left Sharpe's actual cell though.

"How do we open it?" she asked Gravel.

"Combination," he said. "This many turns that way, so many turns this way. Here, let me."

There was a loud clank as he grabbed the wheel, the immediate sound of the mechanism hitting the bar. Violet's heart sank.

"It's locked." Gravel strained at the wheel pointlessly.

"That's the idea, isn't it? Said you could unlock it."

"I can! I could . . . something's changed," he frowned, trying to turn the wheel more.

"You said you could open it!" Violet almost cried.

He turned to her. "Violet . . ."

"The hells are you two doing out there," Sharpe's voice called to them.

"Sharpe!" Violet crouched by the door. "The door's locked."

"You only just figured that?"

"Locked different, I mean."

"Good to know. That important?"

"Is if we're gonna get you out."

"Who's we?" Sharpe asked.

"Never mind. Hold tight, need to think here."

"I'll just stay here then, shall I?"

Violet faced up to Gravel. "How do we get this open?"

He shook his head. "I don't know, Miss. Think we'd need a key as well as a combination. Must be worried about something. Someone. Aristeia and the captain would be the only ones with any keys, don't see that happening for us."

"Is there another way in?" Violet asked.

"For us? No. Maybe our small furry friend could find a way but that don't help us any. Might need to rethink this, Miss

Violet."

"No," Violet shook her head. "Has to happen and has to be now." She leaned on the doorway with one hand. It felt so solid under her touch. Sharpe just on the other side. So close.

"Shall we go fetch the loompa then?" Gravel asked. "Should be down in the hold hunting rats and knocking chips off the big rock."

"Big rock," Violet repeated, drumming her fingers.

So many echoes on this ship. So many secrets and hidden places.

"I have an idea," she said.

Chapter 21

THEY DIDN'T FIND a body. Nel hadn't really expected to. If she was right then Lock, whatever her name was, had known what she was doing. Body would be proper hidden or food for sharks. There was blood though, what Stoker had tracked through. Maybe a person, maybe chicken. Or pig. No way to be sure. No neat little bow for her moral quandary. Didn't matter. If Nel was right, she was right. And if not . . . she'd given the woman a fighting chance.

And I ain't taking no more chances. Not with people I like.

"How long until we make port, Quill?" Nel asked her navigator. The Kelpie had made himself at home, his own charts and those he could find lamp-shaded around the bridge. He appeared to have made a nest for himself as well; several hammocks were bundled in one corner. Didn't even have to leave the room to sleep. Nel stamped her foot to get his attention.

"What?" He didn't look away from his work.

"Haven. How long?"

"We are not going there," Quill raised his eyes briefly. "There is no need. We have enough provisions. Enough air and water. This is where we are going." He jabbed at a point on one of his charts.

"Port Autarch."

"It has been called many things. I believe that is the most

current name."

"Fine."

"Was there something else?"

"Haven was where Sharpe met up with Stoker, yes?"

"As I said, we no longer have need of visiting."

"Wasn't my meaning. Was curious why."

"Why what?"

"Why you suggested it. Haven's as big as they come. It's not a backwater port or some rural moon. Smack damn in the middle of the cross-lanes. Got more ships coming and going than some of the High and more folk than Piper had . . . all right, fine, maybe that weren't so daft, Quill."

"Thank you," Quill sniffed. Nel had to admit it was a begrudging compliment at best. The Kelpie's idea had been more than a bit clever.

Haven was big, deep in the Free Lanes. A planet bigger than most, it had originally been established as a charter mine. Rich veins of ether shallow in the planet's crust, easy to get at. Easier than most. Mines and miners needed food, lots of it. Soon it was more expedient to make farms than it was to make runs. Farms led to towns and towns to communities. These days it was one of the most densely populated planets outside of the Central Band of the High. Still did a decent export of ether though the flood had slowed to a modest stream, last she'd heard. But that many folks all crammed into one place led to industry and the mother of inventiveness. So there was always coin to be made.

Place like that, a couple of ships full of refugees and children and runaway Draugr could blend right in. Get lost in the crowd and never be looked at twice.

Damned clever, in fact.

Too clever.

The kind of clever we're going to need.

"We're up against it, Quill," she told him quietly. "You realise that."

Quill nodded stiffly.

"You given it much thought?"

"No." He raised his eyes. "I gave my word. There is nothing to think about."

"Don't stop you complaining about it."

"Apparently I have more than one word to give then."

"That a joke, Quill?"

"Was it funny?"

"Almost."

"Then it was not."

Nel chuckled. "You thought about after? If we live through this?"

"There is no need. We will live through it or we will not. What happens after will take care of itself."

"Just like that?"

"I believe so."

"Why'd you stick with me, Quill?"

The Kelpie grimaced. Looked away.

"Quill," Nel growled at him. "Something you not telling me?"

"As I said," Quill replied. "I have more than one word to give."

"Who'd you promise, Quill? What'd you promise?"

He didn't answer.

The captain. Couldn't be anyone else.

"Is that all I am to you, Quill? An obligation? All any of us are?"

"No."

"Then what?"

"That is all I am."

"Life was easier when we just yelled at each other, wasn't it?"

"I will try to continue the tradition of yelling, Vaughn."

"You do that, Quill."

"DON'T LIKE THIS." Gravel rubbed his bare arms with both hands, crossing them over his chest. Bandit rode his shoulders, one leg dangling and the other draped over the front. The loompa's hands were in his hair but it didn't seem to bother Gravel any.

"Be brave," Violet told him.

"Brave as can be," Gravel muttered. "Else I'd be running for ma and asking for the brown trousers. Be brave, she says."

"And be quiet," Violet told him. "Had our close call already. Don't need the whole crew knowing what we're doing down here. Don't need anyone knowing."

"This works then everyone is gonna know," Gravel kept talking. "Gonna hear, gonna know, gonna get all mad at us."

Violet stopped and faced him. "You can go back," she told him. "Go back to your hammock. Forget this. Won't think any less of you.”

Gravel shook his head, without hesitation. “Ain’t about being thought less of, Miss Violet. About being more, being better.”

“Why?”

“What happened below,” Gravel said. “That ain’t right. Waking up one day and finding the Alliance just took over your town. Seen that before. Didn’t like being part of it though.”

“What you said about Autarch though,” Violet said.

“I knows what I said. The right thing the wrong way for the wrong reasons makes it a lot less right. That’s why I’m with you, Miss Violet. Figure this is the more right thing. For all of us.”

“This works,” Violet said, holding him by the shoulder. “Then we’re gone. With Sharpe, Bandit too. Off this boat.”

“And then what?” Gravel’s eyes were bright in the darkness, almost as bright as Bandit’s when the loompa opened them all the way. Like small moons in a pale and furry face.

“Don’t know, have to get to then first. Worry about what after then. But . . . I’m glad you’re coming. With me. Us. Bandit likes you.”

Gravel turned his head towards Bandit. The loompa tapped him on the nose.

“Aye, I like you both too.”

Violet started to reply but was stopped short by the skittering ahead. Scrabbling, like little claws, exactly like a smaller Bandit.

“Easy there,” Gravel reached up to soothe Bandit as he tensed to pursue. “Just a rat, nothing to worry about.”

“Used to be his job,” Violet said. “On . . . back on . . .”

“Your old ship, aye. Loompas are good for that, better than cats even since they can climb.”

“Cats can climb.”

“Not rigging they can’t.”

Violet shrugged. “Come on,” she said. “It’s up ahead, unless they moved it.”

“They didn’t.”

Been back checking, have you? Kaspar wouldn’t like that. Wouldn’t like none of what we’re doing. Shame though. He could be here too then. Then it’d be him that . . .

“Here,” Gravel said, holding the light higher.

Violet shaded her eyes with one hand. The light wasn’t needed, her eyes had adjusted just fine. Probably because of all the time she spent down here she saw better in the dark now. Saw more where there was just shadows and didn't trip over things others didn't see.

And now she saw their goal. Onyx.

There was, she had to admit, a sleek, polished beauty to the black golem. What light there was sheeted over the smooth contours, the cast meant to resemble a person. But the arm protrusions that came to such deadly tapered points showed the truth. The golem was a tool, a weapon, meant to sow death and destruction.

And you work for me now, crag-face. See if you don't.

Violet sucked in a breath. "Ok," she said. "Make it . . ."

"What?" Gravel answered. "Dance? Curtsey?"

"Try walking. Walking would be good."

Gravel made a face at her. "Walking, she says. Fine, walking it is."

He took a step closer, which prompted Bandit to dismount in a hurry, taking up an aggressive posture and squawking at the golem. Gravel waved him off, then clasped his hands together, cracking his knuckles.

"Don't like that sound," Violet winced.

"Helps me think," Gravel said. "Now . . ."

He raised his hands. There was light crackling around his fingers, thick bolts. They ought to be blue, coloured, but it was too dark to see them. Just the faintest tinge to them. The bolts were thicker though, faster too, compared to what Violet had seen on other thaumatics. Did that mean he was stronger? Or something else? He wasn't trained like all the others—even Gabbi had been taught the proper how to this.

Nothing happened.

"Make it walk."

"I'm trying," Gravel said through gritted teeth. He clenched his fists and pulled them back towards his belly. Still Onyx refused to move.

"Seen it done," Violet said. "It's thaumatics that make it move, can't do it without them."

She rolled the captain's ball in one hand, inside her shirt pocket, as she thought quickly. It helped her think. Focus. Even made the headaches less. This could work. She'd seen it work.

He moved you before. And Quill moved you before that, she

thought hard at it. *Moved you right across the ship and back. Would have cleared you off the deck if she hadn't been there to save your craggy behind.*

Gravel dropped his hands and stepped back in disgust. It was an expression Violet was so familiar with it took her by surprise. Maybe it was a navigator thing.

Thaumatic, not navigator. Not the same thing. Not all thaumatics are navigators.

"Maybe it's something else then."

"Like what?"

"How should I know? A key, everything locked needs a key."

"It's a big rock. It don't lock."

"Maybe a word," Gravel continued, thinking aloud, ignoring her. "Maybe it only works for certain people. Special people. Like owners and them that made it."

"Raines made it," Violet said.

Gravel blanched. "How'd you know that?"

"'Cause he told me. Brought me down here to show it off. Felt like that anyhow, didn't make much sense."

Gravel was very pale, even under the lack of lighting. "Violet, this is bad. We can't use this thing. Can't trust it. Not if Raines made it."

"Have to," Violet said, not willing to argue beyond that. "I need to get Sharpe out. This is how I do it."

"The fox scares me, lass," Gravel told her simply. "He ought to scare you."

Yeah, he scares me. But . . .

"So you won't work for my friend," Violet said. "Fine, don't do that. Be stubborn. But Raines made you. And he's my kind. He made you for Scarlett, for her. But he made you. So . . ."

"Lass," Gravel cautioned as she moved closer to Onyx, hands outstretched, palms flat and facing forward. She ignored him.

"So you're gonna work for me, rockslide," she whispered, touching her hands to the smooth black chest. It felt cool to the touch but there was something under the surface. Not warmth, but . . . an attraction. Something pulling at her hands. Felt like quicksand, soft snow. Mud. Just waiting for her to sink in. Violet squeezed her eyes shut, concentrating. She could see red when she thought hard enough, red through the lids of her eyes. And still that sinking feeling.

I made you move before, didn't I? Looked out through your eyes. Smashed the ship up good. Well, we're gonna do that again. Just let me in. Open the door and then let me in.

Open the door and step inside, little one.

Her face was screwed up in concentration. She knew this because she could see it herself, looking down. Through the golem's eyes.

It brought her headache back with a blinding stab. She staggered, hand to her face and clutching. The golem did the same, mimicking her pose.

"Damn," Gravel whispered, taking a step back.

Violet grinned fiercely.

Got you now.

SNEAKING A HULKING stone behemoth through the labyrinth that was the *Fata Morgana* was not something Violet had thought through. Fortune favoured them that it was a dead watch and that Sharpe's holding cell was close enough to where Onyx had been stored. But for the most part it was plain dumb luck that kept them from being discovered.

"This is the one," Violet said, in front of Sharpe's cell.

"You're sure he understands?" Gravel asked, looking sceptically at the golem.

"She's sure," Sharpe's dry voice called back from the other side of door, his voice a hoarse whisper. "You all wearing steel-soled boots out there or you just bring a marching band with you? Heard you coming from half the ship away."

"Shush your face," Violet told him, holding a hand to her head. Her headache was getting worse. Like there was too much thinking going on in there. Was it the stress or something to do with ordering Onyx around? Couldn't worry about that now. Just had to get Sharpe and make for the boats. Then Onyx wasn't going to be a worry. In fact the blighter could take a long walk off a short pier back into the mist for all Violet cared. And fall.

Fall. Falling . . .

Not now. Can't think about that now.

"Sharpe, move away from the door," Violet told him.

"Vi, I can barely lie down in this pen, there is no *away* from the door."

That was a problem.

"You planning on kicking the door in, Miss Violet?" Gravel asked her. "Might not be too healthy for your friend there."

"Who's that?" Sharpe asked. "I know that voice."

"Name's Gravel, Mister Sharpe, or Brandon, if you prefer."

"What do you prefer?"

"That we hurry the hells up."

"Smart lad, I approve. Hurry up it is. No kicking, though, so we're clear."

"Try the wheel," Violet said, half to herself. She made the gesture, thought about what she wanted, tried to channel her inner lightning. It all made no sense and she still hadn't figured it out yet. Onyx put hands to wheel and wrenched. The wheel came away with the sound of protesting metal, there was no way it hadn't woken half the ship. Onyx took a step back, holding the dismembered handle. The was a hole maybe two hands wide in the door that buckled outwards but it wouldn't open. No way anyone was fitting through either, except maybe Bandit who bounded for the gap, hanging on by his paws and lifting his face to peer inside.

Sharpe's face appeared on the other side of the gap, to Bandit's delight. Sharpe's hairy, bearded face.

"Hello, my friend," Sharpe beamed at the loompa as it batted at his whiskers, trying to pull him through the gap. "Good to see you too."

He caught Violet's eye and grinned. "And aren't you the sight, Vi. Think we might need a bigger hole though. And . . ."

That was when he saw Onyx. His face paled and he jerked back from the hole.

"Sharpe," Violet hissed. "Get back here."

"Why is the rock here?" he called back. She dropped down and peered through the hole. Sure enough he was backed up as far away as he could in the cramped confines of the cell.

"Helping," she told him.

"Since when?"

"Since now. Stay there. Gonna fix the door."

"You too," she said to Gravel, who swooped up Bandit, taking a step back. Then another, to be sure.

"All right," Violet took a deep breath, talking mostly to herself. She imagined, thought, compelled Onyx opening the door.

And nothing happened.

She glared at the golem. The golem stared blankly back at her. *You have no idea what you're doing.*

"Hells damnit!" Violet slammed her fist against the door in frustration. She recoiled in pain, clutching at her hand, then brought the whole arm up to cover her face as Onyx struck out at the door, driving the point of its blade into the lock mechanism. Onyx jerked its fist back, taking the whole mechanism and the locking bars with it. The door tottered, creaking, then fell with a sound that shook the corridor, revealing Sharpe.

Bandit and Violet both launched themselves at him in tandem, wrestling with each other as they wrapped limbs around him. Violet buried her face in his shoulder. It was damp and when she lifted her face she realised it was from her own leaking eyes. Bandit made little mewling sounds so there was that. At least there was that.

"Good to see you too, Vi." Sharpe held on tight, even with Bandit pulling at his clothes.

"Happy as y'all look, we should break this reunion up and move," Gravel told them. "Can hear alarms going off all over the ship."

"Come on, little ones," Sharpe said, finally letting go of Violet. "What's the plan?"

Violet took a moment. Her migraine was gone, forgotten, but she found herself short of breath. Sharpe took her hesitation to mean something else.

"You have a plan, right? Tell me this isn't as far as you thought this through!"

Violet grimaced at him. "Course I got a plan, a good one."

HE HAD NO business being here and Mors knew it. The Luscan's eyes were boring into him, making Kaspar fight the urge to keep his hands at his side. He waited for one of the other officers to call on him or dismiss him.

They were all there, which concerned him. Aristeia never called meetings of the officers, and Raines had addressed the crew twice since taking over. And yet they were all gathered in the wardroom, what had formerly or should have been the wardroom. Now it was Raines' workshop.

There were three other ensigns there, a marine lieutenant subordinate to Mors who acted as their captain, Aristeia as skipper, and a mix of junior officers and mates. All somewhere between attention and ill-at-ease. Waiting for Raines to finish his conversation.

The Kelpie captain had not come alone. She had a companion, an unfamiliar Korrigan woman. Kaspar recognised her from the mess hall but couldn't name her.

The conversation was clearly important, above his pay grade, and unless Kaspar read the tension wrong, meant to be much more private.

Both Heathen and Aristeia had just raised this very point.

Raines looked up from his chair, frowning. He looked irritated, dismissive.

"Fine," he waved his hand. "Go away, all of you. Away."

"Dismissed," Aristeia said for good measure.

"You too, Coldstream," Heathen added. Mors narrowed his eyes at her but Aristeia nodded, reluctantly. He joined the procession of officers.

"Not you," Raines called out as Kaspar was halfway towards the door. He winced, pausing mid-step, feeling the eyes of his fellows on him. He turned the heel and stepped back to stand at attention. He heard the door shut behind, ominous and echoing.

"Captain, this is irregular," Aristeia protested.

"I have questions."

"They can wait until after this meeting."

"Or I could ask them now. Ensign, your report."

"Sir?" Kaspar looked between them. Aristeia glaring, Heathen studying him. And then there was the stranger. Probably Guild.

"Your charge, the girl, report," Raines leaned back, waving his hand again.

"Violet?"

"Yes," Raines said impatiently. "Her, what have you noticed?"

"Little, sir," Kaspar said, shifting uncomfortably.

"Nothing? Nothing unusual, out of the ordinary. Nothing of note?"

"Just that . . ." Kaspar hesitated.

"Yes?" Raines leaned forward.

"She still has the falling, sir. Trouble with colours, dizziness, a fear of heights."

"That is to be expected, Ensign," Heathen said. "She was pulled from the black, barely alive."

"Yes, sir."

"Nothing else?"

"Not much of a report," the newcomer grinned. "Hardly worth staying around for."

Kaspar hesitated. The woman had come in with the Kelpie, almost certainly Guild. The golem, hidden though it was below, had also come via Heathen. And when they'd chased down the *Tantamount* . . .

Bad things follow her. That hasn't changed.

"I think we can dismiss the ensign," Aristeia said pointedly.

"Yes, yes," Raines shrugged. "To other matters. Heathen, Verity, what have you to tell me? How much longer do we have to—"

"*Captain*," Aristeia growled.

"The ensign is still here? Off you go, my lad, off you go."

Kaspar saluted, turning for the door again. It opened before he could reach for it. Mors. The Luscan glared at him, then past him.

"We have a situation," he announced.

"THE HELLS IS that thing?" Sharpe's voiced echoed around the deck. His words made Gravel turn and stare at him, stopped short, a bemused expression plastered on his face.

"You sound . . ."

"Sound like the skipper," Violet said. "But then you were sweet on her, weren't you?"

Sharpe flinched. The man actually clutched at his chest, gripping at his shirt. He faced Violet with wide eyes.

He started to say, "Violet, I—"

"No," Violet shook her head. "Not now, shouldn't had said anything. Talk about it later."

"Later would be good," Sharpe managed a smile. "Later, I have something . . . and . . . later. After we get away from *this* ship."

He turned and pointed. "But *that* is not a ship."

Gravel had cleared the tarps around the test ship, the tender that was going to carry them away. And it truly didn't look like much, just the bones of a vessel cleared of all mast and rigging. Incomplete and all the more worrisome for it. And there was the problem of how they were going to get it outside in the first place.

"It's a launch," Gravel pushed him towards it, tugging Violet along by the hand. "Don't stop."

"No sails, where are the sails?" Sharpe did stumble to a halt. He twisted half around. "Raines made that."

"And I sailed it, now move," Gravel pushed him again.

"No sails," Sharpe repeated, stumbling towards the launch.

"Mister Sharpe," Gravel held him by the shoulders, staring him down. "Need you to focus here, sir. Can't be doing this without you."

Sharpe stared back at him, blankly or with focus, Violet couldn't see.

"Controls are right simple, least until we get going. Need you to operate them, work them just so."

"Me?" Sharpe pulled back.

"Aye, you. Little tug is all locked up, and I have to see to that, don't have time to say how. Lowered just so. Miss Vi, need you to open the hatches, no, not now, if you please. Those are the levers there. Yank them and the floor's going to open up under us. At the last, or they'll know we're here, won't take them long as it is to figure without us ringing more bells."

"Just say what, Captain," Sharpe clapped him on the shoulder. The grin was back in his voice. "Give the orders."

Gravel looked at him with surprise, then grinned back. Violet looked away, shaking her head, fighting off a grin herself.

Time for that later. Once we're away in the black.

She had to reach out and steady herself, holding onto the launch at that thought. Squeezed her eyes shut till her balance returned. The black was just below them. Huge and empty, the same thing she'd fallen through, almost died in.

Time for that later.

"Here's how," Gravel was saying. "This drops the keel, keeps her steady and plugged full of ether. Enough air for a week, but maybe three days with all of us. Those valves control the pitch and the thrust, like a sphere tender. Doesn't use up our air, runs off those tanks there."

Gravel rapped his knuckles on the metal cylinders set into the floor. The sound echoed around the lower hold. Loudly. It reminded Violet of Sharpe's own tapping.

"We need to go," she called out in a loud whisper.

"Right you are, Miss Violet," Gravel agreed. "You ready there, Mister Sharpe?"

"No," Sharpe shook his head. "But we'll manage. Let's away."

"Aye, let's away," Gravel grinned. He hesitated a moment still. It wasn't hard for Violet to guess what he was thinking.

"He wouldn't have come," she reminded him.

"Aye, maybe. Worry about him, what might happen after, is all."

"He'll be fine. Worry about us."

"Aye, you remember the lever?"

"Big brass knobbly one, far side by the wall."

"Aye, big brass and knobbly, lass. I'll see to our ropes. Just leaves one thing." He pointed at Onyx, standing silent watch over them all.

For a moment something pulled at Violet. She half toyed in her head with the idea of bringing Onyx along. An indestructible bodyguard. She'd just gotten Sharpe back, part of her old life. Could she risk that? No, the golem was too heavy. Gravel had said so.

But then . . . what does he know?

He could be wrong.

If he weren't the only one who could work the launch . . .

"Stay there," Violet said, still not sure if it was her words or thoughts or actions that were driving the golem. "Once we start, don't let anyone else on the ship, understand? No one else gets on."

No golems on the ship.

Violet smiled. Onyx turned its head, a twist from a featureless waist, to face her. She felt judgement there.

There was no way to tell if the golem understood, and Violet ran to the far side of the hold, straight for the brass lever. It was ratcheted, linking up to gears and cogs in a way she didn't understand but unlike the pulleys and winches used to manage normal cargo holds, it could be operated by a single person. She took hold of it and waited, watching Gravel removing the mooring ropes. That only left the ones suspending the tender. Gravel waved at her to pull the lever before he released them.

The lever stuck at first, refusing to budge. Violet threw her weight against it but then the hells broke loose.

Armed sailors burst into the deck, pouring out from walkways and stairwells. The dark interior lit up with wandfire; no questions were asked or warnings given. Perhaps it was the sight of Onyx, a black silhouette in the shadows. Shots fired and ricocheted off its skin, and Violet winced at the memory of that happening before.

Different ship, different time.

Sharpe and Bandit ducked down inside the tender. Gravel dropped to the deck, lying low. He waved frantically, swinging his arm in low sweeping motions, at Violet. She tried again, wrenching at the lever. This time it gave, throwing her off balance and onto the floor. The floor lurched, the axis actually shuddering as the hold doors opened, splitting apart and opening up to the mist.

Violet scrambled to her feet, and a stray shot almost took her head off. It couldn't have been aimed. She hadn't been there a moment ago and it was almost impossible to see her. It caught her in the shoulder though, spinning her round and dumping her back onto the cold, metal deck.

The light was changing. Could make out faces now, voices too. Orders being shouted. She saw Mors at the head of a pack, brandishing a wand in one hand, the other giving directions with sharp, savage motions.

Violet started to crawl on her elbows and forearms, making her way towards cover. From there she could dash to the tender. Sharpe must have found a weapon because he was shooting back. She couldn't see Gravel. Hopefully he was aboard too.

Just me then, better hurry, be a long cold jump.

Someone grabbed her from behind, an arm wrapping around her waist and another over her mouth. The breath whooshed out of her lungs as she was dragged backwards, away from Sharpe and Bandit. Back in the dark.

Violet bit down on the hand covering her mouth. She felt blood spurt out between her teeth, hot and metallic, and felt the shudder of pain from whoever held her. But they didn't let go, they gripped tighter and took another step back. Violet fought but it was useless. It was wrong. It was all going wrong.

Violet grabbed at the arms holding her. Too strong. Her feet were lifted off the ground, flailing, kicking at the air. She threw her head back, collecting something of her attacker's face, rewarded with something that might have been pain. Still nothing.

Her eyes found Sharpe, across the deck. Through the dark and the confused fire-fight raging around them. He saw her. He was reaching out one hand, the other gripped the side of the tender. Realisation, horror. Then a decision. He was going to come for her. She saw it in his eyes.

Quill looked at me like that . . .

The lines holding the tender shuddered, then began to uncoil at a rate of knots, ropes zipping through the pulleys. The boat, Sharpe inside, dropped through the thin outer envelope. Violet blinked and it was gone. They were gone.

He was gone.

Gravel had pulled the releases. She saw him then, one hand on the switches, the other hoisted above him. Onyx dangled him, holding him tight and feet above the ground. Gravel's face was defiant but screwed up in pain.

Let him go. Let him go!

The words screamed inside Violet's head but never emerged. She fought to plant her feet on the deck, intending to run to Gravel's side, to force Onyx to let him go. She saw the light arcing around both of them as Gravel pried at the black fingers holding him. It flared out in a crazed spider web around Gravel, and he began to convulse. He cried out once then went limp, ribbons of smoke drifting off his body.

Violet did scream now. Into the hand covering her mouth. Even that was denied her. Muffled. Unheard.

"Be quiet!" Kaspar's voice. Right in her ear. He was the one who had her, pulling her back. "Or they'll hear you!"

Back. Away. Out of sight.

Sharpe was gone. Gravel wasn't moving. He was passed out. Violet felt herself do the same. Slipping into the black.

She no longer cared if anyone found her there.

Chapter 22

"Ship feel quiet to you?"

"Feel?" Nel turned her head to look down at Sharpe. She stood atop the rails near the bowsprit, one foot extended out over the edge of the ship. It was a pose she'd often found Violet in, face first into the black, holding onto the lines and leaning out over the stars.

Sharpe looked much the same as he had back then. He'd found a razor or scissors or maybe borrowed a knife from Jack's galley. Shorn himself clean. Maybe not clean—there was blood on his collar, nicks and cuts on his face. But the long hair and beard were gone.

"Quieter. Empty."

"Ship is empty, Sharpe," Nel told him. "And the crew don't talk much."

It was eerie, the way the Draugr went about their duties with hardly a word. They could and would talk just fine if asked, but the banter and catcalls that would normally fill the top deck and rigging were nowhere to be heard. Every few hours something might set them off and they'd jabber like a crowd of gossiping fisher-folk. All of them talking at once, over one another. The air would buzz with words for a few minutes and then the silence would drag again. It was those long silences Sharpe seemed to struggle with. And not just him—Quill and Jack had been conspicuously quiet. They'd had one spectacular verbal sparring match, blowing out at each other. Then both had come to the same conclusion; that they were yelling at each other from across an empty deck. With no one paying any attention. The two had slunk back to their respective corners to sulk about it.

Nel wasn't even sure what they had been fighting about.

"Yeah," Sharpe said. "That is the problem."

Nel turned back to the stars. She didn't let Sharpe see the smile tugging on her mouth as he fidgeted next to her. He paced. Drummed his fingers. Took hold of a line, tugging on it to test the slack. It wasn't meant to be slack.

Someone can't handle the quiet.

She took pity on him. "Something on your mind?"

"You never asked me," he said.

"Asked you what?"

"About me. Me and Raines."

Nel kept looking out to the black. "Talking to you about you is like trying to drink rain water. Doesn't do much for your thirst."

"What's that mean?"

"Means I gave up asking because you never answered."

"Ask me now."

Nel faced him. "Meaning you'll answer straight?"

Sharpe nodded. "Told Violet. Through a cell door aboard the *Morgana*. Might be nice to tell someone, face to face."

Nel grimaced. "I ain't Violet. Besides, I don't care no more."

Sharpe blinked, eyes widening in surprise. "What?"

"Said I don't care."

Sharpe grabbed her by the arm. "Nel, I want you to know. I want to tell you."

"And I said I don't care."

"But . . ."

"Let me tell you this once," Nel said, lowering her voice. She could feel eyes on them. "I don't care what you did, or what you were. All I care about is who you are now and you don't get to tell me that. You show me. And so long as you're on this ship and my crew that's all we're going to say about it."

She turned to leave, scowling when she caught the eyes of her navigator watching her from across the deck. Right after all.

Sharpe still had her arm, pulled her back around to face him. She couldn't read the expression on his face. Even though it was right up close. Uncomfortable close. And getting closer.

"Chanel, I need to tell you—"

Nel put up a hand between them. "Sharpe, I don't know what you're thinking, but I will warn you that if you so much as try and kiss me right now I will knock your teeth so far back you'll be chewing biscuits through your nose."

She could read the expression now as she pulled away. Shock, disbelief, a little bit of fear. All good things. Better than what she saw on Quill's face when she made her way to the bridge.

"I will never understand the mating habits of your kind," he shook his head.

"No mating on the ship, Quill," she told him. "Very important rule."

"A new rule?"

"Old rule. Just reinstating it."

"Ah, yes. Were you not the reason that rule came about?"

"Shut your face, Loveland."

"Of course. I have no interest in discovering whether chewing through one's nose is indeed possible."

Damned Kelpie.

IT WAS ARISTEIA who escorted her to the captain's chambers this time. It felt wrong to call it a cabin. It was a double room in the centre of the ship, not the traditional grand cabin along the stern. Violet recalled it was because it provided equal access to all parts of the ship and the network of speaking tubes converged in the area, giving Raines access to whoever or wherever he needed. It was not a break with tradition she approved of.

Aristeia was not a tall woman, Violet realised. When she looked at her she was looking the first mate in the eye. It only made the walk uncomfortable. No one had yet accused her of being involved in Sharpe's escape but surely it was only a matter of time. The long walk to her trial and likely execution. Aristeia her solitary escort; she hadn't seen Kaspar since he'd assured Mors and Aristeia that Violet had been with him during the whole event. He was probably a suspect too with how close he and Gravel were. Might hold him responsible as an officer in any case.

They were all waiting for her. Mors and Heathen opposite one another. Raines pacing the length of the room, his arms folded across his chest and clutching his elbows. He stopped when Violet was ushered in, becoming keen and attentive.

"Ah, here she is."

Aristeia wasted no time. From behind Violet she spoke. "The escape of the prisoner. What was your involvement?"

Violet did her best not to react. She clasped her hands behind her back, standing at near attention the way an enlisted sailor might. Her response drew a frown from Raines.

"The girl is acquainted with both the prisoner and his accomplice?" Heathen asked. She gave nothing else away.

"Also the ensign," Mors said quietly, tapping the hilt of one of his hands. He paced out from behind the desk, moving to flank Violet. "He is being questioned now."

Violet turned her head towards him, lifting her eyebrows. "And?"

"And what?" Mors scowled.

"What did these questions tell you?"

"He claimed he was with you," Mors answered at a look from Raines.

"Convenient," Aristeia growled.

"Do you believe him?" Violet asked.

No one answered her.

Violet shrugged. "If you believe him there's nothing to discuss. If you don't then let's get on with it."

"You were both aboard the *Tantamount,*" Heathen said. Her voice was cool, steady. Indifferent. "I remember seeing you there. There is no link between the prisoner and the man who helped him escape. Other than you."

Violet shrugged.

"The prisoner is unimportant," Raines dismissed Sharpe. "A path once taken that leads nowhere. I would pay him no further mind. However—"

"I disagree," Aristeia interrupted. "If only for the implicit treachery from one of our own in his escape."

"I agree," Mors said. "I dislike loose ends."

"Fine, fine," Raines sighed. "Then by all means, do tidy them up. I would ask that we resolve the matter with our young friend here though, so that she and I may continue our work."

"This work is making progress?" Heathen asked. Her attention had shifted, Violet realised. She wasn't the focus.

"Very much so," Raines smiled, nodding at Violet.

"I see."

"Another matter then," Aristeia said. "Mors."

Mors raised his hand, clutching a rolled-up parchment. At first glance a map.

"We would have you explain this." He placed it on the desk and motioned for Violet to approach. She unrolled the parchment, spreading and flattening it, glancing at Raines before bending to see what it was. The officers waited expectantly.

"This . . . this is . . . ," Violet stared, her skin growing cold. She couldn't move, her arms were locked in place, touching it. The paralysis lasted a few seconds then she recoiled, stepping back and putting distance between. The parchment rolled up.

"Yes?" Aristeia's voice. "This is?"

Violet grabbed her own hand, clutching it to her chest. Shaking. Eyes hot. Vision blurry. She shook her head angrily.

You are not going to cry. What sort of weak, mewling girl child cries at a time like this?

"The deed," her voice came out choked, sobbing. She hated herself for it. "To the *Tantamount.* That . . . that were the captain!"

Violet stared at the deed in utter horror. It was the captain, tattooed on his back, his skin. That was Captain Horatio Phelps' skin she'd been touching.

"Where'd you get that? Where . . . ?"

"Enough," Raines snapped. Violet flinched at his words but they weren't directed at her. "This is most . . . upsetting. It avails us nothing, the very opposite."

"Not the reaction you were expecting," Heathen commented, though it was not obvious who she was directing her words at.

"This is the first time you have seen this?" Mors asked, leaning over the desk. His hand pushed down on the map, fingers splayed and locking it in place.

"Clearly," Raines told him.

"That question wasn't for you," Aristeia said. "Captain."

The room fell silent as the two locked gazes. "This was found after the escape," Aristeia said. "Not on our turncoat but picked up from the hold. It was most likely lost during the fracas. Again, our young friend here is the only link between a ship gone to the black and what has occurred. So I will ask again—"

"You never use my name," Violet spoke up. All eyes turned to her. She looked around at all of them in turn.

"None of you do," she said. "None of you ever use my name. Not once."

Stony faced glares all around. Raines covered the loss of control quickly. Heathen . . .

That was a smile.

"Do not presume to talk to any of us here with such insolence, girl," Aristeia warned her, grabbing her by the shoulder. Violet shook off the hand, turning on her heel to face the woman.

"Say it," she said to the ship's second in command. Then emphasising each word, "Say my name."

Aristeia's eyes narrowed to mere slits. She moved close enough for Violet to see the scars on her face turn white over clenched jaw muscles. Still the woman didn't speak or address her. Not by name.

"Who am I?"

"You are not—" Aristeia started.

"I gave it to him."

All eyes turned to Heathen. She blinked once, a horizontal wisp across her eyes.

"What?" Mors was the first to speak. "You?"

Heathen blinked again. "I gave it to him. To Sharpe, the prisoner. In his cell. Before."

"Why?" the captain asked.

"I was seeking a reaction."

Remember the last thing you saw of Sharpe.

"He escaped," Mors said.

Reaching for something. Something important.

"Quite the reaction."

You thought it was you.

"Tearing apart the brig," Aristeia added.

It wasn't you.

"That would be the golem," Heathen said.

It was never you.

"A golem you delivered to us. The golem and prisoner both. Who then broke free after you visited them."

"So perhaps the girl is not the connection," Mors took up the thread of conversation. Something in his words grabbed Violet's attention. "Perhaps you are."

He was right close to Heathen now, almost in her face, one hand clenched on his weapon.

"An interesting thought," Heathen told him. She held up her hand, closed but for one finger. "I suggest you forget it."

Violet looked to see if Raines would move to stop the confrontation, as sparks literally flew. It appeared so.

"This talk is pointless," Raines stepped between the two. Mors jerked his hand away from his wand, surprised. Heathen's step down was more gradual, the glow disappearing from her hand much slower than it had appeared.

"The golem could not act on his own unless given instruction," Raines said, gesticulating as he talked. He seemed to need to talk with his hands as much as his mouth. "And these are instructions that cannot be given by just anyone. They require a connection with the golem, with Onyx. And they require a specific skillset."

"Thaumatics," Heathen said.

"Just so."

"The prisoner is not such a person," Aristeia said.

"No, he is not. But the boy who helped him escape is," Heathen said.

Raines frowned. "I was not aware of that. You are sure?"

Heathen nodded. "An easy enough thing to recognise, if you know what to look for."

"Which I imagine you do," Raines agreed, considering. "Interesting. The entire purpose of this ship was to eliminate the dependency upon such people. It seems we have left ourselves with a blind spot because of that. So the traitor could in fact have manipulated the golem into his plan? Most curious. Most . . ."

"Why then was it responsible for detaining him?" Mors asked.

"Residual instructions," Raines shrugged. "From the previous partner."

"Partner?" Heathen asked pointedly. "Not owner? Master perhaps?"

"As I said, there is a connection required. A relationship, of sorts."

"Of sorts," Heathen repeated.

"It is a complicated one."

"Concealing unregistered thaumatics within the fleet is a black offence," Aristeia spoke up.

"Is it?" Raines sounded bored. "Given the consequences here I can see why that might be. I assume there is a punishment?"

"There is," Aristeia said. "But the mutinous actions take

precedence over it."

"Nothing too drastic, I presume," Raines said. "I would like some time to investigate the boy's connection to Onyx further. It bears some interest."

"The creature should be jettisoned," Aristeia insisted. "It's done enough damage."

"The *construct* will be staying aboard," Raines told her. "It will be staying aboard because *I* say it will. Is that understood?"

"No, it is not bloody well understood, Raines," the first mate said to him. "That's twice now that damned thing has run riot on this ship. Or are you so distracted you can't make the connection?"

"You said it was a ray attack," Heathen broke in.

"Only officially. Unofficially . . . the boy was seen in the hold where the damage was done, immediately after. I didn't think anything of it at the time, but now . . ."

"Ah," Heathen said. "I see."

Violet was watching Raines. The expression on his face, cold, calculating. "You believe the incidents are connected, well then, our course seems obvious. Dispose of the boy and there will be no further connection. And I need hear no more complaints about the construct. *My* construct."

"Captain," Mors appealed, moving to stand with the first mate. "These are serious incidents."

"Yes," Raines repeated. "*Captain*."

Violet watched, waiting. And then Aristeia and Mors saluted. Like good officers.

"And the girl?" Heathen said, not looking at Violet. "You seem to have had nothing but trouble since she came aboard."

"It is in hand," Raines told her.

"I disagree," Aristeia said. "*Respectfully*."

"And I do not care whether you agree or not, first mate. Respectfully or otherwise."

"Violet," Heathen said, directly. The word drew a look of ire from Raines. "Perhaps it would be better if you removed yourself to my ship."

"That will not be . . . necessary," Raines said firmly. "She is my—that is, she is under my protection. Safer . . . better off with her own kind."

"And that is you?" Heathen asked. She shrugged. "I was

merely making an offer."

"We decline. The girl stays, Captain," the captain of the *Fata Morgana* told his fellow officer. "That is not why we requested your help."

"My ship stands ready to assist you."

"It's not *your* ship, Captain," Aristeia said. "The *Mangonel* is a fleet ship of the line."

"Nor is it your ship that we require, as you well know," Raines said.

"Of course not," Heathen agreed. A smile. Cold. The mask was back. "Let us continue our discussion then? In private?"

"Aristeia, take the girl away," Raines dismissed them both. "Make the arrangements. We will be with you shortly."

Aristeia bristled at her orders. She exchanged a curt nod with Mors then grabbed Violet roughly by the arm. The Luscan fell in behind them.

"Move," she ordered. Violet had time for one last look around the room before she was hauled out. Raines seemed to have already forgotten her, deep in his own world of thoughts. It was Heathen who watched her leave. And she'd never been good at reading Kelpie expressions.

THEY'D BEATEN HIM in the hold. Beaten him more since Violet had seen him dragged off to the brig. One eye was swollen shut, a lump of blue and purple that mottled the rest of his face. Blood had dried on his neck, crimson running down his chest. Two marines supported him, in fact dragging him along the deck, manacled feet trailing limply.

His escort stopped in front of the portside winch. No cranes on the *Fata Morgana*, instead a grooved chute framed by rails that led directly to an oversized porthole. Three glass spheres were lined up like cannonballs waiting to be fired. Gravel collapsed to his knees when the marines released him, his forehead coming to rest against the curved wall of the bubble, sliding down as even his knees gave out. His descent left a smear of red on the glass, and when he fell he exposed his hands to Violet and Kaspar. Copper wire was wrapped tightly around his wrists, cutting deeply into the flesh.

Shock himself if he tried so much as a whisper of breeze, right into his veins. Might even stop his heart.

Aristeia Quinn knelt in front of Gravel. If she was concerned about any last-minute reprieves or escapes she didn't show it. Almost disdainful, she unlocked his leg restraints, passing them to the nearest marine before untwisting the copper with her own fingers. This Aristeia bundled around her own hand, stepping back to take one last look at her former crew member.

The restraints were unnecessary. Gravel was barely conscious, certainly not capable of any sort of action. Whoever had worked him over had made sure. Nor did he make a sound. There was a whimper, a cut-off groan, but it came from Kaspar, not his friend.

"Quiet," Violet whispered, perhaps harsher than she had intended. She unwrapped her arms from around herself and grabbed onto the ensign's wrist. She could feel his trembling, feel the tendons move under her fingertips. She tightened her grip as the captain stepped forward.

Don't be an idiot. You can't help him.

Somewhere in her head she heard the sound of disappointment. But there was nobody else here, nobody who could do anything.

Raines didn't say anything, just stood over Gravel, as if considering. And then he was done, turning around to face his crew.

They're not his crew. Look at how they wait for the first mate. Their skipper . . .

Aristeia called out, "Proceed."

The marines opened the bubble, proceeding to roll Gravel inside. They operated with military efficiency, one was pushing his feet inside and a heartbeat later the other was slamming the hatch closed, setting a bar to seal it from the outside. The marines turned and saluted, stepping away. Inside, Gravel twitched, struggling to rise on the inside of the curved glass.

"Captain!"

Godsdamnit.

Kaspar pulled free of her grip, stepping forward, back straight and heels at attention. "Captain, I protest."

Raines turned his head a fraction his way. He seemed perplexed as to how to respond. "Ensign Vaughn protests," he said to Aristeia.

"Mors," the first officer replied.

The Luscan smiled. "The ensign's protest is so noted."

"Captain," Kaspar tried again, only to be cut off as one of the marines pulled the lever. The ratcheted tension unleashed and the bubble cell was throw out into the black. Violet caught a last glimpse of Gravel thrown violently around inside, the bubble starting to spin as it sped away.

"It seems there is nothing more to protest," Raines shrugged. "Carry on, my dear."

"Mister Coldstream," Aristeia said. "You may fire when ready."

And there was Mors, standing silent but poised by the wand battery. The starboard battery, shiny metal and charged crystal pointing out into the black. Mors stood alone, needing no crew to man the single weapon, or perhaps it was a choice that he did this himself. Was it a preference or did the first mate want her trusted officer to carry out the deed?

The Gunner's Daughter. Do you remember how she got that name?

Aristeia walked up beside Mors, leaning in to whisper a quiet word. She held up a finger.

One shot. No wasted fire.

Mors nodded, with a glance in Violet and Kaspar's direction. His expression was hard to read. Cold. Alien.

The was a glint of reflected light from Aristeia's hand. The copper wire wrapped around a palm. It made Violet's hand itch, where rope had been tattooed on her skin. Her link to a ship, now gone. To the deck crew, gone. It was broken with scar tissue, where a rope had threatened to burn it away. Aristeia only had scars, no tattoos.

She took the copper, one shot for the kill. For the example. But they don't care about the tender. They could have just blacked him, thrown him overboard. But it wouldn't be the same. This is deliberate. This is cruel. This is for . . .

She heard Kaspar's ragged breathing beside her. Barely restrained.

This is for who?

Mors bent to his task, sighting along the gun barrel itself. His head came up, he adjusted. The wand fired.

The light was incandescent, burning a path through the black. The mist tore and frayed where it passed through. And it struck the glass sphere floating in the void, unerringly.

There was no sound. The deck was unnaturally quiet, so subdued. Nothing carried back to them when the sphere cracked and fell apart. Slowly, pushed in a hundred different directions by the escaping air inside. A broken body, drifting in the black. And then swallowed up by the mist.

"Bring us about," the first mate ordered, soft words that carried far. Raines, the captain, was already gone, slipped away before the display was done.

The bubble was little more than a gleam in the black now. Violet was distracted from searching for it by the sound of leather striking metal. Kaspar running down the hallway, after the captain maybe. Violet heard herself cursing and running after them both.

VIOLET FOUND HIM hiding in the dark. She'd misplaced her glasses again. Her eyes were getting worse, and the longer she wore the glasses the worse her eyes were without them. These days, the interior of the ship was little more than smudges and shadows, a series of greyed out obstacles lurking in the dark to bash her shins at any opportunity. She was hobbling by the time she found him. Followed the sounds; a faint, wheezing sob, a racking cough. An irregular banging.

It was him, Kaspar, huddled in a corner, sitting down with knees pulled up to his chest. There were tears running down his face, he looked awful. She saw what was causing the banging, when the sobbing reached a certain point he threw back his head, hard, repeatedly, against the interior metal wall. And then he'd bury it forward on his arms and begin again.

Bandit was beside him. No surprises there, he'd made these dark corners his home. No one else knew about him. Half the people he would show himself to were now gone. She'd thought him gone with Sharpe but he must have jumped out at the last.

Violet didn't talk when she walked up to Kaspar, nor did she try to be quiet about it. She crouched down in front of him, balancing on the balls of her feet, resting one of her hands on his arms. He stilled at her touch but did not look up. Maybe he was collecting himself. Maybe he wanted to be alone. Maybe he just didn't care.

"The captain called you Vaughn," Violet said at length. "Ensign Vaughn."

Kaspar went even stiller under her touch. She heard him draw a long, shuddering breath before finally raising his head. His eyes were puffy, shot with swollen blood vessels.

Violet reached out, plucking a lock of hair between two fingers. It looked drab to her in the pale moon lighting of the ship. Like mud, a sort of brownish green, but she remembered the vibrant red it would look like under real sunlight. What it should look like if she were wearing her glasses.

"You have her hair," she said. "Just like her. I can see her in you now. I don't know why I couldn't before."

"Maybe you didn't want to."

"Maybe I didn't," Violet nodded. "You don't use her name. You have that in common. What is it with names, with you Vaughns? What shameful secret are you carrying around that you are afraid of? So afraid you try and hide from your own name?"

Kaspar pulled his head away from her, back as far as his cramped position would allow him.

"What's in a name, Niko?"

"My name," he said through gritted teeth, "is Dominik Kaspar Vaughn. And I am nothing like my sister."

"Really?" Violet said. "You know she's dead. That's how you knew about me, because you knew she was first mate aboard the *Tantamount*. The ship you helped shoot down."

Kaspar glared at her.

"Did you keep my secret for my sake or for yours?"

No answer.

"She killed me," Violet said. "She left me to die. In the cold. In the black. Your sister."

"I don't want to hear," Kaspar said, "about my sister."

"Just like Gravel," Violet said. "Alone. In the cold."

Kaspar stared. "Why are you saying this? Why are you talking . . . like that?"

Violet shrugged. "Because it's the truth." She turned around, sitting down beside him. Their shoulders were touching, and she could feel him trembling, wanting to pull away from the contact. He was the only warm thing in the room.

"Did you love them?" she asked. "Gravel?"

"He was my friend."

"That's what he said about you. But did you . . ."

"It doesn't matter. He was my friend and he's dead. And I

couldn't stop it."

"No."

She waited.

"What are you going to do about it?"

Again he didn't answer. So they stayed like that in the dark, in the hold. Somewhere, in another part of the ship, probably some place she hadn't been and would never find, she imagined they'd taken Onyx. Somewhere secure and hidden. The golem was probably chained now, wrapped in iron. There had been two incidents. They wouldn't allow a third. She could imagine them, Raines and Aristeia, arguing over the golem, what Raines called the construct. So vivid she could even hear the words they might use.

The chains are unnecessary, first officer.

I disagree, Captain.

More than that, they are pointless. The construct could snap them if it chose.

The boy is dead. Who would make it do so?

Ah, yes, the boy.

We both know it wasn't the boy.

The girl then.

Yes, the girl.

And not the girl, we must remember that.

I am tired of your experiments and the toll they are taking on my ship.

Your ship is one of my experiments. And do not forget that I speak for the Guild in these matters.

You speak for the Guild but I speak for the fleet. And what of your other experiment? That's twice he has escaped you now.

A loose end to be dealt with. I have made arrangements.

What arrangements?

Guild arrangements.

How many of your damned arrangements am I to have aboard my ship?

My ship, first officer.

Heathen has made a request.

Has she?

There are other loose ends.

They are of no concern to me.

Maybe not to you but to . . .

Fine. Fine, I will speak to the agent involved. If the opportunity arises.

Heathen says it will.

Perhaps Heathen should have been the captain of this ship then.

"You are an abomination."

Violet stopped, facing Heathen. There was no one else around. The Kelpie captain appeared to have been waiting for her.

"What do you mean?" Violet asked.

"No games," Heathen said, reaching for her. The woman grabbed her around the throat, lifting Violet off her feet and slamming her against the bulkhead wall. "I want to talk with you."

Violet clutched at the hand around her throat, the one choking her. More than that, her skin burned. She could barely control her hands as live current ran through them. Then all of a sudden it was gone, Heathen dropped her. Violet drew in shuddering breaths, one hand clutching her chest. Her heart hammered away but more, she held something. A glass sphere, one that sucked all the charge that Heathen had sent running through her body.

"Children use those," Heathen commented, her voice calm but cold. "Young children who can't yet control their powers. Some who don't even know they have them."

"I am," Violet snarled, "not a child."

"Yet you hide in the body of one."

"Not for long."

"If I had known what Raines had planned I would have left you there. Drifting until you fell into the sun."

Violet chuckled, still clutching the sphere between her fingers. "He didn't plan this."

"Yet it happened."

Violet smiled at her.

"That boy is dead because of you."

"He shouldn't have listened to small voices," Violet said. "And who are you to talk, Heathen? How many are dead because of you?"

"Thousands," Heathen frowned. "Tens of thousands."

"Do you remember what you said to me? Before the battle at Rim?"

"There are worse things than dying," Heathen nodded. "I am looking at one."

"Then why don't you do something about it?" Violet challenged her. She held up the sphere, crackling and encircled with blue and white lightning bolts. "You could rip this ship apart from the inside, couldn't you? Or do what you did at Rim. Oh wait, you can't."

She laughed. "Raines built this ship to conduct thaumatics, but you knew that, didn't you? If you tried, even if *you* tried, it would dissipate throughout the hull. It's like a giant children's ball really, isn't it? And this place, it's special, isn't it? Nothing quite works the way it should here. I thought it was just me but it's not."

"Very little is what it should be," Heathen stared down at her with narrowed eyes. "It must hurt you, all that pain, the memories. The girl fighting to reject you. And all that power you can't bleed off aboard this ship. What do you do with all that hurt? Doesn't it make you feel . . . helpless?"

Violet held up the children's ball mockingly. "There are what, half a dozen in the whole of the High Lanes anywhere near as strong as you, aren't there?" Violet reminded her. "And you *still* can't do anything. How does that make *you* feel, Captain? Helpless?"

"The same, I imagine."

Violet grimaced. "What made you so eager to break from the fold?"

Heathen didn't answer.

"This?" Violet pointed at herself. "This makes you squeamish? After everything else. Everything you've done."

"Imagine your own answers."

"But you wanted them from me."

"I wanted to see for myself."

"And?"

"I think your control is more fragile than you would have Raines believe."

Violet frowned at her. "For now. And not for much longer."

"Best hurry, Raines is not known for his long-standing patience. It will take weeks to repair the damage done to the *Fata Morgana*. Damage you were responsible for."

"Not me," Violet said quickly. "Her."

"Ah. So there is a difference?"

"No."

Heathen looked down at her. "What Vaughn would say to you."

"A shame I'll never get to see the look on her face," Violet said smugly.

"Look now," Heathen told her, raising her eyes to somewhere behind the girl. Violet spun, catching Kaspar standing not too far away. He stared at her, then walked away without saying anything.

"And what does that prove?" Violet turned back to Heathen.

"That you should be more careful," Heathen said. "It's dangerous to stay in one place for too long. You know what's coming. And neither one of us can stop it."

"That's not true," Violet smiled. "There's one thing you could do. What you always do."

Heathen glanced aside involuntarily. On most ships she would have seen the black, the world below. The world now part of the High. But there was only the metal shell of the *Fata Morgana*.

CHAPTER 23

"WHAT IS A cold sun?" Sharpe asked. "Does it burn cooler than other stars? Is it made of ice instead of fire? Should we have brought warmer clothes?"

"Are you cold?" Nel gave him a sidelong glance.

"Only when I'm away from you, Skipper," he managed with a straight face. Nel rolled her eyes at him. She didn't have the energy to give more of a response right now.

"Gonna be like the ice run?" Jack asked, having made an unusual visit to the bridge as they approached the realms of thin mist.

Probably wants to know if he needs to start getting cosy to the stove again, Nel thought. *Spent half that run sleeping next to it and the other half hugging the rum jar.*

"It will be," Quill told him, "nothing like the ice run. Something, and I believe this to be a first, we can both take solace in."

"Good." Jack looked unhappy and then, unusually thoughtful.

Point Quill, managed to ruin Jack's happy moment after all.

"So what makes it a cold sun?" Sharpe asked. His arms were folded, rubbing his hands up and down. Talking himself into thinking it was cold.

Except he shouldn't feel it anyway.

"Cold is just what they call it," Nel told him. "More about the mist than the sun, doesn't gather like it should. Currents run strange. No mist or not enough mist, ships can't fly."

"There are places that run both thick and thin. As you said, currents and tributaries run between them, across all the Lanes. For the most part they are to be avoided," Quill added.

"Like the Edge," Nel said quietly. "And the Morgana. The Fata Morgana."

Damn, but I don't like where they took their name from. Not that I like anything about this.

"But they are colder," Sharpe said, still stuck on the concept. "Shouldn't we be feeling that?"

"You feel heat in the black from the hot ones?" Nel asked him pointedly.

"No," Sharpe admitted.

"I crack your head harder than I thought back in Vice?" Nel asked him. "Or you just trying to play the part of jabbering cabin girl till I get mine back?"

"Six of one and a half-dozen of the other," Sharpe grinned. "Just think, when it's done there can be two of us. Can get matching tattoos and do our hair the same, won't be able to tell us apart."

"No," Jack said immediately.

"I agree," Quill said almost as quickly. "And I do not like agreeing with Jack. Nor does Jack like it when I agree with him."

"Stop making us agree, Sharpe," Jack warned him. "Kelpie's right, don't like him. Never did."

Sharpe gave Nel a helpless look. She had no sympathy. Even though he had done the impossible. She couldn't recall Quill and Jack ever agreeing on anything.

Hells, don't like it any more than they do.

"What is your plan?" Quill asked her, directing the conversation to something more meaningful. "Shall we engage them head on? It has worked so wonderfully for us in the past."

"Helpful thoughts, Quill," Nel reminded him.

"In truth, I am not so attached to this vessel," the Kelpie admitted. "I would weep no tears should you order ramming speed."

"Be crying on the inside, I know, Quill," Nel winked at him. "You're close, but oh so far."

"Enlighten me," he said huffily. "You have a plan. There is always a plan. Often it is a maddening, illogical fallacy of a plan.

Sometimes it is swill, the kind found at the bottom of a bottle, but there is always a plan."

"You want to hear this plan, Loveland?"

"Yes."

"Then stop talking rot about my plans."

"Is that an order?" Quill asked. "A captain's order, perhaps?"

"No captains," Nel scowled.

"Then I will continue to voice my concerns about your inane concepts of what a plan should be," Quill said.

Damnit. More points for Quill.

Instead of using Quill's maps, as the area was sparsely charted in any case, Nel stood on the brightwork, toes hanging over the edge of the black. She pointed at the curve of the mist, the faint outlines of banks where it had floated away enough to form up in density. It was not unlike how clouds formed.

"There," Nel pointed, careful not to throw herself off balance. She looked over her shoulder at her crew. Just the three of them. *Two really . . . and Sharpe.* In the background she could see Stoker's people, not quite able to bring herself to think of them as crew yet.

"The mist is denser there where it coils. We take the long route, circumspect, take our time and make sure they don't spot us. Stay to where the mist is thick."

"There are rays in the mist," Quill pointed out. "An unusual number."

He was right, Nel hadn't seen them clearly but had sighted the giant shadows kiting through the miasma. She could hear their songs and crooning too.

"Not here for the rays, here for Violet and the *Morgana*. Once we're above them, we dive."

"Dive," Quill repeated. "We are back to the ramming?"

"Not exactly. Just need to get us closer, give us the right angle. Jack, want you on the crane. Sharpe, you and me, we're in the tender."

The three were silent while they took this in.

"Am I correct," Quill was the first to respond, "believing that you intend to board the *Morgana . . .* from a bubble?"

"You are correct, Mister Quill."

"This is the ship that shot us down last time we encountered it. Left us floating in a cracked glass ball. And you intend to . . ."

"Irony, Loveland, explain it to you someday."

"This new-found fondness you have for throwing people overboard is irony."

"I'm staying on the ship?" Jack asked.

"Need you on it, so yeah," Nel told him.

"What happens after? You coming back?"

"Plan to, need you waiting and hiding. Cut the angle right, Quill. Enough so that Jack can throw us where we need to be but keep your time in the big drop to as short as you can. You can do that, right?"

"Of course I can . . . yes, I can do that. We will need to hoist all sails before we . . . and then . . . yes, I can do it. But there is a problem. You see it, even Jack sees it."

"Be getting out the same way we go in," Nel told him. "Need you to watch for us and come gets us after."

Quill craned his neck, squinting at the grey outline of the *Fata Morgana*. "And should they see us?"

"Won't be looking for us, not at first. Whole point in this place is that you're not meant to be able to sneak up on them. Not expecting many on watch."

"That is an Alliance ship," Quill reminded her. "There *will* be lookouts."

"Quill's right," Sharpe said. "And that ship . . . Nel, it's big. Twisted. It could take days to find Violet in there even if it wasn't full of people who are going to shoot us on sight."

"This is the plan," Nel said. "Unless someone has a better idea?"

No one did.

"So long as I'm staying on the ship, don't care what you do," Jack said.

"That hurts my feelings, Jack," Sharpe told him.

Quill grumbled something, but he didn't repeat it so anyone could understand him.

"Do you remember the Fata Morgana?"

Violet frowned. "The ship? This ship?"

"No, apologies," Raines shook his head in a negative. "I should have been more clear. The Morgana itself, that which lies at the centre."

Violet frowned. The words were familiar. The idea conjured

up images, sensations. But . . . no.

"I don't."

"A pity. Still, that first trip was many years ago. Perhaps that memory is buried deeper yet."

They were alone in the workshop again, if one didn't count the Mandragora, silently going about their inscrutable duties. The only noise came from her relentless tapping. Violet stared at her fingers on the trestle table between them. Fingers drumming that same pattern, again and again. *Tap, tap, tap.* Mindless repetition. Whenever her attention wandered she would find herself doing it.

Or am I? Which one of us? It's become hard to tell.

"I have . . . gaps," she said, to break the silence. "Holes, blanks where I know things should be. Things I believe I should know, but it's like someone told me about them. Second-hand memories."

"You have experiences like this? Perhaps with the golem?" Raines looked at her from raised brows. Concern or curiosity, she couldn't tell.

"No, not like this. That was different."

"Even your time in the black? Until we found you again?"

"Like a dream. A nightmare. Until I woke up."

She looked down, at her hand, the whole body, so unfamiliar. So wrong. But better than what had come before. The black, the falling . . .

"I worry I'm still not awake," she said honestly, grimacing at the tremor in her voice. How quiet she was. "Still half asleep, not sure if I might drift away, or wake up somewhere . . . somewhere . . ."

The ship shuddered around them, a sudden jolt accompanied by a drop in her stomach. A sharp course correction to avoid something in the black. Glasses rattled on the shelves and the furniture shifted. She grabbed for the arms of her chair, fighting down the blind panic the sudden turbulence threw up.

It was over in a moment. The Mandragora tending the room unfrozen, resuming their duties.

"You are still with us?" Raines watched her carefully.

She nodded, not trusting words. Slowly, she relaxed her hands.

"I see there is still some ways to go, some remnants. Perhaps it will always be so. But I imagine you will become more fluent in this body. Such a remarkable transition. Unique, so far as I am aware."

She grimaced. "Distractions, instinct. Sleep and dreams. They all . . . all triggers."

"I see." Raines considered. "Do you recall the announcement after my return from the Edge? The discussions that followed? Such controversy."

"I remember the surprise."

"Yes?"

"People believed you. That was a surprise."

"I came bearing evidence. Why should they not? Evidence and explanations."

"People never believe the prophets. Not when they speak of doom."

"This world is doomed," Raines motioned towards the window. The triple layers of glass, glazed and bolted between them and the outside. The world they floated above and its cold sun.

"It was doomed before we arrived. You just hastened the end. Besides, what was the alternative? To let it spread?" she asked.

"That is the answer they have come to in the High. How to avoid their fate. To flee and spread to other worlds. They think they can save everyone."

"They think no such thing. All the ships in the Lanes, it will never be enough. It was never going to be enough."

"It will be. For some. Those who know how to survive."

"They don't know. Those people on the world below. You brought *her* here. To do it again."

"The fog would have been here soon anyway. They would never have survived it." Raines smiled. "We know how to survive, don't we, my dear?"

Violet didn't answer, tapping her fingers. Her gaze was fixed on the outside, through the porthole. The black outside, faint and wispy around the cold sun. But that would change soon.

"Violet?" Raines called out to her.

The girl shrugged. "No."

"ALL OF YOU feeling that?" Stoker asked, shuffling in place to turn around. "Or is it just me feeling my skin peel off?"

"That is disgusting," Quill said.

"No, I feel it too," Nel said. The hairs on the back of her hand were standing up, alive and writhing. Tingling all over, like she was standing too close to Quill. But the Kelpie was distant enough and wasn't using his powers, too focused on making sure they cleared the thin edge of the miasma. And the higher they rose, the deeper into the mist bank, the stronger the feeling became.

Quill had been right and nervous about the rays, they'd been buffeted once or twice when one had strayed too close. Dark shapes in the mist, a breeze where there shouldn't have been one, and the song of the black.

This was something else.

She recognised it now.

"Quill!" she yelled in alarm. "Envelope! We're meshing!"

She couldn't see anything, just dense, roiling mist. It parted like water when it struck their own envelope, but was so thick there was nothing visible a dozen feet out. They'd chosen this direction for that reason, it was already haunting them. Nel looked for the telltale, the shimmer where another envelope might be or where it might be joining them.

Timbers were shaking, the whole mainmast creaked. The wind was turning, no longer under Quill's control. The ship was in danger. Whatever was out there was bigger than them.

Much bigger.

There were voices in the mist, she realised. Shouting. Orders. Hails.

"Hold!" She raised both hands to her mouth to yell. "All hands stop. Stop!"

Dead or alive, sailors still turned the world blue. The deck and rigging came alive with words as sails were reefed. Quill brought the wind to a head, leaving them in irons, before throwing the brakes on. The ship tilted forward at the sudden change in direction, the half sails flapping before they caught. The crew held fast, all of them waiting.

"Quill," Nel called out, loud enough to be heard. "Give us a breeze. Starboard side."

The Kelpie did his trick, a gust of thaumatically created wind tearing down the flank of the ship, blowing a passage in the mist.

The *Mangonel Falling* was alongside them. The name emblazoned and garish as ever, man-high letters taller than Nel when up close. And they were up close. Half a hundred cannon stared down at them. A broadside that wouldn't just cripple their ship, splintering masts and tearing holes in sail. At this range it would kill them all, riddle them with splinters and debris. A sailor who took a direct shot would be the lucky one.

There were sailors lining the deck above, looking down on them. Close enough to make out faces. Heathen was there, because of course she was. She'd been waiting for them. Her crew were already preparing a gangway. Not just a boarding plank, an actual bridge lowered on ropes to cross between the two ships. There was no permission asked, no threats or ultimatums. There was no need.

And everybody knew it.

"YOU UNDERSTOOD MY message," Heathen said, hands clasped in front of her. The three of them sat in the captain's cabin, facing her. Nel and Sharpe at Heathen's request. Quill because he'd insisted. Heathen was alone. Her crew waited outside, under orders to do nothing unless provoked.

Nel trusted Stoker to keep his lot under control. It was only Jack that gave her concern. For now he'd barricaded himself in the galley. A last stand holdout. Everyone was content with the stalemate.

"What took you so long?"

Sharpe's fingers drummed on the table. It was the only response. His nervous habit.

"What do you want?" Nel asked when she saw Quill about to launch into some tirade.

Heathen blinked at her. Slow, liquid blinks, one set of eyelids then two. "What do you want?" her former captain repeated at Nel.

"I'm here for my crew," Nel said. "The ones you haven't killed yet."

Narrowing eyes. *A hit.*

"How many of mine are dead because of you?" Heathen asked.

"Didn't take you long to acquire another ship," Sharpe pointed out.

"Nor did it take you long to return to your usual position," Heathen retorted. "Tell me, do you come at your master's beckon or is it some basic drive instilled in you? A seasonal migration perhaps? You know what he is? Both of you?" This last was to Nel and Quill.

"We know," Nel said. "He told us. Don't care."

"Good," Heathen dismissed the issue. "Then we need say no more on that. But you realise why your escape failed."

Sharpe looked confused. "What do you mean?"

"You were betrayed."

His face hardened. "I wouldn't call the golem a betrayal. Violet lost control of it. That thing . . ."

"She never had control," Heathen said, watching him critically. "And the golem did what it was told, what it wanted to. The only surprise is that you managed to survive, let alone escape. Not everyone was so fortunate."

"Violet is why we're here," Sharpe said.

"I gathered that. I was not talking of your erstwhile cabin girl."

"You talk too much," Quill told her.

Heathen's eyes snapped to him. "And you are a fool. If you had listened to me back on Vice instead of—"

Quill rose up, leaning over the table. "When I saw you with that same creature? I regret only that—"

"Enough," Nel told them. She didn't raise her voice, but did reach out to pull Quill back. Then to Heathen, "You obviously want to talk. So talk. Say your piece."

"Very well," Heathen cast one more wary look at Quill before beginning. "You made a mistake, Chanel. Not finishing off the Guildswoman. That's where this all started."

"Quill hit her with an anchor," Nel said. "Dropped her and the golem both into the black."

"And there lies the problem," Heathen said. "The golem. We . . . recovered it. After."

"Figured as much. Surprised it still works," Nel scowled.

"It works because its master survived. Scarlett, her name, I believe."

"No," Nel said flatly. "She's dead."

"I said survived. I didn't say alive."

"Hells," Nel muttered. She looked around the cabin. All the drink was gone. She'd made sure of that.

"I don't understand," Quill said.

"Golem worked 'cause Scarlett made it work, Quill," Sharpe explained. "When you sent her for a long walk some of her survived inside Onyx."

"Some," Heathen confirmed. "A fragmented, tormented, insane part."

"And you took her aboard," Quill sneered. "More the fool."

Heathen sighed. "Yes. More the fool. She made her intentions known. We arranged a meeting, a transfer. With her Guild associates. At Port Border."

Quill made a strangled sound. His eyes almost bulging out of his head.

"What?" Nel demanded, twisting in her seat. "Quill, what? What do you know?"

"The girl," Quill gritted. "Border. She thought she saw . . . it. The golem. I dismissed her claims. Paranoia."

"Idiot," Heathen told him.

"Enough of that to go around," Nel glared at them both. "What happened? Everyone start filling in the gaps here before I start making gaps in people's faces."

"The rest merely follows," Heathen said. "The girl encountered the golem at Port Border. What was left of Scarlett, inside, attempted to take control of her. Possess her. In the same way it did the golem. An opportunity presented itself. Perhaps she was fixated on the girl, perhaps it was just a suitable . . . replacement. It was not a very successful attempt."

"I don't believe you," Nel said. "Something like that had happened to Vi, we'd have known. I'd have known."

Heathen studied her closely. "Would you?"

"Yes."

"Nel," Sharpe interrupted.

"What?"

"How'd they keep finding you?"

"Dumb luck, at Border," she said. "The dumbest of bad luck."

"And after?"

"How?" she demanded of Heathen.

"Signs were left," Heathen told her. "A trail. Breadcrumbs, if you like."

"Violet," Sharpe said.

"An unsuccessful attempt. But a connection was made. It did not do what was left of the Guildswoman any favours. She was unable to communicate after Port Border. A creature of simple rage, for the most part."

"Yet you kept pursuing us," Nel said.

"Do you wish to hear the rest?" Heathen asked her. "Once you hear it all you can throw your accusations around as you like. But I will not be reprimanded before."

"And after?"

"We will have words."

"Talk," Nel said. "Tell me about the *Fata Morgana*. How the hells did we end up getting chased by a Guildsman and the Gunner's Daughter?"

"Quinn is a lapdog," Heathen dismissed the woman with a growl. "A fearsome reputation propped up on a vindictive streak the wrong people saw fit to encourage. The woman is not even trusted to be master of her own ship. Arlin Raines is master, commander, and architect of the *Morgana*."

"Sharpe mentioned him," Nel said. "An inventor for the Alliance brass."

"A Guildsman," Heathen told her. "Very senior. Not someone to be trifled with. Not someone . . . you say no to."

"That includes you?"

Heathen nodded. "You would find his hand fitting the glove behind many things, Chanel. He is someone I would happily never hear word of again. Someone I thought I was quit of."

"He was your contact to hand over the golem," Nel said.

"Nel," Sharpe said quietly, "he *made* that golem."

"Wasn't the only thing was it," Nel looked down.

Sharpe looked at her unhappily. "I wanted . . . I tried to tell you."

"Tell us what?" Quill glared at him.

"Never mind, Quill," Nel told him. "I said it didn't matter then and it don't matter now."

"And you said he did tell you," Heathen rasped.

"Said it didn't matter."

"That is something Raines would say. Very little matters to him. Golems, Draugr, ships that do not require crew or navigators," Heathen said. "These are the themes of his work. He has little love or attachment for people. Unless they intrigue him. What happened to your girl intrigued him greatly. He would see if the intrigue can be taken any further."

"She has a name," Quill growled at her.

"I have yet to hear you speak it."

"She's his own kind, Vi is," Nel said. "A Kitsune."

"That wouldn't matter. It doesn't matter. Be grateful, for your girl's sake, that they are in fact nothing alike."

"I want Vi back, doesn't matter what's happened to her. Maybe more because. But what do you want, Captain?" Nel asked her again. "You sent a message. Why?"

Heathen gave a slight smile. "I'm not your captain anymore, Chanel. I want Raines dead. For that I need you."

"Far as you knew we were dead."

"The killing blow came from the *Morgana*. We pursued you, yes, but for effect only. I saw your escape, a fact I chose to keep from Raines and Aristeia."

"Maybe. But I don't remember you ever needed help killing anyone," Nel reminded her.

"Raines is the reason behind much of that."

"What do you mean?"

"Misery. The orders for what happened, they came from him."

Vintage, Nel thought. *Not Misery.*

"That is . . . convenient," Quill spoke up.

"And what would you know of it?"

"I know the responsibility for what happened there that day lies with one person," Quill said.

"Cut away that which is sick so the whole might live," Heathen quoted at him. "Misery was sick, we could not risk that spreading to the rest of the High. Or is that not a tenet of your ways? The *old ways*?"

Quill hissed at her, baring teeth. He slammed something to the table between them. "Cut away?" he repeated. "You cut this from my captain's body!"

Heathen stared down at the deed, unflinching. "I believe that was what he intended."

"Hells of a long shot, Captain," Nel told her. "There was no way you could have known that would make it to me. Or that I'd figure out your message. It could have been months before anyone even took notice. *And* when you gave it to Sharpe he was still locked up."

"He was," Heathen agreed. "But he had escaped before. I trusted he would likely find his way back to you. If not, it was a worthwhile gambit."

"With little chance of paying off," Quill snorted. "All could have been long gone from here before we discovered your cipher.”

“The cipher was to lead you here.”

“To the cold sun. Why?”

“Because of what you were to see. The fact that you find us all still here is fortuitous, not intentional.”

“And if we hadn’t?” Nel asked.

“There were other options on the table,” Heathen told her.

“Why him?” Nel asked. “Why Castor?”

“And why not Violet?” Sharpe added.

“I feared the girl a lost cause. Or at least too far gone to be an acceptable risk. As I said, options. Thus the deed and its hidden map. If you had arrived later there would have been . . . signs.”

“You always did like your schemes, Captain,” Nel sighed.

“I was trying to make contact with you. I will not apologise for the means.”

“You were saying Raines had something to do with the fog,” Nel said. “With what happened there, at *Vintage*. You expect me to believe someone can cause that to happen?”

“Not the fog,” Heathen said. “What happened there was a plague. Nothing more or less. The actions taken to contain it, those were driven by him, by Arlin Raines.”

“There were no Guildsmen on the blockade at Vintage,” Nel allowed. “I would have heard of a seven-tailed Kitsune. Didn’t hear nothing.”

Heathen shrugged. “I have no evidence. But when you served under me, have you known me to be cruel?”

“Yes.”

“Needlessly so?”

Nel hesitated. “No.”

“I left the Alliance not long after you did,” Heathen told her. “As your companion says,” this to Quill, “there was only one face of what happened there.”

“Explain Marching to me,” Nel said. “Thatch. Rim. History repeats and to me it looked like nothing had changed.”

“No.”

“No what?”

“No, I will not explain, Chanel. I have said what I intended to say. You are the one who has to make a choice.”

Nel glared over the table at her former captain. There was something there. She could almost see it if not for the . . .

"Vintage," she said. "I remember afterwards. What you said."

Heathen gave her nothing back.

"Not the first and won't be the last, you said."

"This is irrelevant," Heathen told her.

"This is the last, isn't it," Nel guessed. "You left because you wanted out. And they pulled you back in. This is you trying to get out again."

"Craven," Quill muttered. But he looked away when Heathen faced him.

"We all have to live with ourselves," she said.

"Yeah," Nel said. "We do. Those of us still alive."

Heathen shrugged her shoulders at that. "There is one more thing," she looked at Sharpe, "you are familiar with Aristeia Quinn's sense of discipline?"

"Was on the blunt end of a few beatings," Sharpe said carefully.

"Woman likes to make examples," Nel said. "Her crew are loyal, because they know what happens to those that aren't."

"What do you mean?" Sharpe asked.

"An example was made after your escape," Heathen told him. "The young man who helped you. They set him adrift. Then fired on him."

Sharpe went very pale. Very quiet. Mouth open but no words. Trembling.

"And Violet?" Nel asked, because she had to. Her heart had lurched at the implications, though her mind was already reeling torrential thoughts in with icy cold logic. *She's fine, has to be fine. Or there's no reason to go through with this. Except revenge. Maybe Heathen's counting on that. Or maybe she's about to lie to my face. Hells damnit, stop thinking, stop thinking, woman!*

"Alive," Heathen said. "If not well. As I said, she intrigues Raines. The experiment continues. Now the question is, what will you do about it?"

"Nothing's changed," Nel said. She looked around at all of them. "Violet is crew. I'm getting her back."

"And Raines? Aristeia?" Heathen asked her.

"If they get in my way, I'll handle it," Nel said. "But I won't do your wet work for you."

"The *Fata Morgana* is a remarkable ship, as you have gathered," Heathen said. "It is a match, perhaps more, for either of ours. Perhaps both."

"Thin mist, enough to negate your powers," Quill accused her. "You are afraid of a fight that is fair."

"Of one I could lose, yes. Inside the influence of a cold sun or the ship itself, thaumatics are mostly useless. Outside, restored to working order, then yes, I doubt the capabilities of this ship are comparable to the *Fata Morgana's*. Only a fool without any options enters a conflict they cannot be confident of winning. But with you, perhaps that is possible."

Heathen looked at Nel once more. "You want your girl back. I want Raines and that ship removed from the board. And we have little time before they are gone, before everything here is gone."

Nel said it, for the last time. "What do you want from me?"

ABOARD THE *DANCERS Poignard* Jack worked with Nel and Sharpe to make the tender ready. It turned out there was but one glass sphere aboard the small ship. Which only reinforced what a one-way trip this was going to be.

"How much of that did you believe?" Sharpe asked Nel as they fitted the crane onto the bubble.

"Some," Nel shrugged. "Enough."

"She was lying."

"Everybody lies."

"But you still agreed," Sharpe pushed.

"You've been lying to me since I met you," Nel reminded him, brushing hair out of her eyes. It had gotten long again. Dry and brittle from hard living too. *Need to tie it back, be embarrassing to be brought down because I can't see nothing.* "Still here because of you, aren't I?"

"Thought you were here because of Violet. Besides, it's different when I do it."

"How so?"

"I'm prettier for one. And I tell it better."

Nel actually chuckled. Sharpe didn't, man was still glum after what he'd learnt. Banter must be habit.

"Not your fault," she told him. "Wasn't your idea to get rescued. Girl did that all on her own and whoever signed up to help did so of their own free will."

Sharpe regarded her sceptically. "I hope you hear yourself talking, sometimes."

"Never listen to myself. That's everyone else's job."

"Ball's ready," Jack called out to them. "You going now?"

"Trying to get rid of us, Jack?" Sharpe asked him.

"Yeah. You talk too much. The both of you."

"Just gonna be you and Quill here after we're gone," Sharpe reminded.

"Naw, got those grey fellas now. Good silent types. Don't drink much though. Working on that."

Sharpe shuddered. Nel gave him a quizzical look.

"Horrible thought," he admitted. "Think Stoker might leak if he drank anything."

"You didn't need to share that with me."

"You asked."

"I did not."

"You looked like you wanted to ask."

"Not the same."

"Doin' it again," Jack complained. "Talking."

"Shut up, Jack," Nel told him. "Lend me a tie, before we go."

Jack reached up and undid one of his long braids, handing over the strip of tanned hide that had bound it. "Am I getting this back?"

"If we make it back."

"So I ain't getting it back."

Nel scowled at him as she bound her hair in a sailor's ponytail.

"There's tar on that," Sharpe told her. "You're getting it all greasy."

"It's meant to be, you hogfish," Nel rolled her eyes, securing her hair. She wiped her hands off on her breeches. "Quill, come to say goodbye?"

"I have," the Kelpie approached, his head twisting from side to side. There was no sign of the *Mangonel* again but that hadn't stopped Quill looking. "I want one thing understood."

"What's that?"

"That I am in charge. Until you return." He looked meaningfully at Jack.

"Ship's not going anywhere without you," Nel conceded.

"Good," Quill was mollified. "Do not take too long. And do not lose *her*." He held out a pair of carabineers to Sharpe, joined by a length of cord. Sharpe took them, briefly clasping hands with the Kelpie.

"There is a certain symmetry to this." Sharpe held open the hatch to the bubble.

Nel adjusted her belt one last time, making sure the fastening strap on her wand was in place. *Don't need to lose another one.* She had a knife tucked into her boot as well, a midshipman's dirk Stoker had provided.

"Make sure you both come back," Quill told them, pacing in front of the bubble, hands clasped behind him, stooped, tail lashing. He was a bundle of nervous energy, almost ready to bolt. Still with the searching too.

"You know what to do if we don't," Nel told him.

"I am not being left alone with Jack," Quill snapped at her. "That will not be happening."

"Good," Sharpe said. "Then if this rescue goes south you be sure the next one don't."

"Ready when you are, Jack." Nel pushed Sharpe inside, climbing in after. "See you both soon."

She shut the hatch before either could reply.

Chapter 24

THEY WERE FALLING at the same rate but at different angles. Quill, Jack, Stoker, all those left on the ship vanished out of sight. It was a strangely skeletal look, almost ghostly, as the sails were drawn and stowed, bundled against the stays by Draugr linesmen. They worked well, Nel thought. The ship started to fall away, and with her back against the curve of the glass, Nel couldn't follow them anymore. She resisted looking down. There was little they could do now, other than trust that Jack and Quill had done their jobs right.

"Nel," Sharpe said, grimacing with the same falling sensation she was feeling. "How do we even get onto the *Morgana*?"

"Jump," she told him. "You waited till now to ask that?"

"Too much talk going on," he said. "Figured it was best just to get on with it."

"No other way," Nel said. "Either we miss the ship and it's moot, or we come too close and smash into them. You don't want to be in here if that happens."

"So we cast the hatch open and get sucked out?"

Nel nodded. "Yes."

"And if we jump and miss our landing?"

"Don't do that."

"Right. Only . . . aw, hells," Sharpe whispered, staring through the glass cage they were travelling in.

Nel saw it too. They'd misjudged their fall, badly. The *Fata*

Morgana wasn't where they'd thought it was, it wasn't even where she would have sworn it was a minute ago. They were going to miss it, by a lot.

"Get the hatch," she told Sharpe. There were no other words, they both knew they had only a few moments to get this right. Sharpe took the turn-wheel, feet set against the inside of the sphere. If he opened it too soon they would miss their chance. He looked at Nel to say when that chance was.

Nel grabbed onto the rope tethering the two of them together, a thin and fragile thing. But it had held her fast on more than one occasion. Once even with Sharpe, what seemed so long ago.

A sort of symmetry.

A few hundred feet now. There was a decent supply of air inside, it wouldn't all gush out at once. Though she wasn't sure how the outside environment, the lack of mist, might affect that. *Faster or slower? Probably faster. Hells, no second chances here.*

"Open it," she ordered. Sharpe swung the wheel, the hatch flew wide open, and even braced as he was it sucked Sharpe out after it. The rope tugged and Nel followed right after.

She caught the wheel with one hand, ripping skin from her palm, almost doing the same for her shoulder. Wind rushed past her, cold and instantly icy, a blizzard to go with the cold sun.

Too far, still too far!

She could see the *Morgana* now, closer, bigger, still too far. Her fingers were starting to slip. Sharpe dangled below her. He was bent back almost in half, dangling from the rope around his waist, unable to look up at her. Caught in the same flurry, just the one hand supporting the both of them.

It wasn't enough. She let go.

The last breath of air leaking from the bubble pushed them away, then the sense of falling was gone. Just drifting. Nel closed her eyes, already feeling frost starting to form over her lashes and eyelids.

So close. Too far . . .

And then they were falling again, Sharpe first, and the line went taut again, pulling her down. Nel's eyes snapped open and she tried to twist, looking for which way they were going to land. She barely had time to sight the incoming wall of metal, huge and filling her vision, when her shoulder slammed into it followed immediately by her back. She half rolled with the impact when the rope pulled her up short. She hadn't even seen Sharpe strike the hull first, pulled in by the *Fata Morgana's* envelope.

Nel rolled flat onto her back, arms out. She wanted to groan as the pain hit her but there was no air in her lungs. They were definitely inside the envelope, she was just winded.

Just winded.

She heard something beside her. Hysterical. Laughter. Choking, gasping laughter. She managed to roll her head to see Sharpe in the same spread and flatly prone position. His head rolled to face her, split wide by a grin.

"Hells, woman," he said. "You trying to kill me?"

Nel looked up at the black. Sharpe was right.

She started laughing too.

THEY FOUND A hatch after venturing forth onto the hull, taking their steps slowly. Nel could imagine her footsteps must sound like the inside of a bell on the other side. There were several ways in, but they chose one a third of the way down the deck, though Nel disliked the dual-side decking arrangement. It was nothing she hadn't heard of before, or seen, but the sheer aesthetic of it rubbed her wrong. It wasn't a ship they were standing on, it was a metal box.

"Any idea where this will take us?" she asked Sharpe.

"No," he shook his head. "Didn't let me out for walks much. The bow and stern should be the busy parts though. The midship, this is our best bet."

Nel nodded, finding herself taking shallow breaths as Sharpe twisted the hand wheel open. Possibly it could be locked from the inside but it seemed nobody had bothered.

Because nobody would be daft enough to try what we just did, that's why.

They exchanged a look as Sharpe cracked the seal on their entry. Sharpe's face must have mirrored hers, tight-lipped and pale, already wincing against the shouts of alarm and discovery. But nothing happened. He pulled the hatch the rest of the way open.

Sharpe went first, taking the ladder that was revealed inside then dropping the last few feet to the floor. He landed lightly, crouching all the way down. One hand on his weapon, the other poised on the ladder for the first sign of trouble.

They came rushing from both sides, but first the corridor lit up with a flash of wand fire. Sharpe dropped flat to avoid it and just barely got to his feet when the first man tackled him. A Korrigan, built squat and low to the ground, almost took Sharpe down. Two more piled on, going for his arms. Somehow he fought them off and was scrambling for the ladder. Nel started to reach for him, pull him to safety but other arms reached up first. Wrapping around him, pulling him down. Sharpe stretched out with both arms, not for her but for the wheel lock, slamming the hatch closed. Her last glimpse was of him crashing back inside the ship.

"Oh, the hells with that!" Nel shouted to the empty deck. She ripped the hatch back open, jumping straight down into the rolling fracas. Her elbow connected with someone's head and she found herself atop two collapsing bodies. There was no room for wandplay in the cramped confines, only knees and fists. She could barely see who she was struggling with, other than it wasn't Sharpe. Someone's neck wrapped under her arm. Slammed back against the wall, that body slipping limply from her grasp, dead or unconscious or broken, no way of telling. Someone connected with her, to the face, the light she saw wasn't real. Yelling.

And then they were running.

Dashing down the corridor, footsteps ringing out. *Inside of a bell, never lose them now.* Twists and turns, Sharpe's hand on hers, pulling her forward. Then he stumbled, buckled at the knees, rolling and coming up again. She almost ran into him, then bright, hot pain in her knee. She went down too.

She saw him, looking back. The Luscan from Vice, dual armed, two wands dropping sparks, glowing hot in his hands. He'd winged them both. Another step towards them as she reached for her weapon, arm drawn back, a lazy roll of the shoulder.

The lights went out.

"YOU NEED TO come with me."

"You sound angry," Violet said to Kaspar. Looked angry too.

"Why do you think that is?"

"Because I got Brandon killed," Violet said simply.

Kaspar flinched, looked away. Biting down on his lip before he replied. "You shouldn't call him that. Only his friends called him that."

"I was his friend. Wouldn't have asked for his help otherwise."

"His help—" Kaspar started, then cut himself off. He stepped up to her, right in her face. "I heard you! Talking with Heathen, I heard you, Violet!"

She frowned at him. "Heard what? I never talked to Heathen, except when I got dragged in front of the captain."

"I saw you," he said harshly. "And you saw me, why the hells would you even bother denying it?"

Violet shook her head, then reached up to steady her glasses. She tried to think, but couldn't recall what he was talking about. "I don't know," she said. "Honest, Niko, I don't know what you mean."

Kaspar glared at her. He wanted to be angry, she realised. But was perplexed. She just didn't know what, other than it was somehow her fault.

"You need to come with me," he said, grabbing her arm. "Everyone's been called out, we're to meet on the gun deck."

Kaspar dragged her down the hallways, the twisting corridors of the *Fata Morgana*. They passed more crew, more marines, on their way. All of them headed to where they themselves were going. And there was a crowd gathered. Kaspar pushed them both through it.

"Skipper," Violet heard herself whisper. It couldn't be anyone else, the shock of hair red against the pallor of her skin, a match for the blood running down her face, almost drying and flaking like rust. The colours, so bright and vivid. Violet reached up, clawing the glasses off her face. She could hear her own breathing, harsh, laboured. The world was easier in grey, painted all in silver. Just like being belowdecks, the light of a glowstone. No need for the harshness.

She felt calmer now, different. Like rough waters, with someone else steering. It wasn't her concern. She just had to let it ride.

"Violet," Kaspar whispered to her, holding her arm. His grip was tight, she had to grab at his hand when the blood stopped flowing. White-knuckled hands she could feel.

You're alive.

Kaspar. Vaughn.

Skipper . . .

Oh no . . .

She wasn't alone. Sharpe was with her, bound and tied again, manacles around his wrists. Thrown down onto his knees and collapsed next to the skipper.

Why did you come back? Why didn't you stay away? You and the skipper.

Except she wasn't the skipper anymore. There was nothing left to be skipper of. No ship, no crew, no *Tantamount.* She was just Nel Vaughn. All alone now.

Aristeia Quinn was there, the skipper of the *Fata Morgana.* The Gunner's Daughter. Flanked by marines and looking down at her prisoners. Raines too, standing further back, safely away. Mors flanked him like a good guard dog, watching.

"I expected better."

Nel looked up, face battered and bloody, strands of hair stuck to her face. "You *expected* us. Meant it to be a surprise."

"It was a careless plan. Even if we hadn't been warned, you would have been found as soon as you came aboard. What did you hope to accomplish?"

Warned? Who warned us? Them . . . who warned . . .

Nel smiled, thin and sickly, teeth still covered in a film of blood. She'd been hit hard. "You took my ship from me, *Skipper.* My crew. Thought I'd . . . return the favour."

"You were a commendable officer once," Aristeia said. "A pity."

"Yeah."

The first mate waved to Mors. "Deal with this."

"You want a fight?" Nel struggled to her feet before anyone could take action. "I'll fight *you.* Here, now, I'll fight you. Draw your damned weapon and show me you can still use it."

Aristeia measured her up and down, considering. "A duel? Why? What would be the point?"

Nel turned her head and spat, staining the deck crimson. "You're a coward."

"Are you trying to goad me, Vaughn? You'll have to try harder than that." The first mate turned to go, putting her back to Nel.

"Afraid of a few more scars? *I* expected better." Nel pushed herself to her feet, hands still bound in front of her. A sailor moved to restrain her, and she elbowed the man in the face, her eyes never leaving the first mate. The marine holding Sharpe moved to help restrain Nel. Aristeia stopped but didn't turn to face her.

"All the stories I ever heard about you, the great dread captain who's not a captain. Child of the black, gunner's daughter, hero of the Bells. It's all rot. I got the drop on you *and* your little friend back on Vice."

Nel took a step forward. "And I heard you cried like a little girl," she said, "when they held you down to paint a shellback on you—"

"Someone put that woman down," Aristeia snapped, turning, moving to do so herself. She charged straight past Sharpe who chose that moment to stand up himself. He raised his bound hands high and looped them over the woman. She started to struggle, half drawing her weapon. Sharpe grabbed for it, dropping his hands and wresting it from Aristeia's. He stabbed down, triggering the discharge and both their bodies lit up.

A miniature lightning storm enveloped them both, and the *Fata Morgana*'s first mate went into convulsions. The wand flew through air, and with the slightest nudge from Sharpe, straight into Nel's outstretched hands. She didn't waste the moment, aiming directly for the captain in a savage whipping gesture.

Raines, to his credit, did not flinch, did not move. But his bodyguard did, stepping into the path, smooth as silk. The Luscan half-breed caught the wand fire on one tip, sending it flying off to the side. His face cracked in a predator's savage grin.

Violet could see Nel grind her teeth in frustration, squeezing the wand hilt tight. Like Violet, she'd only ever seen a Guildswoman pull that trick before. But Nel had seen it, knew what it meant. Mors drew his second duelling wand, holding them crossed in front of himself, daring her to try again.

Aristeia Quinn's limp body slumped to the deck with a thud, the only sound. Smoke drifted off of her. Sharpe stood tall above her, still wreathed in electricity. His body shook but he didn't go down. Surrounded by the *Fata Morgana*'s crew, all of them with weapons bared. No one moved to touch him yet.

"Do you want to persist in this pointless charade, my dear?" Raines asked, stepping around Mors. "I despise duels. The bravado, the pantomime. But very well, have it your way. Ensign, cut her free. And someone do see to your first mate."

Aristeia was already being attended to by marines. Scorch

marks and blisters marred her already scarred skin. Worse for it, she made it to her feet, unsteady and supported, but still standing.

"Captain," she called out.

"Enough, later," Raines ignored her. "Let us be done with this. Mors."

The Luscan twirled his matched wands eagerly. Nel barely acknowledged the young ensign stepping up to her until the knife flashed between her wrists. Severed rope hit the deck.

The skipper shoved Kaspar away fiercely, growling something Violet couldn't make out. He returned hurriedly to where Violet was standing.

"She doesn't like you very much," she said to him.

His response was tight, pale and choked. "We killed her crew."

And you had no idea.

Did she?

Violet focused on the upcoming duel, thoughts running through her mind. "Mors commanded the cannon during the battle. Do you think *she* knows that?"

She hadn't spoken loudly but Nel's head turned to her slowly, her eyes dead and flat. She returned that gaze to Mors Coldstream.

"She knows now," Mors said, his grin becoming even wider. "Thank you, girl, you just made this interesting."

"I've heard a lot about you," Nel said to Mors, loudly. "I wanted your captain, but I'll settle for you first."

"You were lucky, before, on Vice. Think you'll be so again?" Mors laughed. At the same time Nel whipped her wand in a horizontal cross, stepping forward close behind the salvo.

"Hells!" Violet heard Kaspar curse beside her. Nel closed the distance between herself and Mors in a matter of heartbeats, and the duellist reeled, sending her attacks left and right, forcing the crew to scurry for cover. Kaspar dragged Violet down.

When she looked up again, Mors and Nel were pressed almost against each other. The duellist was panicked now. He still ducked and weaved as the woman lashed out with her wand in close like it was a knife but he seemed to lack the ability to match her at this range.

Violet saw it coming, even if Mors didn't. Nel dropped down to the deck, taking a knee as his backhand arced over her head, and then she came back up, leading with her fist. Her punch nearly lifted Mors off his feet when it connected with his chin. He staggered, dropping a wand. Nel hit him again and he dropped like a stone. She stood over him, wand raised for the killing blow.

The *Fata Morgana's* first mate stepped in then, grabbing Nel's wrist with one hand and smashing it back into her face. She stumbled, tripped, fell. Aristeia stamped down on her hand, trapping the wand against the deck.

"Hells," Kaspar whispered again.

"*That* was well fought," Aristeia said. "Clever."

The woman was breathing hard, still injured herself, yet she'd intervened. For Mors. Violet was, she had to admit, surprised. The two women were a lot alike.

Aristeia motioned to her crew, and they swooped in and picked up Nel. She struggled briefly but gave it up.

The first mate assisted Mors as he rose groggily to his feet, the two leaning on each other. "I truly am disappointed," she said to Nel. "You could have been great, the kind of officer I'd want to serve with. Unfortunately for you, Mors' aim with cannon is better than his tavern brawling."

"Skipper, no!" Kaspar took a step forward, his voice raised in protest.

"Step back, Ensign," Aristeia glanced over her shoulder, eyes narrowed.

Kaspar took another step forward, making a strangled sound, still reaching. For Nel, but she wouldn't look at him.

You couldn't stop this last time. Why should this time be any different?

"Ensign Vaughn, I will not tell you again. Step back!"

Nel showed no reaction. Sharpe was the most telling, looking from Nel to Kaspar and back again. Violet could imagine the connection he was making. Saw the words his mouth formed silently. She knew exactly how he felt. Seemed so obvious after the fact.

Would knowing have made any difference?

It would have, wouldn't it.

Too late now.

CHAPTER 25

THE CREW OF the *Morgana* set them in front of one of the wand batteries, rolled back and out of the way to expose the raised port. Open to the black. And there truly was nothing else outside, not so much as a hint of miasma to break the black. And by a fluke of their angle, no stars either. Just black.

"Any preferences?" Mors grinned. "Ladies first or would the condemned like to buy his captain a few precious breaths more of sweet, sweet life?"

Sharpe chuckled, rolling his head so he could look Mors in the eye. "She's not my captain. Not anyone's captain."

"You'll be going first then?"

Sharpe shrugged. "You talk too much. Always annoyed me. Thought that tap to the jaw might have quieted some."

"There is no before or after, Mors," Raines berated him. "Bad enough we're wasting one sphere on them. There are quicker and cleaners ways to do this. This showmanship—"

"Sets the proper example," Aristeia growled. "Mors, do it."

To Nel's surprise, their restraints were removed. There was no way to take advantage of this fact though, not with half the crew assembled to watch the spectacle.

Might even be more than half, if what Sharpe said is right, about them not needing so many hands. Tough-looking bastards though, marines and shellbacks all of them. All except . . .

"Did you know your brother was aboard?" Sharpe asked her,

rubbing at his wrists. They were raw and bloodied from the restraints. Starting to resemble Jack's.

"No."

"Feel like I should have known, guessed maybe," Sharpe said. "I'm sorry. If I'd known . . . suspected . . . I would have said."

"No reason you should have," Nel still avoided looking at Dominik. "It's a big realm out there. Could never have guessed . . ."

Doesn't even use his name any more. Ha. Guess we have that in common.

"I presume you have a ship out there," the first mate said. Hard to tell where all the scars and burns and scowls ended on her face. Had to be mostly rage keeping her upright. "I won't insult you by asking where. We'll find it. I will ask how you got aboard. I am that curious."

"Fired a bubble straight at you," Sharpe told her, before Nel could stop him. "Tell you the truth, lady, had to swim the last part. Wasn't fun."

Aristeia's brows lifted. "Truly? I am impressed. Your ship must be somewhere in the coreward bank then, above us. Thank you, that simplifies the search greatly."

Sharpe winced, casting an apologetic look at Nel. "Sorry."

"Idiot," she told him.

Nel turned away in disgust. *Always with the talking, running his mouth. Always!*

Her gaze found Violet, the first chance she'd had to really look at the girl.

It was a kick to the guts. The girl was different. Taller, older. Beaten. Hurt. She stood with Dominik, hands clasped in front of her. She didn't wear colours but her clothes had a military cut to them, Alliance cast-offs, sourced from the slop chest. She was cradling something in her hands, a ball, maybe. Rolling it back and forth. And she wore bifocals now, glasses.

The hells?

The glasses had a tint to them, pale red, almost pink. Rose.

Seen those before. Violet, lass, what happened . . .

I left you.

That's what happened.

"You look tired, my friend," Aristeia said to Mors. "Let me save you the effort. We'll dispense with our usual practice. They can retrieve their own tender. From out there."

Mors frowned, looking down at his own hand. It was shaking. Reluctantly, he nodded.

Aristeia waved to her marines. "Do it. Throw them to the black."

"Wait!" Raines stepped forward, holding up his hand to forestall the marines. "A moment, a moment yet."

Nel looked to Sharpe. Out of the corner of her eye she caught the look of distress on his face before it bristled into anger.

Anger. That's new.

It was the Kitsune, the captain, seven-tailed. Which was . . . impressive.

"Raines," she heard Sharpe mutter beside her.

Raines pushed his way through the crowd of sailors. Or rather they parted ways for him, if grudgingly.

"What is it, Raines?" the first mate asked. Nel caught a touch of irritation in her voice.

"This one," Raines pointed at Sharpe, "this one is mine. I still have a use for him."

"I ain't yours, you shifty little weasel." Sharpe was visibly restraining himself. Wands were already levelled at him. A decent shot and he'd be knocked straight out the gun port. Nel was in no rush to experience the black again so soon. Inevitable as it seemed right now.

"He's done," Aristeia told Raines. "And you're done with him. Caused enough trouble, the both of them."

"Got you good, didn't he?" Nel grinned, drawing a dirty look from the scarred mate. *Hells, can't resist either, can I? May as well get our shots in while we can.*

Raines was in no way deterred by the first mate's objections. "You are going to throw them overboard? Again? Fine, fine, I am not objecting to the what, merely the how. I want my protégé to do it."

"This is absurd," Mors told him.

"Then take a moment to appreciate that," Raines said. "Now I believe I gave you an order, Aristeia."

Dark storms on the first mate's face. *He's not in control here. Someone doesn't like it. Bad look in front of the crew? What does Raines have here? And his protégé? Does he mean . . .*

"The girl used to serve under this woman," Aristeia said pointedly.

"Exactly," Raines clasped his hands together, eyes fever bright. "That is exactly who she used to be. Let us see who she is now. Come here, little one."

Violet walked over, obediently. One hand fell to the side, still holding something. Nel saw Dominik's hand reach for her briefly, snatched back of his own accord. There were things going on here Nel couldn't take into account.

How much longer can this drag out for?

Raines was speaking with Violet, and the girl looked past him, towards Nel and Sharpe. It was impossible to meet her eyes through the glasses.

"This is bad," Sharpe said.

"Wait," Nel told him. "Let them."

"Yeah, sure."

The bell was ringing again, footsteps, but too loud for any one person to make. It would take a whole squad marching in perfect step to make the walls ring like that. The marine crew turned with Nel, watching the door as it squeezed through, turning sideways with barely a pause in step.

"Godsdamnit."

Onyx, still dark as the black. Headed for them. Headed for her.

That thing holds grudges.

"And here we are," Raines pronounced happily.

The crew were not so happy, wary glances exchanged, weapons held raised and ready. Mors and Aristeia faced the golem together, both to the side of Raines.

The hells is going on here?

"Crew's still jumpy," Sharpe explained. "Big rock tore through the ship last time."

"How?" Nel asked.

"Violet. She's . . . in control."

No. Didn't wanna believe it but . . .

"It's not Violet."

"If you would all humour me for but a moment longer," Raines announced to the crew. He put his hand on Violet's shoulder and pointed towards Nel and Sharpe.

"Kill them."

The golem thundered towards them, shaking the ship with every step.

The first mate was good. So too was her second, in fact the

whole damn crew. Most of Nel's attention was fixed on the golem, the thing trying to separate her head from her spinal column. It hesitated when she and Sharpe darted in opposite directions, giving Nel a moment to check her blindsides.

She saw the crew's reaction.

There was a brief moment when an object passed through the envelope at speed. A half second of warning when sound returned. Most of the crew heard it, an unmistakeable sound once you'd experienced it, of incoming fire. The first round hit the hull, further up-ship, the sound rippling out, followed immediately by a rainstorm of other impacts.

Then the real fire began. The heavy-bore weapons salvo arrived and the ship rocked, caught at an angle and set into a slow spin on its axis. Nel lost her footing, falling flat on the floor with all limbs spread. She was lucky. The next impact threw everyone else, including the golem, off their feet.

Mors was covering Aristeia's body with his own, then helping her up. No time for pride under attack. Mouths were moving but Nel couldn't hear the words. The crew responded without orders, rushing to guns and stations in other parts of the ship.

Violet, where's Violet?

Thrown off her feet like everyone else, facedown on the deck. The girl picked herself up, one hand cradling her face. The glasses had survived, cracked maybe. The girl staggered to her feet, staring at something in her hand. Nel saw it now, a globe, one she'd seen the captain with.

Horatio. My captain. Our captain. Vi, that belonged to his daughter, why did he . . .

Dominik was there, by Violet's side. Hands on her shoulders, helping her up. Violet stumbled as he lifted her, dropping the sphere. She grabbed for it and missed, and Dominik caught it where it rolled on the ground and her hand closed over his. Sparks flew where they touched, then not just sparks but a bright sheet of light, blue and white and crackling. And it didn't stop.

Sharpe grabbed Nel, throwing them both into the shadow of Onyx, which had fallen and showed no signs of getting up. The expanding wave of thaumatic energy, unmistakeable as anything else, washed over the deck. People cried out in pain; the metal under them buzzed with stinging electricity.

The two of them, her and Sharpe, peered over the chest of the golem. To her relief both Violet and Dominik were alive, centred at the nexus of what had just happened. Violet looked dazed, almost out on her feet and only held up by Dominik. Her brother was smoking. Parts of his uniform were charred and crisped, thin tendrils of smoke wafting but he seemed mostly unhurt.

How long has that bauble been leeching her? Just caught the edge of it and everything's quivery. Don't know if you meant it for that, Captain, but thank you.

Sharpe nudged her. "And now?"

"Same plan as before, get Violet!"

The golem stirred. Nel and Sharpe both scrambled away from it. Onyx caught sight of them and smashed one hand down on the spot where Sharpe had just been. Drunken and uncoordinated but no less dangerous for it.

Nel searched for and found Violet. The girl was fixated on them, and Nel could see the eyes now, even through the glasses. She saw murder in those eyes.

"Go!" Sharpe yelled at her, narrowly avoiding another swipe. He'd acquired a broken pipe from somewhere, a few feet of torn metal. His battering didn't do much against the polished rock skin but he was keeping it focused.

Nel covered the distance between her and Violet. Dominik was shaking her, yelling at her. Nothing seemed to have an effect.

"Violet!" Nel yelled at her, grabbing her by the shoulders. The girl shook like a rag doll, head rolling atop her neck like it was barely attached. Nel glanced behind her, saw Sharpe backed into a corner. He had nowhere to go.

She slapped Violet. Hard. The girl's eyes widened then focused on her. Narrowed.

"You," she snarled. The voice was ugly. Mean.

Hells, not Violet.

"It's no good," Dominik told her. "She can't hear you, not when she's like this."

Gods, when did he . . . he was so little last I saw him.

Can't think that now.

Violet, not-Violet, grabbed Nel by the throat. And squeezed. Nel grabbed at her hand, still the stronger of the two, but she felt nails digging into her throat.

"Give me that." She snatched the globe out of Dominik's hand. Pulled her arm back.

"Sorry, Vi," she managed, before slamming it into the side of the girl's head. Violet's eyes rolled back, her body spasmed and collapsed. Dominik caught her before she hit the deck.

Nel checked on Sharpe. Still alive, putting space between him and Onyx. The golem was frozen, like she'd hoped. No, not frozen, already stirring, turning to face them.

Face her.

"Vaughn."

The voice was Violet's but laced with pure hatred. Nel met the eyes, grabbed the hand clawing for her again.

"Get out of her, Scarlett," Nel growled. "You get out and let my girl go."

Lips pulled back, feral grin. Unsteady on her feet but no lack of determination. Violet reached up, pushing the glasses into place.

Had enough of those too.

Nel hit her again. Square to the face and cracked the frame of those damned rose-tinted glasses. Violet's head snapped back and she gave a cry. That sound tore at Nel. She held the girl up by the wrist.

"You hit me!"

That voice could have been either one of them. Nel wanted to believe who it was.

"Vi?"

"Get down!"

Her brother tackled her to the ground, and Onyx crashed over the both of them, catching her in the ribs with a passing leg. Nel's whole side went numb and she curled around it, swearing. When she looked up Violet was back on her feet, supporting herself by clinging to Onyx. The glasses were gone but the look on her face was no less ugly for it.

So much for that idea. Nothing is ever that easy.

"That's enough," Violet snarled, reaching for Nel one more time. But this time she wasn't trying to throttle her. There were blue and white sparks wreathing the girl's hand—she was reaching for something else. Nel twisted her head, trying to see what would come flying her way.

Dominik threw himself forward, and Nel thought he was trying to tackle Violet or knock or her out like her own failed attempt. Instead he grabbed Violet by her outstretched hand.

No, not grabbing, what's he got there?

It was the sphere, the captain's sphere. Dominik shoved it right into Violet's outstretched hand and her fingers closed around it reflexively. All that miniature lightning coalesced around the ball, drawn to it. And unlike last time, Nel realised, it had no direct connection to the metal hull. It had nowhere to go except back into the two people touching it.

Dominik and Violet were thrown apart, explosively and with a flash of light that seared Nel's eyes. She caught her brother, or more like he collected her on the way. They both skidded to a stop along the metal floor. Dominik groaned in her arms, and she held on protectively. His skin was hot and shocked to the touch.

"You alive there?" Sharpe appeared over her, holding her head up. "Both still breathing, that's something."

"Violet," Nel pushed herself up.

The girl was on hands and knees, cradled under the crook of the golem. Her golem, Nel realised. Because it wasn't really Violet. Hadn't been for a while.

"Damnit," she said. She saw the knife on Dominik's belt. That would do.

"Wait, Nel, what are you doing?" Sharpe called out as she took long strides towards Violet.

"You are never going to beat me," Nel called out to Scarlett, her voice grim, not slowing. "Not with that damned golem, not with your stolen body. Not ever."

Scarlett wiped away blood from a mouth that wasn't hers. She stared at it distastefully, unhappy with what she saw. "I think, Vaughn," she said, the voice sounding nothing but wrong, "that so long as I have this body, you lose."

"Then I'll fix that." Nel held up the knife. Scarlett's eyes widened and her golem stepped between them. But it was slow, groggy, like her. Nel ducked under its lumbering arms and kept going for her target.

"Nel, stop!" Sharpe yelled at her, getting between them too. Nel hit him with a back-fist, the knife's pommel to his temple. He veered away, clutching at his head. Scarlett could only back up now, faltering steps. The face, the eyes, the cry she made.

It's not her.

"I'm so sorry, Vi," Nel whispered. She grabbed the girl by the shoulder with her free hand. And stabbed forward with the other.

"Skipper," Violet whispered. Her eyes were big and wide. Disbelief. Confused.

Hers.

Nel looked down. There was hot blood running over her hand. Red and vivid. Two hands clutching hers. A body doubling over, falling to their knees.

Hells.

"I told you to stop," Sharpe looked up at her.

He collapsed at her feet, both hands wrapped around the knife buried in his side. Violet cried out, clutching at him, blood staining them both.

Nel was ripped away from him and Violet. She twisted, found herself face to face with Onyx. The golem's eyes were lit up. Fiery and animated.

"I win," it said with Scarlett's voice.

Nel clutched at the arm holding her, her blood-slick fingers failing to even hold onto the rocky limb. She gave up, but still grinned back in the face of the golem.

"Made you flinch."

She enjoyed the part where those fiery red eyes widened just then. The arm came up, spiky protrusion levelled at her. Nothing for it now.

The arm shook, struggling. Shaking. The pointy end was still aimed at Nel's throat. The golem's attention had shifted to behind her. Nel craned her neck to see.

Violet, looking somehow frail and fierce all muddled together. One hand outstretched, holding the golem's arm back. The concentration was bringing beads of sweat to her face. Scowl lines that were carving themselves into her forehead. But she'd pushed Scarlett to a stalemate.

Huh. Didn't figure on how this just happened.

Nel turned back and met those red eyes again.

So what now, bitch?

There was a scream, Nel couldn't tell who, then both she and the golem were lifted off their feet, thrown across the deck. The violent movement ripped her free and she tumbled end over end, but free.

Hands pulled her away, up onto her feet. Sharpe? Violet? Turned out to be neither, it was her little brother instead.

"Dominik," she started to say.

"Don't call me that," he snapped at her, instinctively. He manhandled her towards the other two, a dozen feet away. "Hells, but you've made a mess of things," he berated her.

Nel glared at him but was interrupted by Sharpe.

"You stabbed me!" he accused her. *More than an accusation.*

He was clutching his side, shirt sodden with blood and face gone chalky. But he was standing, with help from Violet.

"Talk about it later," Nel told him. "Vi, you with us now?"

The girl blinked. Nodded. Seemed lost for words.

Unlike the rest of everyone else. The deck was still a madcap of chaotic action. Nel could hear cannonballs striking the ship, the twang of metal then the slow drift off as they scrapped down the hull. Shouting. Screaming. Wandfire sounding off. And then, just for a moment, it all went quiet.

Things went dark for that moment, when a shadow swept over them, then the whole ship screamed and shook as something massive slammed into it. All of them were thrown to the deck and the screaming started again.

Nel groaned. Everything hurt and her side was one giant bruise. She managed to get her knees under her, hand to the timbers, pushing herself up. She grabbed for the first hand she saw, Violet's.

"We need to get off this ship."

CHAPTER 26

"STOP PACING, KELPIE," Korrigan Jack grumbled at Quill. The navigator pivoted, facing Jack, taloned feet gouging deep scratches in the deck.

"This offends you?"

"Makes me look at you, don't wanna do that."

"Imbecile," Quill shook his head. He turned to Stoker, much preferring the Draugr's mannerisms. "Are there any signs of them?"

"No," Stoker told him. "Just like before. Big hairy light show going on."

Quill grabbed onto the bridge rails, leaning far out over the edge, for what little perspective it granted him. Below them, in a well absent of mist, the two Alliance warships were locked in their dogfight. The *Mangonel* had the element of surprise, size, and sheer firepower, while the *Fata Morgana* was able to manoeuvre within the cold sun's well, bringing its lances to bear on the traditional timbers of the dreadnought. By contrast, impressive as the hundred strong broadsides were, much of it was deflected off the steel hull.

Quill had expected a short and brutal takedown of the metal ship. Now his concerns had swung in the other direction. There was a thin trail of mist, or whatever filled the pipes within the *Fata Morgana,* that leaked out from some rupture. Stark against the depth of the black but it did not seem to impede the ship any.

301

"Not sitting right, is it?" Stoker voiced what they were both thinking. "The waiting."

"I did not come all this way," Quill gripped the woodwork tightly, leaving more gouges, "to sit on the sidelines and observe."

"Well, what we gonna do about it?" Stoker asked him. "Got cannon aboard, thinking we should use them?"

"Short range cannon," Quill reminded him.

"Aye, true, this here's a carronade-class we've stolen. Meant for getting in close and poking the bear. Right grizzly one down there."

"We would only get one pass," Quill said. "I can steer us into range but once we leave the edge of the mist we will fall."

"How far?" Jack asked.

"Until we return to the mist," Quill glanced back at him. "And then some more, until it becomes thick enough to buoy us."

"So once we leave we ain't coming back, you saying," Jack said.

"More or less," Quill allowed grudgingly.

"Open to better ideas," Stoker said. "Otherwise, you want I should get Powder and Chit to warm up the cannon?"

"Got one," Jack said.

Quill hesitated. *But why not*, he thought. "What?"

"That one there ain't falling," Jack pointed at the *Fata Morgana*.

"Yes," Quill said testily. "But we are not that ship. That ship is different to us."

"Yeah, it's different. Don't like different. Not the only one."

"What do you mean, Jack?" Quill asked him.

"Rays don't like it neither," Jack pointed.

Quill looked, following where Jack led him. He saw a ray leave the cloudbanks of mist above the *Fata Morgana*, diving hard and fast, straight between the duelling Alliance ships. It struck the hull of the *Morgana*, hard, shaking the whole vessel, then fell away, sailing through the thin black until it reached the safety of the mist again. A fever of them circled below now.

Quill watched as another began the journey from above. This one did not make it to the *Fata Morgana*, falling prey to the gunners. The tattered body fell and dropped swiftly.

Jack chuckled, darkly. "That's where we wanna go to. So let's go there. Right in their faces."

Quill exchanged looks with Stoker, then both of them looked to the front of the ship. The pointy end.

It seems they had a plan after all.

"And after we poke the bear?" Stoker asked.

Jack grinned. "Got an idea for that too."

VIOLET STARED AT her hand. Still tingly, still blue. Like everything she looked at, blue and tingly. She blinked her eyes repeatedly, still blue. But there were other colours as well. Greens and reds. Especially . . .

"Sharpe!"

He was back. On the *Fata Morgana,* and there was vividly red blood pouring down his side. One leg and the arm he was trying to hold the red in with were stained crimson.

"What happened?" she demanded of him, rushing to catch him when he tottered.

"She happened," Sharpe said through gritted teeth. "You stabbed me!"

Violet looked up, saw the Skipper and her brother. Kaspar was holding her up much the way Violet was supporting Sharpe. Violet had to shake her head at the sight of the two red-headed siblings—the colour was too strange and foreign to her now.

"Talk about it later," she heard the skipper dismiss his complaints. "Vi, you with us now?"

Violet could only nod, still trying to make sense of things. Felt like she'd just woken up, still trying to sort out which parts she'd dreamed.

The ship rolled under her, throwing her down, never a chance to get her bearings. Everything was loud and violent, her head hit the timbers and there was pain. She groaned, or someone did. Felt someone take her hand then, squeezing.

"We need to get off this ship," the skipper told her. "I need your help, lass."

Violet nodded. *Help, get off the ship. Easy.*

She made it back to her feet.

"Don't bleed on me," the skipper was saying to Sharpe, taking his weight on her shoulders. Violet stumbled and Kaspar grabbed her arm. Seems they'd traded partners. The world kept changing.

"Shouldn't have stabbed me," she heard Sharpe tell the skipper. When had she stabbed him? Violet put a hand to her head, trying to puzzle out what the hells was going on.

He was between us. Was looking over his shoulder. At Vaughn. Nel. The skipper . . . why would she . . .

"Violet!" Kaspar had one arm around her waist, pulling her forward. She bashed her face on his shoulder, the pain helped her focus. Her face felt bruised, bloodied. All from that one knock?

"Where are we . . . ?" she tried to ask.

"There," Kaspar pointed. Towards the tender, the glass bubble the captain had been going to execute Sharpe and the skipper in. Just like he had Gravel.

The deck twisted under their feet. The ship was banking but being raked by cannon fire.

"Who's shooting us?" Violet demanded.

"No idea," Kaspar replied.

"It's the *Mangonel!*" the skipped called back to them.

That made no sense to Violet. None of this did. The deck was filling with smoke and there were tears in the hull. She glimpsed the *Mangonel Falling* through one of the breaches, still massive and fearsome but taking as good as it gave. The mizzenmast had been severed and several of the sails were burning. Half the ship disappeared in smoke then as a broadside was fired. She braced but like everyone else was thrown from her feet when the impact hit.

"Move, move, move!" Kaspar was yelling at her, almost straight into her ear. His arms were wrapped around her tight and they rolled. Seconds later one of the tender spheres rolled past them, free from its restraints and loosing havoc on the gun deck.

"Damnit," Kaspar looked over her shoulder. Violet didn't have to turn to conclude the bubble had smashed against the far wall. She pushed herself up, pulling Kaspar up with her.

"I must say, this is disappointing."

The gun deck was chaos, smoke and debris. The battery crews, those Violet could make out, were occupied with returning fire in the running battle outside. Raines looked out of place amidst it all. Calm, almost serene, hands clasped behind his back, seven tails splayed out behind him. Seeing him gave Violet her first clear emotion. Anger.

"You," she growled at him.

"Scarlett was my very favourite agent, did you know?" Raines met her eyes, almost making conversation. "Imagine my excitement when it seemed there was a way to get her back. Such a shame. Do you even realise what a remarkable—"

The skipper swung at him, brandishing a pipe. Went straight for the face and didn't hesitate but Raines was quick, twisting out of the way. Then Onyx again, stepping out of the smoke, batting the weapon away, looming protectively over the elder Kitsune. The skipper tried to dodge around, going for Raines again. Onyx wasn't alone though: Mors was there, the duellist down to one wand but it was enough. A thaumatic flash and the skipper tumbled back towards them, groaning in pain. Sharpe knelt by her side quickly.

"A valiant attempt," Raines said. "A pity. I abhor waste. But this has gone on long enough. Scarlett?"

Once more the golem advanced on them, snapping both arms out to the sides, scraping the lethal points of the arm blades along the deck. Each step was slow but deliberate. Whatever confusion or lack of control had affected the big rock before was gone. Mors circled them as well, sidestepping, wand held ready.

Violet clenched her fist but there were no sparks now. Just her. Kaspar squeezed her other hand.

"Skipper," Violet called to her.

The skipper looked up at her voice. And flinched. The woman pulled hard on Sharpe's arm, bringing him down on top of her. Violet heard Kaspar cry out and suddenly she was being pushed down to the deck as well, the ensign covering her body with his own.

It felt like the ship was being torn apart, the metal decking creaked and tore around them. Steel sheeting protested as it ruptured, and for all Violet knew the *Fata Morgana* had split in half around them. The only thing Violet could imagine might come close to it was an earthquake. No one could have stayed on their feet throughout it.

When she looked up she could see even less, but she knew why. Multiple pipes had cracked, the same lines the crew had spent so long repairing were gushing their condensed miasma into the ship's envelope. It rushed like smoke in a chimney, seeking the newly created gap in the *Morgana's* skin. A hole caused by the prow of a ship Violet had never seen before and had no business being inside like that.

Her first thought was the *Mangonel Falling*, but if that were the case there really would be nothing left. The ship was much smaller, the bow wrapped in iron and the extension fashioned into a woman's face. Too delicate a thing for the brutal purpose it had been put to but the figurehead was mostly intact.

A familiar face appeared in the breach. The long-jawed head twisted from side to side, surveying the innards of the *Fata Morgana,* searching. Standing right in the mist funnel. Quill.

"What the hells."

Kaspar. Somehow she'd ended up top of him. Violet beamed down at him—she could feel the grin splitting her face. "Come on," she said. "Time to go."

Violet climbed off and over him, almost putting her foot in his face. No time for that. She grabbed his hand, hauling him along behind her. He'd get his feet to the deck or be dragged across it. Quill was here. She'd never expected to feel joy at the idea but there it was and there he was. And was that Jack beside him? What ship was this? Who was crewing it? Had they really just rammed the *Morgana?*

The Kelpie's eyes locked onto her as she ran across the deck, pulling Kaspar with her. Even from this distance she saw those eyes narrow, the scaly glare. The Kelpie raised his hand and something floated up beside him.

Is that . . . a cannon ball?

The only thought that there was room for on her mind was there were no cannonballs on the *Morgana.* So Quill had brought his own. And Quill didn't need a cannon to fire it.

The Kelpie gestured and the cannonball flew, straight towards her. No, not her, she realised. Towards the boy in blue and white Alliance colours chasing her. Because that's what Quill would have seen.

Violet spun, skidding to a stop and threw her arms around Kaspar as he crashed into her. She wanted to squeeze her eyes shut but refused to do so. That was when she saw Onyx behind them. Arm raised, ready for the killing thrust. The cannonball took the golem's arm clean off, shearing it at the elbow. Even Onyx stared at the stump, dumbfounded. And screamed in horror, in a woman's voice.

The cannonball came back for another pass, ricocheting off the head then thumping solidly into the chest. Not nearly the momentum it had on the first pass but it was enough to send shards of rock flying and drive the golem down to the deck. It covered its head protectively, just like a person would've. The cannonball struck once more and Onyx flailed, grabbing and hugging the projectile to itself.

"No!" Violet heard Raines scream, spotting him just a few feet away. The Kitsune was livid, watching his prize creation taken down. "Kill them! Somebody kill them!"

Marines in the mist. Armed marines. *That's right, we're still on the gun deck. Not much point manning the guns when another ship has rammed you. There's Mors, again. Doesn't anybody stay down on this ship?*

Raines snatched a wand from one of the marines, firing wildly at them in his rage. Violet flinched but the shot went wide. Whatever Raines' talents, wandplay wasn't one of them. But he was so close it was hard to imagine him missing again. Mors and the marines held back, letting it play out.

"So many failures," Raines shook as he spoke. "The fault must lie with me. I suppose one must accept that some experiments are simply—"

Several things happened together, all at once. The *Morgana* shifted, rolling, trying to dislodge the ship impaling it. A shrill, manic shriek, then Bandit launched himself atop Raines' head, clawing at his face and eyes as he had once tried to do to Onyx. Violet couldn't tell if the shriek came from either or both of them. Sharpe tackled Raines around the middle. The Kitsune had already dropped his wand in his efforts to remove Bandit from his person. Kaspar swooped on the wand, ignoring Raines and swinging for the Luscan behind him. Mors barely reacted in time; the battle must have taken its toll on him.

"Would you move, girl!" A clawed hand on her shoulder, Quill's ugly maw looking down at her. He'd left his ship and boarded the *Morgana* itself.

"But . . . ," Violet protested. She saw the skipper now, in the midst of it all. Woman had two wands, who knew where she'd acquired them. Had come at the marines from behind. She made eye contact, not with Violet but with Quill, standing above her. Time to go, those words everyone kept saying.

Sharpe and Raines grappled, and the Kitsune slammed an elbow into the man's bloodied ribs. Kaspar was on top of Mors, pummelling him, almost crying. *For Brandon*, Violet realised. The skipper pulled him off, running towards Violet and Quill, bent low. Violet saw Bandit scampering at their heels. The body of Onyx tumbled over them, just inches above the Vaughns' heads, on its way to collecting Raines and any stray marines. Quill again, the static from his thaumatics making her fur stand on end. The golem kept tumbling, striking another bank of piping across the way. Mist started to leak out. Then Jack was there, throwing an injured Sharpe indifferently over his shoulder.

"I told you to stay with the ship!" Quill snapped as the Korrigan trotted past. Jack ignored him.

"I told *you* to stay with the ship!" the skipper yelled at him. "Not crash the damned thing into us!"

"You were taking too long!" Quill defended himself, grabbing Violet by the collar and pushing her towards the foreign ship.

"Get off me, Kelpie." She swatted his hand away.

"All of you shut up and get on!" Jack bellowed at them, heaving Sharpe over the side and into the relative safety of whatever vessel they were escaping on. "Ship's still here, time it wasn't."

Violet hesitated, just a moment. There were bodies lying around the ship. Marines, all of them with stab wounds. Jack's work.

"Come on, Vi," the skipper called her, already over the railing and holding out her hand. Violet reached up and grabbed it, no more hesitations, jumping up and aboard.

"Quill!" the skipper yelled. "Time to go!"

THE KELPIE BROUGHT his hands together, a slow, drawn out clap at Nel's command. The *Poignard* rumbled, wood grating against steel. It seemed like they were stuck, moving by inches. Nel saw Violet run to the bow, that mad dash that made her heart lurch thinking the girl was going to continue over the side without stopping. Half of her did, the girl's top half bending far out over the rail, feet leaving the deck.

Hells, she back to being not-Violet now?

Violet twisted around, almost in the air and nothing but her hands tethering her to the ship itself. "Down!" she yelled, a second before belching mist came tumbling out of the innards of the *Fata Morgana*. Nel crouched, feeling something solid strike the outside of their hull.

Felt like we hit a reef.

But that impact, combined with the outpouring mist and Quill's efforts, finally dislodged them. The ship was free. Then falling.

"Quill!" Nel yelled for her navigator, holding on for life. She felt the plane starting to shift as the *Dancers Poignard* plummeted stern first through all too thin black and mist.

But there was nothing he could do and they both knew it. Nothing but hold on. Which was what Nel did, grabbing a line.

She saw Violet, to her relief, in the headsail lines. There was no sail, fortunate since it would only have become tangled after Quill had rammed the *Morgana,* but that left plenty of rigging for the girl. Above her, rapidly receding, Nel could see the battle still unfolding. The *Morgana's* lance batteries were like lightning to the *Mangonel's* thunderous cannon. Some of the sound was even reaching their own envelope.

Damn, but they made that ship tough, was all she could think. Wounded, gutted, pierced, and bleeding profusely, the *Fata Morgana* was still a wonder of design. She watched as it dove and barrel-rolled, using the same thin mist that was affecting them, to escape the *Mangonel Falling's* firing line. Those barrel rolls served another purpose, bringing not one but two broadsides to bear, bright streaks of light that bit into the wooden hull of the dreadnought. And not just the *Mangonel.* There were rays in the black, diving out of the mist. They were swirling all over the *Morgana,* crashing and butting into it, then falling away. The wandfire discouraged them but the ship was in a dance for survival, pressed in on all sides.

Good luck, Heathen, was all the thought Nel could spare for her former captain. The battle was out of their hands now and they'd gone above and beyond in providing the promised distraction.

One of the rays dove past them then, wings bigger than their sails stretched out and pale as the mist. Nel swallowed hard as one great eye faced her. The eye itself was bigger than she was, maybe only a passing glance before the ray dropped past them, wings flaring as it swept by.

"Mist bank, coming up!" Sharpe yelled from further down the ship. He'd slid all the way down to the main mast, with the ship close to vertical in its descent. Lashed himself to the woodwork as well. Nel realised there was no one else beyond him. Not a single soul of her crew to be seen. She had to look up to the rigging to find them.

And every sail furled.

They were coming to the edge of the thin mist. In a few hundred feet it was thick enough to lose yourself in.

"Drop sail!" Jack bellowed. He was hanging from the rails, one arm and one foot hooked into the brightwork, same as he would in the rigging, waving to the Draugr in the spars. Nel watched them; Boxing swung on a line, unfurling the main, Horse up in the nest working on the top gallants. Jack called out orders and the sails dropped, one after the other, to hang loose and full.

"Aw, hells," Nel muttered, realising what the plan was. Jack turned, faced her, and grinned. He held on with both hands now and mouthed one word.

"Brace."

The jolt when the sails filled was wrenching. The ship suddenly had mass again, real weight, and the free fall came to a jarring stop. They couldn't have put more stress on the ship if they'd driven the bow into a cresting wave and found a reef the other side. The timbers protested, creaking, but Nel found herself matching Jack's primal grin in return. The ship held fast.

"You little beauty," Nel whispered to her, feet finding the deck as the ship started to level off. Quill had somehow made his way to the bridge and was doing what he did.

"Jack!" she called. "That your madcap idea?"

Jack only laughed, one of the few times she could recall seeing him genuinely happy. He pointed up to the rigging.

"Lost a couple," he told her. "Forgot to hold."

"What?" Nel started. Had she heard that right? They had crew overboard? She started searching the black, but it was all white. White misty miasma—anyone overboard was gone.

"Calm down, Skipper, were all tied on. Ain't none of us stupid," Jack assured her. He pointed, and she spotted a swinging body, Yarn, going by the beard. He was stuck hanging until the ship finished righting itself.

"Don't worry," Jack grinned, pointing. "Got my best man on it."

"Is that . . ." Nel stared. And it was. Bandit, scampering up the mast, already into the rigging and down the rope. Yarn stared at him, nonplussed, when the loompa parked himself on the Draugr's chest. And then there were two of them, just swinging on the end of the rope.

"Of all the . . ." Nel shook her head. She didn't have the words. *Shoulda known.*

"Make sure they all get down," she told Jack.

"Aye, Skipper, I'll do that," he said.

"And Jack . . . well done."

Jack chuckled.

Happy Jack, strange world this is.

Quill met her eyes across the length of the deck. He had seen Bandit too. His expression resigned.

"Chanel," Sharpe called to her, back up against the mast, still holding his side. Bleeding looked to have stopped, something for Jack to have a look at once he was done pulling in their Draugr fishing lines.

"Don't—" she started to say.

"You stabbed me," he interrupted her. "Don't start with the name thing."

Nel glared. "Fine," she relented. "But don't make a habit of it."

"Stabbed," Sharpe pointed, with a grimace. "With the stabbing. By you."

"Wasn't trying for you," Nel told him, almost sullenly.

Sharpe's eyes flicked past her. Violet, presumably. He put his hand on Nel's shoulder, leaning in closer. "I figured what you were trying to do, after the fact. You think of that all yourself? You think it all the way through?"

"Scarlett," Nel said. "Woman jumped bodies, rather than let herself go. Powerful fear of dying that speaks to. Powerful."

"Powerful," Sharpe nodded. "Thing of it though, if I hadn't gotten in the way, would you have stabbed Vi like you did me? Or were you bluffing? 'Cause I've seen you at cards. You're a lousy bluff."

"Wasn't a card game, Castor."

"And that wasn't an answer."

"Oi, Skipper!" Nel heard her name called. Twisted just enough to take the impact in the front as Violet cannonballed into her, and then it was all arms and legs and wrapped up. Sharpe grunted as he took some of the impact too.

Violet pulled back, looking up at her. Not so much as before, girl had gotten taller. Same girl slapped her in the chest.

"You hit me! In the face!" Violet exclaimed.

Beside her, Nel saw Stoker mouth the word *stabbing* again. She tried to shush him with her eyes.

"Wasn't you, Vi," Nel said, tilting the girl's face up. She tried not to wince. There was going to be black and blue and more than one shiner come tomorrow. Maybe not even that long.

"Was still my face! Just wasn't steering." Violet hugged her again, then another punch, to the arm this time. Couldn't seem to make up her mind.

"Sorry, lass," Nel told her. She said it fast, but it wasn't enough. If she said it again, for what mattered, her voice might let her down. "I'm so—"

"It's fine, s'okay," Violet said, trying to sound gruff. "Talk about it later."

Sharpe almost had a coughing fit at that.

"Who else?" Violet asked. "Who else is here?"

"Us and Quill," Nel said. "And Jack. Picked up Stoker and some friends. Good hands, all of them."

"Gabbi," Violet said. "The captain. All the rest."

Her eyes were bright. So big and liquid. She wasn't asking. It was something else.

"Brought Bandit," Violet pointed up. "He came through it with me. Through it all."

Nel sighed, but didn't let it show. *Damned loompa's going to outlive all of us. Probably end up captain at this rate.*

Hells, why'd I have to go think that?

"And this one," Violet looked over her shoulder. Dominik, waiting awkwardly behind her. "Figure you two might wanna talk. Gonna go see Quill and Jack."

One more hug and the girl darted past her. Then stopped.

"Hey, Skipper," she called, tilting her head.

"Yeah, Vi?"

"Kissed your brother."

"Who," Quill asked her suspiciously, "is that?"

"Who is who?" Violet stared at him, not understanding.

"That," Quill pointed. Pointed with his eyes. Glared. "They appear familiar. Why?"

"Means the lad with the skipper," Jack chuckled. Jack was grinning, an ear to ear smile. Bandit was perched on his shoulder, fussing over Jack's braids Grooming him. Both seemed to be enjoying the exchange. "You know, pint with the same locks as her."

Quill squinted at Jack. "These follicles, the shade is significant, it holds some meaning?"

Jack shook his head, still grinning, setting his own braids in motion. Bandit squawked his protest until he stopped.

"That'd be the brother, Quill. Her brother," Violet told him. "On account of them looking alike when you stand them up together like that."

Quill frowned. "I do not see it. You are sure?"

"Sure as he's a Vaughn."

"A Vaughn," Quill looked troubled. "There are two of them now. Two Vaughns."

"Just don't go calling him that then," Violet suggested. "Keep you both happy."

"What am I supposed to call him if not that?"

"How's about little skipper?" a voice called from above. Violet looked up, recognising Stoker but not the other Draugr with him up in the rigging. "Hello, little Miss. Welcome back, welcome aboard, I should say. At your service, we are, but need some help with these top lines if any of you are free to oblige?"

"You go," Jack said. "Lines up top are flimsy. Suit you, both of yous," he nudged Bandit meaningfully with the side of his face. "I'll stay here and keep the Kelpie company."

"I would much prefer if you did not," Quill said.

"Why do you think I'm doing it?"

Violet's head swivelled back and forth between the two. "This feels very awkward," she said in a loud whisper.

"Kelpie missed you," Jack told her. "All this fuss, coming to get you, was his idea."

Violet cocked her head. *Couldn't have heard that right, Jack's just messing.*

Quill glared at them both. Familiar, comforting. "Violet, go and help Stoker with the lines. Now!"

Rigging, Violet thought, gazing up towards the topsail. *Ropes and cordage. Tackle and blocks. Swaying masts and crows nests. Oh, I missed you . . .*

She didn't bother trying to keep the smile off her face as she climbed hand over hand up into them, Bandit right by her side.

Halfway up; Violet paused. Hooked her knee, holding on with just the one hand, leaning out and looking up at the black, past the nest, past the flights of rays swarming above, up into the mist.

How I missed you . . .

"I do not like you, Jack," Quill told the Korrigan once Violet was out of earshot.

"And I still think you're ugly. But you missed me, Kelpie, same as you missed the girl."

"I admitted to no such thing," Quill snorted.

"Didn't have to," Jack said. "You called her by her name."

"Shut up," Quill snapped at him.

Jack just laughed.

CHAPTER 27

ARISTEIA QUINN STEPPED back onto *Fata Morgana's* gun deck, taking in the carnage. The starboard side had taken the most damage. The gun ports were traditionally a structural weakness, and the enemy had breached the hull with a carronade-class frigate as well. Faux-mist from the ruptured piping still leaked in faint bursts despite being sealed off closer to the source tanks.

The first mate nudged a prone body with her foot. The marine rolled over at the touch, exposing puncture wounds and a slashed throat. This drew a frown. The soldier-sailor still manned one of the ship's heavy weapons, the wand battery having come loose from its restraints and rolled across the deck, facing the battered innards of the ship.

"Mors, see this weapon secured," she ordered her Luscan shadow. "You have eyes on the *Mangonel Falling*?"

"Still retreating," Mors confirmed. "De-masted and aflame."

"And the creatures?"

"They stopped their attacks when we moved into the thin void. We have some time."

"I see," Aristeia nodded. "Your thoughts?"

"I would not risk a pursuit," Mors said bluntly. "Here we have the option of safe anchorage. Firing lines. If we were to stray into the black . . ."

"Yes?"

"We would lose."

"Aristeia!"

A dark look settled over the first mate's face. She turned stiffly towards the call, facing Raines. The Kitsune was trailed and flanked by his pet golem. Both looked to have fared badly in the battle. Raines had someone else's blood splattering his clothes and matting his fur, and the golem was missing the better part of one arm. That last fact was impressive.

"Aristeia," Raines said without preamble. "You need to follow that ship."

"Mors and I have discussed it," Aristeia told him. "We are in agreement that any further engagement with the *Mangonel* would be tactically unwise."

Raines visibly bristled, his black eyes bulging. "Tactically? That is irrelevant, besides which I was not referring to Heathen's archaic scow. The other ship, that is who we must follow."

"The other ship," Aristeia repeated. Her gaze strayed meaningfully to the gaping breach in the hull.

"The *Dancers Poignard*," Mors supplied.

"Yes?" Aristeia mused. "Masona Flint's command. I will assume formerly. A shame. I knew her."

"Even in this state of disarray," Raines threw his arms out, "this ship is more than capable of contending with such an inferior vessel. Give the order."

Aristeia's brow furrowed into a deep vee. The mouth a thin, lipless line. "No."

Raines stepped forward. "Need I remind you, first officer, that—"

"No, you need not remind me who is captain of this vessel. You may have designed her, Raines, but she is under my command. And I say we are done with battle for today."

"Then perhaps," Raines lowered his voice, "it is the strain of the recent battle I hear. Taking its toll on you."

"Doubtful," Aristeia told him. "You are captain in name only, Raines. I suggest you push the issue no further."

Raines smiled. It was not a nice smile. "In *name* only. It seems we have suffered from an unclear chain of command. Our performance in the battle just now proves my point. A battle where we took losses. Most heavy losses. The fleet would grieve the loss of such a renowned officer. Don't you agree . . . Scarlett?"

All attention turned to the obsidian golem. Formerly known

as Onyx, now Scarlett. The head turned slowly, from Raines to the first mate and back again. Considering.

Consideration that was cut short by the convulsions of Raines. His body jerked into a series of spasms, lifting up onto the tips of his toes, limbs thrust out like a starfish. He toppled forward, falling flat and face-first upon the deck. Mors stood behind him, recently reclaimed wands in both hands. He looked down at the still-twitching form of the Guildsman.

"Choose your next words carefully, Scarlett." Aristeia raised her eyes to meet the golem's. She was met with impassive rock features. The head moved down, considering Raines, before speaking.

"Raines does not speak for me, or the Guild."

"That is good," the first mate nodded. "It is a great loss though. Arlin Raines was a brilliant inventor. His death in a minor and pointless border skirmish along the Free Lanes boundary will be considered a great tragedy. His knowledge and insight will be sorely missed in what is to come."

All eyes on her, Aristeia Quinn showed no expression. On the deck, Raines no longer twitched, but a faint moaning could be heard.

"Alas, his body could not be recovered," the first mate raised her voice. "Lost as he was during a valiant attempt to affect repairs to his final contribution, this ship. So the record will duly reflect."

Aristeia turned on her heel, parade-ground snap, with arms clasped behind her back, to face the breach. "If one of you would make it so."

The eyes of the crew turned to Scarlett. It was a long moment before she stooped, picking up the limp form of Raines with no discernible effort. The Kitsune hanging by her one arm no different than a sack of produce would have, the golem made the short journey towards the edge of the ship.

Scarlett stopped there, Raines underarm, looking out at the black expanse. She cast Raines out, leaving his body to drift amongst the stars.

Mors fired the moment Scarlett turned around. The loose battery, still primed from the battle, lit the inside of the deck for a moment. The discharge struck the one-armed golem full on the chest, hurling it out after its maker. If the Scarlett-golem was capable of showing surprise, it did not.

It did scream. Right up until it passed outside the envelope. A long, despairing wail.

Aristeia looked at her second, Mors. "I believe I said for that cannon to be secured."

"Apologies, Captain," Mors saluted gravely. "Marines, secure the weapon."

He waved the nearest marines over and they proceeded to lash the cannon, wheeling it back to its original mounting.

"Any further orders, Captain?" Mors asked.

"Begin repairs, second," Aristeia told him. "And then plot us a course for the Central Band. We have a long journey and dark days ahead of us. Time enough to properly reflect the record."

"Aye, Captain."

"Carry on."

"Dominik."

Her brother made a face. "Don't call me that. That's Da's name. You oughta know better than anyone."

"Kaspar," Nel corrected herself, switching to his preferred middle name. She didn't know what else to say.

"The hells are you doing on my ship?"

"Your ship?" he bristled. "You mean to tell me with a straight face it belongs to you? That you didn't steal it? It's got fleet branding and colours and it's been a long time since that meant you. Not to mention your crew looks like you spun them out of a bad song about pirates."

"Had a ship," Nel stared him down. "Then I didn't."

Kaspar flinched, looking haunted for a moment. "I didn't know that was you."

Nel sighed. "And I saw you," she admitted. "Before. Probably should have said something."

Kaspar's head came up. "Saw me? When? Where?"

"Port Border," Nel said. "Ran away, rather than talk. Good at that."

Kaspar shuffled uncomfortably. "I probably wouldn't have wanted to talk to you." He made a face. "Then. But after."

His eyes drifted, following Violet going up the rigging. "That was the day I met her. Never thought all this would follow."

"About her," Nel said. "About what she said. Anything you

want to tell me?"

To her immense surprise, her brother flushed crimson. Between hair and complexion it was not flattering. "No," he shook his head vigorously.

"Anything you need to tell *her* then?"

Kaspar gave her a withering look, somewhat undercut by the barely faded blushing. Nel held up her hand in peace offering.

"Nothing she doesn't already know," he said curtly.

"Fine. Good." Nel frowned. "You met her? Vi? In Border?"

"Yes. During the riots. I was looking for . . . someone. They turned out to be drinking with her, with Violet."

"Someone?" Nel asked him. It was hard to miss the pain in her brother's voice.

"A friend," Kaspar smiled. Sadly. "You remember how good I was at making those."

Hells. She patted him awkwardly on the shoulder. His expression said he felt as uncomfortable about it as she did.

"You were looking for us?" she asked.

"No," Kaspar shook his head. "We were shaking down the *Morgana.* Aristeia Quinn was supposed to take her out to the Amber Lanes, work on curbing the pirates that have been striking there. But we were contacted by a Guild spokesman to divert to Border. We had Raines aboard as our contact. He built the ship, he—"

"I know about him," Nel interrupted, earning a dirty look from Kaspar.

"We were to retrieve a golem that had been delivered to Port Border," Kaspar said. "It went on the run during the riots. Almost killed me and Brandon, might have if Raines hadn't stopped it."

Kaspar shrugged, a grimace. Too many bad memories. Nel thought better than to ask who Brandon was. "Next thing I knew we were all hands aboard tailing some ship. Yours, it turned out. Talk aboard was how we even knew how to find you. Guess we know now."

Nel nodded. *Yeah, we were all slow on that one. But how was anyone to guess that?*

"We left markers. Our contact from Border was supposed to help run you to ground. Things got complicated once we were inside the Free Lanes. When you tried to run at Vice . . ."

"I know," Nel said. "Things went bad."

"Weren't supposed to," Kaspar said. "Raines wanted to take you on the ground. Everyone alive. Not in a good way, I guess, but alive. Aristeia was the one who gave the order to shoot you down under Vice. Things went dark between her and Raines afterwards."

"Those shenanigans back aboard," Nel said, remembering. "You and Vi, the sphere and the light show. The hells was that?"

Kaspar gave her a very sidelong glance. And just the hint of a smile. "Something a former captain of yours might have suggested, let's say."

Nel opened her mouth to follow that line up when they were interrupted. Sharpe yelled out in pain, followed by a bellowing from Jack. Nel turned to see Sharpe batting at the Korrigan with one hand while Jack liberally applied brandy to the man's wound. She recognised the bottle.

"You're wasting it," Jack growled, trying to hold him down and pulling the bottle out of reach. "Don't. Don't do that."

"Easy, lad," Nel came up behind him, wrapping an arm around his chest and trapping one of Sharpe's own behind his back. "Hold still, man's right, can't be wasting top-shelf grog like that."

Sharpe screwed up his face, breathing sucking between his teeth as Jack poured.

"Drink?" Jack offered the bottle, still half-full.

"No," Sharpe winced.

"Skipper?"

Nel just made a face, making Jack laugh. He swigged some for himself then set to work with needle and thread. Nel made sure not to let Sharpe go before he was finished.

"You wriggle more than a bait fish," she told him at the end.

"That a good thing?" he asked, gingerly exploring Jack's stitches.

"No, and stop that." She slapped at his hand.

"Now what?" Sharpe asked.

"Find yourself a new shirt and don't touch those for a week," Nel told him. "You don't want Jack double stitching you, believe me."

Sharpe made a face at her. "Not that, can figure the sewing out for myself. Got Violet back, that's what we set out for, right? Where to now?"

"Away," Nel said. "Put some distance between us and what's

behind us, that's all I'm thinking."

"I would suggest Haven," Quill said.

Nel glared at him. "Wasn't asking, Quill. But thanks for announcing yourself. Saves me telling you to mind your business."

"I can hear you from the bridge just as easily," Quill told her. He nodded at Sharpe. "This one from further. If there was further."

"Still not minding."

"And I am still the navigator so you may as well take my advice now so you do not need to take it later."

"Agree about Haven." Stoker climbed down from the rigging to stand beside Jack. "Know some folk there. Good folk. Especially if you've an eye for a new ship."

"What's wrong with this one?" Nel asked quickly.

"Nothing," Stoker told her. "Sails straight, she does. But a bit distinctive, if you don't mind me saying. Could be the colours or the lines but truth is she don't look like a Free Lanes trader to most folk."

Jack laughed at the Draugr's words and held up his bottle again. "Drink?" he offered.

"Aye, be pleased to," Stoker accepted, taking a free-pour sip, the bottle not touching his lips. He wiped at his mouth with the back of his hand.

"Thought you didn't need to drink," Nel said.

"Ah, Skipper," Stoker sighed, almost happily, "man doesn't drink a drop like this because he needs to. Drinks it because he can."

"Just hope it doesn't come leaking out of you right away," Sharpe said.

"Believe you're the only man here with holes poked in him, Mister Sharpe," Stoker grinned. He waved to the other Draugr up in the rigging. "Care for a drop, my lads and ladies?"

Nel sighed, raising her voice. "Anyone not here?"

"I'll have some," Violet dropped to the deck, landing in a ball of fur that was all gangly arms and legs. She was half reaching for the bottle when Nel snatched it away.

"Oi!" Violet protested, echoed by Bandit. "What gives?"

"Please don't give her any," Kaspar sighed. "She's a mean drunk. The girl can't hold her liquor."

"Oh and you can?" Violet retorted. "You ain't the boss of me. Either of yous."

"In fact *she* is," Quill told her. "Whether *she* is prepared to admit it is another thing."

"Shut up, Quill," Nel told him.

"I think not," Quill said. He reached into his knapsack, pulling out rolled parchment.

"What's that?" Violet asked quickly.

"Be still and be quiet and I will tell you," Quill said as he unrolled it carefully. He looked up and met Nel's eyes over the tattoo deed before speaking again. "This is the deed to the *Tantamount*," he told them. "It is from the captain and of the captain. He leaves the responsibility of her to one," Quill grinned, showing all his teeth, "Chanel Dominica Vaughn."

"That's all well and good," Kaspar was the first to speak, "and not to rub salt in your wounds, truly, but the ship you're talking about is gone."

"The *Tantamount* was never really a ship," Nel muttered. "Captain just couldn't remember the actual damned name. Kept saying whatever he thought it was at the time was close enough. Tantamount to. Just as well since the actual ship was wanted for blockade running."

"The *Tantamount* is not a particular ship," Quill agreed. "It is the people aboard her, her crew. That is what Captain Horatio left."

"Skipper?" Violet asked. "What's it mean?"

Nel made a face. Then, reluctantly, "*Dancers Poignard* is a gods awful name anyway."

"Hear hear," Jack chuckled, claiming the bottle back from her. He raised a toast and then a cheer.

"Does that make you captain then, Skipper?" Stoker asked. "Ship ought to have a captain."

"Shut your mouth, Stoker," Nel told him.

"It makes her captain," Quill confirmed. "All in favour?"

A chorus of ayes.

"The hells it does," Nel glared at them all. "I say nay."

Quill shrugged. "If there is no captain the crew votes. You have been outvoted. Captain."

"Gods damn you, Loveland," Nel told him.

"To a miserable life with the likes of you," Quill nodded. "Such is their will. Shall we vote on a second next? A skipper?"

"Me!" Violet said quickly. "I'll do it. I can do it. Can it be me?"

"I vote for Bandit," Jack put forward. "Already my second mate. Can be the captain's too. Got the experience."

"That is not how it works," Quill stared at him. "That is not even . . . no."

"Why not?" Jack asked.

"Why can't it be me?" Violet pressed.

"Maybe that's for another time," Stoker suggested. "Perhaps we should be underway, discussions to be continued?"

"Sounds like something a good first mate would say," Sharpe grinned at him.

"Begging your pardon, Mister Sharpe, was that you volunteering yourself?"

"Me? Gods no, man, I can't even sail."

"Ah, makes you a fine choice of an officer then."

"Enough!" Nel shouted at them all. "All of you, back to work."

"Aye, Captain," Stoker saluted her. "Trust you'll be wanting us all to stay on for a bit, then?"

"Just . . . man the lines, Midshipman. Man the lines."

"Aye, Captain," Stoker grinned, climbing back up to join his crew in the rigging.

"Good man, Stoker," Sharpe said. "Always did like him. Hope the new captain keeps him on."

"I will lay in a course for Haven," Quill said while Nel ground her teeth in frustration. "Jack, a word with you."

Jack followed the Kelpie towards the bridge, grinning broadly, a bottle in his hand.

"So I can be skipper, right?" Violet began again. "If you're captain that makes me skipper, aye?"

"What about you, lad?" Sharpe asked Kaspar. "Fancy a promotion? Would seem to make sense."

"What?" Violet reacted with shock. "No! He can't be skipper. He just got here. He doesn't even want to be skipper . . . do you?"

"Kas," Nel said, following the thread in the girl's ramblings. "She's right, I haven't asked. I'm sorry. What do you want? Where do you go from here?"

"There's a place here," Sharpe offered. Nel frowned at him but didn't object to what he'd said.

Kaspar hesitated. Finally he said to Nel, "Da would be proud of you.”

Nel couldn't help herself. She started to laugh, and after a moment her brother joined in.

Violet sulked. “Did the captain mention me? Did he say anything about me in the deed? Never mind, see for myself. Quill. Quill!”

And the girl was gone, a madcap dash to the bridge, tangled hair flying out behind her.

“She seems better,” Sharpe commented. “Better than she did before, I mean. More her old self.”

Nel pursed her lips, eyeing Violet thoughtfully. *But is she? How do we know she's her again? Violet, not Scarlett. Our Violet.*

“She's not quite right,” Kaspar told her.

“What do you mean?” Nel asked, alarmed.

“None of you are.”

Sharpe laughed. “Come with me, see if we can't wrestle that bottle away from Jack. Let's talk, you and I. About Violet, seems I missed a few things. And your sister. Let's talk about our dear captain. Tell me everything there is to know about Chanel Vaughn.”

“You should know she hates being called that.”

“I do know that! Now why is that, exactly?”

Kaspar looked back over his shoulder as Sharpe steered him away, mouthing something.

Nel looked out, over the black. Her ship. Her crew.

Hells, Captain, what have you done to me?

There was a squawk. From behind. Nel sighed, turning to find Bandit perched there on the railing. Just him and her and the brightwork.

The loompa had something in hand.

A hat. A captain's hat.

From Nel's new cabin.

“Give me that,” she scowled, snatching it away from him. The loompa just chirped, not troubled at all.

It really was similar to Horatio's. Same style, same colour. Not as faded or as tattered.

She was painfully aware of the rest of the crew watching her. She put her back to them so she could face the black again. Bandit made the jump to her shoulder, grabbing for the hat. She didn't care for his weight on her back, and it reminded her of how he'd used to ride around on Piper.

Bandit retrieved the hat and set about trying to place it on his own head. It was far too big and covered his face. Nel just stared ahead. She preferred it to looking back.

Another chirp and she felt something placed awkwardly on her head, pushed and patted down until it stayed. Unfamiliar and the wrong fit. Nel reached up with one hand to adjust it, turning her face to fix the loompa with a scowl. Bandit cautiously withdrew his hands, waiting for her response.

"That'll do, Bandit."

The End

Acknowledgements

First of all;

Mum, stop skipping to the end of the book and go back and read it from the start, the way it's meant to be read.

And second;

To all the people who said no. And to the ones who said yes.

But mostly to those who said, 'This could be better. You could do better.'

About the Author

Thomas J. Radford is a New Zealand author and frequently introduced at social gatherings as 'our friend the author' in exchange for social currency. His personal circumstances have no probable bearing on the likelihood of happy endings and character deaths, despite any rumours to the contrary.